CLIVILIUS

INTERCONNECTED STORIES. INFINITE POSSIBILITIES

© 2024 Nathan Cowdrey. All rights reserved.
First Edition, 26 April 2024
ISBN 978-1-4457-6771-0
Imprint: Lulu.com

Step into Clivilius, where creation meets infinity, and the essence of reality is yours to redefine. Here, existence weaves into a narrative where every decision has consequences, every action has an impact, and every moment counts. In this realm, shaped by the visionary AI CLIVE, inhabitants are not mere spectators but pivotal characters in an evolving drama where the lines between worlds blur.

Guardians traverse the realms of Clivilius and Earth, their journeys igniting events that challenge the balance between these interconnected universes. The quest for resources and the enigma of unexplained disappearances on Earth mirror the deeper conflicts and intricacies that define Clivilius—a world where reality responds to the collective will and individual choices of its Clivilians, revealing a complex interplay of creation, control, and consequence.

In the grand tapestry of Clivilius, the struggle for harmony and the dance of dichotomies play out across a cosmic stage. Here, every soul's journey contributes to the narrative, where the lines between utopia and dystopia, creator and observer, become increasingly fluid. Clivilius is not just a realm to be explored but a reality to be shaped.

Open your eyes. Expand your mind. Experience your new reality. Welcome to Clivilius, where the journey of discovery is not just about seeing a new world but about seeing your world anew.

Also in the Clivilius Series

Luke Smith (4338.204.1 - 4338.209.2)

Luke Smith's world transforms with the discovery of a cryptic device, thrusting him into the guardianship of destiny itself. His charismatic charm and unpredictable decisions now carry weight beyond imagination, balancing on the razor's edge between salvation and destruction. Embracing his role as a Guardian, Luke faces the paradox of power: the very force that defends also threatens to annihilate. As shadows gather and the fabric of reality strains, Luke must navigate the consequences of his actions, unaware that a looming challenge will test the very core of his resolve.

Paul Smith (4338.209.4 - 4338.214.3)

Paul is a tale of survival, leadership, and the enduring power of family ties in the face of overwhelming odds. It's a story about finding light in the darkness, hope in despair, and the unyielding strength of the human spirit in the most challenging of environments. Join Paul and his family as they navigate the treacherous and transformative landscape of Clivilius, where every decision could mean the difference between survival and obliteration.

Kain Jeffries (4338.207.1 - 4338.211.2)

Kain Jeffries' life takes an unimaginable turn when he's thrust into Clivilius, far from the Tasmanian life he knows and the fiancée carrying their unborn child. Torn between worlds, he grapples with decisions concerning his growing family. Haunted by Clivilius's whispering voice and faced with dire ultimatums, Kain's resolve is tested when shadowy predators threaten his new home. As he navigates this new landscape, the line between survival and surrender blurs, pushing Kain to confront what it truly means to fight for a future when every choice echoes through eternity.

Beatrix Cramer (4338.205.1 - 4338.211.6)

Beatrix Cramer's life is a delicate balance of contradictions, her independence and keen intellect shadowed by her penchant for the forbidden. A master of acquisition, her love for antiques and the call of the wild drives her into the heart of danger, making her an indispensable ally yet an unpredictable force. When fate thrusts her into the clandestine world of Guardians, Beatrix must navigate a labyrinth of secrets and moral dilemmas. Caught in the crossfire of legacy and destiny, she faces choices that could redefine the boundaries of her world and her very identity.

Gladys Cramer (4338.204.1 - 4338.214.3)

In a world frayed by tragedies, Gladys Cramer seeks solace in wine, her steadfast refuge amid life's turmoil. Tethered to a man ensnared by duty and love, she stands at a pivotal crossroads, her choices poised to weave the threads of her fate. Each glass of wine deepens her reflection on the decisions looming ahead and the silent vows brimming with untold consequences. Amidst tragedy and secrets, with wine as her guiding light yet potential harbinger of misstep, Gladys's journey veers onto a path set for an inevitable collision.

Karl Jenkins (4338.209.1 - 4338.214.1)

Plunged into Tasmania's most chilling cases, Senior Detective Karl Jenkins confronts a string of disappearances that entangle with his clandestine affair with Detective Sarah Lahey. As a dangerous obsession emerges, every step toward the truth draws Karl perilously close to a precipice threatening their lives and careers. "Karl Jenkins" is a riveting tale of suspense, where past haunts bear a perilous future.

Sarah Lahey (4338.209.1 - 4338.214.2)

In the grip of Tasmania's eerie disappearances, Detective Sarah Lahey's quest for answers becomes a personal crucible. As her investigation draws her deeper into the shadows, her tangled relationship with fellow detective Karl Jenkins blurs the lines between ally and liability. Together, they face a darkening path that tests their bond and the very heart of their resolve. "Sarah Lahey" weaves a tale of relentless pursuit and suspense, where the quest for truth risks more than just a partnership—it tempts a treacherous fate.

4338.209.3 - 4338.214.3

LUKE SMITH

"Life, my friends, is a cosmic tapestry waiting to be unfurled. Each thread woven with dreams, decisions, and the dance of interconnected destinies."

- Luke Smith

4338.209

(28 July 2018)

A PHASED APPROACH

4338.209.3

Phase 1: Phone Call

The phone felt heavier in my hand than it ever had before, as if the weight of the world had settled upon it. Its cold, lifeless surface contrasted sharply with the turmoil that was boiling inside me, a storm of emotions that seemed ready to burst forth at any moment. The device, once a simple means of communication, now felt like a lifeline to a past I both yearned for and dreaded to revisit.

"Hello, this is Nial," the calm voice on the other end echoed through the line, oblivious to the storm raging within me. His voice, steady and unsuspecting, flowed through the receiver, sounding like a distant echo from a life that once was. *How could he sound so serene when my world was on the brink of collapsing?*

Despite the residual tremors coursing through my hands from the pain that had mercilessly ripped through my chest moments ago, I summoned a smile. A façade, a feeble attempt to cloak the turmoil churning within. *This must be done*, I reminded myself sternly, pushing back the tendrils of doubt that threatened to entangle my resolve. My heart pounded in my chest, a relentless drum echoing the fear and desperation that I fought to keep at bay.

"Hi Nial. This is Luke Smith. Not sure if you remember me, but you did a small fencing job for me a few years ago, out in Berriedale." The words hung in the air, suspended between the present reality and the memories I desperately sought to keep at bay. Each syllable felt heavy, loaded with the weight of the past and the uncertainty of the future. I could almost see the sun setting over the fence he had worked on, a fence that marked the boundaries of a life that now felt so far away.

Nial's response was surprisingly prompt, as if he had been expecting my call, anticipating the reunion of our fates. "With the small dog that followed me like a shadow and had to keep poking his nose into everything, yeah?" His voice held a chuckle, a recollection of canine antics that brought a fleeting warmth to the conversation. For a moment, I could picture that small dog, its curious eyes and wagging tail, a stark contrast to the heavy heart I carried.

"That's the one," I replied, mirroring the lightheartedness, though my eyes tightly closed in an effort to banish the memories of my beloved Duke. The image of him, so vivid and heart-wrenching, threatened to overpower my composure. *Be brave. Be bold. Do it for Henri.* I repeated the mantra in my head, a lifeline in the swirling sea of emotions that threatened to engulf me.

"I remember it well," said Nial, his voice dancing with a light and energetic cadence. It was as if his words were imbued with a liveliness that I desperately yearned for, a reminder of simpler times. "What can I do for you?"

"I have an urgent job that I need done in the next couple of days," I replied, the necessity of the situation pressing against the constraints of time, making each second feel more precious and perilous.

"Hmph," scoffed Nial, a deep sound resonating in my ear. His skepticism was a tangible force, an obstacle that I needed to overcome. "That's not enough lead time. I need at least two weeks." His words were like a cold splash of reality, dousing the flicker of hope that had started to ignite within me.

"You'll be well compensated for it," I lied. As the words left my mouth, a part of me recoiled at the ease with which the lie had surfaced. My brain raced to concoct any reason that might sway Nial's decision, for Henri's sake. The stakes were too high to be hindered by scruples.

"How much?" Nial inquired, a hint of curiosity cutting through the skepticism in his tone. There was a shift in his voice, a subtle but noticeable change that hinted at the potential to sway his decision.

"One hundred thousand dollars," I replied, a figure that hung suspended, briefly questioning its own audacity. The number felt surreal, almost fantastical, yet it was the bait I hoped would clinch the deal. "In cash," I added, the words spilling forth, a commitment made before I could second-guess the weight they carried. The enormity of the promise loomed over me, a towering wave that threatened to crash down at any moment.

"Shit! What sort of job is it?" Nial's curiosity grew, echoing my own internal interrogation. *What was I getting myself into?*

"It's... uh... it's a pretty big job. Look, why don't you meet me in Collinsvale, and we can go over the rough plans. Tell me what you think before you give your yay or nay." My voice faltered slightly, betraying a hint of the unease that I was desperately trying to mask. The suggestion to meet was a gamble, a play to gain time and perhaps, in some way, validation for this madness.

"Oh, you're not in Berriedale anymore?" The question struck a nerve, a reminder of the intricacies of the web I was weaving. The past and present seemed to collide in that moment, each battling for dominance in my mind. I had to keep my story straight, had to maintain the façade.

"Yeah, I'm still in Berriedale. Just helping a friend out." The lie slipped out smoothly, a practiced deceit that I hoped would cover my tracks. Each word felt like a step further into a maze of my own making, with no clear path back to the truth.

"Cash?" Nial echoed, seeking reassurance. His repetition of the word 'cash' reverberated in my ears, a reminder of the enormity of what I was proposing. It felt like a test, a measure of my commitment to this precarious plan.

"That's right. One hundred thousand of it," I asserted, my confidence belying the turmoil beneath the surface. I forced strength into my voice, projecting an assurance I was far from feeling. "On top of the cost of materials," I added hastily, as if to further justify the exorbitant sum. The words felt like a lifeline, a way to make the deal more palatable, more real.

"I'll meet you there in thirty," declared Nial, his eagerness for an immediate meeting catching me off guard. His quick acceptance and readiness to act sent a jolt through me, a mix of relief and apprehension. *Was this really happening?*

"Great. I'll text you the address." My response was automatic, a reflex in this rapidly unfolding scenario. I was committed now, the pieces set in motion, a game that I had to see through to the end.

"Okay," said Nial, concluding the call. His words, simple and final, marked the end of our conversation, but the beginning of a path from which there was no return.

As the line went silent, I inhaled deeply, the air thick with the weight of my own deception. It felt heavy, almost suffocating, as if the very act of breathing had become a chore in this new strategy I had crafted. The phone in my hand, once a mere device, now felt like a symbol of the deceit I had woven, its surface cold and impersonal against my increasingly clammy palm.

I clutched the sides of the bench, my knuckles whitening under the strain. The bench, once a place of respite in my kitchen, now felt like a confessional, a witness to the web of lies I had spun. My eyes burned like an uncontrolled bushfire, ready to consume everything in its path. The intensity of my gaze reflected the turmoil raging inside me, a wildfire of emotions that scorched every rational thought.

Thick, black billows of smoky guilt smothered my mind, a relentless reminder of the choices I had made. The guilt was suffocating, a dense fog that clouded my judgement and choked my conscience. It was a stark contrast to the clear, moral guidelines I had once adhered to, now obscured by the complexity of my situation.

"Why!?" I screamed out in agony, the anguished cry escaping the confines of my being. The sound tore through the quiet of the house, shattering the serenity of the morning. It was a raw, primal sound, born from the depths of despair and regret. The cry was not just a question, but a lamentation for the path I had chosen, tortured by the deadly impact of my actions.

Yet still, amidst the tempest of regret, I knew the wheels had been set in motion. There was a bitter acceptance in this realisation, a resignation to the new course I had set.

For Henri, I reminded myself. *It was for Henri.*

❖

Phase 2: Collection

"For fuck's sake!" I swore, the exclamation escaping my lips as my foot collided with one of the precarious stacks of nature magazines lining the narrow hallway of the Owen's home. The sudden contact sent a jolt through me, a physical manifestation of the turmoil inside. Gravity asserted its dominance, and I found myself tumbling to the floor, the magazines sprawling out in front of me like a mocking reminder of my own clumsiness. They fanned across the floor in a chaotic array, a vivid metaphor for the disarray in my life.

In a fit of frustration, emotions spilled over once more, and I unleashed my anger on the periodicals, tossing every goddamn magazine I could see into the open maw of the Portal against the hallway wall. Each magazine flung felt like a release, a futile attempt to rid myself of the frustration and desperation clawing at my insides.

My pacing did little to ease the ache in my heart or the nervous energy escalating within me. The hallway, now stripped of its paper clutter, felt like a confined space, the walls closing in on me with each passing minute. The bareness of the corridor only served to amplify my sense of isolation and entrapment, a physical echo of the mental prison I had built for myself.

Up and down the now-empty corridor, I retraced the steps of my restless journey, the details of the strategy replaying in my mind like a broken record. It was a simple plan, a precarious dance of deception. I had promised Nial a hundred thousand dollars in cash, but my pockets were barren of such wealth. The lie weighed heavily on me, a deceitful burden that I bore with every step.

The real agenda was to coerce him into Clivilius, where he could contribute to building secure fences for the settlement. In my mind, I could see the fences, a tangible symbol of safety and security in a world that felt anything but. Nial's fencing business would serve as a legitimate source for supplies, minimising the risk of raising any alarms. It was a calculated move, a strategic manipulation of resources and people.

As for his wife, a ruse using Nial's phone would keep her at bay, thinking he had gone away for a few weeks for work. The thought of involving his wife, of weaving her into this web of lies, added another layer of guilt to my conscience. It was a necessary part of the plan, but that did little to ease the weight of it. Every step, every decision, felt like a further descent into a moral abyss from which there was no easy escape.

"It's the perfect plan! I'm certain of it," I muttered to myself, the conviction in my voice wavering beneath the weight of doubt. The words, meant to be a reassurance, felt hollow, echoing in the empty hallway. Each syllable was a feeble attempt to bolster my own crumbling confidence, a mantra that lacked the certainty it desperately tried to convey.

As I grappled with my thoughts, the sound of tires rolling across wet ground cut through my contemplation like a sharp knife slicing through the thick fog of my mind. It was a jarring, yet grounding reminder that the time for action had arrived. Peering through the front screen door, I watched Nial park his ute beside the large gum trees, their leaves glistening with the remnants of a recent rain. The sight of his vehicle, so mundane and yet so pivotal to my plan, sent a fresh wave of anxiety coursing through me.

Wiping my face clear of residual tears, I forced a smile onto my face. The action felt mechanical, a mask put on for the world to see. It was a smile that didn't reach my eyes, which still held the echo of the turmoil I was trying so desperately to suppress. *You just need to get him inside. That's all you have to do*, I reminded myself. The thought was both a command and a plea, a focus for the swirling storm of thoughts and emotions that threatened to overwhelm me.

My gaze momentarily shifted to the swirling colours on the hallway wall behind me. They were a vivid representation of the turmoil within me, a physical manifestation of the internal disarray. The colours, so bright and jumbled, seemed to mock my feigned composure.

Each step towards the door felt like wading through treacle, my movements slow and deliberate as I tried to maintain the façade of normalcy. The plan, a delicate house of cards, hinged on my ability to persuade Nial, to draw him into the web I had spun.

"Hey Nial," I greeted him as cheerfully as I could muster, stepping onto the front verandah. The words felt like a costume, ill-fitting and uncomfortable, yet necessary for the role I had to play. The pounding of my heart left no room for patience, and I covered the distance between us before he could take a step. Each stride was an effort to appear casual, to mask the urgency that thrummed through my veins like an electric current.

"Hi Luke," replied Nial, accepting my hand with a firm shake. His grip was solid, grounding. His presence, so real and tangible, was a reminder of the stakes at hand.

"I'm glad you came," I told him, dropping my hands to my sides. My fingers commenced a nervous tap against my legs, a rhythm born of anxiety. It was a small, almost imperceptible movement, but to me, it felt like the drumbeat of war.

"No worries," replied Nial. "I'd be lying if I said I wasn't more than a little curious about the job." His words carried a hint of suspicion, an undercurrent that made my stomach clench.

"Good. That's... that's good," I stammered, my words fumbling in their attempt to mask my inner turmoil. My eyes averted from Nial's penetrating gaze, afraid that he might glimpse the deceit lurking within them.

"The Owen's home?" Nial inquired, his voice carrying a subtle nervousness. The question felt like a probe, a test of the ploy I had so carefully constructed.

My eyes raised, determination flickering within, "Oh, I've got the plans lying on the kitchen table. You'll love them!" I said, giving Nial's shoulder a playful slap. The action was a desperate attempt to inject some lightness into the situation, to steer the conversation away from dangerous waters. "Shall we?" I gestured toward the house, my movements overly animated, betraying my eagerness to get him inside.

"So, a hundred thousand?" Nial asked as we walked in step.

"Cash," I replied calmly, projecting a confidence I did not feel.

"Must be a pretty important job then." His tone was casual, but I could hear the underlying curiosity, a probing for more information.

"Probably the most important you'll ever do," I said, my eyes fixed on the front door, a silent plea for focus. The words were a mix of truth and fabrication, a cocktail of desperation and determination.

Nial's heavy work boots made a solid clomp as he ascended the wooden steps leading to the verandah that stretched the length of the modest cottage. The sound was steady and reassuring, a counterpoint to the erratic beat of my own heart. As we approached the door, the reality of what I was about to do settled over me like a heavy cloak, each step forward sealing my commitment to this nefarious plan.

I held the front screen open, ushering Nial inside. The door's familiar creak seemed louder than usual, reverberating through the tense silence between us. The weight of the moment pressed down on me, each second stretched thin with anticipation.

"Thank you," said Nial, stepping into the doorway. His large frame seemed to fill the space. Gripping the doorway, he paused and turned back to me, a rush of panic coursing through me. His hesitation was like a physical barrier, a wall that threatened to block my carefully laid plans.

"Look, Luke, I'm not sure I can do this," he said, shaking his head. The words hit me like a physical blow, a sudden and unexpected obstacle. My heart raced, panic clawing at the edges of my carefully maintained composure.

"Oh?" I asked, attempting to conceal the panic. *Just a few more steps*. My voice was a mask of calm, belying the turmoil within. "What's wrong?" The question was an attempt to reel him back in.

"I dunno. It's just... it's a lot of money. And in cash," Nial explained, exhaling deeply. His concern was palpable, a mirror to the doubts that gnawed at my own conscience.

"I get it," I said with a short chuckle. "I suppose I have been a little mysterious about it all, haven't I?" It was a gamble, an attempt to disarm his reservations with humour.

"Maybe just a little," agreed Nial, his face softening slightly. The shift in his expression was a small victory, a crack in the wall of his hesitation.

I smiled widely, a show of confidence I was far from feeling. "I promise it's legit. It'll all make sense once you see the plans." My words were a bridge, an offer of understanding and reassurance.

"You sure?"

I nodded eagerly, my movement a bit too quick, a bit too desperate. "And the Owen's? They're not home?" He was probing, looking for assurance, for stability in the shifting sands of this situation.

"Come, let me show you," I replied, sidestepping Nial's question and urging him to continue into the hallway. It was a delicate dance, leading him on while avoiding the pitfalls of his questions.

"Okay." His acquiescence was a relief, a sign that he was still on board, albeit tentatively.

"The kitchen's just down the end of the hallway and to the left," I directed.

A pleased grin spread across my face as Nial's pace slowed, his attention irresistibly drawn to the mesmerising colours of the Portal that still swirled across almost the entire length of the hallway wall. The Portal, a riot of colours and shapes, was like a siren's call, drawing him in with its otherworldly beauty.

"That's a remarkable piece of work," said Nial, unable to pull his eyes away. His fascination was evident, his guard momentarily lowered in the face of such wonder.

"I know. I've seen it a dozen times now, and I still think it's spectacular," I said. My words were a lure, keeping his attention fixed on the Portal, away from the lingering doubts and questions.

Sensing the growing strength of Nial's ease, like a fearless lion, I lunged at him. It was a calculated move, a culmination of strategy and desperation. Having learned from earlier encounters, my shoulder collided forcefully with Nial's side. The impact was a release, a physical manifestation of the pent-up tension and fear.

Unable to stop the inertia, and with nowhere to grab onto, Nial fell into the spectacular artwork and vanished. The sight of his disappearance was surreal, a moment frozen in time, both triumphant and terrifying.

Closing the Portal, I breathed a deep sigh of relief. Despite Nial's larger frame, that was much easier than Kain's episode, and as easy as I had hoped for. The relief was short-lived, quickly replaced by the weight of what I had just done.

Now, that's phase two of the plan done. The thought was a cold comfort, a reminder that the path I had chosen was irrevocable, each step forward a further descent into a world where the ends justified the means.

❖

Phase 3: Confirmation

The ute roared to life, a thunderous sound that shattered the serene atmosphere, startling the several geese that had ambled up from the small pond behind the house. Their flapping wings and hurried quacks added a layer of liveliness to the scene. As the engine hummed with power, my eyes performed another three-sixty, absorbing the scene that had once been a sanctuary. The thick native Tasmanian trees encircling the property cocooned it in a shield of protection, warding off the prying eyes of distant neighbours. Their towering forms, stoic and silent, seemed to watch over me, a reminder of the world's beauty that lay just beyond the chaos I had ensnared myself in.

In this moment, amidst the rustling leaves and the occasional quack of the geese, tranquility blanketed the landscape, momentarily eclipsing the weight of the dramas I had initiated and had no idea how to stop. It was a bittersweet solace, a fleeting escape from the relentless advance of my own machinations.

"I love this spot," I whispered to myself, a fleeting attempt to find solace in the familiar surroundings that had become a backdrop to my tangled endeavours. The words were a caress, a soft touch against the harsh reality of my actions. They were a reminder of what I was fighting for, a plea for forgiveness from the land that bore witness to my deceit.

Having meticulously filled Nial's ute to the brim with supplies collected from the Owens' house, a peculiar readiness settled within me. It was a readiness tinged with resignation, a preparation for the next phase of my plan. Ready to face the man I had deceived, yet secretly hoping that time had worked its magic, and someone else had taken Nial to camp. Perhaps, in some twisted way, I could absolve myself of the direct consequences of my actions. Perhaps, I could conveniently leave the ute by the Portal, a silent testament to the deeds done in the shadows.

But the practicalities nagged at me. "But I need him to tell me where his office is," I sighed, acknowledging that avoidance was not an option. The realisation was a weight, a heavy cloak that settled on my shoulders. With the key still nestled in the ignition, I extracted it from its chain. Stuffing the remaining keys into my pocket, I felt the sharp edges against my thigh, a constant reminder of the choices made and the path that lay ahead. Each step, each decision, felt like a further entanglement in a web of my own making, a journey through a landscape that I had altered irrevocably with my actions.

The Clivilian dust erupted into a plume as I drove through the Portal, signalling my arrival in a manner as dramatic as the circumstances that had compelled me here. The landscape of Clivilius, with its rugged terrain and the fine dust that seemed to hang in the air, greeted me like an old friend, albeit one whose embrace was tinged with the complexity of my intentions. And to my surprise, Nial was standing nearby, engaged in conversation with Kain, an unexpected juxtaposition of my old life against the backdrop of my current predicament.

"Why is he here?" Kain demanded the moment I emerged from the ute. His voice, laced with accusation, cut through the air. I could feel the tension, palpable and charged, a silent standoff in the dust.

"He owns a fence construction business," I replied curtly, aiming to truncate the conversation, to shield Nial from the complex intricacies that had woven themselves into the fabric of the last few days. Each word was measured, an attempt to navigate the minefield of questions and implications that Kain's inquiry had unearthed.

Kain nodded, a silent acknowledgment of the necessity to bring another person into Clivilius. It was a gesture that carried the weight of acceptance, albeit reluctantly, a concession to the dire needs of our community.

"These include your office keys?" I turned to Nial, presenting the keys I had retrieved from my pocket.

"Yeah," Nial replied, his expression a canvas of confusion. His voice, tinged with uncertainty, echoed the tumultuous thoughts that I imagined were racing through his mind. The situation, so far removed from the ordinary, must have seemed like an unfathomable puzzle to him.

Kain can deal with Nial's introduction to the camp, I reassured myself, resisting the urge to unravel the convoluted events of the past few days to bring Nial up to speed. It was a decision born of necessity, a way to distance myself from the immediate fallout, to preserve what little integrity remained in the web of lies I had spun.

"Where's your office?" I inquired, cutting to the chase. The question, direct and devoid of any prelude, was my attempt to steer the conversation towards practicalities, away from the moral quagmire that threatened to consume my mind.

"It's a home office. Why?" Nial questioned, his brows furrowed in a mix of curiosity and concern.

"Great. The key is still in the ignition," I informed the two men, the words hanging in the air as a precursor to my departure. It was a statement of finality, a closing chapter on this phase of the plan, leaving the intricacies of what came next for Nial, in their hands.

Without further ado, I walked through the Portal, the threshold between worlds swallowing me whole. Stepping back into the familiar yet now alien landscape of my own world, I was acutely aware of the bridge I had just crossed, a bridge that spanned not just worlds but the vast expanse of my own moral compass. The journey back was a solitary one, filled with the echoes of my actions and the unyielding path that lay ahead.

❖

Phase 4: The Office

The day already felt like it was slipping through my fingers, a realisation that weighed on me as heavily as the morning dew clinging to the blades of grass along the driveway of Nial Triffett's house. The visit to his home had taken longer than I anticipated, an unfortunate reminder of the unforeseen challenges that seemed to proliferate with each step I took deeper into this tangled web of responsibility. I had naively expected to find his address plastered all over the internet, but reality, as it often does, had different plans. An old invoice from a small job Nial did for me years ago became my unexpected saviour, its fine print holding the key, quite literally, to his whereabouts. His business address, assumed to be his home address, was a treasure buried at the bottom of the invoice, a breadcrumb in my quest that I had almost overlooked.

Parking discreetly a few doors down, I found myself now striding somewhat confidently down the driveway, keys to Nial's home and office clutched in my hand like talismans. The plan, in theory, was straightforward: let myself in and transport Nial's entire office to Clivilius. There was no need for covert break-ins this time. With Nial's office situated in Clivilius, he could assist in ordering supplies to fortify the settlement with much-needed fencing. The practicalities of executing such a plan, however, danced on the edge of my consciousness, a ballet of moral and logistical dilemmas.

After a series of knocks to confirm the absence of occupants, the first key I tried slid into the front door, turning with a reassuring clunk. The sound was a symphony of progress, a promising, yet fleeting moment of things going according to plan. The ease of entry brought a rare smile to my face—a welcome departure from the complications that seemed to haunt every Guardian task.

The last time I had ventured into someone's home under such circumstances was to collect clothing for Glenda, Kain, and Joel, a task that should have been simple but proved otherwise. The memory served as a poignant reminder that nothing is straightforward about being a Guardian. Each step taken, each decision made, seemed to unravel in unexpected ways, weaving a fabric of complexity that I was constantly struggling to keep from fraying.

As I stepped into Nial's home, the air heavy with the silent stories of its inhabitants, I couldn't shake the feeling of intrusion, a violation of privacy that weighed heavily on my conscience. Yet, the urgency of our situation in Clivilius, the lives depending on these actions, propelled me forward. It was a delicate balance, navigating the thin line between right and wrong, each action a testament to the sacrifices demanded by the role of a Guardian.

Once inside, closing the front door behind me, a deep growl pierced the air, shattering the silence with its menacing promise. I turned to face a lanky Dalmatian, teeth bared in a warning that left little room for misunderstanding. My heart leaped into my throat. Swallowing an initial surge of panic, I addressed the dog with calm authority, an attempt to mask my inner turmoil. "Sit," I instructed, my voice steady, projecting a confidence I scarcely felt. To my surprise, the dog obeyed, its posture shifting from aggression to cautious obedience.

"Stay," I commanded, my voice imbued with a hope that its trained obedience would grant me passage through this unexpected obstacle. My gaze then shifted to the closed door off the hallway, which I assumed led to Nial's home office. Carefully, I slid another key into the lock, my attention divided between the task at hand and the watchful eyes of the Dalmatian.

As the dog darted past me, a sudden chiming from my phone caused me to startle, the abrupt sound jarring in the quiet of the house. Retrieving it from my pocket, I read the message.

14.17PM Jane: *Luke, Thelma is with me. We need the key back that she gave you.*

"Shit," I muttered under my breath, the timing of the message adding another layer of complication to an already precarious situation. "They'll just have to wait," I whispered to the dog at my feet, trying to convince myself more than the animal. My gaze then settled on what I presumed to be Nial's cluttered work desk. The mahogany surface, polished to a sheen, hinted at craftsmanship that could only be Nial's —a testament to his attention to detail and skill.

My fingers traced the smooth surface, inadvertently displacing several papers that drifted to the floor in a gentle cascade. The dog emitted a quick bark as the papers fell, a sound that seemed more curious than threatening now. A closed laptop occupied a central position on the desk, its presence a beacon of hope amidst the clutter. *Finally, the universe is on my side*, I thought, a rare flicker of optimism surfacing amidst the layers of challenges and moral quandaries.

My phone chimed again, a shrill sound that seemed to echo the urgency of the situation.

14.23 Jane: *It's urgent. Come now.*

"For fuck's sake," I hissed under my breath, my frustration mounting with each passing second. The words on the screen felt like a tether, pulling me back to a reality I was desperately trying to navigate. Torn between aiding my newfound grandmother, Jane, and bolstering the settlement's security, I found myself at a crossroads, each path laden with its own set of implications. My gaze returned to the desk, a symbol of the task I had set out to accomplish. *A few more hours' delay won't make any difference*, I reasoned with myself, trying to find justification in my decision. *They can't order materials and build a fence in that time anyway,* I continued, my mind seeking solace in the logic of my own argument.

"Nial, are you home?" a woman's voice echoed from the direction of the front door, slicing through the silence of the house like a cold draft. My heart skipped a beat, the sudden intrusion of another human voice igniting a spark of panic within me. The Dalmatian, previously my reluctant ally, trotted out, betraying my presence with its movements. The loyalty of pets, it seemed, was not to be underestimated.

The pounding of my heart felt as if it might burst through my ribcage, each beat a thunderous reminder of the precariousness of my situation. Realising the decision had been made for me, I hastily seized the laptop. The device, so central to my plans, now felt like a heavy weight in my hands.

With no time to spare, I made my exit through the swirling colours of the Portal, activated inconspicuously on the side of a tall filing cabinet. The transition between worlds, normally a moment of awe and wonder, now felt like a desperate escape, a leap into the unknown driven by necessity. As the familiar yet always unsettling sensation of crossing through the Portal enveloped me, I couldn't help but feel a sense of loss, a poignant reminder of the world and responsibilities I was momentarily leaving behind.

KEY RELATIONSHIP

4338.209.4

The sterile scent of disinfectant enveloped me as I walked through the glass doors of the nursing home, a familiar yet always slightly jarring welcome. Each step resonated in the hushed corridors, the sound of my footsteps a solitary beat in the quietude of the afternoon. Though the visit was familiar, today held an unusual sense of anticipation, a deviation from the ordinary that sent a flutter of unease through my stomach.

Passing the reception desk, the receptionist's courteous smile masked the monotony of her daily tasks. It was a smile I had come to recognise, one that spoke of long hours and the ceaseless flow of visitors, yet today it seemed to carry an extra layer of significance. Navigating the maze of hallways, a gravity seemed to hang in the air, an unspoken understanding that this visit held something significant. The weight of the impending meeting pressed down on me, a tangible presence amidst the antiseptic smells and muted sounds.

The pale walls adorned with idyllic landscapes attempted to inject warmth into the clinical environment. Paintings of lush fields and tranquil rivers contrasted starkly with the reality of the nursing home, a poignant reminder of the world outside these walls. Hushed whispers of caregivers and the occasional wheeled walker created a subdued symphony of life, a backdrop to the profound moments within these walls. Each sound, each movement, felt imbued with a deeper meaning, the ordinary moments of care and support weaving together to form the fabric of daily life here.

Leaving the main thoroughfares, I entered a narrow hallway, its stark white walls echoing the untold stories of ageing and solitude. The hallway felt like a liminal space, a bridge between the bustling activity of the nursing home and the private world of its residents. Quickening my pace, my mind focused on the impending meeting with Jane and Thelma. The anticipation of what was to come—a mixture of dread and a desperate hope for resolution—gnawed at me.

Interrupted by Ben's voice, calling out as he pushed an old lady in a wheelchair down the corridor, irritation simmered beneath my surface. The sound of his voice grated against my already frayed nerves, an unwelcome distraction from the tumult of thoughts swirling in my head. Suppressing the urge to ignore him, I waited for his approach, impatience etching my features into a mask of barely concealed annoyance.

"What?" I asked curtly, my tone reflecting the irritation that bubbled within me. Each word was clipped, a verbal manifestation of my desire to be anywhere but here, dealing with anything but this.

"Is Jamie alright? I've not seen him at work the last week," inquired Ben, his question innocent enough but to me, it felt like an intrusion, a needless poking at the one place he most certainly did not belong.

"Jamie's fine," I replied, my words a tightrope walk between irritation and the need to maintain some semblance of composure. If not for the old lady with him, my response might have been less guarded, my politeness replaced by outright hostility. Her presence was a reminder of the decorum expected here, even if my patience was threadbare.

The old woman's unsettling gaze intensified my discomfort. Her eyes, sharp and penetrating, seemed to bore into me, seeing through the façade of calm I struggled to maintain. Something about her seemed eerie, her stare sending a shiver down my spine, as if she could glimpse deeper than the tumultuous sea of emotions I was desperately trying to navigate.

"Can you tell him I say hi, and that I hope he's back at work soon?" Ben's request came through, his concern genuine but to me, it felt like another weight added to the burden I already bore.

"No," I said bluntly, my patience waning. The word was a barrier, a line drawn to protect the scant peace of mind I clung to.

Ben's pout only fuelled my frustration, his expression one of wounded confusion. "Is everything okay with the two of you?" he probed further, his curiosity piercing the thin veneer of my self-control.

That was the final straw. Reacting instinctively, I slammed Ben against the wall, my anger boiling over. The suddenness of my own action startled me, but the rage that had been simmering beneath the surface found its outlet. His laboured breathing echoed in the corridor, a stark counterpoint to the silence that had preceded our altercation.

"You've got a nerve asking something like that," I seethed, my grip tightening as I leaned in, my words laced with venom. The corridor, once a place of transient passage, became a stage for the drama that unfolded between us.

Ben's face soured, contorting with a mix of fear and defiance as he struggled to breathe. "Get over it, Luke," he retorted scathingly, his words a sharp jab aimed at my most vulnerable spots.

My free hand delivered a warning, squeezing Ben's crotch. "If you want to keep these functional, I suggest you learn how to keep them in your pants. Or I will stew them like a pair of overripe plums on a sweltering summer day."

Releasing Ben, he dropped to the floor, nursing his aching gems. The tension in my muscles eased slightly, but the turmoil within me did not. "Have a nice day," I told the old woman, forcing a smile as I passed her. The effort it took to muster that smile felt monumental.

Turning the final corner, my heart thumped in my chest, a relentless drumbeat that seemed to echo the tumult of my emotions. An unspoken greeting passed between me and Virginia in the hall, a silent acknowledgment of the gravity of the moment. "Don't be long," Virginia called over her shoulder, her voice laced with concern. "She needs rest." Her words, meant as a gentle reminder, felt like a weight, adding to the sense of urgency that compelled me forward.

My face softened as I considered Jane's declining health, nodding my agreement. The reminder of her fragility, of the preciousness of the time we had left, brought a momentary clarity to my thoughts, a brief respite from the maelstrom of guilt and duty that battled within me.

Arriving at the door marked "Lahey," I took a deep breath before knocking, trying to steady myself for the encounter ahead. The air was infused with the faint scent of aged wood and a distant hint of lavender, a reminder of the life and memories that permeated these walls. The door reluctantly swung open with an annoying squeak, a sound that seemed to underscore the tension of the moment.

Jane's piercing gaze met mine as she held out her hand, "Where's Thelma's key?". Her question, direct and laden with expectation, cut through the air between us. "It's in a safe place," I replied, my voice steady, though I could feel the weight of anticipation in the room. The sunlight filtered through the window, casting a soft glow on the worn carpet, a visual contrast to the tension that filled the room.

Jane's eyes narrowed with a hint of panic, a clear sign that my refusal to hand over the key without getting the answers I sought was not part of her plan. "You didn't bring it with you?" she asked urgently.

"No," I said softly yet firmly, my resolve unwavering. I needed to set the tone for this conversation, to assert that the time for evasions was past. "I want some answers first." My words hung between us, a challenge, a plea for transparency in a situation that had been anything but clear.

Jane sighed heavily, the sound carrying years of burden, a testament to the complexity of the secrets she held. "I don't think we have time for answers." Her words were a deflection, an attempt to push past my demands, but they only served to heighten my curiosity and my concern.

I eyed Jane curiously, unsure of the urgency she implied. The atmosphere in the room hung heavy with unspoken secrets and so many unanswered questions. It felt as though the very walls were witnesses to the mysteries that lay just beyond my grasp.

"Let the boy in," an old croaky voice instructed from inside the room, resonating like the rustle of autumn leaves. The command, unexpected yet authoritative, cut through the tension, introducing the second player into this intricate dance of revelation and concealment.

Stepping aside, Jane ushered me into their world, the door closing behind me with a finality that echoed through the narrow hallway. The room was a tableau of memories – faded photographs adorned the walls, capturing moments frozen in time; an armchair with worn armrests stood as a sentinel of the past, its fabric telling tales of countless hours spent in contemplation or companionship; and a threadbare rug underfoot whispered stories of years gone by, each worn fibre a testament to the life lived.

Thelma sat at the table, her hands clasped in front of her, a cup of steaming tea untouched. The scene was one of waiting, of preparation for something yet to unfold. The air carried the warmth of nostalgia, mixed with the faint aroma of brewing tea leaves, a scent that evoked memories of simpler times, of afternoons spent in quiet solitude. The room, with its relics of the past, felt like a bridge between the world I knew and a world I was only just beginning to understand, a place where the threads of our stories were interwoven with the fabric of time itself.

"Hello, Thelma," I greeted her, taking a seat at the table as indicated by Jane. The room, with its layers of history and personal stories, enveloped me, making the moment feel both intimate and imposing. Thelma's eyes, though aged and bearing the weight of many years, flickered with a glimmer of recognition as she smiled faintly. It was a smile that seemed to bridge the gap between the present and a past replete with memories.

"Have you seen my key?" she asked gently, her voice soft yet carrying a weight that seemed disproportionate to the simplicity of the question. Her words, woven with an air of confusion, hinted at depths and mysteries that lay just beyond reach.

"You gave it to me, remember," I reminded her, gazing into her aged eyes, attempting to forge a connection lost in the labyrinth of time. The effort to connect, to find a shared point of reference in the muddled sea of her memory, felt like reaching across a vast chasm.

"William will be most pleased," Thelma said, her words echoing like a distant melody that refused to fade. The repetition of the cryptic phrases mirrored the tangled web of thoughts swirling in my mind, a puzzle that seemed to grow more complex with each exchange.

"I can hear him, you know," Thelma continued, her voice dropping to a spectral whisper that danced on the edges of comprehension. The claim, so casually stated, sent a shiver down my spine, a chilling reminder of the unseen connections and hidden truths that lay just beyond the veil of the ordinary.

A hefty sigh escaped Jane's lips, a sound heavy with the weight of unspoken burdens. It settled into the room with a palpable presence, as she leaned into the back of a dining chair, her posture one of resigned watchfulness. I looked to Jane, seeking answers in her eyes, but was met with a wall of silence. Her expression, while guarded, was tinged with a silent plea for understanding, a wordless communication that spoke volumes of the complexities we were navigating.

"Do you know what she's talking about?" I asked Jane, my voice laced with concern and a hint of desperation. The situation, already fraught with confusion and unanswered questions, seemed to deepen with each passing moment.

Jane shrugged gently, her gesture one of resignation mixed with an undercurrent of sorrow. Her gaze, distant yet piercing, was filled with a silent plea for understanding, a recognition of the shared burden of knowledge and the pain of secrets long held.

I hesitated, reluctant to probe further in front of Thelma, but the nuance of the situation demanded clarity. The room felt charged with the weight of unspoken truths, each breath a moment of decision. "Is it dementia?" I asked, the question slipping out more gently than I had intended, my words hanging in the air like delicate threads vulnerable to the slightest disturbance.

Jane shrugged again, her face a mask of emotionless resolve that offered no comfort or denial. The ambiguity of her response left me floating in a sea of uncertainty, grasping for any semblance of understanding in the complex web of their lives.

Thelma's hands slammed against the table, the sudden motion igniting a spark in her eyes that belied the calm of moments before. "You know darn well that I don't have dementia," she asserted with a vigour that startled me. The fire within her, so at odds with the fragility of her age, spoke volumes of the strength and defiance still residing within her.

"Then what's going on?" I asked, my confusion and impatience growing in equal measure. The puzzle before me seemed to expand with every attempt to piece it together. "And who the heck is William?" The question, borne of frustration and a desperate need for answers, felt like a key turning in a lock, unsure if it would open the door to understanding or further mysteries.

A smile crossed Thelma's wrinkled face, a brief flicker of something other than the confusion and shadows that seemed to dominate our conversation. "William Jeffries is my father-in-law," she revealed, the simplicity of the statement catching me off guard and redirecting the flow of my thoughts.

With the fondness that Thelma seemed to speak of him, I had expected a more personal connection, a story interwoven with her own in a way that suggested a deeper bond. "The two of you were close?" I asked, my curiosity piqued, leaning forward slightly as if the space between us could shorten the distance to the truth.

"No, they weren't particularly," Jane answered on Thelma's behalf, her intervention abrupt, her face stern. Her words, decisive and final, felt like a door closing on a chapter of the story that remained shrouded in mystery. Jane's demeanour, guarding a trove of untold stories, suggested layers of complexity and hidden depths to their family history that were not mine to easily uncover.

I rubbed at my brow, feeling the physical manifestation of my inner turmoil—a mix of frustration and intrigue that seemed to knot tighter with each passing moment. "You two are making this a little confusing," I admitted with a slight chuckle, an attempt to lighten the mood that felt heavy with unspoken histories. "Why don't we just start with the key? Why is it so important? What is it for?" The questions tumbled out, each one a lifeline thrown into the depths of their mysterious past, hoping to catch on something solid.

"You never met James, my husband, did you?" Thelma asked, her voice carrying the weight of a love lost to time. The question, seemingly out of place, hinted at a story that stretched far beyond the confines of the present moment, reaching back into the tangled threads of their family history.

"He's too young for that nonsense, Thelma," Jane interjected sharply, her tone a mix of protectiveness and impatience. "Just tell him about the key." Her words, meant to steer the conversation back to more immediate concerns, nonetheless added layers to the mystery, suggesting a history rich with emotion and significance.

Thelma touched her neck gently, a tender gesture that seemed to connect her to cherished memories, to times and people long gone. "Oh," she said with a chuckle, a sound that carried both warmth and a hint of sadness. "That's right, you have it."

"The key?" I pressed, my curiosity now a flame fuelled by their cryptic exchanges.

"Yes," replied Jane, the word hanging in the air, a key in itself unlocking the door to a tale entwined with the echoes of the past. Her affirmation, though brief, felt like a pivotal moment, a turning point in the unravelling of this intricate web of family, memory, and loss.

Slowly, Thelma began her story of the key, her voice crackling with the fragility of old age, yet underscored by a strength that seemed to defy it. The room seemed to hush in reverence to her words, and I leaned in, captivated by the secrets about to unfold, each detail painting a vivid picture in my mind.

"Only a few years into our marriage, I stumbled upon a strange trapdoor in James's study. I was never supposed to enter the study, but then I discovered the exciting news of my pregnancy," she paused, her words laden with the weight of both joy and trepidation. The pause, filled with the echo of memories long past, seemed to stretch on, bridging years in moments.

Jane reached out, placing her hands gently atop Thelma's. The sight of the two close friends comforting each other, their hands a silent conversation of support and shared history, warmed my heart. Their bond, clearly forged in the fires of shared experiences and enduring loyalty, was a testament to a lifetime shared, adding depth to the narrative unfolding before me.

Thelma continued, her gaze drifting to a point beyond the walls of the room, to a time and place only she could see. "We'd been trying since our wedding night to fall pregnant, but there had been complications." She looked to Jane as she spoke, seeking not just understanding but perhaps validation of the emotions that still ran deep. "I thought James would be pleased to hear the news. Just once, I'd convinced myself, he would allow an exception." Her voice, tinged with hope and a hint of naivety, spoke volumes of the love and expectation that had once filled her heart.

"What happened?" I asked, my voice barely above a whisper, completely transfixed by the unfolding tale. The story, more than just a recounting of events, felt like a window into Thelma's soul, offering glimpses of her hopes, fears, and the love that had driven her actions.

"After knocking on the door several times and getting no reply, I let myself inside," said Thelma, her voice carrying the weight of a forbidden secret, as if the very act of recounting the tale was a trespass into forbidden territory.

"And that was when you saw the trapdoor?" I asked, excitement bubbling within me, my earlier frustrations forgotten in the wake of my burgeoning curiosity.

"Yes," said Thelma, her face growing serious as she recounted the moment of discovery. "It was exposed by a section of carpet that had been moved to the side." A soft chuckle escaped her, a sound that seemed to carry both fondness and a touch of irony. She closed her eyes, lost in the memories. "Looking back now, it all seems so cliché. But back then, there was nothing cliché about it whatsoever." The nostalgia in her voice painted a vivid picture of the past, a time of innocence abruptly confronted with the shadows of secrets.

My face mirrored the seriousness of Thelma and Jane's expressions, the room now enveloped in an aura of mystery that seemed to thicken with each word spoken. The air felt charged with the weight of their history, a tangible presence that drew me deeper into their world.

"The discovery almost cost me my life," said Thelma, her voice low, each word a heavy stone dropped into the still waters of the past.

"Our lives," Jane corrected softly, her intervention a reminder of the bond they shared, a connection forged in the crucible of shared adversity. The lines on their faces, etched by time, seemed to deepen, telling a story of struggle and resilience.

Thelma nodded softly in agreement. "In revenge for the horrors we uncovered," she began, her words hinting at dark secrets that lay buried beneath the surface.

I interrupted Thelma, my curiosity now a living, breathing entity that demanded satisfaction. Turning to Jane, I asked, "You were there too?" My question, hopeful for clarity, sought to piece together the fragments of their tangled past.

"It's a little more complicated than that. Far too complicated than the time we have left now," answered Jane, her eyes a deep well of unspoken truths, hinting at layers of complexity that stretched far beyond the confines of this conversation.

"In revenge for the horrors we uncovered," Thelma repeated, picking up the thread of her narrative with a resilience that commanded respect. She continued, "I managed to steal the key to the trapdoor."

My eyes widened considerably at her admission, the pieces of the puzzle clicking into place with the clarity of revelation. "That's the key you gave me?" I asked, the weight of the revelation pressing down on me, a gravity that pulled me further into the depths of their story, creating ripples of disbelief and wonder that spread through my consciousness.

"Stop interrupting," Jane scolded, her words cutting sharply through the air, emphasising the weight of the tale unfolding before me.

"No," answered Thelma, her voice soft yet resolute, a faint smile tugging at the corners of her weary mouth. It was a smile that seemed to carry within it the resilience of a life fully lived, the wisdom earned through the passage of time and the trials it brought. "I made three copies and then returned the original before James realised." The room seemed to hold its breath, absorbing the confession like a well-kept secret finally making its way to the surface. The significance of her actions, the forethought and courage it must have taken, resonated deeply with me, painting a picture of Thelma not just as the elderly woman before me but as the keeper of profound secrets.

My eyes darted to where Jane's fingers fidgeted with a delicate gold chain around her neck, the metal seemingly warm with the stories it held. It was a subtle indication, a silent testimony to her deep connection to the unfolding narrative, like another hidden key waiting to unlock yet another door to the past. The gesture, almost unconscious, spoke volumes, intertwining her own story with that of Thelma's in ways I was only beginning to understand.

"Clearly, you have one of those keys," I observed, my voice carrying a new level of understanding as I nodded in Jane's direction, acknowledging the intricate dance of secrets and revelations that had characterised our meeting. The room, charged with the weight of history and the anticipation of discovery, felt like a crossroads of past and present.

Carefully, Jane pulled the chain from her bosom, revealing an old key in the palm of her hand – the same key Thelma had entrusted to me. The sight of it, so similar yet uniquely its own, bridged the gap between generations, between the secrets of the past and their implications for the present. The room echoed with the clink of metal against metal, each sound resonating like the ticking of an ancient clock marking the passage of time, a reminder of the enduring connections that bind us, the choices that define us, and the stories that continue to shape our understanding of ourselves and each other.

"So, who has the third key?" I asked, leaning forward slightly, my curiosity growing like a flame fed by the enigmatic revelations that filled the room. The air seemed thick with anticipation, each word spoken adding fuel to the fire of intrigue that burned within me.

"Bob," both women's voices croaked in unison, their timbre a shared acknowledgment of a figure looming large in their collective history. The name fell between us like a stone into still water, sending ripples through the air.

"Bob?" I repeated, surprised, my voice echoing my astonishment. "Bob Gangley? The old guy down the corridor that annoys you so much?" It was as if the pieces of the puzzle were falling into place, yet each piece revealed only deepened the mystery, forming a mosaic of interconnected lives that extended far beyond the confines of this room.

"He's not that bad, really," said Jane, her quick defence of Bob carrying a note of fondness that seemed at odds with their previous complaints. Her words hinted at a nuanced understanding of shared burdens and a history that ran deeper than mere annoyance.

"He's just old, like us," Thelma chuckled, the sound rich with the resonance of shared experience. Her laughter carried the weight of time, each ripple revealing the complexity of existence in their twilight years. "None of the simple things in life seem so simple anymore when you're our age." The truth of her words struck a chord, painting a picture of life's complexities magnified by the passage of years.

I smiled understandingly, my expression a silent acknowledgment of the intricate tapestry woven by the years gone by. Yet, as the warmth of shared understanding faded, my brow creased with the return of unanswered questions. "What happened to the original key?" I asked, my voice carrying a mix of curiosity and concern. The mystery of the original key seemed central to the unfolding story, a linchpin that held together the threads of their tale.

"How would making copies of the key satisfy revenge? And revenge for what?" My questions spilled out, driven by a desire to understand the heart of the mystery that intertwined their lives. The concept of revenge, mentioned so casually yet loaded with significance, hinted at past wrongs and the lengths to which they had gone to address them.

The room seemed to contract around us as the weight of my questions hung in the air. The story of the key, far from being a simple tale of discovery and consequence, hinted at deeper currents of emotion and action, of secrets held close and the lengths to which they had been willing to go in pursuit of justice or reparation. As I awaited their response, the silence that followed felt charged with the weight of stories yet to be told, of truths that lay just beyond the veil of the past. The intertwining of their lives with Bob's, the mystery of the original key, and the shadow of revenge that loomed over their narrative promised revelations that would likely challenge the very foundations of what I thought I knew about them, about the nature of justice, and about the complexities of human relationships.

"I think that's enough for today," said Jane, rising abruptly from her chair, a clear signal that the day's conversations had come to an end. Her weariness was apparent, not just in the lines etched deeply on her face but in the slow, deliberate way she moved. The room seemed to exhale with her, the weight of the revelations hanging in the air like lingering echoes of a long-forgotten song.

"But," I tried to coax more of the tale from them, my thirst for answers unquenched. The stories and secrets they held felt like pieces of a puzzle I was desperate to complete, each piece a fragment of their lives, and now, somehow, of mine too.

"Come back next week. Bring the key, and we'll tell you more," Jane promised, her words a lifeline extended to me, linking our stories across the chasm of generations. It was an invitation, or perhaps a challenge, to dive deeper into the mystery that bound us together.

I looked to Thelma for any sign of further details, finding instead a quiet resolve in her aged eyes. There was a depth there, an unspoken understanding of the importance of what was being shared, and what was yet to come.

"Next week," Thelma reaffirmed, her voice a whisper yet carrying the weight of anticipation. It was a confirmation, a pact sealed with the simplicity of her words.

Nodding slowly, I agreed, "Okay." The commitment sealing our connection as the keepers of a shared secret. It felt as if I was being entrusted with a part of their legacy, a link to the past that was both an honour and a burden.

"Promise that you'll bring that key with you," Jane told me, her gaze intense, boring into mine. It was a plea for trust and continuity, a bridge between the past they had lived and the future yet to be written. Her eyes held a mixture of hope and apprehension, as if the key was not just a physical object but a symbol of the trust she was placing in me.

I squirmed a little uncomfortably under her gaze, the responsibility of holding their history, even just a part of it, settling heavily onto my shoulders. "Yeah, I promise," I responded, the words heavy with the weight of the commitment I was making. The key, once an innocuous piece of metal, had become a talisman, a beacon guiding me through the murky waters of their past, and now, it seemed, of my future as well.

PHASE 5

4338.209.5

Phase 5: Office Relocation

The urgency to act propelled me forward, a feeling as unfamiliar as it was intense. An uncommon anger surged through my veins, a testament to the stakes at hand. Waiting for nightfall, a tactic of patience and caution, now seemed an impractical option given the critical misstep I had made earlier. My haste had led me to retrieve Nial's personal laptop instead of his work laptop, a mistake that could potentially derail our efforts to protect the settlement. Arguments about the significance of business conducted online paled in comparison to the immediate need for action; the settlement's protection hinged on Paul and Nial starting to order fencing materials as soon as possible.

Taking a gamble, fuelled by the pressing need for haste, I chose to enter the Triffett residence through the Portal already activated in Nial's office. This decision sidestepped the need for another front door entry, cutting down on the time and reducing the risk of being caught. A quick glance around the space confirmed that the office door was once again closed, presenting a window of opportunity for a swift retrieval of Nial's work laptop. The room, quiet and undisturbed, seemed almost complicit in my mission.

Clambering through the side of the filing cabinet, the entry point from the Portal into Nial's lost world, I navigated awkwardly and briskly toward Nial's large desk by the window. The desk became the focus of my frantic search.

Papers and notebooks shuffled in rapid succession as I sought the elusive second laptop, each movement a mix of determination and desperation.

The act of sifting through Nial's belongings, a violation of privacy under any normal circumstances, felt justified in the context of our situation. Yet, as I moved papers aside, my actions fuelled by the ticking clock of urgency, I couldn't help but feel a twinge of guilt. This was Nial's personal space, his sanctuary of work and thought, and here I was, disrupting it in my quest to correct a mistake.

The room, bathed in the muted light from the window, felt like a silent witness to my actions. The tension of the task at hand was palpable, a mixture of fear, anticipation, and the pressing weight of responsibility. The need to find the work laptop and ensure the settlement's safety was a burden I carried alone in that moment, navigating the fine line between right and wrong in a world that had become far more complicated than I ever anticipated.

In less than five minutes, success crowned my efforts. The laptop, snugly ensconced in its bag along with the power cable, was firmly in my grasp. As I pondered the logistics of charging the laptop in Clivilius, a realisation dawned on me, adding the task of getting electricity to the settlement involuntarily to my never-ending mental list of things to do. The complexity of life in Clivilius, already a tapestry of challenges, seemed to grow with each passing moment. With a resigned sigh, acknowledging the precarious position I found myself in, I stuffed the power cord into the bag, a small but significant action in the grand scheme of our efforts.

Activating the Portal once again on the side of the filing cabinet, the only obvious clear surface in the room, a wave of relief washed over me. The portal, a doorway between worlds, felt like a lifeline in that moment, offering an escape back to a place where the stakes were immeasurably high, but where I felt a sense of purpose and belonging. The confirmation of a swift and incident-free mission bolstered my spirits, a brief respite in the constant push and pull of my struggle to secure the settlement's future.

The silence in the office, a partner to my clandestine activities, was abruptly shattered by the ringing of the phone in my trouser pocket. Panic, swift and unforgiving, gripped me. In a rushed attempt to answer before the sound could betray my presence, my movements became clumsy, nearly resulting in the laptop bag slipping from my grasp. The phone, an innocuous object in any other circumstance, felt like a beacon of danger in that moment.

With the phone in hand, ready to reject the call and silence the immediate threat it posed, a momentary pause overcame me. "Gladys' mum," I mumbled under my breath, feeling a knot tightening in my stomach. Calls from Wendy were a rarity, an exception rather than the rule, and the unexpectedness of this one heightened my anxiety. My gaze flickered to the Portal, its silent swirl a tempting offer of escape. Yet, the thought of ignoring a call from Wendy, especially under such unusual circumstances, gnawed at me with an urgency that couldn't be dismissed.

Convincing myself that a brief call to Wendy, simply telling her that I'd call her right back in a few minutes, would be harmless, I answered the phone. "Hello," I hissed, my voice barely above a whisper, the fear of discovery pressing down on me with a weight that made my breaths shallow and quick.

"Oh, Luke!" Wendy's words tumbled through the phone at a frantic pace, a cascade of concern and urgency that made it impossible for me to find a moment to interject.

Several attempts to interrupt proved futile, her torrent of words sweeping away my planned reassurances until the mention of Duke seized my attention. At the sound of my dog's name, tears unexpectedly welled in my eyes, blurring the edges of my calculated composure. Duke, always the unsuspecting anchor of my emotions, now the focal point of Wendy's call, tightened the knot in my stomach into a constrictive loop.

I need to take this call, I acknowledged internally, frustration etching wrinkles across my forehead. The situation, underscored by the unexpected emotional surge at the mention of Duke, left no room for half measures. Continuing the call inside the house risked my voice alerting someone to my presence, a risk that grew with each passing second.

Glancing at the portal, I grappled with the realisation that going that way would sever the connection, cutting off this crucial lifeline to Wendy and the situation at hand. My eyes then shifted toward the office door, a sliver of hope in a plan forming rapidly in my mind – *if I can sneak outside, I'll be free to talk without fear of discovery.*

"Wendy," I hissed sharply, cutting through her rambling with a desperation that finally caused a pause. "I've got bad reception in here. Just give me a couple of secs to get to a better spot." My words were a blend of urgency and subterfuge, a makeshift excuse that bought me the precious seconds needed to navigate this precarious situation.

"Okay," Wendy tentatively agreed, her voice carrying a hint of confusion and concern.

Cringing as several floorboards creaked beneath my feet, betraying my movements, I opened the office door and peered into the hallway with cautious eyes. Despite the car in the driveway that I had seen from the office window, signalling someone's presence, the house seemed eerily quiet, as if holding its breath alongside me.

Breathing a little easier but with a resolve to stay vigilant, I crept toward the front door. Each step was measured, a careful dance with the unseen eyes I feared might be upon me. The soft grunt of someone dozing in the living room on the left brought me to an abrupt halt, my heart skipping a beat. The realisation that I couldn't reach the front door without passing the open living room directly—a gauntlet laid out before me—prompted a quick reassessment of my plan.

Pivoting on my heel, I moved stealthily in the opposite direction, my mind racing with alternatives. The need to escape unnoticed, to preserve the secrecy of my presence, was paramount. Peering into the bedroom as I approached, the darkness within served as a veil, revealing only the outlines of a small child asleep in his bed. The sight of the Dalmatian from my previous visit, resting on the floor beside him, brought an unexpected pang of warmth to my heart amidst the tension. The dog, a silent guardian in the quiet of the afternoon, seemed at peace, a stark contrast to the turmoil within me.

The presence of the child, innocent and unaware of the complexities that shadowed the adults around him, underscored the gravity of our situation in Clivilius and the risks I was willing to take. It was a reminder of what was at stake, of the lives touched by my actions, both directly and indirectly. The need to protect, to secure a future against unseen threats, was never more palpable than in that moment, a silent vow made in the darkness of a child's bedroom doorway.

Taking another step, the floor beneath me betrayed my presence with a creak that seemed louder than thunder in the quiet house. The Dalmatian looked up at me, its eyes sharp and assessing, emitting a short growl that threatened to shatter the fragile silence. Instinctively, I motioned for the dog to be quiet, a silent plea for discretion. Remarkably, it obeyed, lowering its head back to its paws, a silent accomplice in my stealthy departure.

Suddenly, the young boy's eyes opened wide, a startling awakening that froze me in my tracks. Half sitting, he stared directly at me, his young eyes a complex mix of fear and curiosity, a silent question hanging between us. Without a word, I pressed my finger against my lips, signalling for him to remain silent. Understanding, or perhaps just subdued by the strangeness of the situation, the child rested his head back on his pillow, a silent agreement to our unspoken pact.

With my heart thundering in my chest, a cacophony of beats that felt loud enough to betray me, I decided it was time to move faster. *Much faster!* The urgency of the situation, compounded by the young witness to my clandestine activity, spurred me into action. Hoping that the toddler would keep our secret, I made haste toward the back door, every step a calculated risk.

With a small amount of luck that seemed to be on my side, I quickly unlocked the door, a small victory in the escalating tension. Stepping out into the chilly late afternoon air, a welcome escape, I closed the door softly behind me, a silent farewell to the scene of my covert operation.

Bringing the phone to my ear as I began to walk into the backyard, the open space a brief respite, I spoke, "Wendy, I can't talk for long," my voice quivered, betraying the adrenaline and anxiety that coursed through me. "What's wrong?"

"Why the hell is Duke wrapped in a bloody towel in Beatrix's bathroom!?" Wendy's voice, a mixture of screech and sob, pierced my eardrum, a shocking revelation that jolted me to my core.

My back stiffened, a reflexive reaction to the unexpected and alarming news. Every hair on the back of my neck tingled eerily, a physical manifestation of the shock and urgency that Wendy's words invoked.

"I'll be right there," I promised Wendy, promptly ending the call.

With burning eyes, the urgency of the situation igniting a fire within me, I turned on the spot in the backyard, desperately searching for a suitable place to activate the Portal. The garden, full of trees and enclosed by a wood-paling fence, offered little in the way of clear space, making my options for escape look bleak. The limitations of my surroundings, once an inconsequential detail of Nial's home, had become critical barriers in my quest for a swift departure.

The sudden opening of the back door gripped me with a terror so profound it felt as though it could swallow me whole. Spinning around, my heart sank as I found the little boy standing in the doorway, the protective Dalmatian by his side. The sight, so innocent yet so daunting, underscored the complexity of my predicament.

With each warning bark from the Dalmatian, I winced as though each sound physically penetrated my skin, a reminder that my presence was neither welcome nor unnoticed. The realisation that my borrowed time was about to expire sent a chill down my spine, the stakes of my mission suddenly framed in stark relief against the domestic backdrop of the Triffett home.

Launching itself from the steps, the dog barked furiously as it bounded in my direction, a blur of motion and sound that seemed to close the distance between us with terrifying speed. Caught in the firm clutches of panic, my instincts took over. I turned and I ran, desperation lending speed to my legs as I sought refuge.

Approaching the small shed at the back of the yard, my heart pounding in my ears, I finally caught a glimpse of my escape. Casting a glance over my shoulder as I activated the

Portal, the sight of the Dalmatian almost upon me, its teeth bared in a primal display of protection, and the toddler not too far behind, painted a scene straight out of a surreal chase.

With the only other choice being to remain and face the consequences of my intrusion—a scenario that could only end in disaster—I darted through the Portal. The decision, made in a fraction of a second, was a leap of faith, driven by the primal urge to survive. I'd barely commanded it closed before the collision of human flesh and dog fur ensued, sharp yips of pain filling the air as we both tumbled through the dust on the other side.

❖

"Fuck!" The exclamation escaped my lips, an embodiment of frustration and self-condemnation echoing through the air, reverberating with each syllable as if to underscore the seriousness of my mistake. Each word pounded into the ground like a personal rebuke, mirroring the turmoil inside me.

The Dalmatian, now with a limp and a final growl of resentment, distanced herself from me. Her injured leg demanded attention, and she sat, licking it with a mixture of pain and defiance. The sight of her injury, a consequence of my actions, weighed heavily on my conscience, a disappointing reminder of the unintended harm my presence had caused.

"Buffy!" A surprised voice called from a distance, breaking through my introspection.

I took several deep breaths, attempting to rein in the whirlwind of emotions that threatened to overwhelm me. Nial and Paul approached from the Drop Zone, their expressions a mix of confusion and irritation.

"What the hell!?" Paul exclaimed, exasperation littering his tone. "Duke hasn't even been dead for a day, and you're already bringing another dog here!?" His words, sharp and accusatory, struck a nerve, igniting a fury within me that I couldn't contain.

"How dare you bring Duke into this!" I yelled, my anger manifesting in a hard shove against Paul. The mention of Duke, a sore and fresh wound, felt like a low blow.

"Let me guess, it was another 'accident'," Paul slurred the insult at me, his arms preventing a second assault. His words, dripping with scorn, were designed to wound, to cast blame and stir guilt within me.

"As a matter of fact-," I began, my voice tight with anger, ready to defend my actions before cutting myself short. Swiftly changing tact, I realised that trying to defend Paul's accusation would get me nowhere. "Where is Duke?" I asked, accusation laced in my tone, reminding Paul of his own 'accident.' The question, though simple, carried with it a weight of implications, a challenge that sought to redirect the focus of our confrontation.

Paul's face dropped, his mouth working in silent overtime, searching for words that seemed to elude him in the moment. The tension between us was palpable, a tangible force that filled the air with an electric charge of expectation.

"Was there an 'accident'?" I sneered, unable to hide the bitterness and suspicion that laced my voice. The word 'accident' felt like a barb, a pointed reminder of the fragility of trust and the consequences of actions left unexplained.

Shrugging in defeat, a gesture that seemed to carry the weight of resignation, Paul admitted, "Beatrix took him."

"I know," I replied, my voice steady, masking the turmoil of emotions that churned within me. My affirmation, a declaration of my awareness, seemed to catch Paul off guard.

"Oh," said Paul, life springing back into his face as if the acknowledgment had rekindled some spark of connection between us. "So you've spoken to Beatrix?"

"No," I said bluntly, cutting off any assumption of direct communication. My denial, sharp and to the point, seemed to puzzle him further.

"Then how-?" Paul questioned, a curious brow furrowed.

I sighed, the weight of the confrontation beginning to exhaust me, each breath feeling heavier than the last. "It would seem that Wendy has found him." My admission, a revelation of the chain of events that had unfolded outside of our immediate circle, introduced a new player to the complex game we found ourselves in.

"Who's Wendy?" Paul asked, his question highlighting the widening gap of misunderstanding and miscommunication that lay between us.

"Beatrix's mother," I answered.

"Oh," Paul replied sheepishly, the realisation dawning on him. "That might be a little awkward." His understatement, an attempt to grasp the nuances of the situation, barely scratched the surface of the potential complications that lay ahead.

"You don't say," I sighed again, the redundancy of our exchange mirroring the cyclical nature of our challenges. "Anyway," I continued quickly, gesturing towards Nial who crouched, comforting his injured dog. "That really was an accident. I'll tell you about it later." My promise, a deferral of explanation, felt hollow even to my own ears.

"We've got time now," Paul remarked, his eagerness to delve deeper into the narrative clear. Yet, his interest, though genuine, seemed incongruent with the urgency of my own priorities.

My lips pursed in frustration. "You might have time, but I don't," I snapped more harshly than intended, the stress and pressure of the moment fraying the edges of my patience.

Paul's head tilted, and he sighed unreassuringly, a nonverbal acknowledgment of the divide that had formed between us. "Guess I'll talk to you later, then." His resignation, though tinged with disappointment, was a necessary concession to the unfolding crisis.

For a long moment, we stood in silence, our gaze locked in a silent exchange that seemed to acknowledge the chaos I had thrown us into. With my eyes, I tried to convey a message of hope, a silent plea that it'll get better. *For my own sake, it has to!*

"I guess," I echoed Paul's sentiments, handing him Nial's laptop bag. The act, simple yet significant, was a tangible representation of the complexities of our intertwined lives. With a heavy heart and a mind burdened by the weight of what lay ahead, I walked away.

SECURE MELTDOWN

4338.209.6

"Damn it," I muttered under my breath, my steps echoing heavily on the soft carpet of Beatrix's bedroom as I moved swiftly toward the door. Each footfall felt like a hammer striking the ground, marking my presence in this place that I had no right to be. My abrupt halt mid-step mirrored the sudden realisation that I couldn't just materialise in Beatrix's house without raising serious questions from Wendy. The logistics of my movements, once a matter of practicality, now bore the weight of consequences I hadn't fully considered.

As I contemplated returning to Clivilius to find a different entry point to Earth, a strategy to mitigate the potential fallout of my actions, raised voices from the other side of the doorway seized my attention. Duke's name sliced through the air, sending a jolt of anger and concern through my chest.

"I have no idea where Beatrix is. Or Luke. Or Jamie. Or..." Wendy's voice, thick with frustration and confusion, paused, her words trailing off into a heavy silence. The weight of our Guardian activities on those we concealed our secrets from hit me like a punch in the gut. This realisation struck me with clarity and force: *This isn't just about protecting Bixbus anymore; it's affecting everyone around us.* The ripple effects of my actions, once contained within the boundaries of each mission, now extended into the lives of those we loved and interacted with, casting a shadow of complication and distress.

"I want that poor dog out of this house immediately!" Wendy's demand reverberated through the passageway, her voice a mixture of indignation and resolve.

After a beat of silence, Brett's weary voice replied, "I'll go and take-" His response, cut short, left the outcome hanging in the balance. Brett, another unsuspecting participant in the web of our Guardian responsibilities, now tasked with a role he hadn't asked for.

The hairs on my arms bristled, an instinctive reaction to the sudden appearance of Beatrix, as the bedroom walls briefly reflected a glow of colour from her Portal, momentarily distracting me from the unfolding conversation outside. Spinning on my heels, the sight of Beatrix standing before me, with the colours of her Portal vanishing into the ether behind her, anchored me back to the immediate crisis.

"What the hell is Duke doing here?" I blurted out, my words harsh whispers that barely contained the mix of confusion and anger swirling within me.

Raising her hands defensively, Beatrix attempted to placate the situation. "Luke, I can explain," she began, her mouth moving in a dance of starts and stops, as if her voice was lost in a sea of explanations she couldn't quite bring to the surface.

Impatient and too stirred by the urgency of the moment to wait for Beatrix to find her own words, I prodded further. "Whose idea was it? Jamie's?" My question, pointed and direct, sought to unearth the rationale behind the bewildering decision to bring Duke here.

"No," Beatrix replied, shaking her head fiercely, her denial swift and unequivocal.

"Paul's?" I continued, my determination to uncover the culprit driving my questions.

"It was mine," Beatrix hissed sharply, frustration and a hint of defiance etched on her face. Her admission, delivered with a sharpness that matched the intensity of the situation, halted me in my tracks.

"What... where... what the hell were you thinking?" I stammered, my initial whispers transforming into a voice strengthened sharply by disbelief and frustration. My tone increased, a reflection of the incredulity and concern that Beatrix's revelation evoked within me.

The sudden flick of the bedroom light switch bathed us in its bright glow, a stark contrast to the dim ambiguity we'd been cloaked in just moments before. "Beatrix!" Wendy called out in surprise, her voice cutting through the tension like a knife. "I didn't hear you get home."

Silently pleading with Wendy to maintain her assumptions —that Beatrix and I had entered the house like normal people should—I slowly turned to face her.

"And Luke... when did you..." Wendy stammered, her surprise growing as she pieced together the unexpected scene before her. The realisation that I was here, under such bizarre circumstances, seemed to add layers of complexity to her understanding of the situation.

"We haven't been home for long," Beatrix cut her off, sparing us from further questioning with a swift interjection. "Luke and I were just discussing where we should bury Duke." Her words, a fabrication meant to provide cover, hung heavily between us.

We were? I couldn't help but cast Beatrix a silent question over my shoulder, my gaze laden with confusion and a hint of admiration for her quick thinking.

"Your father is taking care of it," Wendy replied, a hint of disappointment in her voice as she pouted, hands resting squarely on her hips. Her words implied a disconnect, a gap between her expectations and the reality we presented.

Eyes widening, I could only glare at Beatrix, the implications of Wendy's words and our fabricated story weaving a complicated web I wasn't sure we could untangle. The sudden sound of a car door slamming outside, followed by the engine roaring to life, added an urgent punctuation to the moment.

Impulsively, Beatrix and I dashed to the bedroom window, driven by the instinct to gather as much information as possible from the audible clues. However, we were greeted only by the darkened silhouettes of trees in the back yard, a silent reminder of the limitations of our current vantage point. I forgot that Beatrix's bedroom didn't face the front of the house, a detail that, under different circumstances, might have been inconsequential but now almost encouraged a faint smile to pull at the corner of my mouth.

"Where is he going?" Beatrix asked, her movements a bit frantic as she turned back to face her mother, accidentally bumping into her dresser in the process. The urgency of the situation was palpable, each of us caught in a tangle of emotions and decisions that seemed to pull us in different directions.

Wendy's face softened as her gaze met mine, a brief moment of connection. "To yours, Luke," she said, her voice carrying a mixture of concern and resignation before she quickly looked away. The implication of her words weighed heavily on me, the realisation that my home was now another stage for this unfolding drama, and I wasn't present for it.

"Tell him we'll meet him there," I blurted out, the words escaping me before I could fully grasp their implications. My small Portal Key, a symbol of the extraordinary life I led beyond the bounds of normalcy, rolled between my fingers in anxious anticipation for my imminent departure. The urge to act, to prevent whatever was about to unfold at my home, was overwhelming.

Beatrix grabbed my arm fiercely, her grip a physical manifestation of her concern. "Luke!" she hissed, pulling me back from the precipice of a decision that could unravel the delicate fabric of secrecy we'd woven around our lives.

"What!?" I snapped, my impatience and frustration boiling over. The logic was simple in my mind: *Brett might have a car, but I had a Portal Key. If I left now, I could get there before he did.*

Beatrix's eyes dropped to the device in my hand, her voice dropping to a whisper, "Not here." The caution in her words was a timely reminder of the risks involved.

With Wendy watching us closely, the realisation that Beatrix was right hit me like a wave. Opening the Portal here and now, in front of Wendy, would not only expose our secret but could potentially draw her into a world of danger and confusion she was unprepared for. Had I acted on impulse, Duke's situation would be the least of the complications we'd face.

Feeling like a trapped animal, my fist clenched around the device hard enough to turn my knuckles white. The frustration of being cornered by circumstances beyond my control, of having to navigate a minefield of secrecy and urgency, was infuriating.

Beatrix turned back to her mother, quickly shifting gears in an attempt to manage the situation. "I'll call dad and ask him to come back here," she said, reaching for her phone with a speed that spoke of desperation.

"I doubt he'll answer you while he's driving," Wendy replied, her skepticism a reflection of the everyday realities that suddenly seemed so mundane compared to the whirlwind of Guardian activities.

Either unconvinced of her mother's knowledge of her father or out of sheer desperation, Beatrix didn't hesitate to dial her father's number anyway. Almost immediately, a faint ring echoed from downstairs, a sound that seemed to carry dread in its tone.

"Oh, I think that might be your father's phone," Wendy said, her voice carrying a mixture of realisation and surprise as she hurried out of the room. The possibility that we might just dodge further scrutiny offered a sliver of relief, yet my gut still twisted in an agonising knot. The complexity of our situation, the thin ice upon which we skated, seemed all too likely to crack under the weight of one wrong move.

"Shit," Beatrix muttered under her breath, a sentiment I echoed internally as she followed her mother out of the room.

"Beatrix," I hissed sharply, catching her immediate attention before she could make it out the door. "Let's get out of here," I urged her back into the room, my voice low and urgent. In response to my plea, I sent a swirl of vibrant colours reflecting on her bedroom wall, the Portal activating as a testament to our need for a swift escape.

"What about mum?" Beatrix hesitated, her concern for Wendy evident in her voice. It was a valid question, one that tugged at the edges of my resolve.

I frowned, the complexity of our situation pressing down on me. "I'm sure she'll just assume that we left through the front door," I said desperately, my eyes pleading for Beatrix to agree with me. My assurance was more a hope than a conviction, a fragile solution to the myriad of problems we faced. The ease with which Wendy had accepted Beatrix's earlier explanation, that we had recently arrived home in a normal manner, offered a thin veneer of hope that perhaps we could slip away unnoticed this time as well.

"Fine," Beatrix shrugged, a glimmer of hesitation lingering in her eyes. "I'll meet you there in a minute."

My eyes narrowed suspiciously at Beatrix. I knew we would have to activate our Portals separately, but that would require less than thirty seconds.

"I'm just going to run downstairs and slam the front door. It'll make it more believable," Beatrix explained with a loud huff, her determination evident in her voice. The strategy, designed to reinforce the illusion of our conventional exit, carried an inherent risk of drawing Wendy's attention directly to her.

"Okay," I conceded, my tone laced with skepticism. The necessity of her actions was debatable, but at this juncture, as long as it didn't delay my departure, I was willing to let it slide. The thought of Duke, on his way back to me, overshadowed any lingering doubts about the plan.

"But in case she catches me, don't wait for me," Beatrix added, a serious undertone to her voice that underscored the potential complications of her manoeuvre.

Not that I was planning on waiting around anyway, but her comment stirred a sense of solidarity within me. "We've got nowhere else to be," I found myself replying, my voice betraying a hint of the fatigue and resignation that had settled over me. The weight of our situation, the constant balancing act between our secret lives and the façade we maintained, pressed down on me, causing my shoulders to slump in a somewhat depressing acknowledgment.

"I know," agreed Beatrix, her voice carrying a mix of resolve and apprehension. "But you know mother's not going to let me get away so easily without a full assault of questions."

"Don't get caught, then," I grunted the obvious reply, a mixture of advice and hope that she could navigate the impending interrogation without complication.

With a final nod, Beatrix departed from the room, her steps quick and purposeful as she embarked on her risky endeavour to reinforce our cover story. As soon as she was gone, I didn't waste another second contemplating the potential fallout of our actions. Walking into the wall of colour, I let the vibrant hues envelop me, the Portal's embrace a familiar sensation that signified both an escape and a return to the responsibilities that awaited me.

❖

I barely had time to down a shot of whiskey before the insistent knock at the front door demanded my attention. The fiery liquid did little to calm the frantic beats of my heart, its warmth a stark contrast to the cold dread settling in my stomach. The weight of the glass felt strangely insignificant in my trembling hands, a reminder of my vain attempt to find solace in something, anything, before facing what was to come.

Taking a deep breath, I willed myself to keep it together, to face the news that Brett was bringing to my doorstep. My hand on the door handle felt like a metaphorical turning point, the moment before stepping into a reality I wasn't sure I was ready to confront.

Swinging it open, my attempt at joviality felt hollow, a poor mask for the turmoil churning inside me. "Brett, what a surprise to see you here," I greeted, my voice straining to maintain a casual tone. My eyes skimming over him, I avoided looking directly at what he carried, afraid of confronting the inevitable. I hoped my feigned nonchalance concealed the dread clawing at my insides, the fear of facing a truth I didn't want to acknowledge.

Brett's face sagged with an unspoken burden, his eyes carrying the weight of news that no one should ever have to deliver. Ignoring the heaviness in his gaze, I pressed on with feigned ignorance, clinging to the thin hope that pretending not to know might somehow alter the reality of the situation. "What's wrong?" I asked, the words feeling like a betrayal of the truth I already understood.

"Look, Luke," Brett began, his voice heavy with emotion, the struggle to maintain composure evident in every line of his face. "I really don't know how else to say this." His arms extended towards me, and in that moment, my heart sank. The bundle he handed me, wrapped in a blood-soaked sheet, was a tragic embodiment of my beloved Duke—a sight that pierced through any remaining defences I had.

The hot prickle of tears burned my eyes as I accepted the weight in my arms, the bundle that was once Duke. The fabric of the blood-soaked sheet clung to my skin, cold and sticky, a visceral reminder of the loss that I now held. "He, uh… he-" I tried to articulate the swirling storm of grief and confusion, but the words lodged in my throat, too raw and unspoken to find their way out.

"You don't have to explain," Brett offered, his voice carrying a blend of empathy and sorrow. His own grief was etched across his features, a mirror to my turmoil, as he braced against the porch railing, seeking support from the inanimate to bear the weight of our shared sorrow.

A heavy silence stretched between us, a chasm filled with words suspended in the air, unspoken yet understood. "I… I should get going," Brett finally murmured, his voice barely above a whisper, stepping back hesitantly, as if wanting to leave but uncertain that he should.

"Yeah," I agreed, the softness in my voice barely concealing the storm within.

Our eyes met briefly, and in that moment, Brett's warmth and understanding spoke volumes – a shared comprehension of a pain too profound and consuming for words. "Will you be okay?" he asked, his eyes reflecting genuine concern.

"Yeah," I repeated, nodding gently in an attempt to reassure him, or perhaps myself. The affirmation was automatic, a reflex, though I was far from believing it.

Brett retreated, the sound of the car door closing with a final thud that echoed through my shattered world. It was a sound that seemed to mark the end of an era, a definitive closing of a chapter that had meant everything to me.

Closing the front door behind him, an unfamiliar numbness began to envelop me, a cold, creeping detachment that sought to shield me from the rawness of my emotions. The immediate reality of Duke's absence, the silence of the house that once echoed with his presence, settled around me like a suffocating blanket. The emptiness was overwhelming, a void where warmth and companionship once resided.

❖

The bedroom's darkness enveloped me, a fitting backdrop for the abyss of sorrow that had claimed me. Sitting on the bed, my back pressed against the headboard, I cradled Duke in my arms, a silent vigil for a friend whose presence had filled my life with joy and companionship. Slowly unwrapping the sheet that encased him, the sight of his lifeless eyes and matted fur twisted my gut with a pain so acute, it was as if I was being hollowed out from the inside. Every breath was a struggle, the air around me feeling thick and suffocating, as if the very atmosphere had been vacuumed from the room.

In this moment of profound loss, I found myself yearning for impossibilities – to black out and awaken to a reality where everything was fixed, where Duke's joyful kisses would greet me, his tail wagging with unbridled happiness. But the harsh truth of his absence, the finality of his stillness, pressed down on me with an unbearable weight.

Leaning toward my forever faithful friend, tears streamed down my cheeks, each one a testament to the bond we shared. They fell onto his head, mingling with his fur, as I whispered, "It's okay, Duke. You're home now." The words, barely audible, were drowned amidst the echoes of grief that filled the room, a feeble attempt to offer comfort to both Duke and myself. In that moment, speaking to him as though he could hear me, I sought not just to reassure Duke, but to find some semblance of peace.

❖

"Luke?" a soft voice pierced the shroud of darkness that had enveloped me, but I couldn't muster the energy to respond. Overwhelmed by a grief so tangible it felt like a physical weight pressing down on me, I continued to sniff loudly, the act of sucking back the snot a desperate attempt to prevent further soiling Duke's lifeless form cradled in my arms.

The figure of Beatrix approached the doorway, her presence a reminder of the world beyond my immediate sorrow. "Luke?" she called out again, her voice laced with concern as her hand found the light switch and slapped it on.

My swollen eyes blinked rapidly against the sudden burst of bright light that filled the room, an intrusion that seemed almost violent in its intensity against the backdrop of my mourning.

"Oh, Luke," Beatrix said, her voice soft, carrying a blend of empathy and sorrow as she took several tentative steps towards me. Slowly, she seated herself on the edge of the bed, her presence a silent offering of support in a moment when I felt utterly alone.

"I could have done more," I sniffled, my voice barely a whisper, choked by the dryness of my throat and the effort it took to voice my guilt and regret.

Reaching out, Beatrix placed a soft hand on my shoulder, her touch a gentle reminder of the connection and understanding that existed between us. "I know you did everything you could, Luke. You're a great dog dad, and Duke was lucky to have you," she assured me, her words meant to comfort, to heal the raw edges of my grief.

Finally lifting my eyes to meet Beatrix's, I found a well of emotions reflected back at me. "I just wish I could have done more. I feel like I let him down," I admitted softly, the admission a confession of my deepest fears. In that moment, sharing my sorrow with Beatrix, I felt the first fragile threads of connection weaving through the isolation of my grief.

Approaching a realm of vulnerability I seldom visited, Beatrix wrapped her arms around us, creating a haven in the midst of my turmoil. "You did everything you could. Duke knew how much you loved him, and he was grateful to have you and Jamie as his family." Her words, imbued with sincerity and warmth, aimed to bridge the chasm of my grief. I knew Beatrix meant every word she said, and deep down, a part of me clung to the truth in her assurances. Duke was indeed a well-loved dog, his life a testament to the joy and unconditional love he brought into ours. Yet, the harsh reality that this wasn't supposed to happen, that it wasn't supposed to end like this, gnawed at me relentlessly.

Several minutes of silence enveloped us, a respectful homage to the depth of sorrow that words could scarcely touch. It was Beatrix who broke the silence, her voice soft, yet carrying the weight of practical concerns. "What are you going to do with him?" she asked gently, her inquiry pulling me back from the edge of despair to consider the immediate reality.

"I don't know," I replied, the admission slipping from me as I tried desperately to shake the overwhelming pain that embattled my weary heart. The path forward was obscured by grief, each thought of the future tinged with the ache of Duke's absence.

Beatrix continued, her voice steady, "That Charity woman said it's too dangerous to bury Duke in Clivilius. His body will attract creatures worse than shadow panthers." Her words, a harrowing reminder of the complexities and dangers that lay beyond the familiar, cast a new shadow over the already daunting task of honouring Duke's memory.

Remaining silent, I nodded, the weight of her words settling heavily upon me. *Guardians, Shadow panthers, and Portal Pirates*, I mused silently to myself, the list of threats and mysteries of Clivilius growing longer by the day. The realisation that our new world, one already fraught with danger and secrets, held even more perils than I had known, was a sobering thought.

What other secrets does this strange world hold? The question echoed within me, a reflection of the uncertainty that seemed to permeate every aspect of my life as a Guardians. The challenges I faced, the losses I mourned, and the secrets I kept, all intertwined in a tapestry of duty and devotion that was as complex as it was compelling. As I sat there, enveloped in Beatrix's comforting embrace, I grappled with the reality of my existence, the sacrifices made, and the uncharted waters I navigated in my quest to protect those I loved and the worlds I yearned to call home.

Cradling Duke in my arms, I felt the heavy burden of reality pressing down on me. A heavy sigh escaped my lips as I brought myself to my feet, the physical act of standing up feeling like a metaphor for the resolve I was trying to muster. *You know what must be done, Luke,* I silently told myself, the internal dialogue serving as both a command and a source of encouragement as I made my way to the back door. The path ahead was clear, though fraught with emotional landmines.

"Beatrix, I don't want to go back yet. Can you get me a shovel or something from the Drop Zone?" I asked, my voice strained under the weight of grief but beginning to regain some semblance of strength. The request felt like a tangible step toward facing the reality of Duke's passing, a necessary action in the process of letting go.

"Sure," Beatrix replied, her voice laced with hesitation. The pause, though brief, spoke volumes of the unspoken understanding between us, a shared grief and the heavy task ahead.

While Beatrix vanished to retrieve what I had asked for, Duke and I headed outside into the embrace of the early evening. The outdoor lights, sensing our movements, sprang to life, banishing the heavy darkness that mirrored the tumult within me. Old wooden slats groaned beneath my feet as we walked across the back decking, each step a reminder of the countless times Duke and I had traversed this space together in happier moments.

Making our way carefully down the cement blocks that served as rustic steps, Duke and I stopped when we reached the bottom. The cement was cold beneath us as we sat, the chill seeping through, grounding me in the moment. We gazed at the apricot tree that grew nearby, its presence a silent witness to the countless memories we had created in this garden.

Fond memories of Duke and Henri playing in the garden flooded my mind, a welcome respite from the pain. Duke was always so full of energy, so fearless. He was the first one to discover the over-ripe apricots falling off the tree - it was his way of coaxing Henri to move beyond the decking. I had never figured out whether it was initially fear or laziness that stopped Henri from attempting the concrete slab steps, but

Duke always had a way of encouraging him. Henri would always do anything for food, and the memory of their antics, so full of life and mischief, brought with it a light chuckle, a brief flicker of warmth in the cold shadow of loss.

❖

Beatrix and I worked in mostly silence as we dug the hole beneath the apricot tree, the earth yielding to the rhythmic rhythm of our shovels. The act was methodical, each scoop a weighted acknowledgment of Duke's lifeless form resting beside us, a silent tribute to the boundless joy and companionship he had brought into our lives. With every shovelful of earth, the reality of what we were doing sank in deeper, the clinking of dirt against metal serving as a sombre melody that underscored the finality of our actions.

The physical exertion of digging, normally a task I might have undertaken with a mind focused on the job at hand, was instead imbued with a profound sense of ceremony and mourning. The hole we created, a final resting place for Duke beneath the apricot tree, felt like both an end and a testament—a physical manifestation of the love and memories we held for him.

As the depth of the hole grew, so too did the silence between Beatrix and me. It was as if words had become superfluous, inadequate in expressing the mix of grief, remembrance, and the shared weight of loss that enveloped us.

The finality of burying Duke cut through the air with each impact of dirt against metal, a reminder that this small act was a farewell not just to Duke's physical presence, but to the era he represented in our lives. The joy, the unconditional love, and the countless moments of companionship we had shared with him were now memories, treasures to be carried in our hearts as we navigated the world without him by our side.

After a few words of farewell, spoken more out of necessity than any belief that they could encapsulate the depth of our loss, Beatrix and I stood there, the void left by Duke's absence feeling like a tangible presence among us. The air around us seemed to thicken with unspoken grief, a silent testament to the sorrow that enveloped us both. Then, as if a dam had finally given way under the pressure of the accumulated pain, my emotional reserves broke, and sobs violently shook my shoulders. Collapsing at the base of the apricot tree, my head buried in my hands, I was completely overwhelmed by grief, each sob a raw, aching testament to the love and memories shared with Duke.

As the initial torrent of despair began to ebb, leaving me drained and hollow, I slowly lifted my head. The despair etched on my face mirrored the frustration and helplessness I felt, staring at the freshly disturbed ground that now served as Duke's final resting place. "We have no resources, almost no money, no security," I muttered, the words heavy with anxiety and the daunting reality of our situation. "What are we going to do? Do we really have any hope of helping Bixbus survive?" The questions, rhetorical yet laden with desperation, voiced the deep-seated fears that threatened to consume me.

Beatrix knelt beside me, wrapping her arm around my shoulder in a gesture of comfort and solidarity. "We'll figure something out," she said, her voice a beacon of reassurance in the darkness of my despair. Even if uncertainty lingered in the air between us, her presence and words offered a glimmer of hope, however faint.

Leaning my head against hers, I let out a heavy sigh, the simple act a silent admission of my vulnerability. "I don't know, Beatrix. It feels like everything is falling apart." The words, barely a whisper, conveyed the depth of my fear that the foundations of my worlds, both the one I knew and the one I fought to protect, were crumbling beneath me.

She hugged me tightly, her whispers a soothing balm trying to mend the fractures of my spirit, reassuring me that somehow, we would navigate this storm. Yet, even as she spoke, the feeling that I was drowning, overwhelmed by challenges that seemed beyond my grasp, refused to be silenced.

Suddenly, Beatrix suggested, "Hey, why don't you grab your laptop? I have an idea." Her words, imbued with a hint of determination and hope, pierced the fog of my despair. Skeptical but willing to clutch at any straw that might lead me out of this morass, I slowly brought myself to my feet. Casting a final glance at the small mound beneath the apricot tree, a silent farewell whispered through my heart to Duke, and we headed inside the house.

❖

Seated at the kitchen table, its black shiny surface reflecting the imprints of countless family dinners and shared conversations, I watched Beatrix's focused expression, bathed in the gentle glow of the laptop screen. The hum of the machine and the rhythmic tapping of keys became the soundtrack to our collective dive into the digital world. The open screen before us transformed into a portal to potential solutions, a flickering beacon in the dimly lit room that whispered the promise of a way forward.

I settled into the chair beside Beatrix, the creak of the worn wood beneath me breaking the silence that had settled around us after bidding Duke farewell. It felt like crossing a threshold from the palpable grief into a space of action and potential hope. Beatrix's eyes, alight with a fusion of determination and purpose, meticulously navigated through websites, her focus unwavering as she searched for temporary fencing solutions. The soft glow of the screen played upon her face, highlighting her features with shadows that added a contemplative edge to her serious expression.

"Look," she said, her voice breaking through the quiet, a beacon of hope amidst the darkness of our predicament. "They have next-day delivery. I think this might work until we can figure out a more permanent solution." Her words, infused with cautious optimism, seemed to lift some of the weight from my shoulders. The prospect of taking concrete steps, however small, towards safeguarding what we held dear in Bixbus, offered a sliver of relief in the overwhelming tide of challenges we faced.

The spark of hope that ignited within me felt like a beacon in the stormy darkness of recent trials. "Do you think we could order enough to protect the entire settlement?" The question, born out of a burgeoning sense of possibility, seemed to hang in the air between us, charged with the potential of what could be.

Beatrix's gaze met mine, a flicker of uncertainty lingering in her eyes as she contemplated the enormity of the task. "I'm not sure," she admitted, her fingers dancing across the keyboard with a grace that belied the gravity of our situation. "But it's worth a try. And in the meantime, we can look into other options." Her words, though measured, resonated with an inspiring determination.

As Beatrix skilfully navigated the online store, placing a small order that included the delivery address at the Owens property in Collinsvale, I felt a subtle sense of hope begin to sprout within me. The laptop, once merely a tool for mundane tasks, now became a vessel for possibilities, a lifeline that connected us to solutions beyond our immediate reach.

"I know this is just a temporary solution, but it's a start. It should be enough to give the settlers the security and protection they need," Beatrix said, her voice carrying a note of gratitude for the small victory we had secured. Her optimism, grounded in the practical steps we were taking, infused me with a renewed sense of purpose.

I nodded, a genuine smile tugging at the corners of my lips for the first time in what felt like an eternity. "Yeah, it will. And it will give them some peace of mind too. They've got every right to be worried about the shadow panthers and other unknown dangers that might be lurking around."

The hope that had begun as a mere spark within me swelled into a quiet confidence. *We have each other, and now, with two Guardians standing side by side, we'll tackle Clivilius head-on.*

4338.210

(29 July 2018)

BAD CONNECTION

4338.210.1

My body tensed, every muscle coiling as if ready to spring into action. The hairs on my arm bristled, standing on end like sentinels on alert, and those on the back of my neck tingled with a foreboding sense of anticipation. *Was it merely coincidence? Or was there someone, or something, lurking within the supposed sanctuary of my home?* The very thought sent a shiver down my spine. Given the recent upheavals in our world—where Portal Keys and Pirate technology blurred the lines between friend and foe—the idea of an intruder wasn't just paranoia; it was a plausible threat.

With a caution that felt more akin to the stealth of a cat, I poked my head into the hallway. The shadows seemed to dance at the edges of my vision, making the familiar feel unfamiliar. "Hello?" My voice, though intended to be firm, carried a tentative note as it echoed slightly off the walls. The silence that greeted me was almost more unnerving than any response could be.

"Hey, Luke," came the unexpectedly comforting voice of Beatrix, cutting through the tension like a beacon of normalcy.

A sigh of relief escaped me, so profound it seemed to uncoil the tightness in my chest. I let my body relax, feeling the adrenaline dissipate as quickly as it had surged. In an almost subconscious move, I found a t-shirt and pulled it over my head, covering my bare chest. It was a subtle act, but it was as if dressing could somehow restore a sense of order to the morning.

"You're up early," I announced, stepping into the convergence of the kitchen and living areas. The space felt too quiet, the air holding a stillness that was almost tangible.

Beatrix, looking more weary than I'd seen her in a long time, managed a yawn that seemed to embody exhaustion. "I didn't sleep very well," she confessed, her voice tinged with the strain of enduring pain. "I've already taken more pain killers than I probably should, and my head is still pounding." There was a vulnerability in her admission, a crack in her usually unbreakable façade.

As she spoke, I found my hand drifting to my left temple, mirroring her discomfort. "Tell me about it," I replied, a camaraderie in shared pain, even as I realised the growing ache in my own head that had gone unnoticed until now. It was a strange connection, one that underscored the undercurrents of unease that was becoming all too common.

Beatrix's frustration with the contents of our fridge—or the lack thereof—was palpable as she swung the door open and then shut it with a definitive huff. The sound echoed slightly in the quiet of the kitchen, a testament to her irritation.

"Alcohol already?" My question hung in the air, tinged with incredulity.

"Fuck off. I'm not Gladys," Beatrix snapped back, her voice sharp, cutting through the calm like a knife. There was a fire in her eyes, a spark that spoke of her fierce independence and stubborn pride.

"Sorry," I said, the corners of my mouth betraying me as I fought back a smile. There was something about her spirit, even in moments like these, that I couldn't help but admire. "There's muesli bars?" I offered, trying to shift the mood, as I opened the pantry and retrieved an unopened box. The mundane solution seemed almost comical given the earlier tension.

Beatrix's displeasure was evident, her face scrunching in a way that was both endearing and exasperating. I couldn't hold back any longer; a soft chuckle escaped me. "They're choc-chip," I added, a playful tease to lighten the atmosphere.

"Hmm. Fine," she conceded, extending her hand with a reluctance that was almost theatrical. Her pride was a fortress, but even fortresses have gates.

Ripping the box open, I tossed her several bars, each movement punctuated by the simple, unspoken connections that defined our relationship. "Thanks," she mumbled, the first package already being devoured. Muesli filled her mouth, a temporary peace offering that seemed to bridge the gap between frustration and the day's demands.

"Any plan for today?" Beatrix's voice, muffled by food, carried a note of curiosity as she began to navigate through the living room, her movements a dance of grace and purpose.

"You're going to visit Grant Ironbach and bring him to Clivilius," I replied, the words coming out more brusquely than I intended. My own muesli bar was torn open in a moment of distraction, my stomach betraying my hunger with a loud growl.

Beatrix stopped and turned, her scowl deepening, a storm brewing in her gaze. It was a look that could have made lesser men flinch.

"It'll be good practice for you," I encouraged, attempting to smooth over the abruptness of my earlier statement. There was a challenge in my voice, but also a belief in her capability, a faith in her strength.

"People aren't my thing," she declared, her tone matter-of-fact, as if that simple truth could excuse her from the task at hand.

"I already have to get Adrian," I replied, matching Beatrix's bluntness with my own. There was a certain gravity to my words, a recognition of the increasing complexity of our situation that seemed to hang heavily in the air between us.

"Who's Adrian?"

"He's a construction engineer. Runs his own company," I explained, feeling a sense of pride as I spoke of Adrian's expertise. "He did the building inspection for this place when Jamie and I bought it. Nial is great with fences, but I think the group needs more... professional help." It was an admission of the limitations of our current capabilities, a concession to the reality that the challenges we faced required a level of skill and knowledge that went beyond our makeshift solutions.

Beatrix, her attention momentarily captured by her muesli bar, bit into it before responding. "I suspect you're right there."

"I'm going to arrange to meet with him at the Collinsvale property tomorrow morning," I continued, outlining my plan with a sense of determination. The strategy was forming, piece by piece, in my mind, each step a move towards fortifying our position.

Suddenly, a long, loud honk shattered the morning's relative peace, its abruptness startling in the quiet of our surroundings. Beatrix reacted instantly, her movements quick and sharp as she poked her head through the blinds to investigate the source of the disruption, only to quickly withdraw.

"I wouldn't worry about it," I told her, trying to inject a note of reassurance into my voice. The brevity of her movements had not escaped my notice, and it concerned me that the tension of our circumstances might be pushing her towards paranoia. "There's always hoons on that road."

Beatrix shook her head, her expression one of conviction rather than reassurance. "No. I think the house is being watched." The certainty in her voice was unsettling.

I rubbed my brow, a gesture borne of a deep-seated need to remain patient and composed in the face of mounting pressures. "Did you recognise the person?" I asked, hoping for some clue, some indication of who might be taking such an interest in us.

"No," she replied, her head continuing to shake, her eyes reflecting the frustration of uncertainty. "It was too quick."

"Have another look then," I told her, my hand gesturing towards the window. It was an encouragement, a push to confront our fears directly rather than let them fester in the shadows of doubt.

Sliding her palm between the vertical blinds, Beatrix's movements were deliberate. She pulled one back slowly, her actions careful and measured as she peered out the window. "He's gone!" she hissed, a whisper filled with a mix of relief and lingering concern, as she let the blind snap back into place, restoring the veil of privacy between us and the outside world.

"Gone?" I echoed, my voice laced with confusion. *Why was Beatrix still so concerned if the car had driven off?* The small dirt pull-over area across the road was frequently a hub of minor commotion; it was hardly unusual to hear or see something odd there. Yet, the urgency in Beatrix's voice suggested this was no ordinary disturbance.

"Yeah. He's not in the car anymore," she continued, her voice still a hiss, barely above a whisper. The tension in her words was palpable, a clear signal that she perceived this as more than a fleeting threat. "We'd best get out of here for a while," she declared. Her decisiveness was characteristic, a reflection of her instinct to act swiftly in the face of danger. Without waiting for any reaction or response from me, Beatrix opened her Portal against the living room wall. The air seemed to ripple as if reality itself was bending, and then she stepped through, leaving me standing there, alone, in a room suddenly too quiet.

The wall soon returned to its original state, an ordinary, charcoal-coloured wall, as if nothing extraordinary had just occurred. But the illusion of normalcy was shattered by a loud knock at the front door. "Shit!" I whispered under my breath, the sudden noise spiking my adrenaline. My fingers instinctively sought the cool surface of my Portal Key in my trouser pocket, a lifeline now seemingly useless with the immediacy of the threat at our doorstep.

There's no time to activate it now, I realised with a surge of panic. *If the person at the door decided to peer through the windows, they'd spot me for sure*. Acting on impulse, I hastily crouched behind the kitchen's island bench, seeking the scant cover it provided. From my crouched position, I was acutely aware of how vulnerable I felt, hidden yet exposed, my heart racing as I contemplated my next move.

My breathing deepened, each inhale and exhale more deliberate than the last, as a whirlwind of questions raced through my mind. *Who the hell is it? Is it someone I know? Am I in danger?* The weight of the unknown pressed heavily upon me, the anticipation gnawing at my very core. Yet, amidst the swirling tide of anxiety, a spark of curiosity flared, urging me to uncover the truth behind the intrusion.

Moments later, the sound of the wooden gate rattling shattered the eerie silence, an unsettling breach of my sanctuary. The unwelcome visitor had effortlessly jumped over the barrier that was supposed to protect the backyard. Anger began to simmer within me, a slow boil of indignation at the audacity of the intrusion. Yet, I fought to keep my curiosity in check, channeling it into a focused determination to understand who dared to encroach upon my space.

Staying low, with the agility of a predator in its element, I stealthily moved into the hallway, each step measured and silent. My aim was clear: to catch a glimpse of the intruder without revealing my presence. I peered briefly into the bathroom doorway, hoping for a vantage point, but the frosted glass thwarted any chance of a clear view, offering nothing but blurred shadows.

Pushing along the hallway, the suspense tightened its grip with every step. I reached the end, where the corridor branched off, presenting a choice: the master bedroom to the right, or the small toilet and corner bedroom to the left. My heart pounded against my ribs, a drum of war echoing the tension that filled the air. Straining to hear any hint of movement, I was met with an unnerving silence that seemed to cloak the intruder's actions.

Slowly, cautiously, I edged my gaze around the bedroom's doorframe, the need for stealth paramount. And then, I saw him—a tall man standing outside the window, his presence casting a dark, ominous shadow across the venetian blinds. The sight of him, so unexpectedly close yet separated by the thin veil of glass, sent a jolt of shock through me. I gasped, the sound escaping before I could clamp down on the reaction, and yanked myself back, retreating into the shadows of the hallway.

The man's presence, a tangible threat now just metres away, sent a surge of adrenaline coursing through my veins. The reality of the situation hit me with the force of a thunderclap—this was no mere curiosity. I was potentially in grave danger. My mind raced, considering the possibilities, the motivations for his intrusion, and the implications for my safety. In that moment, hidden yet exposed, I realised the delicate balance between curiosity and survival, each decision from here on out could determine a new fate.

Deciding to capture any memory of the intruder, a surge of resolve coursed through me as I pulled out my phone and activated the camera. My hands, albeit steady with intention, betrayed a slight tremor of adrenaline as I held the phone as low as possible, navigating its lens toward the doorway. Using the viewfinder as my eyes beyond the wall, I slid my finger across the smooth, cold surface of the screen toward the 'capture' button, preparing for a quick snap that might serve as crucial evidence later.

"Who the hell are you?" The sudden, gruff call of a man's voice from outside pierced the tense silence, startling me. My grip faltered, and the phone slipped through my sweaty fingers, crashing to the floor with a sound that seemed far too loud in the quiet of the moment. "Shit!" I hissed under my breath, the curse a whisper of frustration and panic. Quickly, I slammed myself onto the carpet, my heart pounding in my ears. Retrieving the phone, I cradled it close, hoping desperately that my clumsy movement had gone unnoticed.

A moment of silence ensued, thick with anticipation, before the intruder spoke again, his voice carrying through the still air. "I'm Karl Jenkins. Detective Karl Jenkins," he finally revealed.

Shit! Why the hell is a detective sneaking around my backyard? The question hammered in my mind, a whirlwind of confusion and suspicion. *Was this a routine investigation, or had our activities attracted unwanted attention from the law?*

Realising that there were two voices outside, a new wave of urgency coursed through my veins. I pressed my back against the closed toilet door in a desperate bid for concealment. The cool surface of the door offered a stark contrast to the heat of my racing thoughts.

"And who are you?" the detective inquired, his tone authoritative yet tinged with a hint of curiosity.

"Oh. I'm terribly sorry to have interrupted you," the other man replied, his voice carrying a note of apologetic formality. "I'm Terry. I live across the street."

So, that's what the old guy actually sounds like. The realisation struck me with a mixture of surprise and intrigue. I had seen him frequently, tending to his front garden with a quiet dedication, yet our paths had never directly crossed, our interactions nothing more than distant acknowledgments.

Eager to hear more, to understand the unfolding dynamics outside my makeshift hideaway, I edged my head closer to the doorway, my curiosity now intertwined with a cautious calculation. Every snippet of conversation, every tone of voice, could offer insight into the situation at hand.

"I am looking for Luke Smith or Jamie Greyson," Karl's voice carried a professional edge, each word deliberate, hinting at the seriousness of his inquiry. "Have you seen either of them?" The question hung in the air, a tangible weight that seemed to press down on me from my concealed position.

Good question, I mused internally, my heart rate accelerating as I processed the implications of his visit. Saliva caught in my throat, a physical manifestation of my sudden anxiety. *Was Terry, the seemingly innocuous neighbour, actually an overlooked liability for our Clivilius efforts?*

"Not in the last few days," Terry's response came, his voice carrying a casualness that belied the gravity of the conversation. A moment of relief washed over me, fleeting and fragile. It seemed Terry might not be as astute or protective of his street as I initially thought. *Or perhaps,* I speculated, *he is just feigning ignorance to protect his neighbours.* The idea that nobody likes police poking their noses where it doesn't belong floated through my mind, a sliver of hope clinging to the possibility of Terry's discretion.

"But their friend has been here a lot recently. She's made a few trips here in a small truck," Terry continued, and with those words, any semblance of relief I'd felt shattered. *Fuck!*

Terry's observation skills were evidently neither lacking in astuteness nor inclined towards neighbourly protection.

"A small truck," Karl repeated, his tone reflecting a mixture of curiosity and suspicion. "How odd. Do you have any idea what for? Are they moving?" The detective's questions probed deeper, each one a potential unravelling of the carefully constructed semblance of normalcy that I suddenly realised we probably hadn't put as much effort into maintaining as we should have.

"Not sure. I don't think so. I think she's been making deliveries of some kind. I've not noticed anything leaving the house," Terry's reply came, his tone suggesting a blend of curiosity and neutrality. His observations, while accurate, painted a picture of our activities that I hadn't anticipated becoming public knowledge, least of all police knowledge.

"Very odd indeed. Well, do call me if you see anything else, sir," Karl instructed, the professional veneer firmly in place as he concluded his line of questioning.

"Of course," Terry replied with a promptness that felt like a betrayal, despite his earlier semblance of neutrality. "I'll make sure you're the first person I call." His assurance to the detective sent a chill down my spine.

Shit! The realisation hit me like a freight train: *We definitely have to start using the Collinsvale property now. My house has been compromised.* I sighed heavily, the weight of this revelation pressing down on me like a physical burden. The safety of our operations, once a given within the walls of my home, was now a gaping vulnerability. The thought of moving our base of operations wasn't just a tactical shift; it was a stark admission that the world outside was closing in on us, inch by inch.

"Brilliant!" The word, laced with sarcasm or perhaps genuine satisfaction, came from Karl. His tone was hard to pin down, a reflection of the complex dance of cat and mouse we found ourselves entangled in.

"Well, I'll leave you to it, then," Terry's voice signalled a conclusion to their exchange, his departure perhaps a brief respite in the mounting tension.

"Terry," Karl called out, a moment before Terry could retreat into the ordinariness of his day. "Yes?" Terry's response was prompt, a signal of his readiness to assist further if needed.

"Have you seen anyone else around here? Last night or this morning?" Karl's question was pointed, a direct probe into the comings and goings in our neighbourhood. His inquiry hinted at a broader search, a net cast wider than just my immediate circle.

"No, sir. Only you," Terry replied. His answer, straightforward and seemingly innocuous, offered a temporary shield, a momentary veil of ignorance that I desperately hoped would be enough to deflect Karl's suspicions.

A thick, heavy silence enveloped the space again, the tension palpable. The only exception was the constant thumping of my heart, a relentless drumbeat echoing the fear and uncertainty coursing through me. *Was Terry's interruption enough to make the detective leave?* The question lingered, a hopeful thought amidst a sea of dread.

Unable to muster the courage for even a fleeting glance around the bedroom doorframe, I once again turned to the silent witness in my hand: my phone's camera. The digital eye became my proxy, a way to brave the world outside without exposing myself to further risk.

A soft, metallic scraping sound abruptly shattered the silence, snapping my attention upwards. It was quickly followed by the loud clatter of the bedroom window's fly-screen crashing to the concrete below—a sound of intrusion, of boundaries breached. A deliberate, "Shit!" from the detective punctuated the moment, a rare slip that revealed his own frustration or perhaps surprise.

I let out a soft "Shit!" of my own, the expletive a whisper of mirrored frustration and rising panic. Without hesitation, I leapt into action, propelling myself into the hallway and scrambling toward the kitchen. The thought was clear and urgent: *I can't afford to get caught now. Especially not by a detective!* The stakes were too high, the consequences too dire. My movements were a blend of fear and determination, a desperate bid for safety in a world where every shadow could hide a threat, and every knock could be the prelude to a downfall.

Returning my phone to my trouser pocket, I fumbled frantically to retrieve the Portal Key. My fingers, slick with a sheen of sweat and trembling with adrenaline, slid across its small button. "For fuck's sake! Why aren't you working?" I growled at the stubborn device, my voice laced with panic. Each failed attempt to activate the Portal Key and escape from the imminent danger sent a new wave of despair crashing over me.

The sound of shattering glass from the bedroom window reverberated down the hallway, a chilling reminder of the escalating situation. *This Detective is insane!* The thought screamed in my mind as I bolted onto the small landing, my heart pounding in my chest like a drum of war. I clambered down the stairs, each step a desperate bid for safety, my mind racing with the need to evade the unforeseen threat that had breached my sanctuary.

"Shit! I'm an idiot!" The self-rebuke came as I stumbled clumsily into the only downstairs room, the realisation of my hasty and ill-considered escape plan dawning on me. "Where the fuck am I supposed to go down here?" I tormented myself, casting a frantic glance around the room. My eyes settled on the door that guarded the small, dark space under the stairs. *Taking that option would be my final move*, I warned myself. There'd be no escape from such a confined space, a trap of my own making.

The large, glass sliding door that led to the grassy backyard beckoned to me, its presence offering a glimmer of hope, an obvious escape route that screamed both opportunity and danger. With a surge of determination, I reached for the deadbolt at the top of the door, pulling it down with such fervour that I felt the tip of my fingernail bend backward.

"Fuck!" The hiss escaped my lips, a sharp intake of breath following the acute pain. I shook my hand fiercely, trying to dispel the sting, before pausing to examine the damage. A moment of relief washed over me as I saw the nail remained intact, a small victory in the midst of evading a detective. *Thankfully*, I thought, my focus returning to the task at hand. The physical pain was a jarring reminder of the reality of my situation, a tangible anchor in the whirlwind of fear and desperation that threatened to overtake me.

Unlocking the second latch, I pulled the heavy door open with a determined tug, releasing the pent-up tension in my muscles. As the door glided open, a fresh, cool morning breeze greeted me, a brief moment of respite that caressed my face with its soothing touch. Standing in the doorway, I hesitated, caught between the urgency to flee and a momentary pause of relief. Then, abruptly, the tranquility was shattered by the roar of a car's engine coming to life, its tires screeching across gravel in a hasty departure.

Was that the Detective? The thought barely had time to form before instinct took over. I darted from the doorway, my body propelled by a mix of adrenaline and fear. It took almost no time to reach the back fence, my back slamming against the ageing wood with a thud that echoed the rapid beating of my heart. Desperate to catch a glimpse of the car before it vanished from view, I peered over the tall fence, stretching every muscle in my attempt to see.

My foot kicked against the fence involuntarily, a physical manifestation of the tumult of emotions swirling within me as I watched the silhouette of a dark car disappear in a cloud of dust. *Bugger!* The word was a silent scowl in my mind, a mix of frustration and resignation. I knew it hadn't been an official police car—its departure was too hurried, too lacking in the ceremoniousness of law enforcement. Yet, I didn't get a clear enough view of the vehicle to know what to watch out for in the future, a missed opportunity that gnawed at me.

Exhaling loudly, I allowed myself a moment to process the events. There was a relief, albeit a temporary one, in the realisation that today would not be the day I come face to face with the law—a law that I seem unable to keep myself from breaking. *But it's not my fault,* I reminded myself with a defiant inner voice. *It's for Clivilius.* This justification was a shield, a way to reconcile the actions I deemed necessary for a greater cause with the societal norms I found myself at odds with.

❖

After confirming that Detective Jenkins had indeed vacated the premises, and witnessing the undeniable evidence of the bedroom window's violation, my heart sank. The shattered glass lay scattered like a crystal carpet, a stark reminder of the intrusion into my once secure haven. Ignoring the fragmented remains, I promptly exited the exposed room, pulling the door closed behind me with a finality that echoed my resolve. The house, already compromised, stood as a silent testament to the urgent necessity of vacating it. Cleaning up now seemed a futile gesture, an attempt to mend what had already been irrevocably broken.

Entering the study, a room once filled with the quiet hum of contemplation and strategy, I aimed the Portal Key at the far wall, the device in my hand my only ticket to a swift escape. I pressed the button, once, twice, several times, each press a desperate plea for action. But the Portal Key remained obstinately silent, its failure to activate sending a wave of frustration through me.

"Shit!" The exclamation burst from me. My temples throbbed with a pulsing rhythm, mirroring the panic that gripped me, paralysing and potent. The words that followed trailed off, leaving my mouth as a mumble, the intensity of my emotions rendering me incapable of the bold declaration I had intended. "Why the hell won't you work? Clivilius, what the fuck is going on?" My voice, laced with desperation and confusion, filled the study, a room that had once been a sanctuary of planning and progress now a witness to my moment of vulnerability.

PORTAL CONFLICT

4338.210.2

Circling the island bench for what felt like the thousandth time, a sense of déjà vu enveloped me, each turn a repetition of dwindling hope. I pointed the Portal Key at the living room wall once more, my movements mechanical, driven by the desperation of the situation. I slid my finger across the button, the air around me charged with tension, a tangible representation of my growing despair. My chest tightened with each futile attempt, a physical manifestation of the frustration that threatened to overwhelm me. Again, there was no response from the device. No ball of energy shooting from its end. No wall exploding in a spectacle of colour, just a bland vacancy that mocked my efforts.

The phone on the bench vibrated loudly, its sudden noise a jarring contrast to the stillness of my failed attempts. My impatience and frustration reached a boiling point, culminating in a loud huff as I swiped the phone from the bench. The notification screen greeted me with a message from Gladys. I silently read her name at the top, a sliver of distraction in the sea of my turmoil.

11:07AM Gladys: *I'm at Collinsvale. Where are you?*

Shit! Nial's Bunnings order. The realisation hit me like a wave, a forgotten obligation surfacing amidst the drama of the morning. I scolded myself, feeling the weight of my oversight. My shoulders ached from prolonged tension. *I can't leave here until I know what's going on with my Portal Key*, I firmly told myself, the resolve hardening within me. Knowing that the luxury of almost instant travel to the Owens' property was currently beyond my grasp, I typed out a quick reply to Gladys.

11:09AM Luke: *Bring it around home. Sorry.*

11:09AM Gladys: *Seriously!?*

11:10AM Luke: *Yes please. I'll get you some wine. I promise.*

The negotiation, if it could be called that, hung in the balance. "Come on, Gladys," I murmured softly, an undercurrent of hope in my voice as my fingers tapped the benchtop nervously. The wait for her response felt interminable, each second stretching out before me.

11:12AM Gladys: *I want two bottles*

A smile broke across my face, a brief respite in the tension of the day. *Easily persuaded.* The thought brought a chuckle, a moment of lightness. Confirming the deal, I typed out my response.

11:13AM Luke: *Done*

Making a concerted effort to cease my anxious pacing around the living room, I began the arduous task of preparing the house for an abrupt departure. The echoes of our recent struggles were everywhere: a broken window in the back room, a smashed light in the study, traces of Beatrix's blood smattered along the hallway and door frames. Despite our best efforts to clean it all up, these marks of conflict rendered the house less like a home and more like a battleground. With the unwanted attention of a detective now part of our reality, the urgency to relocate our belongings to Clivilius felt not just practical, but necessary.

As I gathered, sorted, and packed our lives into as many bags and boxes as I could find, the weight of our situation pressed heavily upon me. Each item I touched was a reminder of the life we were being forced to leave behind, of the safety and security that had been shattered as easily as the glass of the back window.

Staring at the three-seater couch downstairs, I wrestled with the logic and emotion of the decision to empty the house. The rational part of me knew that moving our belongings to Clivilius was the smart move. *The tents there are huge,* I reminded myself, trying to bolster my resolve with the practicality of the plan. *They can easily fit a few couches, especially in those central, shared spaces.* The thought of making the new, albeit temporary, accommodations a little more comfortable offered a small relief.

Yet, as I stood there, contemplating the logistics of moving a couch among other things, a deeper, more poignant realisation took hold. This wasn't just about physical comfort or the strategic necessity of consolidating our resources. It was about clinging to a semblance of normalcy, about creating a space that felt like home in a world that was becoming increasingly unrecognisable. The couch, an ordinary piece of furniture under normal circumstances, had become a symbol of the life I was desperate to preserve, a life that was slipping through my fingers with each passing moment.

"Hey, Luke," Gladys's voice pierced the silence, her sudden presence in the room jolting me from my thoughts. The element of surprise sent a wave of adrenaline through me, momentarily heightening my senses.

I turned to face her, my expression morphing into one of suspicion. "How–" I started, my confusion palpable. The ease with which she had entered, combined with the disorienting swift passage of time, left me grappling for answers.

"Front door was open," Gladys offered an explanation, her tone matter-of-fact.

"Open?" The word echoed out of me, my mind racing to the worst possible scenarios. My eyes widened, the panic that someone else might be in the house, an intruder lurking in the shadows, momentarily seizing my thoughts.

"Not open, open," Gladys clarified, catching the edge of alarm in my voice. "Just unlocked."

Her clarification brought a wave of relief, washing over me like a cooling breeze. "You had me worried there," I admitted, letting out a loud exhale that carried the weight of my temporary fear.

Gladys's response was a shrug, her nonchalance a stark contrast to my momentary panic.

"So," she began, drawing out the word in a way that signalled her curiosity was piqued. "What's with all the packing? Why not take it straight to Clivilius?" Her gaze swept the room, taking in the clutter of boxes and bags, her fingers absentmindedly brushing small clumps of dirt from the couch.

Her question and the casual gesture of cleaning the dirt from the couch brought a silent frown to my face. That dirt, so inconsequential to her, was a tangible reminder of Duke's existence.

"My Portal Key isn't working," I snapped, the frustration and helplessness I felt bleeding into my tone, sharper than I had intended.

"Do you know why?" Gladys's question followed, her attention shifting from the task of cleaning to me. She moved along to the recliner, her actions methodical as she began to dislodge the dirt that had clung to the fabric.

Feeling the frustration and anger bubbling up inside me like a tempest, I knew I needed to divert Gladys's attention before the emotions overwhelmed me, before the burning behind my eyes turned into something visible. Desperation clawed at my insides as I reached into the near-permanent home of my wallet in my front trouser pocket, retrieving the cash I had taken from Kain's wallet—a reminder of the lengths I was willing to go for the cause.

"Move the truck onto the vacant block and then you can take Jamie's car to go and buy yourself some wine," I said, my voice a mixture of command and plea. I thrust the wad of notes under her nose, a tangible symbol of dismissal and necessity. The truck, temporarily in Gladys's possession until my Portal Key decided to function again—if it ever would—left her with little else to do here. The thought sent a shiver of anxiety through me, the reality of our situation, the dependency on such a small device for such significant parts of our lives, was terrifying.

"Sure," Gladys responded, her voice carrying a note of surprise, or perhaps it was just acceptance. She snatched the cash, her fingers quickly thumbing through it as she counted, the action so mundane yet so starkly contrasted with my current Portal Key dilemma.

Anticipating the direction of her next question, I interjected, "spend all of it," cutting off her inquiry before it could fully form.

Gladys, with a nod, shoved the notes into her back pocket, a simple gesture that marked the acceptance of the task. As she glanced over her shoulder, leaving the room, her gaze inadvertently caught mine. For a moment, her eyes lingered on me, witnessing the vulnerability I so desperately tried to hide—a single tear I hastily wiped away before it could betray the turmoil inside. She hesitated, perhaps sensing the depth of my struggle, before disappearing up the stairs.

The front door closed with a loud bang, a definitive sound that marked Gladys's departure. The noise echoed in the empty space. Left alone with my thoughts, the weight of my predicament pressed heavily on my shoulders. The brief interaction, the exchange of cash for a temporary reprieve, felt like a bandage over a gaping wound. It was a fleeting solution, a momentary distraction from the relentless tide of challenges I faced.

Slowly making my way to the recliner, I moved through the room as if each step was a journey through the memories that clung to every piece of furniture, every corner. Ignoring the little dirt that remained on the dark fabric, I allowed myself the simple act of sitting down, letting my body sink into the cushy softness that promised a brief respite from the turmoil of recent events. The recliner, an island of comfort in a sea of chaos, welcomed me, its familiarity a balm to my frayed nerves.

As I settled in, my breath catching in my throat, a single strand of white fur caught my eye, its tip ensnared in the fabric on the arm of the recliner. Carefully, I picked it up, the action both deliberate and tender. Bringing the fur to my nose, I inhaled deeply, closing my eyes to better savour the moment. The scent was unmistakably Duke's, that familiar dog smell that had become as much a part of this house as the walls that sheltered us. For a moment, Duke's furry brown and white face hovered in front of me, vivid in my mind's eye, his pink tongue lolling from his panting mouth, a picture of joy and boundless energy.

I could almost feel the weight of his body, his paws performing a delicate balancing act on my thighs as if he were right there with me. The sensation of his rough tongue running across my cheek elicited a broad smile from deep within me, a spontaneous reaction to the memories of his affection. A light chuckle escaped my lips at the thought, a sound of pure joy amidst the sorrow, as I playfully fought to push his face away before he could lavish me with more of his enthusiastic kisses. Duke always was the more affectionate of the two boys, his presence a constant source of comfort and love.

Then, as quickly as the memory came, it faded. Duke leaped from my lap in my imagination, his skinny front legs extending outward like a sugar glider, landing with a soft thump on the carpet before vanishing from my view. The vividness of the memory was so acute, so real, that for a fleeting second, I half-expected to see him there, looking up at me with those trusting eyes.

Pressing the strand of white fur against my chest, I felt the pounding of my heart, a physical ache for the loyal companion I knew I would never hold again. The weight of that realisation, the permanence of the loss, settled over me like a heavy cloak. "I'm so sorry, Duke," I whispered into the silence, a vow of remembrance and regret. The words were a tribute, a soft-spoken prayer for a friend whose loyalty and love had been a beacon of light in the darkest of times. In that moment, sitting alone in the quiet of the house, the depth of my grief for Duke was a poignant reminder of the fragility of the bonds we forge and the pain that their breaking brings.

❖

Taking a moment to gather my thoughts and steady my breathing, I continued with the grim task of stripping the house of its contents. The realisation that, apart from one of the beds and one of the leather couches in the upstairs living room, nothing else warranted staying any longer weighed heavily on me. It was a poignant acknowledgment that the house, once a sanctuary, had been reduced to little more than a shell, its essence to be carted away for the sake of safety and secrecy.

Standing in the solitude of the study, I found myself staring at the blank wall before me, my fingers twitching with a mix of anticipation and anxiety. The thought of the Portal Key continuing to malfunction loomed large in my mind, a spectre of isolation and immobility. "Just bloody do it already!" I chided myself, the stern self-admonishment a reflection of the internal battle between fear and the necessity of action.

Emboldened by a surge of determination, I listened to that more confident part of myself, the part that refused to be cowed by uncertainty. My trembling finger slid across the small button at the end of the device, an action that felt both defiant and desperate. Then, with a bright flash that momentarily banished the shadows of doubt, the study wall came alive with comforting swirls of colour, a beautiful spectacle that heralded the portal's activation.

Without hesitation, I stepped through the newly opened portal, the urgency of confirming its destination to Bixbus pressing heavily on my mind. The transition was instantaneous, the familiar sensation of passing through the portal a strange mix of disorientation and relief.

As I emerged on the other side, warm swirls of dust danced about my feet, the sight of the Drop Zone not far off bringing a wave of calming relief. *What the hell had happened?* The question echoed in my mind, a silent query amidst the tranquil scene that greeted me. My eyes scanned the surroundings, searching for any clue, any indication of what might have caused the earlier malfunction. Yet, finding nothing out of the ordinary, I was left with nothing but an accepting shrug and a burgeoning hope that such a failure would never repeat itself.

Back in the study, the relief of knowing my portal passage was restored mingled with a new uncertainty. *Could objects traverse as freely as before, or had the recent malfunction altered something fundamental?* This question lingered, adding a layer of complexity to the already daunting task of emptying the house.

My hands gripped the white desk, the surface cool and unyielding under my fingers. With a determined grunt, I pulled the desk toward me, its weight more formidable than I had anticipated. *Shit, this thing is heavier than I realised.* The effort it took to move it even slightly was a burdensome reminder of the physicality of my task. After making another hefty pull, I paused, my breath heavy with exertion. The memory of dismantling the desk six months ago surfaced, a task undertaken in a moment of wanting change, craving a different perspective from the mundanity of my then-routine.

I had moved it from the back room to this room, drawn by the desire to gaze out the window that overlooked the main road. There was something inherently relaxing about watching the native hens emerge from the nearby thick scrub to feed by the roadside. It was a simple pleasure, a momentary escape from the complexities of life. The desk, in its assembled state, hadn't fit through the doorway, turning what I had hoped would be a straightforward task into a painful exercise of deconstruction.

"Actually," I mumbled to myself, a faint smile playing on my lips as I recalled the ordeal. Dismantling it had indeed been the easy part, a process of undoing, of breaking down into manageable pieces. It was the reassembly that had tested me, the challenge of putting all the pieces back together in a way that made sense, that restored its purpose. That was always the challenge. While I had the strength and determination to tear things apart and start anew, building things, creating order from chaos, was definitely not my forte.

This realisation, while not new, hit me with renewed force as I contemplated not just the physical task of disassembling the desk once more, but the broader metaphor it represented. In our efforts to navigate the dangers we faced, to dismantle the threats and rebuild a semblance of safety, the real challenge lay not in the tearing down, but in the rebuilding.

But now is not the time for rebuilding a desk, I mused to myself, a light chuckle escaping. Channelling what felt like an endless supply of determination, coupled with a reasonable addition of grunting for good measure, I pushed and pulled the heavy desk through the portal into Clivilius. The effort was monumental, each step a testament to the will to persevere. Stopping to wipe the salty sweat from my brow, I realised that the desk and I had barely made it more than a few metres beyond the portal before the thick ochre dust of Clivilius clogged our path. "This'll do," I grumbled, giving the desk a slap across its white surface. It shone bright under the warm sun of this new world, a stark contrast to the dim study it had once inhabited.

"Guess what?" Paul's voice suddenly broke through my focus, causing me to jump. His presence was unexpected, a sudden intrusion into the solitary task I had set myself.

"I'm not particularly in the mood," I responded tersely, my voice betraying the mix of still-raw emotions and the physical exhaustion that gnawed at my edges. Paul's exuberance, normally a welcome respite, felt overwhelming, his energy almost too much to bear in my current state.

"We can access the internet," Paul blurted out anyway, his excitement undimmed by my lacklustre response. In one fluid motion, he jumped up, sitting on the edge of the desk I had just transported through sheer will.

"Get off," I scowled, my patience frayed, swatting him across the back in a brotherly gesture of annoyance. The desk, despite its journey, was not yet ready to bear the weight of new discoveries, nor was I.

Paul pouted as he slid off, his movement slight, a mere shift given the closeness of his long legs to the ground even when perched on the desk. His reaction, so typical of our interactions, seemed out of place in the vastness of Clivilius.

"What's your problem?" he asked, a hint of genuine concern beneath the casual inquiry.

I sighed, the weight of my exhaustion making it difficult to articulate the depth of my feelings. "I'm just tired," I admitted. It was the simplest truth, an acknowledgment of the weariness that permeated both body and soul.

Paul's impromptu decision to help move the desk wasn't just surprising; it was a testament to the unpredictable nature of our relationship. Pushing me to the side with determination, he grabbed hold of the desk's edge and gave it a firm pull. The desk's stubborn refusal to budge more than an inch from his effort brought a smile to my face, and I couldn't help but chuckle at the look of surprise and mild indignation on my brother's face.

"Help me carry it to the Drop Zone," Paul said, the grin on his face widening as his hands mimed the motion of lifting. It was a request, but one that carried the heavy weight of expectation.

My eyes rolled in a mixture of exasperation and resignation. "Fine," I conceded, recognising the futility of arguing. Together, we positioned ourselves at opposite ends of the desk, our hands finding purchase under its weight. The initial lift was marked by small grunts from both of us. The journey was slow, punctuated by several stops as we paused to catch our breath and muster the strength to continue.

"Did you hear what I said before?" Paul asked, breaking the silence that had settled between us as we focused on relocating the desk.

"Do we really have to talk while we move?" I responded, the effort of carrying the desk making my words come out through gritted teeth.

"Yeah," Paul insisted, undeterred. "It's exciting."

"Fine," I huffed, a reluctant agreement to engage in conversation despite the physical exertion. "You talk. I'll listen."

As I begrudgingly allowed Paul to dive into the narrative of his recent adventures with Beatrix, Nial, and their endeavours with a router, my body was a contradiction of emotions. On one hand, impatience gnawed at me, urging me to dismiss the details as trivial. On the other, curiosity piqued, luring me into the intricacies of his tale. Despite my efforts to maintain a façade of disinterest, Paul's animated recounting of the events drew me in, his enthusiasm infectious even against my will.

The technical jargon of wifi signals and the logistical nightmares of fence supply orders required my full attention. My eyes narrowed, not out of disinterest, but in an effort to piece together the puzzle Paul laid out before me. The frustration within me wasn't directed at Paul's storytelling but at the urgency to grasp the full implications of their technological experiment.

"The downside," Paul noted, his voice cutting through my swirling thoughts, "is that because the router still had to be connected on the earth side, Beatrix had to keep her portal open the entire time."

His words acted as a catalyst, a peculiar coincidence emerging from the fog of details. "And this was today?" I couldn't help but interrupt, the timing of their experiment aligning too closely with the issues I had faced.

"Yeah. This morning," Paul confirmed, his casual acknowledgment igniting a spark of realisation within me.

"Interesting," was all I managed to say, my response so soft it was almost lost in the breeze. My mind raced ahead, weaving together the fragments of information into a hypothesis that demanded exploration.

"What is?" Paul's curiosity was evident, his question an anchor pulling me back from the precipice of my thoughts.

"We would need to test it," I said, more to myself than to him, the idea taking form, solidifying into a plan that held the potential to unravel the mystery of today's anomalies.

"Test what?" Paul's confusion was palpable

"Fuck's sake, Paul, keep up, will you," I snapped, frustration and excitement mingling in my voice as I headed back toward the portal with renewed purpose. My mind was ablaze with possibilities, the pieces of the puzzle beginning to align.

"But you haven't really said anything," Paul protested, his bewilderment a distracting contrast to my burgeoning clarity.

Halting in my tracks, I turned to face him, the intensity of my gaze pinning him in place. "When Beatrix next arrives, tell her to contact me. I have an experiment of my own to conduct with her," I declared, my voice imbued with a certainty that brooked no argument. Beneath the surface, excitement bubbled, a rare feeling of anticipation at the prospect of uncovering new avenues of understanding. In that moment, the frustration and fatigue that had clouded my day began to dissipate, replaced by the invigorating thrill of discovery and the promise of collaboration.

Paul's mischievous grin, a telltale sign of his innate ability to sense the unfolding drama, added a palpable tension to the air. "Speak of the devil," he teased, his gaze flicking to the portal behind me. The anticipation in his voice was infectious, prompting me to turn with a mix of eagerness and apprehension.

As my heels sunk slightly into the soft, ochre dust, my heart skipped a beat at the sight unfolding before me. A large vehicle, with a caravan in tow, emerged from the portal, its appearance heralding the start of something new, something potentially groundbreaking. The vehicle's arrival through the portal, a feat of technology and magic combined, never ceased to amaze me, yet today it felt like a prelude to an even greater revelation.

Beatrix, stepping out of the car, was a sight to behold. She pulled her silver hair back, securing it with a hair tie, an action so mundane yet so mesmerising under the circumstances. Strands of her hair rebelled against confinement, dancing in the breeze, adding a touch of normalcy to the extraordinary.

"Beatrix!" My voice carried across the distance, laden with urgency and a keen anticipation. The moment demanded swift action, and I could scarcely contain the excitement bubbling within me.

"Can you two unhitch the caravan?" Beatrix's request cut through my thoughts. Her struggle with the disobedient strands of hair, a battle against the elements, mirrored our own struggles against the odds.

"I need to test something with you," I insisted, brushing aside her practical concerns with a wave of determination. The experiment I had in mind, sparked by Paul's earlier revelation, held the promise of answers, of understanding that could redefine our approach to the challenges we faced.

"How am I supposed to move the caravan back to camp if it's not connected to a vehicle?" Paul's query, practical yet tinged with frustration, underscored his logistical challenges.

"You've got other vehicles here," Beatrix suggested, her tone a mix of exasperation and practicality as she attempted to tame her hair once more. "Surely one of those has a tow bar you can use."

Paul's grunt, a vocal expression of his frustration, reflected the tension that underpinned their interactions.

"You're doing a lot of grunting today," I teased, a light chuckle escaping me as I gave Paul a playful slap across the shoulder. It was an attempt to diffuse the tension, to inject a moment of levity into the urgency of our tasks.

Despite Paul's initial reluctance, he shifted his attention back to the immediate task, his movements methodical as he began the process of unhitching the caravan. Beatrix's offer to bring another vehicle equipped with a tow bar was a testament to her pragmatic approach to the challenge.

As the caravan was uncoupled, the car bounced slightly. The metallic clinks, each a testament to Paul's determination, underscored the physical reality of our situation, a stark contrast to the theoretical musings that occupied my thoughts.

Turning back to Beatrix, I was eager to explore the implications of my recent technological mishaps. "I can't go through your portal, nor you through mine, right?" I asked, seeking confirmation of our known limitations.

"Right," she replied, her cautious tone matching the narrowing of her eyes.

"So, what if that also means that I can't open my portal if you have yours open, and vice versa?" I posited, laying out my hypothesis based on the day's events and Paul's recounting of their experiment.

Beatrix's gasp was immediate, a spontaneous reaction to the implications of my suggestion. "The router," she whispered, the word heavy with realisation, as if my words had unlocked a new perspective on the problem.

"Exactly!" My response was animated, buoyed by the alignment of our thoughts. "I'm pretty sure my Portal Key wasn't working at the same time that you had your portal active with that blasted router." The pieces of the puzzle were aligning, each revelation shedding light on the mysterious malfunction I had encountered.

"Shit," Beatrix uttered, her expression mirroring my own concern. Her eyes, wide with the dawning comprehension of the potential ramifications of our discovery, reflected a shared sense of urgency. This revelation wasn't just a technical curiosity; it hinted at underlying principles of our portal technology we had yet to fully grasp.

The urgency of the situation and the potential breakthrough in our understanding of how the portals interact with one another sharpened my resolve. "I have a small truck with fence supplies to bring through. Beatrix, go somewhere safe on earth and wait for two minutes. Give me enough time to get this truck here. I'll leave my portal active for another few minutes, and in that time, you keep trying your Portal Key." The plan was clear in my mind, each step calculated to test our theory with precision.

"Yeah, good idea," Beatrix agreed, her voice carrying a mixture of anticipation and a dash of apprehension. The potential of our undertaking wasn't lost on either of us; this was more than a mere experiment—it was a step towards unravelling the mystery that had plagued me.

"What about the internet?" Paul attempted to interject, his voice tinged with desperation. The connection to the wider world, to the flow of information it represented, would be a lifeline for him, yet at this moment, it was a distraction for me.

"Not now, Paul," I snapped, perhaps more harshly than intended. My focus was like a laser, honed in on the experiment and its potential to shift our understanding of portal technology. The intricacies of our digital connection to the earth had to wait; we were on the cusp of a discovery that could impact us in a drastic way if we didn't get it right.

"BYE KARL" - PART 1

4338.210.3

The success of our experiment washed away the frustrations of the morning like a tide receding from the shore. The revelation that Beatrix and I could effectively block each other's portal access if one was active had its implications—potentially dramatic ones for our future operations—but the clarity it provided was invaluable. Understanding the rules of the game, even those that complicated our play, gave us a strategic edge we hadn't possessed before.

Paul, having grown bored and frustrated with our prolonged experiment, had drifted back to camp in search of a vehicle equipped with a tow bar. Reflecting on his earlier irritation, a pang of guilt nudged at me. In a gesture of brotherly conciliation, I opted to drive the small truck loaded with fencing supplies to the Drop Zone myself. It was a small act of consideration, leaving the task of unpacking to Paul but sparing him the additional chore of fetching the vehicle. The decision to leave the small truck in Bixbus was practical, given the increasing police interest back on Earth. It had served its purpose, and with the law's eyes possibly scouring for any sign of our activities, it was safer here, away from prying eyes.

With the day's immediate concerns addressed, I turned my attention back to the house, only to be greeted by the incessant jingle of my phone. Missed messages and calls from Gladys filled the screen, a stark reminder of the world beyond our immediate concerns. The voicemail icon beckoned, and I pressed play, bracing myself for whatever urgency Gladys's voice would convey.

"Luke!" The panic in Gladys's voice was unmistakable, her words rushed and laden with anxiety. "The police are following me back to your place. They're expecting to find Jamie. What do I do?"

"Shit!" The word escaped my lips as I hastily opened the text message from Gladys, her written words echoing the urgency of her voicemail. My heart pounded, a mix of fear and resolve churning within me as I prepared to verify the timing of her messages. However, before I could scrutinise the details further, the soft shuffle of sneakers on the front porch sliced through my concentration.

Gladys? The thought flickered through my mind, a sliver of hope that perhaps she had made it back safely. With cautious steps, I moved across the kitchen tiles, each footfall a calculated risk as I inched towards the front door.

Then, the unmistakable sound of knuckles rapping loudly against the wood sent a jolt of adrenaline through me, propelling me to duck behind the island bench. *Don't answer the door.* The internal warning was clear, born of the realisation that Gladys had house keys and wouldn't need to knock. This left two possibilities: either it wasn't Gladys at the door, or it was, and the police were with her, either scenario fraught with danger and complication.

The muffled cacophony of multiple voices outside the door confirmed my worst fears, a sinister chorus that spelled trouble. The jingle of keys, a sound that should have been innocuous, now served as the catalyst for my next move. Darting back into the hallway, I made my way to the back bedroom, my mind racing with possible escape routes and contingencies.

As I opened the back bedroom door, a cold breeze greeted me, a chilling reminder of the state of neglect the house had fallen into. Jamie was the handyman, the one who kept the house in order, who could fix anything that broke. A frown marred my face as I faced the uncomfortable truth: *without Jamie, the house's days were numbered.* The realisation brought a heavy sense of foreboding, a fleeting mourning for the life we had built and the home that had sheltered us.

Gripping the door handle tightly, I took care to close the door with controlled, deliberate movements, ensuring the wind didn't cause it to slam and alert our unwelcome visitors to my presence.

"Jamie!" Gladys's call, echoing down the hallway, momentarily lifted the veil of tension that had settled over me. "Jamie!" she repeated, her voice a blend of urgency and feigned confusion. I couldn't help but scoff silently at her performance, a slight grin breaking through as I recognised the cleverness of her act. She knew as well as I did that Jamie wouldn't—couldn't—respond. And just as quickly as it appeared, the grin vanished, the reality hitting me with a renewed force. "Jamie is never going to reply," I whispered to myself, a solemn truth that echoed the permanent silence of Duke's absence.

The sudden swing of the bedroom door shattered the brief calm, its creaking hinges a jarring reminder of our precarious situation. I instinctively jumped back, my heart racing as Gladys entered, her calls for Jamie now directed into the room with a palpable pretence.

"Luke! What the fuck," she hissed upon seeing me, her eyes wide, a tumultuous mix of panic and frustration swirling within them. My initial instinct was to respond, to offer some explanation or reassurance, but her hand quickly covered my mouth, silencing any words I might have offered. Her intense gaze held mine in the dim light of the room, conveying more than words ever could.

"There are two detectives in the living room, waiting for me to return with Jamie," she whispered, her voice barely audible, each word infused with the heavy burden of our current crisis.

"Karl Jenkins?" The name slipped out, almost instinctively, the mention of the detective bringing a specific face, a known entity, into the fray.

"Yes," Gladys confirmed, her reply short, her eyes searching mine for something—reassurance, a plan, any indication of what our next move should be. "You know him?"

"Yeah," I responded, the weight of my encounter with Detective Jenkins bearing down on me. A heavy pause filled the space as I grappled with how much to divulge. My decision to shield Gladys from the full extent of my interaction with Jenkins was deliberate, a protective instinct to spare her from additional worry. "I caught him snooping around here the other day," I admitted, leaving out the depth of the ordeal.

"Did he see you? Did you talk to him?" The urgency in Gladys's voice was palpable. Her concern was not just for the immediate issue but for the potential ramifications of any interaction with law enforcement.

"No," I assured her quickly, wanting to alleviate her immediate fears. "Do you know the detective with him?" I redirected, curious about the identity of Jenkins's companion and the role they might play in our unfolding drama.

Gladys's description of the other detective painted a picture, albeit a vague one, that stirred a sense of recognition within me. "No. She's a little taller than me, long, black hair, and quite attractive, really," she offered, her tone laced with a hint of unease at the memory.

"Sounds like Sarah Lahey," I found myself saying, a name surfacing from the depths of my memory, its familiarity prompting a mix of intrigue and concern. *Really?* I questioned internally, doubting my own recall. The name Sarah Lahey hovered in my thoughts, a piece of the puzzle that seemed to fit yet felt oddly out of place.

"Befriend her," I found myself instructing Gladys, an unexpected strategy forming amidst the uncertainty. It was a curveball, indeed, one that carried with it a mix of risk and potential insight. If this detective was indeed Sarah Lahey, then perhaps there was an avenue through which we could navigate this precarious situation with a semblance of control.

"Befriend her?" Gladys's query, laced with evident surprise, echoed the improbability of the suggestion I had just made.

"Yeah."

"What? Why?" Her confusion mirrored the complexity of the situation we found ourselves in.

"We need to find some allies. My gut tells me that Sarah might help us," I explained, the conviction in my voice belying the uncertainty that underpinned such a gamble. The idea of turning potential adversaries into allies was a testament to the desperate times we found ourselves in, a reflection of the unconventional warfare we were engaged in.

"To cover up the disappearances?" Gladys's question, probing deeper into the implications of my suggestion, revealed her quick grasp of the situation.

You surprise me sometimes, Gladys, I mused silently, a flicker of admiration for her astuteness stirring within me, hope reigniting knowing that her messed up brain was already ahead of mine.

"You'd better get back out there," I directed, my hands gently pushing her towards the door. The urgency of maintaining appearances before the detectives waiting in the living room was paramount. "They'll be getting suspicious if you don't get back there."

Gladys's reluctance was palpable, her feet dragging along the carpet as she hesitated. The weight of the task before her, the uncertainty of the outcome, hung heavily in the air between us. "What do I tell them?" she asked, her voice tinged with panic, seeking direction in the mire of deception we were entangled in.

With a final nudge, I pushed Gladys out of the room, the gesture more one of encouragement than dismissal. "I really don't know," I admitted with a shrug. "Just don't tell them about me." My words, a plea for discretion, underscored the delicate balance we were trying to maintain.

As the door closed softly behind her, sealing off the room from the hallway and the detectives beyond, a profound sense of isolation washed over me. The muted click of the latch marked the end of our brief conference, leaving me alone with my thoughts and the weight of the unknown future.

Pressing my ear against the wooden door, I found myself in a state of heightened anticipation, hoping to glean any information from Gladys's conversation with the detectives. The voices, however, remained just beyond comprehension, a muffled cacophony that did nothing but fuel my frustration. The cold air that wafted through the remnants of the broken window caused goosebumps to form along my arms, a physical reminder of the environmental contrast between the warmth of Clivilius and the chill of the Tasmanian winter. The thought of fetching a jumper flitted through my mind, dismissed almost as quickly by the knowledge that the detectives' imminent departure would allow me to move about more freely and warm up in the process.

As I leaned back against the doorframe, conceding defeat to the impenetrable barrier of the door, a stray thought crossed my mind: *This garbage really is beginning to stink.* The realisation was as sudden as it was unwelcome, the metaphorical stench of our situation mingling with the physical discomfort of piling up garbage bags. A whimsical idea suggested itself—registering a portal location at the tip for effortless waste disposal. The absurdity of the notion brought a brief chuckle, the idea of solving our waste management issues with inter-dimensional shortcuts a humorous distraction from the tension of the moment.

The sound of soft footsteps approaching broke through my musings, snapping me back to the present with a surge of adrenaline. The steps were too soft, too measured to be Gladys, her approach usually more pronounced. The realisation prompted a strategic retreat behind the door, my body tensed for a rapid exit. The urge to flee warred with a burgeoning curiosity, the latter holding me in place despite the risks. Karl Jenkins had already demonstrated a propensity for unexpected actions; *what more could he be planning?* The question lingered, a provocative invitation to stay and confront whatever came next, even as the rational part of me acknowledged the potential danger of such a choice. In that moment, poised on the edge of action and observation, I was acutely aware that each decision was laden with potential consequences.

The subtle hint of movement at the door handle sent a clear message: *this was definitely not Gladys*. My instincts kicked in, propelling me to sidestep swiftly behind the door, pressing my back against the wall in anticipation. The handle rattled, a clear sign of someone's intent to enter, the door inching open just enough to confirm my suspicions. The thought of opening the portal in this moment was out of the question; the vibrant hues of its activation would be impossible to hide from Karl's prying eyes.

As I stood there, hidden by the narrow gap the partially opened door afforded, a sly smile involuntarily crossed my face. Karl's attention was wholly absorbed by the black garbage bags in the room, their suspicious appearance evidently drawing his curiosity. It was a surreal moment, watching him from my concealed position, marvelling at his obliviousness to my presence. His cautious approach suggested he hadn't anticipated anyone in the room. Had he suspected otherwise, I was sure he would have entered more forcefully, his weapon at the ready. Yet, it remained holstered, a sign of his perceived control over the situation.

Then, unexpectedly, Karl pushed the door open further, the edge grazing the tips of my shoes before beginning its swing shut. His second push was more deliberate, applying pressure against my shoes hidden behind the door. "Fuck!" The whisper of his frustration filled the room, a soft exclamation that broke the tense silence.

In that moment, the reality of our cat-and-mouse game hit me with renewed intensity. There I was, mere inches from a detective whose investigation could unravel everything I'd worked so hard to protect. The risk of discovery, once a theoretical concern, was now palpable, the physical barrier of the door the only thing separating me from exposure.

I stifled a scoff, the thrill of the moment enveloping me, a feeling reminiscent of those childhood games of hide and seek with Paul in the dark. The blend of anticipation and fear, the exhilarating rush of narrowly evading discovery, was palpable now, reignited in this new version of high-stakes game.

Gladys's angry voice, erupting from below, cut through the tension like a beacon of defiance. "Hey! What the hell are you doing up there!" she yelled, her tone laced with frustration and authority. Her demand, "I think you'd better leave," not only offered a momentary reprieve but also affirmed the effectiveness of our ruse. Her proximity, her voice carrying up the hallway, provided a tangible shield for my secrecy, a reminder of the roles we had all assumed in this intricate dance of deception.

As Karl hesitated, then turned to retreat with reluctant steps down the hallway, a mischievous impulse took hold of me. It was a moment of irresistible temptation, a chance to leave my mark on the encounter. Activating my Portal Key, I initiated a subtle yet unmistakable disturbance. The hallway lights flickered in response, a visual testament to the portal's activation, while Karl's radio crackled loudly, static filling the air with a tangible presence. The hairs on my arms stood on end, a physical reaction to the charged atmosphere I had conjured.

"Bye, Karl," I whispered sharply, my voice barely carrying through the crack in the door, a mischievous farewell to the detective who had come so close yet remained oblivious to the true extent of my capabilities. With that, I stepped through the portal into Clivilius, vanishing from the house and leaving behind only the echoes of my departure and the puzzlement it would undoubtedly cause.

❖

Crouched beside the portal, the release of a loud chuckle felt both liberating and necessary, a valve opening to let the pent-up tension escape. The exhilaration of the moment, of having successfully taunted the detective and then vanished without a trace, was intoxicating. Yet, I knew all too well that any desire to witness Karl's reaction firsthand was outweighed by the very real risk of capture. The decision to retreat was not just strategic; it was vital.

As I stood there, allowing my hands to rest momentarily on my hips, I took several deep breaths in an attempt to calm the racing of my heart. The adrenaline that had surged through my veins began to ebb, replaced by a more measured pace of reflection. From a distance, the sound of raised voices reached me—Paul and Beatrix, their discussion heated as they navigated their way to my position.

"Another caravan?" The words slipped out as a murmur, my gaze narrowing in an attempt to discern the details of the caravan that now accompanied them. It indeed appeared different from the one I had noticed earlier, sparking a mix of curiosity and admiration for Beatrix's resourcefulness. However, this fleeting moment of amusement gave way to a more pressing concern—Beatrix's financial means. The knowledge of her current financial situation added a layer of complexity to the equation, leaving me to wonder about the logistics behind her acquiring another caravan.

"What's got you so cheery?" Paul's voice, cutting through my contemplations, brought me sharply back to the present. His question, straightforward yet perceptive, hinted at his awareness of my momentarily lifted spirits.

"Nothing, really," I responded, adopting a tone of nonchalance. The attempt to mask the whirlwind of emotions and calculations racing through my mind was instinctual—a reflex developed from years of navigating the delicate balance between disclosure and discretion. The truth of my cheerfulness, rooted in the successful navigation of a potentially perilous encounter, was not something easily shared, even with Paul. Instead, I chose to deflect, to maintain the façade of calm even as my mind continued to race with the implications of our current situation.

"I need the car back, Paul!" Beatrix's yell sliced through my brief moment of levity, her voice carrying the unmistakable tone of urgency. I couldn't help but release a chuckle at the situation unfolding before me, the familiar dance of negotiation and frustration between Paul and Beatrix.

Paul's response, a frustrated sigh that seemed to carry the weight of Clivilius, was testament to the complexity of our communal life. "I just want to use it to take the caravan back to camp first," he explained, the beads of sweat on his brow indicative of the physical and emotional toll of his circumstances. "Then she can have the car back." His reasoning, practical yet caught in the crossfire of necessity and demand, left room for little else but compromise.

Choosing to stay neutral in their ongoing dispute was an easy decision for me. The dynamics of their disagreement, while important, seemed minor in the grand tapestry of challenges we faced. "C'mon, Paul, just help me unhitch it," Beatrix pleaded, her hands pressed together in a gesture that spoke volumes of her desperation. When her gaze shifted toward me, laden with a silent plea for intervention, I instinctively backed away, raising my arms in a gesture of surrender. "I have stuff to do," I declared, sidestepping the looming debate with a diplomatic evasion.

"We need more wood, too," Paul interjected, his sigh cutting short as if to punctuate the endless list of tasks that demanded our attention.

Beatrix, undeterred by my retreat, continued to motion toward the caravan, her determination to resolve the matter clear in her persistent gestures.

"I'll take care of the wood," I reassured Paul, hoping to alleviate at least one of his concerns. My hand squeezed his shoulder in a gesture of solidarity before I turned to leave, the silent acknowledgment between us speaking volumes. The squabble between him and Beatrix, though momentarily entertaining, was just one of many such negotiations in our shared struggle for survival.

❖

Entering the study, the ambient noise of distant conversation immediately put me on edge. The sound of chatty female voices sparked a momentary panic within me. *I forgot about the detectives!* The thought sent a jolt through me, followed by a rapid reassessment. *They're not still here, though, surely!?*

With urgency, I moved to press my body against the wall beside the door, a tactical position that allowed me to listen more intently without exposing myself. "At least they're static. Must be in the living room," I mumbled under my breath, trying to make sense of the situation. The realisation that the voices were contained, not approaching, provided a small measure of relief.

Then, the distinct sounds of cheers and clinking wine glasses filtered through the quiet, drawing my attention. *What the hell is Gladys doing?* The question slipped out, a mix of bewilderment and curiosity. Peering down the hallway for a clearer understanding, I caught sight of Detective Sarah Lahey placing an empty wine glass on the island bench. She then moved with a casual grace toward the front door, her departure seemingly unhurried and unencumbered by the weight of her professional duties.

A soft chuckle escaped me as I processed the scene. I couldn't help but admire Gladys's ingenuity and audacity. The very idea that she had managed to engage a detective in such a casual, convivial manner spoke volumes of her skill in navigating tense situations. *If she can get a detective to drink alcohol while on duty, there's still hope for us all yet*, I thought, the amusement mingling with a newfound respect for Gladys's tactics.

This unexpected turn of events, witnessing Detective Lahey's informal exit, reshaped my understanding of our current predicament. Gladys's ability to disarm and connect with someone who represented a direct threat to our secrecy was not just impressive; it was a lifeline, a glimmer of possibility in our tangled web of challenges. The realisation that we might yet find allies in the most unlikely places bolstered my spirits, offering a reminder that adaptability and ingenuity were among our greatest assets.

As the sound of the front door closing marked Detective Lahey's departure, I found myself drawn towards Gladys, who remained a picture of composure seated on the couch. "That was an interesting conversation," I remarked, my tone light, attempting to veil my genuine curiosity and admiration for her handling of the situation.

"You don't say," Gladys retorted, her voice dripping with a dry wit as she downed the last of her drink. The simplicity of her response, paired with the action of finishing her drink, spoke volumes of the day's tension and its resolution.

"Another?" I offered, moving to collect her empty glass.

"Cheers," she responded, a single word conveying her gratitude and readiness to move past the moment. She handed over the glass without a hint of hesitation, a silent agreement to the brief respite we were allowing ourselves.

As I poured another glass, the memory of my parting shot to Karl, "Bye, Karl," lingered with a sense of satisfaction. *Impressive*, I mused internally, a smile creeping onto my face as I reflected on the day's events and Gladys's adept handling of a potentially compromising situation.

"Can you organise a few tons of wood to be delivered to the Owen's property for me, please, Gladys?" I found myself requesting as I filled her glass with the red liquid, the task momentarily redirecting my focus from the earlier victory.

"I guess so," she replied, accepting the refill with a nod.

"Why can't you?" she inquired, a reasonable question given the nature of the task.

"I have business with Bonorong," I answered, my reply brief as I took a gulp of shiraz, the rich taste a small comfort amidst the whirlwind of the afternoon's events. Anticipating her potential curiosity, I quickly added, "I'll text you the

Owen's address," aiming to forestall any further inquiry into my plans.

Without waiting for her response, "Bye, Karl," echoed once again in my mind, a mantra of sorts that encapsulated the day's triumphs and the audacity of our actions. I drained the glass clean, the act a symbolic end to the conversation and a momentary pause in our relentless fight for survival and secrecy. The satisfaction of having outmanoeuvred Detective Karl Jenkins, even in such a small way, was a reminder of our resilience and the lengths to which we were willing to go to protect our sanctuary and each other.

BONORONG EXPECTATIONS

4338.210.4

Arriving at Bonorong Wildlife Sanctuary later than I had originally planned, I found myself stepping out of a taxi instead of behind the wheel of Jamie's car. The decision was a no-brainer, really, given the recent attention from the police. A mental note flickered through my mind, a reminder to relocate Jamie's vehicle to Clivilius sooner rather than later. With two of us Guardians now frequently activating our Portals, the network of our available locations was bound to expand rapidly, easing some logistical challenges but introducing new risks.

I expressed my gratitude to the taxi driver, paying in cash to avoid any unnecessary digital footprints. Before stepping out, I took a moment to scan the area for any signs of trouble, a habit that had become second nature. The coast clear, I exited the cab, a part of me relishing the lack of obligation to return for a car. "This isn't so bad after all," I mumbled to myself, the freedom from the responsibility of personal transportation feeling unexpectedly liberating. The plan to activate a Portal location here at Bonorong made the idea of not having a car seem inconsequential. I stretched, allowing the serene environment of the sanctuary to envelop me, the calls of the birds and the gentle rustle of leaves providing a momentary escape from the complexities of my hidden life.

As I observed the visitors bustling around, their excitement was palpable, a contagious energy that momentarily lifted my spirits. They moved with a sense of wonder, eager to explore the sanctuary and its inhabitants. Taking a deep breath, I steeled myself for the task at hand. Today was not about reliving fond memories but about reconnaissance, about ensuring our operations could continue with as little disruption as possible.

With an unexpected bounce in my step, I headed toward the front office, the prospect of adventure mingling with the practicalities of my mission. It had been years since my last visit here with Beatrix, a memory that brought an involuntary chuckle to my lips. The nostalgia was bittersweet, a reminder of simpler times before our lives had become entangled in the constant dance of evasion and subterfuge.

Surely, Beatrix will be making her way here once she discovers the registered Portal location, I thought, a smile tugging at the corners of my mouth. The idea of sharing this new Portal location with her, of expanding our network and possibly revisiting this place together under less clandestine circumstances, offered a rare glimmer of hope amidst the shadows of our existence. For a brief moment, the weight of our secrets felt lighter, the sanctuary offering not just a physical refuge for its animal dwellers but a symbolic one for us, too.

As I approached the front desk, Emma, a friendly staff member clad in the Bonorong sanctuary uniform, greeted me with a warmth that felt both welcoming and disarming. Her smile, genuine and inviting, was emblematic of the sanctuary's commitment to both its visitors and its mission. She wore the iconic polo shirt emblazoned with the Bonorong logo, paired with practical khaki pants that seemed perfectly suited for a day spent caring for animals and educating the public.

"Hi there," Emma's greeting was as sunny as her disposition. "Welcome to Bonorong. Can I help you with anything?"

"Just a single entry ticket, please," I requested, my voice steady as I handed over the cash. "I'm really excited to see all the animals and learn more about conservation," I found myself saying, the words slipping out with an ease that surprised me. I was fitting comfortably into the role of an eager visitor, a façade that was crucial if I was going to successfully navigate this reconnaissance mission.

Emma's response was prompt, her professionalism evident as she outlined the ticket options. "No problem. We have a few different ticket options available. Do you want to go on a guided tour, participate in a wildlife feeding experience, or just explore the sanctuary on your own?"

Her question prompted a moment of reflection. The mission, while important, didn't have to be rushed. The reminder to slow down and appreciate the natural beauty and significance of the sanctuary resonated with me. "I think I'll go on the guided tour," I chose, the decision feeling right. "That way I can learn more about the animals and the work that you do here." It was an opportunity not just for reconnaissance but for genuine learning and connection with the sanctuary's conservation efforts.

Emma's efficiency was evident as she printed the ticket. "Here you go," she handed it to me along with a map of the sanctuary. "The next tour starts in about fifteen minutes, so you have time to explore a bit before then. Here's a map of the sanctuary, and if you have any questions, just ask one of the staff members that will be roaming around."

"Thank you, Emma," I replied, my smile reflecting the genuine appreciation I felt. Accepting the ticket and map, I felt a sense of anticipation for the adventure that lay ahead. The warmth of Emma's welcome, the promise of learning more about the sanctuary's vital work, and the opportunity to momentarily immerse myself in the natural world offered a brief respite from the complexities of Guardian life.

The first ten minutes at Bonorong Wildlife Sanctuary dissolved into the background as I found myself captivated by a conversation with a lone cockatoo positioned near the entrance. The bird, with its surprising ability to articulate a few words, offered a moment of levity and connection, a welcome diversion from the weight of my usual concerns. Its sporadic commentary, a blend of mimicry and genuine interaction, served as a gentle reminder of the intelligence and complexity inherent in the natural world around us.

As the time for the tour neared, I made my way to the designated meeting spot, finding myself among a diverse group of visitors, each of us united by a shared anticipation for the journey ahead. The tour guide, introducing himself as James, exuded a warmth and enthusiasm that was both infectious and comforting. "James," he greeted us, his smile genuine and inviting. "I hope you're all as excited as I am for this tour."

The group's response was a collective affirmation of our eagerness, punctuated by the spirited shout of a particularly enthusiastic young child. James's playful admonition, "Shh, not too loud," accompanied by a mischievous smile directed briefly at me, added a layer of camaraderie to the proceedings. His comment about the sleeping animals elicited a quiet chuckle from me, a sign of my growing ease in this unexpected refuge.

As the tour commenced, I found myself fully immersed in the experience, the usual preoccupations with Clivilius and the duties of a Guardian momentarily receding into the background. With each step, each new piece of information shared by James, I allowed myself to be truly present, soaking in the stories and facts that painted a vivid picture of the sanctuary's inhabitants.

Occasionally, my thoughts drifted to the possibility of a wildlife sanctuary within Bixbus, the idea sparking a blend of inspiration and contemplation. The parallels between our efforts to safeguard the portals and the sanctuary's mission to protect its residents were not lost on me. As I absorbed the information about the sanctuary's conservation work, the notion of intertwining our guardianship with a similar ethos of protection and preservation flickered through my mind, a seed of an idea that might one day take root in the reality of our hidden world.

During our leisurely walk past the koalas, comfortably nestled within the crooks of gum tree branches, a fellow visitor's curiosity about James's satisfaction with his job prompted a heartfelt response. "I love it here," he declared, his affection for the sanctuary evident as his gaze affectionately swept over our surroundings. It was during this exchange that his eyes briefly met mine, holding my gaze a moment longer than necessary, sparking an unspoken connection between us. "I've been working here for a few years now, and I never get tired of seeing the animals and learning more about them. It's such a rewarding job," he shared, his enthusiasm infectious and his dedication clear.

Lost in the flow of the tour, led by James's captivating narration, more and more, I found my thoughts intermittently venturing to the growing concept of a wildlife sanctuary within Bixbus. The potential for such a place in our hidden world seemed all the more tangible, inspired by the passion James displayed for his work and the sanctuary's mission. As we continued, I noticed the distance between us subtly diminishing, his occasional, light touches—like a brush against my arm while pointing out a particularly interesting animal—sending unexpected shivers down my spine. These fleeting moments of contact, though minor, added an unforeseen layer of complexity to the excursion.

Our interactions, while unexpected and certainly not part of my initial reconnaissance plan, posed an intriguing scenario. Given that my primary objective was to gather information and assess the feasibility of integrating similar conservation efforts into Bixbus, the burgeoning rapport with James presented an interesting dynamic. It reminded me that even amidst the seriousness of my self-imposed missions and the dangers I often faced, there was room for moments of genuine human connection. I rationalised that there was no harm in enjoying the tour and the company, especially if it helped to solidify an internal allegiance with someone as passionate and knowledgeable as James. After all, forging alliances, even those born out of chance encounters, could prove beneficial in the most unexpected ways.

James's sudden halt drew our collective attention to the sight of a large kangaroo grazing in the distance. The animal, upon noticing our presence, stood tall, commanding the field with an impressive stature. "That's our biggest male kangaroo. His name is Bob, and he's the leader of the mob," James announced, his voice carrying a mix of respect and fondness for the creature. As his eyes found mine once again, there was a spark of amusement between us, an acknowledgment of the unexpected majesty we were witnessing.

Amidst the group's chuckles, I found myself voicing my astonishment, "Wow, he's huge," the words slipping out in genuine wonder. My experiences with kangaroos back in Broken Hill and on night drives to and from Adelaide had never prepared me for the sight of such a magnificent specimen. Bob's presence was not just impressive; it was almost awe-inspiring.

"Bob certainly is," James echoed my sentiment, his laughter mingling with mine. "But he's a gentle giant. He's been living at Bonorong for years now, and he's a real favourite with the visitors and staff." The camaraderie in our laughter, the shared appreciation for Bob's gentle nature despite his formidable appearance, wove a thread of connection between us, a moment of mutual understanding and delight.

As we stood there, laughing and exchanging glances, I couldn't help but let my thoughts wander back to Clivilius. *How would a creature like Bob fit into the landscapes of our hidden world?* The idea was whimsical, perhaps, but not without its charm. Our eyes met again, and it felt as though we were sharing a secret thought, a playful speculation on the possibilities that lay beyond the confines of the sanctuary.

As we moved through the sanctuary, the tour unfolded like a vivid tapestry of Australian wildlife. Kangaroos and wallabies bounded with an effortless grace, their movements a dance between curiosity and caution. Tasmanian devils, those enigmatic creatures of the night, alternated between peaceful slumbers and playful snarls, offering glimpses into their complex personalities. Echidnas, with their distinctive snouts, ventured cautiously from their burrows, their slow, deliberate movements a stark contrast to the more dynamic kangaroos and wallabies.

James, our guide through this living mosaic, took every opportunity to illuminate the sanctuary's vital work. His voice carried a passion that was both infectious and inspiring as he detailed the conservation efforts at Bonorong. The commitment to rehabilitating and releasing injured and orphaned wildlife was not just a policy but a mission, a core aspect of the sanctuary's identity.

Listening to James, I found myself deeply moved by the sanctuary's dedication. The stories of rescue, recovery, and eventual release painted a picture of hope and resilience that resonated with me on a fundamental level. It was a reminder of the broader battle being fought beyond the immediate concerns of Clivilius—a battle for the preservation and respect of all life forms.

The sanctuary's efforts echoed the principles that guided me as a Guardian, underscoring the interconnectedness of all endeavours aimed at protecting and nurturing the vulnerable. As James spoke, I couldn't help but draw parallels between our work and that of the sanctuary. Both were centred around safeguarding those unable to protect themselves, whether they be portals hidden from the world or animals threatened by it.

This realisation fostered a deeper appreciation for the sanctuary and its mission, reinforcing my belief in the importance of conservation. The thought of integrating similar principles into Clivilius, of creating a sanctuary of our own that mirrored these values, was both daunting and exhilarating. As we continued our journey through Bonorong, I carried with me not just the sights and sounds of the animals we encountered but the underlying message of their presence: the imperative to protect, to heal, and to preserve for future generations.

As the tour drew to a close, James thanked the guests and received their gratitude in return. With the crowd dispersing, I approached James, unable to resist expressing my appreciation despite the risk of making myself too memorable.

"Thanks, James," I found myself saying, my hand reaching out to him. The words came out with a sincerity that surprised even me, given the layers of my presence here. "That was a really good tour." His handshake, warm and lingering, seemed to echo the connection that had subtly formed between us throughout the tour, his playful glint not lost on me.

"You're welcome," he responded, his voice low, almost intimate, as his gaze locked with mine. There was an invitation there, something that went beyond the usual guide-visitor interaction, leaving us in a moment of charged silence. It was a silence filled with unspoken questions and possibilities, a delicate balance between professionalism and the hint of personal interest.

"And here's the real leader of the sanctuary," James suddenly announced, breaking the moment with a lightness that eased the tension. He called out to a young man passing by, one cradling a small koala with a level of care and affection that spoke volumes of his dedication.

"Grant!" James's voice drew the attention of the young man, who paused and turned towards us with an inquisitive look. "Hey, James. What's up?"

James's introduction of Grant Ironbach as the Director of Bonorong Wildlife Sanctuary caught me off guard. The significance of the role, paired with the casual manner in which Grant handled the koala, underscored the passion that must drive the sanctuary's operations. "Nice to meet you," I managed, halting mid-gesture when I realised Grant's hands were understandably occupied.

"And this is-" James's prompt hung in the air, turning the spotlight on me to introduce myself. The sudden need to articulate my identity, under the gaze of someone as integral to the sanctuary as Grant, left me momentarily cautious. Yet, the warmth of the exchange, the genuine interest from both James and Grant, nudged me towards openness, albeit within the boundaries of my concealed truth.

My response was abruptly cut short by the unexpected arrival of a young woman, her presence like a sudden gust of wind that changes the direction of falling leaves. "Grant! There you are," she exclaimed with a burst of energy, her voice cutting through the tranquility of the moment. "I've been looking everywhere for you." She rushed towards us, her movements filled with a purposeful urgency that seemed to command attention.

"Well, you've found us," Grant replied with a tone that mixed amusement and resignation. He gestured towards himself and the baby koala nestled securely in his arms. "We're right here," he added, as if their location had been a mystery she'd finally solved.

James leaned in closer to me, his voice a hushed whisper that carried a note of caution mixed with intrigue. "And that's Sarah Ironbach. The Assistant Director, and Grant's sister. She's friendly but can be a little feisty at times." His words painted a picture of Sarah that was as vivid as the woman herself, suggesting a depth to her character that caught my attention.

I nodded in response, a silent acknowledgment of James's introduction. However, the truth was, I wasn't entirely sure how I ended up in this situation—a bystander caught in the middle of a familial and professional reunion.

"We're late for the meeting with—" Sarah's voice trailed off as she paused, her gaze shifting to notice James and me for the first time. Her attention suddenly focused on me, as if she was seeing me for the first time. "You must be Brad," she said, extending her hand towards me in a gesture that was both welcoming and assertive.

Confused about my identity, I shook her hand automatically, not fully processing the mistake. Her hand was firm and warm, a stark contrast to the cool, impersonal air between strangers. "James, printed copies of the documents you sent us. I have to say, this sounds like an amazing opportunity. Grant and I are both excited about it," she continued, her words cascading over me like a waterfall, moving faster than my brain could catch up.

"That's great," I managed to reply, my voice barely above a whisper. I was about to correct her on my identity, to tell her I wasn't Brad, but before I could articulate the confusion swirling inside me, James was guiding us towards one of the buildings, a silent shepherd leading his flock.

"Bring Dudley with you," Sarah instructed Grant, her tone leaving no room for argument. Grant looked about somewhat lost, as if he was trying to find his bearings in a situation that was as unfamiliar to him as it was to me. Holding the baby koala, now dubbed Dudley, he seemed to embody the confusion and wonder that I felt inside.

❖

As we shuffled into the small, unassuming building, the air buzzed with the kind of anticipation one feels before the dawn of a significant venture. Sarah, her voice animated and full of purpose, began discussing their fervent enthusiasm for the plans concerning the new sanctuary. She elaborated on how thoroughly they'd reviewed and approved the designs, their readiness palpable in her every word. It was clear that the initial site assessment wasn't just another task for them; it was a leap towards a vision they believed in deeply.

Caught in the whirlwind of information and the rapid progression of the situation, I found myself merely nodding and grunting occasionally. It was a feeble attempt to appear engaged and knowledgeable, but internally, I was scrambling to keep up. The complexity and the pace at which everything unfolded left me feeling like I was perpetually two steps behind, trying to catch up to a train that had already left the station.

"Grant and I have our bags packed and have everything lined up for the two weeks to conduct the initial site assessment," Sarah continued, her enthusiasm undimmed as she moved towards several large backpacks piled in the corner of the room. Her statement, "We're excited to meet your people," felt like a weighty acknowledgment of the collaborative effort this project was poised to be. Yet, her words also served as a stark reminder of the tangled web in which I found myself.

I cast a glance at James, the confusion and disbelief surely evident in my eyes. *How had he let me drift this far into a conversation under a mistaken identity? Did he not realise the gravity of the misunderstanding?* The silence between us grew louder, filled with unasked questions and unspoken clarifications.

I wasn't ready to unravel the entire tapestry of lies that had inadvertently been woven around me. Yet, acknowledging that I wasn't Brad seemed like the first, necessary unravelling of this complex knot. My mind was racing towards crafting a sincere apology for the confusion when Sarah's next words froze me in my tracks.

"I've not been able to get this whole idea of Guardians and Portals out of my head since the last time we spoke with Melanie," she said, her tone shifting to one of awe and wonder. "If she hadn't shown it to us, I'd have never believed that such things were possible." Her words were like a jolt of electricity, sparking a myriad of thoughts and emotions within me.

Perplexed and feeling the weight of the moment pressing in, I reached into the depths of my pocket, feeling the familiar contours of my Portal Key. Its metallic surface, cool and smooth under my fingertips, felt like the only anchor in a sea of uncertainty. With a deep breath that did little to steady my racing heart, I activated the Portal against a vacant wall. The transformation was instantaneous and breathtaking. The once blank and unassuming surface came to life with mesmerising, swirling colours—a vibrant dance of light and shadow that seemed to defy the very laws of physics.

"You've seen this before?" I asked, my voice laced with a mix of incredulity and a faint hope that perhaps they understood more than I credited them for.

"Yes," replied Grant, his voice steady and assured. "We've seen it a number of times now. We're quite familiar with it all."

Are you, really? The skepticism was loud in the silence of my thoughts, my eyes darting between them, probing for any sign that they grasped the true nature of what stood before us. The portal wasn't just a marvel of technology or a gateway to new lands; it was a bridge to Clivilius, a one-way trip from which there was no return. Sarah's casual mention of a two-week trip gnawed at me—*did they truly not comprehend that Bonorong was about to become a distant memory, forever?*

"Well, there's no time like the present," I found myself saying, my voice a mix of resignation and a forced cheerfulness. I gestured towards the swirling colours, the portal's beauty doing little to ease the unease coiling in my stomach.

"Grab the portfolios, would you, Grant," Sarah's voice cut through the moment, pragmatic and focused. Grant, momentarily lost in his farewell to Dudley, handed the koala over to James, a bittersweet exchange that seemed to underline the gravity of their impending departure.

"I'll grab them," I offered, stepping towards the table to collect the folders. My mind raced with questions and concerns, but the immediate task provided a welcome distraction. As I hurried to collect the documents, a part of me sought comfort in the familiarity of the task. *A casual scan through these papers later might shed light on what I was walking into*, I mused silently, hoping for clarity in the midst of the bewildering experience unfolding in front of my eyes.

"See you on the other side," Sarah declared gleefully, her voice brimming with excitement as she walked through the portal, bags in tow. Her enthusiasm, so at odds with my own turmoil, was a stark reminder of the adventure we were embarking on—an adventure that held more unknowns than certainties.

"Don't let this place fall apart," Grant's parting words to James were tinged with humour and a hint of solemnity. He patted the young koala's head, a final gesture of goodbye to a piece of his world.

"You're leaving it all in great hands," James assured, his eyes locking with mine as he gave me a sneaky wink.

Bewildered, I watched as Grant followed his sister through the portal. The sight of them stepping into the swirling colours, disappearing from view, was both awe-inspiring and disconcerting.

"Thanks for all of your help, James," I said, extending my hand towards him, my grasp firm yet warm, conveying a sense of camaraderie that had unexpectedly blossomed between us. My smile was playful, a light-hearted façade that belied the whirlwind of emotions churning inside me. Despite the brief nature of our acquaintance, I felt a sudden, inexplicable fondness for the young man, a bond forged in the midst of this unforeseen adventure. Yet, beneath the surface of this newfound connection, my instincts screamed for caution, a silent reminder of the precarious situation I found myself in. *You can't be Brad forever,* I mused internally, a smirk playing at the corners of my mouth, a silent acknowledgment of the absurdity of the masquerade I had been unwittingly cast into.

Our moment of farewell was abruptly shattered by a knock, the sound a sharp contrast to the low murmur of conversation that had filled the room moments before. Emma's head appeared through the doorway, her expression one of exasperation. "James," she began, her tone laced with a hint of urgency, "Brad Coleman is here to meet with Grant and Sarah about the new confidential project."

At the mention of Brad Coleman, my heart skipped a beat, a jolt of panic coursing through me, rooting me to the spot. My eyes widened, the colour draining from my face as the reality of the situation crashed down on me like a wave breaking on the shore. The room seemed to tilt, the edges blurring as the gravity of Emma's words sank in. James turned to me, his gaze sharp, eyes narrowing as if seeing me for the first time, a dawning realisation etching itself across his features.

"Do you want me to bring him here?" Emma's voice pierced the heavy air, a lifeline thrown into the turbulent sea of my thoughts.

"Uh, hang on a sec, Emma," James replied, his voice a calm in the storm, buying us a moment of precious time. His gaze never left mine, a silent conversation passing between us in the span of a heartbeat.

Part of me was seized by a morbid curiosity about the real Brad Coleman, the man whose identity I had inadvertently cloaked myself in—the apparent Guardian. Yet, as much as curiosity gnawed at me, the realisation hit with the force of a thunderclap—I had a name, and that name was not Brad Coleman. It was a tether to reality, a reminder of the truth behind the mask.

In the few seconds that James was distracted with Emma, a window of opportunity cracked open, a sliver of time in which decisions had to be made and actions taken. With my heart pounding in my chest, a cacophony of beats that drowned out all else, I made my choice. I retreated to Clivilius, the name not just a destination but a declaration, a reclaiming of my identity and my path.

The moment I stepped into Clivilius, the shift in atmosphere was palpable. The air here held a different kind of weight, charged with an energy that seemed to teeter on the brink of anticipation and unease. Grant and Sarah Ironbach, caught up in their whirlwind of excitement, barely acknowledged my presence. They were ensconced in their own world, animatedly discussing the barren beauty that unfolded before us. The vast expanse of Clivilius stretched endlessly, its dusty terrain a stark contrast to the lush landscapes they had left behind. The sky, a canvas of muted colours, hung low over the horizon, adding to the desolation that defined this place.

Anxious energy bubbled up inside me as I contemplated the imminent necessity of explaining not just their presence here but also the tangled web of mistaken identity that had ensnared us all. With a sense of urgency, I scanned the Drop Zone for Paul, hoping to find an ally in this sea of confusion. My gaze finally landed on him, and I managed to catch his attention. A wave of relief washed over me as I realised the Ironbachs remained blissfully unaware of my identity crisis. For now, the masquerade could continue, a temporary reprieve from the inevitable revelations that lay ahead.

"This is almost exactly how they described it," Grant observed, his voice filled with a mixture of awe and recognition as he took in the desolate beauty of Clivilius. His eyes, wide with wonder, swept over the landscape, trying to soak in every detail of this alien world.

"Oh, really?" I found myself asking, my tone laced with genuine curiosity. This was an opportunity to gather information, to understand the depths of their knowledge before the precarious façade they had constructed for me, crumbled away.

"Yes," Sarah responded, her gaze piercing me with an intensity that felt almost accusatory. It was as if she expected me to share in their familiarity of what they had been briefed. Her eyes narrowed, scrutinising me, searching for signs of recognition, of understanding that I struggled to fabricate.

"Paul!" My voice carried across the dusty expanse, laced with an enthusiasm that was as much a performance as it was genuine relief at seeing a familiar face amidst the unfolding uncertainty. He approached, and I quickly introduced him to Grant and Sarah Ironbach, emphasising their connection to the Bonorong Wildlife Sanctuary in Tasmania with a warmth that belied the chaos churning beneath my composed exterior.

As I spoke, I caught the subtle shift in Paul's expression, his brow arching in that familiar way that signalled his curiosity was piqued. There was an unspoken language between us, a lifetime of shared glances and nuances that conveyed volumes.

"As discussed," I confidently continued, locking eyes with my brother in a silent communication that was as clear as spoken word. The look I gave him was a mix of plea and command, a silent entreaty to play along with the narrative I had spun. "They're here to do the initial assessment for the construction of the new wildlife sanctuary here." The words flowed with a rehearsed ease, masking the inner turmoil that threatened to surface with each passing moment.

"Oh, are they?" Paul's response was laced with a skepticism that danced on the edge of disbelief, his brow arching even higher, if that were possible. It was a testament to the absurdity of the situation, the very idea of constructing a wildlife sanctuary in Clivilius's barren landscape teetering on the brink of incredulity.

"Shouldn't take us more than a week or so," Sarah interjected, her confidence and enthusiasm undimmed by the skepticism that hung in the air. Her words, so full of assurance, seemed to carve a slice of reality from the fantastical premise we were all entangled in.

"And then we'll be back to Bonorong. These things don't manage themselves," Grant added, his voice carrying a note of pragmatism that grounded the conversation, if only momentarily. Their commitment to their cause, to the sanctuary, was evident, yet their understanding of the situation was as misplaced as my own presence among them.

Seizing the moment before Paul's astonishment could manifest into something less manageable, I interjected, "Do you mind giving my brother and me a moment or two?" The request was as much for the Ironbachs' benefit as it was for ours—a necessary interlude to confer, to strategise, and perhaps to come to terms with the reality of our predicament.

Pulling Paul away, I felt the weight of his gaze, heavy with questions and disbelief, as if his eyes alone could compel the truth from me. We moved apart from the Ironbachs, stepping into a space where the undercurrents of our conversation could flow freely, away from unsuspecting ears. This was a moment of reckoning, a sliver of time carved out, where truths could be whispered and plans hastily drawn in the sands of Clivilius.

Paul's gaze was like a laser, cutting through the barricade I had hastily erected around myself. His confusion and irritation were palpable. "Luke, what are you doing?" he hissed, his voice a mixture of concern and disbelief. The sharpness in his tone mirrored the severity of our predicament.

"I'm Brad," I shot back, clinging to the alias with a stubbornness that bordered on defiance. My gaze locked with his, a silent challenge, a plea for understanding.

"And what trouble is 'Brad' into this time that I need to bail him out of?" His question, tinged with a condescension born of too many similar past escapades, stung. It was a reminder of the tangled paths my actions often led us down.

"It's not like that," I found myself protesting, the words sounding hollow even to my own ears. This wasn't just another scrape; it was a mire of complexities that defied simple explanation.

Paul sighed, a sound heavy with resignation. "Another 'accident', then?" he queried, the word 'accident' hanging between us, a label too frequently applied to the unintended consequences of my actions.

"Not exactly," I replied, the inadequacy of my response highlighting the depth of the hole I had dug for myself.

Paul's eyes pleaded for further details, and in that moment, I realised the complexities of my situation.

As Paul's eyes bore into mine, pleading for a clarity I scarcely possessed, I realised the weight of the truth I was about to divulge. "They seem to already know about Clivilius and Portals," I began, easing into the revelation with a caution that belied my inner turmoil.

Paul scoffed, the sound loud and disbelieving. "Then why do they have the impression that they're going home in a few weeks?" His incredulity mirrored my own, a reflection of the absurdity of the Ironbachs' misunderstanding.

I shrugged, a gesture of uncertainty in a sea of questions. "I'm not sure. But I think they've been working with another Guardian team. Apparently, Brad is a Guardian," I confessed, the pieces of the puzzle slowly beginning to align, yet still forming an incomplete picture.

"Aren't you supposed to be Brad?" The confusion on Paul's face was a mirror to the conflict raging within me.

"No… and yes," I stumbled over my words, the complexity of my dual identity knotting my tongue. "I was on a reconnaissance mission at the sanctuary. Happened to get myself caught up in a case of mistaken identity. It seems I was there at the right time," I tried to infuse my voice with a confidence I was far from feeling.

"Right time?" Paul's skepticism was evident, his disbelief a tangible force that threatened to overshadow the sliver of optimism I clung to.

"Well, we got the Director and Assistant Director of the Bonorong Wildlife Sanctuary, didn't we?" I countered, attempting to spin the situation into a victory of sorts. My attempt at showcasing our triumph was as much to convince Paul as it was to reassure myself.

"And," I added, my tone shifting to one of emphatic certainty as I held up the folders, "We have their plans for the construction of a new wildlife sanctuary in Clivilius." The grin that spread across my face was an attempt to mask the uncertainty, to project a veneer of success over the muddled circumstances. It was a moment of bravado, a fleeting triumph in the face of a situation that was as complex as it was dangerous. The plans in my hands, tangible evidence of our entanglement, were a token of victory, but the path ahead was fraught with challenges that my grin could scarcely begin to address.

Paul's initial skepticism melted away into a genuine smile, a rare concession that felt like a victory in itself. "I guess that can only be a good thing," he conceded, his tone laced with reluctant optimism. The relief that washed over me was palpable; having my brother finally see the glimmer of positivity was like finding a beacon in a storm. "Great!" I exclaimed, a burst of enthusiasm fuelled by his support. It felt like a weight lifted off my shoulders, the first step towards navigating the complicated path that lay ahead.

Just then, Sarah and Grant rejoined us, their approach breaking the brief moment of camaraderie between Paul and me. "Is everything alright, Brad?" Sarah inquired, her voice carrying a mix of concern and curiosity. The question, innocent as it was, felt like a tightrope walk over the reality of our situation.

"Everything is just perfect," I responded with a smile that was practiced yet genuine, hoping to encapsulate a sense of normalcy in the face of the absurd. As I handed the folders to Paul, I couldn't help but feel the symbolic weight of passing on the baton, of entrusting him with the delicate task of managing our guests' expectations. "My brother is going to accompany you back to camp and debrief you on the situation."

"And you?" Paul's question, his expression morphing back into one of weariness, hinted at the gravity of the role reversal we were about to undertake. The guilt for leaving him to shoulder the responsibility niggled at the back of my mind, yet, the reality was that my role as a Guardian often required me to navigate through unforeseen challenges.

"I have other important Guardian duties to attend to, but I'll see you all later this evening," I assured him, a promise that was as much for myself as it was for them. My words were a veil, a necessary obfuscation of the truth of my immediate tasks, tasks that were as vital as they were secretive.

I could see the familiar struggle in Paul's eyes, the fight against the instinct to express his frustration in no uncertain terms. Instead, he chose professionalism over sarcasm, motioning for Grant and Sarah to follow him with a practiced ease. "We're extremely excited to have you here," his voice carried back to me, a testament to his ability to embrace the role demanded by the moment.

As they walked away, a smile crossed my face, a mix of gratitude and admiration for my brother. Grateful for his unspoken understanding and his ability to adapt, to play along with the guise of normalcy I had crafted. It was a reminder of the unspoken bond we shared, a bond forged through countless challenges and shared secrets. In that moment, I was reminded of the strength that lay in partnership, in the shared responsibility of our duties as Clivilians. My brother's ability to 'play pretend,' to embrace the role required of him, was not just an act of deception but a testament to our commitment to protect and serve, no matter the cost.

4338.211

(30 July 2018)

THE BUILDER

4338.211.1

The morning in bixbus unfolded with a languid pace, a rare luxury in my often tumultuous life. I had been savouring the tranquility, the simple pleasure of a moment's peace amidst the chaos that typically surrounded me of late. Yet, such moments were fleeting, always on the brink of being swept away by the relentless tide of duty and destiny. "Shit! I gotta go," the words tumbled out of me as I caught a glimpse of the time on my phone. The device, stubbornly clinging to a reality that no longer matched my own, hadn't adjusted to Clivilius time, but my internal clock screamed urgency, an undeniable sense that I was precariously close to tardiness.

Activating the massive, transparent portal screen was second nature, a routine action that belied the extraordinary nature of stepping between worlds. Leaving Paul behind, I stepped through with a haste born of necessity, the familiar rush of transition enveloping me. The abrupt stop on the other side, a mere hair's breadth from the Owens' living room wall, served as a jarring reminder of the physical realities that awaited at each journey's end. "I really need to keep that door closed," I chastised myself, the words a muttered reprimand for my carelessness. Securing the door behind me, I closed the portal, a boundary between the mundane and the miraculous.

Stepping out the front door, the world beyond awaited, unchanged by the wonders that lay just beyond its perception. The sight of an unfamiliar ute parked beneath the sprawling canopy of a large gum tree caught my attention, a stark intrusion into the familiar landscape. Its owner, a man named Adrian, presented a study in contrasts—his slim, long-legged frame exuded a casual ease, yet the cigarette dangling from his lips spoke of a nonchalance that felt out of place in the serene morning.

"Hey there, Adrian!" My greeting cut through the morning air, a veneer of cheerfulness plastered over the urgency that pulsed beneath. I offered him a smile and a friendly wave, the universal sign of benign intentions, despite the whirlwind of thoughts churning in my mind. As I descended the front verandah steps, my haste was momentarily arrested by the sight of Gladys, her figure bent in what seemed like a meticulous selection of flowers by the side of the house. The incongruity of the scene struck me—*Why the hell is she picking flowers?* The question ricocheted through my mind, a puzzling distraction from the task at hand. After a brief moment of scrutiny, confirming that she was indeed engaged in floral procurement, I gave her a cursory hello, pushing her presence to the back of my mind as I focused on the more pressing matter before me.

The ground underfoot felt soft and yielding, a testament to the early morning's dampness, as dark clouds began their slow march across the sky, heralding an impending change. Approaching Adrian, who lingered by his vehicle with a languid detachment, I sensed Gladys quickening her pace to catch up. Her voice, a whisper barely audible above the morning's tranquility, carried a note of caution. "I think he's high as a kite," she confided, her words tinged with a mixture of concern and curiosity.

"Good," I whispered back, the response slipping out almost reflexively. Part of me clung to the hope that Adrian's possibly altered state might render him more receptive, more pliable to the extraordinary revelation that awaited him. The weariness of having to persuade, to coax individuals through the Portal had taken its toll, each journey a negotiation between skepticism and wonder. The thought that a more straightforward, unembellished introduction to Clivilius might suffice danced at the edge of my consciousness. *Maybe a more direct approach might work if he's high*, I mused silently, the strategy unfolding in my mind like a new path through familiar territory.

This internal dialogue, a constant companion, reflected the dual nature of my existence—always balancing the mundane with the miraculous, the ordinary with the extraordinary. The prospect of guiding someone through the threshold of worlds without the usual dance of disbelief appealed to my sense of efficiency, and perhaps, my growing impatience with the charade that often preceded the crossing. Yet, beneath the pragmatism lay a deeper thread of empathy; understanding the disorientation and awe that awaited Adrian on the other side, I treaded a fine line between manipulation and guidance, ever conscious of the responsibility that my role as a Guardian entailed.

"This isn't your property," Adrian's voice sliced through the air with a clarity that belied his apparent state. As I drew closer, he took a long, deliberate drag on his cigarette, the unmistakable scent of marijuana mingling with the fresh morning air, setting a backdrop that was anything but ordinary. "What am I doing here? Where are the Owens?"

"I..." My attempt to explain was half-hearted, my hand waving in a futile effort to dispel the smoke that seemed to mark the boundaries of our surreal encounter. "The Owens need your help," I managed to say, the words feeling both inadequate and absurd in the context of our meeting.

"My help?" He echoed, skepticism etched into every syllable, the joint pausing at his lips as if punctuating his disbelief.

Glancing back at Gladys, I sought an ally in this increasingly complex tableau. The recent complications with Portal entries, coupled with a growing concern over police scrutiny, cast a shadow over what I had hoped would be a straightforward mission. *You don't really need to care. You just need to get him to Clivilius,* I coached myself, trying to suppress the rising tide of doubt. *Leave no evidence behind, and everything will be fine.*

Gladys's noncommittal shrug was less than reassuring, her indifference momentarily amplifying my sense of isolation in this endeavour. *Good use you are,* I chastised her silently, the sarcasm lost in the unspoken void between us.

Facing Adrian again, I steadied my resolve. "This is going to sound a little crazy, but we're all grown adults here, and I'm fairly confident you can handle the truth." The words, once spoken, felt like a leap into the unknown, an invitation to cross the threshold of belief and skepticism.

Adrian's response, a cough muffled by the haze of his exhale, was tinged with a cynical amusement. "You and your weird girlfriend here are the ones asking me to meet you on someone else's property, and you want to talk to me about truth." His words, sharpened by the irony of our situation, underscored the absurdity of our predicament.

"Girlfriend?" The question slipped out, my confusion momentarily redirecting the conversation. The thought of Gladys being mistaken for anything other than a reluctant accomplice was almost comical, a misunderstanding that under different circumstances might have been amusing.

"Just show him the Portal," Gladys interjected, cutting through the haze of confusion and redirecting my focus to the task at hand.

Adrian's skeptical gaze, the peculiar juxtaposition of his casual drug use against the backdrop of an extraordinary revelation, and Gladys's impulsive suggestion coalesced into a moment teetering on the brink of the surreal. As the concept of revealing the Portal to Adrian loomed before me, the weight of the decision pressed heavily. The simplicity of her suggestion, to just show him the Portal, was both a solution and a leap into the vast unknown of consequence and reaction. This moment, suspended between the ordinary and the extraordinary, was a testament to the tightrope I walked as a Guardian, constantly navigating the fine line between secrecy and disclosure in a world that was never quite ready for the truth of what lay beyond.

With every ticking second, my patience thinned, the luxury of contemplation a distant memory. Determined, I led the way to the small shed, a sense of finality propelling my steps. The weight of the Portal Key in my pocket felt heavier than before, a tangible reminder of the worlds that lay beyond the mundane. Adrian, curiosity piqued or perhaps just bemused, trailed behind me. As I retrieved the key, the shed's nondescript side transformed, alive with buzzing, swirling colours—a spectacle that defied the dreariness of our surroundings. "That's where the Owens are," I announced, attempting to lace my voice with a casual authority that I hoped would mask the absurdity of the situation.

"Fuck me!" Adrian's exclamation, punctuated by the near loss of his joint, was a mix of shock and disbelief. His words, "I know I'm a little high, but it's not a fucking psychedelic," betrayed a skepticism that no amount of marijuana could dull. The reality of the Portal, so vivid and undeniable, clashed violently with the everyday logic we all cling to.

"I need you to walk through that and help them with a small building job. It won't take very long," I found myself lying, the words tasting of desperation. "They've already got all the materials. They just need your skills." The fabrication, necessary though it felt, left a bitter residue, a stark contrast to the truth that lay just beyond the colourful vortex.

"You must think I'm a fucking nutter," Adrian retorted, his disbelief morphing into a defensive retreat. Watching him hasten to his ute, a sense of failure washed over me, a tide of frustration and self-reproach. My heart sank, the futility of the situation laying bare the folly of my approach. *What a bloody stupid idea this was,* I berated myself, the silent curse a testament to my miscalculation.

"Adrian! Wait!" The urgency in my voice was real as I chased after him, a last-ditch effort to salvage the situation. But the finality of the ute's door slamming shut, a barrier as definitive as any portal, marked the collapse of my plan.

The engine's roar was a harsh goodbye, a sound that seemed to echo my own turmoil. As Adrian wound down the window, his parting words, "But I think you two are the fucking whack jobs!" hung in the air, a judgment that, in the moment, felt like an unassailable verdict on our entire endeavour.

Shouting a frustrated "Shit!" into the void left by Adrian's departure, I spun to face Gladys, my emotions a tempest of irritation and disbelief. Her immediate reaction, a blend of accusation and confusion, only served to fan the flames of my frustration. "What the hell just happened!? I thought you knew what you were doing," she blurted, her words sharp, cutting through the tension like a knife.

"Fuck off, Gladys! I'm not perfect," I growled back, the heat of my frustration boiling over. I began pacing in tight, aimless circles. Each step was a futile attempt to walk off the anger and the embarrassment, to somehow distance myself from the debacle we had just created.

"What do we do now?" Gladys's voice, tinged with concern, penetrated my storm of thoughts. "Do you think he'll tell anybody about what he saw?" Her question, valid and fraught with implications, momentarily halted my pacing.

"Doubt it. He already thinks we're crazy. He'll likely rationalise it as just a hallucination of sorts," I reasoned, attempting to convince both Gladys and myself. The hope that Adrian's disbelief in what he had witnessed would serve as a safeguard, that the extraordinary nature of the Portal would be dismissed as a product of his intoxicated state, was a thin thread of reassurance.

"So we just let him go, then?" Her question hung in the air, a verbal mirror reflecting the gravity of our situation.

My circling resumed, a physical echo of the mental gymnastics I was performing as I weighed our options. The implications of letting Adrian go, the potential risks to the camp, the Shadow Panthers, and Duke, began to pile up, each consideration adding to the weight on my shoulders. My eyes stung, a physical response to the stress and the strain of the moment. Abruptly, I stopped, a decision crystallising amidst the whirlwind of my thoughts. "No," I said flatly, the word cutting through the uncertainty. "We're going after him."

"We are?" Gladys's voice was a mix of surprise and apprehension.

"Come with me, Gladys. You're driving," I instructed, the command leaving no room for debate. My stride toward her car was purposeful, each step fuelled by a newfound resolve. The decision to pursue Adrian, to rectify the misstep, was born not just from a desire to protect the secrets of the Portal and those who relied on it but from a deeper sense of responsibility for the repercussions of my actions.

❖

As we pursued Adrian's ute, Jamie's aversion to being a passenger in Gladys' car suddenly seemed prophetic. The car's interior became a capsule of tension, my grip on the seatbelt a testament to the unease that Jamie had often expressed. Each jerk and swerve under Gladys's unpredictable driving style sent a silent prayer for safety coursing through my mind. The imaginary brake pedals beneath my feet, my desperate wish for control, bore the brunt of my anxiety as we hurtled down the road.

Catching a glimpse of Adrian's vehicle ahead brought a fleeting sense of victory, the quiet roads and his unexpected adherence to the speed limit momentarily aligning with our pursuit. However, this feeling of triumph was ephemeral. As if sensing our approach, Adrian pressed on the accelerator, his vehicle pulling away with a defiance that echoed my escalating worry.

"He's going left," I found myself directing Gladys, my voice tinged with urgency as I pointed towards Adrian's ute veering towards the highway. The blink of his indicator was like a beacon, guiding us yet warning of the unpredictability of his actions. "Keep following him," I urged, my resolve hardening despite the gnawing concern for what lay ahead.

Gladys, with a nod, shifted us into the left lane, her movements precise yet fraught with the same tension that gripped me. I braced against the door, the solidity of the car's frame offering a scant sense of security as we merged onto the bustling highway. The sight of Adrian's swerving ute, a dance of danger on the asphalt, heightened my apprehension. His reckless proximity to a 4WD in the adjacent lane, a near-miss that drew a profane rebuke from its passenger, was a jarring reminder of the potential consequences of our chase.

"Maybe we should stop," the suggestion escaped my lips before I could fully grasp the weight of it. The pursuit, driven by a need to rectify the situation, was veering into recklessness. Gladys, sensing the urgency in my voice, began to decelerate, her actions a silent agreement to the unspoken risks that loomed with every turn of the wheel.

"Wait!" The urgency in my voice startled Gladys, her reaction instantaneous and drastic. Her foot, heavy on the accelerator, propelled us forward with a jolt that pushed me forcefully into the back of my seat. "Jesus, Gladys!" I exclaimed. However, my irritation quickly faded, replaced by a focused alertness as I noticed Adrian's vehicle slowing down. "He's pulling over," I pointed out, redirecting Gladys's attention.

As we eased the car to the side of the road, trailing behind Adrian's ute, I couldn't help but glance upwards at the sky. The dark storm clouds, now ominously close, seemed to mirror the brewing tension below. "Stay in the car," I instructed Gladys, my voice firm, leaving no room for discussion. The atmosphere was charged, a thunderous clap resounding above us as if nature itself was bracing for the confrontation to come. "Things are going to get messy," I muttered under my breath, a reluctant acknowledgment of the inevitable clash.

What am I doing? The question echoed in my mind, a moment of self-reflection amidst the escalating situation. Approaching Adrian, especially given his evident agitation, felt like walking into a storm of a different kind. Yet, as I cautiously moved towards his ute, my resolve firmed, driven by a sense of duty that often demanded navigating through uncertainty.

The driver's door swung open abruptly, its sudden movement halting before Adrian could react. I stood frozen for a moment, the flow of traffic on the busy highway a backdrop to the standoff.

Gathering my courage, I prepared to close the distance between us once more. The ute's door creaked open again, this time with a deliberateness that signalled Adrian's readiness to confront whatever lay ahead. He emerged from the vehicle, his movements embodying controlled aggression.

His advance towards me was marked by a wild glare and fists clenched, a clear indication of his readiness for confrontation.

In a desperate attempt to quell the mounting tension, I instinctively raised my hands, palms outward, in a universal gesture of peace. Taking a few cautious steps back, I aimed to establish a buffer between Adrian's palpable anger and my own rapidly fraying nerves. "Hey... Adrian," I started, my voice strained with the effort to sound both calm and authoritative, a delicate balance aimed at defusing the volatile situation.

But any hope of de-escalation was brutally interrupted by the sudden, inexplicable surge of Gladys's car forward. Adrian's face, previously set in a mask of fury, contorted into an expression of utter surprise as he whirled around, his body tensing in a futile attempt to brace for the impending impact. The collision was swift, sending him sprawling onto the bonnet with a thud that echoed my internal outcry: *What the fuck, Gladys!?*

My mind reeled, unable to voice the shock that gripped me as I witnessed the scene unfold with surreal clarity. Instinct and concern propelled me forward, intent on rushing to Adrian's aid, my heart pounding with the urgency of the moment. Yet, as I scanned the environment for a possible escape route, the realisation that the surroundings offered no viable space for Portal activation anchored me in a mire of frustration and desperation.

Compelled by a mix of duty and panic, I found myself executing an awkward dance of necessity around Adrian, my steps uncertain as I navigated the chaotic aftermath of the crash. My objective became singular—reach the safety of his ute's front seat, a haven amidst the storm of unfolding events.

The sharp knock of my shin against the ute's doorframe elicited a wince, a fleeting acknowledgment of pain that was quickly overshadowed by the urgency to secure myself within the vehicle. Clambering inside, I slammed the door shut with a force that betrayed my inner turmoil, hastily engaging the lock as if it could shield me from the consequences of our actions.

Seated behind the wheel, I found myself momentarily frozen, the echo of my own question ricocheting through the confines of the ute: *What the fuck am I doing?* The breath that left me was heavy, a mix of disbelief and resignation as I grappled with the surreal nature of my actions. The logical part of my mind seemed to recede, giving way to a primal instinct for survival and protection. My fingers, trembling slightly, found the keys that Adrian had conveniently left in the ignition. With a turn, the ute roared to life, a mechanical heartbeat that pulsed in tandem with my own racing pulse.

The sudden, violent rattling of the door handle, followed by a hard thump against the window, jolted me from my frenzied thoughts. My heart skipped a beat, fear and surprise intermingling at the resilience of the glass. Adrian's face, pressed close to the window, his eyes clouded with anger and confusion, was a stark reminder of the reality I had thrust us both into. My rational mind, seemingly adrift from my more primal instincts, dumbly motioned him towards the passenger side, as if this simple gesture could somehow diffuse the volatile situation we found ourselves embroiled in.

The passenger door burst open with a jarring creak, Adrian's forceful entry breaking the tense silence. "Get the fuck out of my ute!" His command, fierce and filled with a raw energy, nearly propelled him onto the seat beside me as he reached in with determined hands. The air was thick with the weight of his demand, his presence an undeniable force that demanded compliance.

But I was not about to yield, not to the threat of violence nor to the fear that gnawed at the edges of my resolve. My foot, almost of its own accord, slammed down on the accelerator, a desperate bid for escape, for control over an increasingly uncontrollable situation. Adrian, caught off guard by the sudden movement, scrambled to secure himself inside the vehicle, his expletives a harsh soundtrack to our frantic departure.

As I steered the ute onto the highway, the closeness of an oncoming vehicle, its horn blaring a warning, underscored the peril of our escape. The stakes were higher than ever, each decision a gamble, each turn of the wheel a potential disaster.

Yet, amid the turmoil, a small, persistent thought emerged, a beacon in the tumultuous storm of my actions: *The Owens*. The mission, the purpose behind this madness, refocused my scattered thoughts. Delivering Adrian to Clivilius seemed the only path that made any sense, the only outcome that could possibly justify the risks I was taking.

This realisation, though it came as a whisper amid the cacophony of our escape, was a lifeline. It anchored me, offering a semblance of clarity as I navigated the treacherous road that lay ahead. The Owens' property represented not just a destination but a responsibility, a duty that I had to fulfil, despite the unforeseen complications Adrian's resistance presented. In that moment, with the road stretching out before us and the echoes of our confrontation still ringing in the air, I understood the gravity of my role, the weight of the decisions I made, and the lives they affected. The journey to Clivilius was more than a mission; it was a test of resolve, a measure of the lengths to which I would go to protect the balance between worlds, even as I struggled to maintain my own.

❖

"There's a fucking chopper in the air," Adrian's voice broke through the tension inside the ute, his announcement sending a fresh wave of adrenaline coursing through my veins. He wiped his hands across the fogged window, pressing his face against the glass as he tried to discern the shape in the sky through the curtain of relentless rain. His actions, born out of a mix of curiosity and concern, underscored the gravity of our situation, the reality of our predicament crystallising with each beat of the chopper's blades overhead.

My concentration was abruptly divided as my phone erupted into a demanding ring, the sound slicing through the heavy atmosphere within the ute. Snatching it up and activating the speaker, I braced myself for more bad news. "Gladys," I called out, hoping for an ally in this escalating madness.

"We can't go back to the Owens'," her voice was direct, her statement cutting off any plans I had been formulating around that very idea.

"Why not?" I questioned.

"Police are there."

"Shit!" The expletive slipped out, the frustration and desperation tightening its grip on me. "Where do we go then?" I asked, my voice tense as my mind scrambled for alternatives, all the while our separation from the safety of the Owens' property growing with each second.

"The Owens' sounds like a fucking great idea to me," Adrian chimed in, his comment laced with a sarcasm that felt wildly inappropriate given the dire circumstances. His subsequent action of finally securing his seatbelt was a small, but telling, acknowledgment of the seriousness of our predicament.

I barely registered his remark, my focus solely on the road ahead, the weight of our situation bearing down on me. The possibility of a safe haven was slipping through my fingers, and with it, my control over the unfolding events.

"Shit! The police are behind us!" Gladys' voice, now tinged with panic, shattered the tense silence that had settled in the wake of our conversation. Her words were a cold splash of reality, the imminent threat of law enforcement's pursuit adding another layer of complexity to our already fraught endeavour.

The urgent flicker of the police lights and the relentless wail of the siren became a backdrop to our desperate escape as we wove through the labyrinthine roads—Collinsvale Road, then onto Collins Cap Road. It was Gladys who broke through the cacophony of panic with a suggestion that felt like a lifeline thrown in turbulent waters. "Myrtle Forest! Go to Myrtle Forest."

Adrian's immediate protest, "Oh, hell no!" was a gut reaction, his voice laced with fear and defiance. Yet, his objection was a distant echo against the pounding of my heart as I veered onto Springdale Road, executing a sharp turn that looped us back, my mind racing as fast as the ute.

"What am I going to do at Myrtle Forest?" The question burst from me. The panic in my chest mirrored in my voice, a tangible manifestation of the dread tightening its grip on me.

Adrian, caught in his own whirlwind of concern, hissed, "Where're the fucking cops gone?" His eyes darted in every direction, searching for any sign of our pursuers. The brief glimmer of optimism in his voice at the mention of the chopper was now all but gone.

Gladys's delayed response, pointing out the large toilet block at Myrtle Forest as our potential salvation, did little to ease the knot of anxiety in my stomach. My mind raced with the implications of her plan. The realisation that the police might have ceased their chase to prepare road spikes was a problematic consideration. "Shit," I cursed aloud, frustration and fear colliding as I envisioned the possibility of using the toilet block to transport both the ute and Adrian to Clivilius—a desperate measure for a desperate time.

But what about Gladys? The question hammered in my brain, its urgency underscored by the realisation that her options were dwindling fast. "What about you?" The concern in my question was genuine. "Are you coming too?"

Her response was immediate, her voice threaded with terror. "I can't." The finality in her words was a stark reminder of her sacrifices being made in the name of escape.

"There's no time to go back now," I pressed, the panic in my voice spiking. "You'll get caught." The reality of our situation was closing in, the window of opportunity narrowing with each passing second.

"Shit!" Gladys' exclamation was a mirror to my own despair, a shared sentiment in the face of the looming consequences. The weight of the decisions before us, the paths chosen and those forsaken, bore down with a gravity that threatened to suffocate. In that moment, the line between salvation and sacrifice blurred, the fate of each of us hanging in the balance as we hurtled toward an uncertain future.

The ute's tires churned up mud, betraying our hasty arrival into the small carpark of Myrtle Forest. As I slowed, my gaze darted about, desperate to locate the toilet block that was pivotal to my plan. The rattle of the seatbelt buckle from the passenger side punctuated the tension, a reminder of the precariousness of the situation.

There it is! The sight of the toilet block sparked a silent triumph within me, a fleeting moment of hope. My foot slammed down on the accelerator, the ute lurching forward with a force that caught Adrian off guard. His attempt at fleeing was abruptly interrupted, his body thrown backward, his elbow colliding sharply with my side. "Fuck!" The exclamation was ripped from me, a sharp intake of breath following the stab of pain. Yet, there was no time to dwell on the discomfort; adrenaline surged, propelling me forward, compelling me to act despite the pain.

With a determined motion, I wound down the window, bracing myself against the cold, wet blast of air that rushed in. Leaning out, I focused intently on the wall of the toilet block, my brow etched with determination, as I activated the Portal. The colours burst forth in an array of beautiful chaos, a testament to the power at my fingertips.

Retracting back into the ute, I called out to Gladys with a sense of finality, "I'm going in!" The urgency in my voice was mirrored by the swirling vortex of colours that now adorned the toilet block's wall, a gateway to safety, to Clivilius, waiting just ahead.

"What do I do?" Gladys's voice, laden with panic, reached me over the roar of the wind and the engine. The desperation, the fear of the unknown, was palpable in her shriek.

"Gladys... Run!" It was the only advice, the only command I could offer in the moment. Our connection, tenuous as it was, snapped the moment the ute crossed the Portal's threshold, the line going dead, leaving me with the weight of her fate and mine entwined in those final words.

INTERCEPTION

4338.211.2

"I'm sorry, Adrian," The words left me in a quiet exhale, a mix of apology and resignation as I got out of the ute. His hand, driven by a cocktail of confusion and anger, reached out towards me, but I evaded, the soft dust around us kicked up into a swirling dance by my movements. The world seemed to pause, the dust particles hanging in the air like witnesses to our confrontation. Pivoting with the car door as my support, I faced him squarely, an unspoken challenge hanging between us. "But we need you here," I declared, engaging in a stubborn stare-down with Adrian across the roof of the ute.

Adrian, his frustration palpable, wiped at the sweat clinging to his brow. "Fuck, it's warm," he muttered, his voice a blend of complaint and disbelief, as he slammed his fist against the ute. The action was a release of his irritation, under the relentless gaze of the sun in a cloudless sky. For a moment, his attention shifted from me to the oppressive heat, providing a brief respite from the tension.

I watched him, a silent sentinel, as he took a step back from the vehicle. My gaze, cautious yet filled with an emerging empathy, followed his every move. When Adrian moved towards the Portal's vast, shimmering screen, a part of me relaxed, letting out a sigh borne of weariness and a deep-seated understanding of the familiarity of his situation. *Another lost soul*, the thought echoed in my mind, a reflection of the unexpected path Adrian's life had taken.

It wasn't his fault, this unforeseen detour into Clivilius—a place as unforgiving as it was unfamiliar. Yet, amidst the desolation that surrounded us, I harboured a vision of the future—a thriving Bixbus, a beacon of civilisation and progress in the midst of vast emptiness. This vision was a guiding light, a reminder of the potential that lay in the very ground beneath our feet.

And if Bixbus was indeed destined to become the new capital of Clivilius, a cornerstone of this newly unfolding world, then the necessity of gathering all available resources and people became undeniable. Watching Adrian, his fists pounding against the Portal screen in a futile attempt to escape his new reality, I was reminded of the sacrifices and the choices that paved the way for progress.

The moment was electric, alive with an energy I couldn't have imagined. The giant screen before us, usually dormant and unassuming, burst alive—a chaotic dance of energised, swirling colours that seemed to defy the laws of physics. It was as if the universe itself had decided to put on a show, with hues that pulsed and throbbed, drawing the eye and the mind into a vortex of impossible beauty.

Paul's voice, sharp with urgency, sliced through the wonder of the moment like a knife. "Get out of the way!" His warning came from afar, his figure a blur as he sprinted towards us from the Drop Zone, desperation etching his every feature. The urgency in his voice sent a jolt of adrenaline through me, rooting me to the spot even as my mind screamed for action.

Before I could even form the words to warn Adrian, reality took a surreal turn. A bright burst of energy, like a star being born, sparked the instant Adrian's flesh made contact with the anomaly. His body reacted as if caught in a tempest, limbs flailing wildly as he was thrown backward through the air with violent force. He landed with a heavy thud, his back striking the ground hard, skidding through the dust as if he were a stone skipped across water. His momentum carried him until he finally came to a rest, a figure marred by the harshness of his landing.

My heart lurched into my throat as the unexpected horror unfolded before my eyes. A motorhome, an intruder from the kaleidoscope of colours, barrelled into reality. Its brakes screeched, a desperate cry against the ochre dust that billowed into the air, a futile attempt to halt its massive form. Yet, it was not enough to prevent the inevitable as the vehicle, a behemoth borne of chaos, engulfed Adrian's legs and torso beneath its relentless advance.

"Adrian!" My voice tore from my lips, a mix of fear and disbelief, as I rushed over, Paul's footsteps echoing my own. Together, we reached Adrian, our hands gripping his shoulders with a strength born of desperation. We pulled, dragging Adrian's lanky form from beneath the motorhome, every second stretching into an eternity.

Beatrix's voice, tinged with remorse, joined the chorus of concern. "I'm so sorry," she stammered. "Are you okay?"

I knelt beside Adrian, my hands moving with practiced precision as I assessed his condition. "I don't see any blood," I noted, a small relief in the midst of overwhelming tension. Despite the gravity of his ordeal, Adrian seemed miraculously spared from visible wounds, his state more dazed and bewildered than physically harmed.

Paul leaned in, his concern manifesting in a direct challenge to Adrian's consciousness. "How many fingers am I holding up?" he demanded, thrusting three fingers into Adrian's line of sight, a simple test laden with the weight of his anxiety.

As Paul's enthusiasm pierced the heavy air, my eyes couldn't help but roll. It felt unnecessary, almost misplaced given the circumstances. Adrian, on the other hand, barely seemed present, his response muted under the influence, his eyes a glazed mirror to his confused mind.

"He's high," I informed Paul with a glance that carried all the weight of our current predicament. The words felt almost hollow, stating the obvious. "And most likely a bit dehydrated. You'd better take him back to camp." The urgency in my voice was a thin veil over my concern. Adrian's well-being was paramount, and every moment we delayed could only compound the challenges he faced in acclimating to his unexpected new reality.

Just then, Nial and Kain arrived, their presence a reminder of the community we were striving to build in the face of adversity. "Everything okay?" Nial's voice was tinged with concern, a stark contrast to what had just unfolded.

Paul, seizing the moment of their arrival, quickly delegated the responsibility. "Can you two take him back to camp?"

"Shit! Adrian. What the hell are you doing here?" The shock in Nial's voice, coupled with the action of slapping Adrian's face, was a jarring but deeply human response. It was an attempt to connect, to break through the haze that enveloped Adrian.

"You know him?" Paul's inquiry, though innocuous, hinted at the layers of interconnectedness that defined our existence.

Nial gripped Adrian's shoulders firmly. "Let's get you to camp," he told him.

"We'll come back," said Kain, assisting Nial in getting Adrian on his feet.

Paul nodded silently, and a sombre air enveloped us as the three men distanced themselves.

"What's going on, Luke? Why the hell is Gladys in a bloody car chase with the police!?" Beatrix's eyes burned with ferocious intensity.

"Things didn't go quite according to plan with Adrian," I began, carefully choosing my words, wary of playing with fire.

"Clearly," Paul said, and Beatrix rolled her eyes.

"We chased after him when he took off," I explained.

"You couldn't just let him go?" Beatrix questioned.

A commotion from the three departed men momentarily drew our attention to Adrian's unmoved ute. "I'm just getting the rest of my gear," Adrian snapped, pushing Nial away.

"He'd already seen the Portal," I said, redirecting Paul and Beatrix's attention. "I know he's high, but I didn't think it was wise to let him go. Who knows—"

"Wise?" Beatrix scoffed, her voice cutting through the charged air like a sharp blade. "You didn't think it was wise to let him go, yet you had no qualms with racing through the streets and attracting the attention of the police?"

I fumbled for words, a realisation settling that Beatrix had a valid point. Hindsight now painted our actions with the brush of foolishness, an uncomfortable truth I couldn't deny.

"And how did you finally get him here?" Paul inquired, his eyes probing for an explanation.

"We came through a wall of the toilet block at Myrtle Forest," I replied, the image of the makeshift portal flashing vividly in my mind.

"And my sister?" Beatrix's sharp gaze intensified, drilling into me.

My brow furrowed, and my face reddened with the weight of the confession. "I told her to run," I admitted, the words carrying a burden of regret.

"Fuck's sake, Luke!" Beatrix huffed, her movements swift as she hurried toward the Portal, which erupted in a riot of vibrant colours.

"Where are you going?" I asked, a genuine concern for her safety colouring my words. "It's too dangerous, Beatrix. The police were right behind us," I answered my own question, assuming her intent.

With a swift middle finger and no words, Beatrix vanished, and the Portal's vibrancy dissipated, leaving behind an unsettling stillness

"You're not going after her?" Paul asked me.

Shaking my head, "she'll be back pretty quick."

The bickering of the three men continued near Adrian's ute. A door slammed shut, and the engine roared to life, its growl a sharp contrast to the tension in the air. Nial stood in front of it, hands braced on the bonnet, a silent sentinel in the midst of ongoing conflict.

"Ridiculous," Paul murmured softly, his voice carrying a mix of exasperation and resignation.

Grabbing Paul's shoulder, I spun him back around as he attempted to leave. His questioning eyes locked onto mine.

"They'll be fine," I assured him, my fingers pressing into Paul's shoulder as I tried to convince myself of the words I spoke.

Paul frowned, disbelief etched in the pout of his mouth.

"Wait here for her, won't you?" It was more of a directive than a question, an unspoken plea for someone to anchor themselves in the tumult.

"And you?" Paul inquired, his nod carrying reluctant acknowledgment.

My brow furrowed as I pondered my next moves. *What a tumultuous day already!* I chided myself, mentally compiling a list of actions. *Nial can settle Adrian*, I noted, glancing over at the ute. *Beatrix can handle finding her sister, if she hasn't been arrested already. Shit! The fence order. I forgot about that!*

"I need to go back to the Owens'. The first delivery of that fence order you and Nial made yesterday is supposed to be delivered today," I informed Paul, hastening toward the Portal.

"Is that safe?" Paul called out, rooted to where he stood.

"I don't have a choice. You need that delivery."

Paul sighed. "Be careful, Luke."

"Always," I responded with a forced, cheery grin, burying the tightening knot in my stomach, a forewarning of the imminent peril I was about to confront by returning to the property.

❖

I had taken a reckless gamble, relying on the hope that the Owens' house wouldn't be swarming with police as I slipped in through the same portal Karen and Chris had used for their unexpected exit. So far, luck had sided with my audacity. Ignoring the lively, chattering voices emanating from the kitchen, I tiptoed through the dim passageway, swiftly advancing toward the front door. The wooden floorboards beneath my feet felt like treacherous ice, threatening to betray my presence with the slightest misstep.

"Shit!" I hissed, instinctively ducking into the bedroom as the front door swung open. The sudden intrusion of light from the hallway felt like a spotlight, exposing my every flaw, every doubt. Perhaps this was indeed a foolhardy idea, a thought devoid of logical reasoning. With heavy footsteps passing the doorway and fading down the hall, I slipped behind the bed, my heart still racing from the close encounter. Pressing my back against the bedside table, I rested my head in my hands, gently rubbing my temples. The texture of the wood against my skin felt grounding, a momentary anchor in the storm of my thoughts.

How am I going to get outside? I mused, the question lingering in the heavy air. *Do I even need to get outside?* A better question emerged, like a beacon through the fog of my panic. On hands and knees, I slid across the polished wooden floor toward the window, the coolness of the boards a stark contrast to the warmth of my flushed skin. *If the fence delivery hasn't arrived yet,* I reasoned aloud, peering between the peach-coloured curtains, *there's no immediate need to step outside. I can wait here until the police depart, then move freely to greet the delivery driver. That's a much better solution.*

The relentless downpour outside painted a grim portrait of the day, the kind of weather that seeps into your bones, uninvited and unforgiving. As I peered through the slightly fogged glass of the bedroom window, the scene on the front verandah unfolded like a silent movie, the lone officer a solitary figure against the onslaught of nature. Watching him shake the raindrops from his black umbrella, a brief, almost whimsical thought flitted through my mind about the futility of such actions against the deluge that enveloped the world outside.

A short-lived sigh of relief escaped me as I noted the absence of a truck in the yard, a small victory in the grand scheme of things. However, that sliver of relief was swiftly replaced by a knot of anxiety in my stomach as the sound of heavy wheels crunching on the gravel driveway announced the arrival of the large truck. Its hulking form loomed through the sheets of rain, a beast awakening, its wheels carelessly navigating the pothole-ridden path, indifferent to the chaos it wrought.

Cussing under his breath, the officer hastily abandoned the shelter of the verandah, racing toward the oncoming truck. It was almost comical, watching one arm struggle to maintain the umbrella over his head, while the other waved frantically for the driver to stop, a dance of desperation and duty.

"This is it," I muttered to myself, bracing for the nerve-wracking minutes ahead. The very idea of leaving the sheltered confines of the house, my temporary haven, and dashing into the thundering rain was anything but appealing.

Yet, the stormy conditions, while daunting, provided a fortuitous distraction, a cloak under which I could make my move.

The officer engaged the truck driver in a lively conversation, their words completely drowned by the roar of thunder, nature's own version of privacy. Not wanting to risk being seen from the hallway, I cautiously opened the bedroom window, the slight creaking of dry hinges thankfully masked by the timely thunderclap that rolled across the property with the authority of an ancient god.

Rain pelted the verandah's corrugated iron roof, transforming it into a cacophony of sound, a drumbeat that was louder and more insistent than I had initially realised. With a deep breath, I slipped through the window, my heart pounding in my chest as I moved left, jumping the railing to land with a squelchy thud in the mud beside the verandah. The ground beneath my feet was a quagmire, eager to claim my boots as its own.

Surrounded by the dense foliage of native bushes, I stayed crouched, a shadow amongst shadows. Every movement was calculated, every step taken with the utmost care to ensure I remained hidden from the prying eyes of the driver and officer in the front yard. The rain was both my adversary and my ally, soaking me to the bone while masking my movements with its relentless symphony. I crept along the side of the house, a spectre in the storm, driven by a mix of determination and the primal urge to evade capture. The world around me was reduced to the sound of my own breathing and the relentless patter of rain against foliage, a reminder that sometimes, the line between hunter and hunted is as thin as the veil of rain that shrouded my escape.

"You need confidence, Luke," I mumbled to myself, the words barely audible above the symphony of raindrops pelting the leafy canopy overhead. My hands were shaking, not just from the cold but from the adrenaline pumping through my veins. I was trying to untangle the knot of fear and uncertainty in my gut, to convert it into something that could propel me forward, something that felt like resolve. "Do it for Henri," I whispered into the damp air, a renewed determination coursing through my veins, mingling with a sharp stab of pain in my chest. The memory of losing one fur baby was a wound still too raw to heal; the thought of losing another was unbearable.

Wiping rain from my eyes, I dashed across the puddle-filled grass, each step squelching underfoot, heading for the edge of the native forest a few dozen meters from the house. The sprint left me panting and soaked to the bone, but the dense foliage offered a semblance of shelter, a brief respite from the relentless downpour. Catching my breath, I pressed on, weaving through the trees and bushes, the underbrush tugging at my clothes as if trying to hold me back.

Securing a clear line of sight to the truck from my makeshift cover, I took another deep, steadying breath. "I'm outside... but now what?" I questioned aloud, the words hanging in the air, mingling with the mist. The truck, with its promise of fencing, seemed like a beacon in the night, calling to me through the rain. *I have to get to that truck!*

From my vantage point, I could see the conversation between the officer and the driver had shifted closer to the house. Their voices, loud and laced with annoyance, carried through the air, punctuated by the occasional frustrated gesture. It was clear things were escalating, and my window of opportunity was closing fast.

Bracing myself for the mad dash back into the rain, I knew that even if I only managed to activate the portal on the back of the truck, it would be enough. I could return later for a more thorough investigation, when the odds might be more in my favour. Barring any unforeseen changes, I couldn't see any other viable options. Attempting to steal the truck was out of the question; a vehicle that size would never escape a police pursuit, not without drawing even more attention to myself.

In that moment, nestled among the trees, with raindrops weaving paths down my face, I felt a mixture of fear and exhilaration. The storm raged around me, both a literal and metaphorical tempest, mirroring the turmoil within. Yet, beneath it all, there was a spark of something that felt like hope. For Henri, for myself, I was ready to take that leap, to dash through the storm and seize the sliver of chance that lay within my grasp.

A loud jingle from my pocket shattered the rain-soaked silence like a glass pane meeting the unforgiving ground. Panic surged through me as I fumbled to silence the intrusive noise, fearing it would herald my discovery. My wet fingers betrayed me, slipping across the phone screen in a hasty attempt to dismiss the call, inadvertently answering it instead. Instinctively, I brought the phone to my ear, heart pounding against my ribcage like a prisoner yearning for freedom.

Beatrix's voice rushed through the line, a beacon of urgency in the midst of the storm. "I'm at the Collinsvale property," were the first words that pierced the fog of my mind. My eyes widened in alarm, frantically scanning the forest surroundings and then back to the house, searching for any sign of her. She was nowhere in sight, her presence as elusive as the shadows dancing between the trees.

"The police are taking it very seriously, Luke. They've bagged evidence and everything," Beatrix continued, her words slicing through the ambient noise of the rain and thunder. A sense of foreboding tightened around my chest, a noose of realisation that the stakes were higher than I had anticipated.

The loud metallic rattling of the truck's back being opened snapped my attention back to the immediate task at hand. *It's open!* The thought surged through me like a bolt of lightning, filling me with a renewed ambition.

"Get the hell out of there, Beatrix," I hissed sharply into the phone, attempting to keep my voice low while conveying the urgency of the situation. My breath fogged the screen in quick, nervous puffs, betraying my rising panic.

"I will as soon as I hang up. Where are you?" asked Beatrix, her voice laced with concern. I paused, deliberating whether to confess my location, the weight of my decision heavy in the air between us.

"I'm at the property," I admitted, a reluctant confession, hoping it might encourage Beatrix to leave, to put distance between herself and the danger that clung to this place like the dampness in the air.

"Where?" she pressed, her determination piercing through the static of the call.

"I'm going to save that fencing order," I replied, withholding the specifics of my location, a guarded secret I was not yet ready to share. My gaze lingered on the truck, its open back a silent invitation and a daunting challenge.

"Let me help you," Beatrix offered, her voice a mix of resolve and worry. But the risk was too great, the stakes too high for both of us.

"No! Go to Clivilius. You need to continue with the missions Paul is giving you," I insisted, my words a desperate plea for her safety, for the continuation of our cause.

Beatrix mumbled something unintelligible, a sign of her frustration or perhaps resignation. And then, as an afterthought, a realisation that jolted me like a cold splash in the face, I added, "And you need to find your sister!" Gladys had momentarily slipped from my mind, a critical piece of the day's puzzle momentarily overshadowed by the immediate crisis.

"Luke, stop being such a stubborn prick. You can't do all of this yourself," Beatrix's voice, laced with frustration, cut through the torrential backdrop like a knife. Her words, meant to pierce my solitary resolve, only served to reinforce the weight of the responsibility I felt.

"You think I don't know how much trouble we're in?" I scolded in reply, my voice a mixture of exasperation and determination. The stakes were impossibly high, and the margin for error was nonexistent. "But if we lose that fencing delivery, those caravans you are sourcing are the camp's only line of protection."

Ending the debate, I powered off my phone with a decisive click, the action symbolic of cutting off any further distraction. The device, now silent, felt like a small, cold stone in my hand - a tangible reminder of the isolation of my chosen path.

With the officer moving behind the far side of the truck and the driver following after him, I swiftly surveyed the area. The coast was momentarily clear, a fleeting opportunity. Seizing the moment, my feet splashed through ever-expanding puddles, each step a grim reminder of the harsh conditions. The irritating feeling of soggy socks against my feet was a minor discomfort compared to the looming threat of discovery, yet it gnawed at me with every squelch.

An unfortunate miscalculation saw my foot catching the edge of a small hole hidden beneath the deceptive surface. Arms outstretched in a futile attempt to brace for impact, my palms slammed into the soggy ground, sliding through the mud as my knees landed with a heavy crash. The world momentarily seemed to slow as I processed the jarring impact, the cold mud seeping through my clothes.

"Shit!" I hissed, the urgency of the situation leaving no time to assess for injury. Through the curtain of rain, a pair of heavy, black boots headed for the back of the truck came into view. I was only a few meters short of the destination, yet in that moment, an instinctual calculation warned me that I was still not close enough.

Extracting myself from the mud with a grimace, I kept a low crouch to the ground, the muscles in my legs protesting as I covered the remaining distance. Finishing off with an awkward drop to the ground, I rolled beneath the truck, a desperate manoeuvre to evade detection. Beneath the metal beast, the ground was a mix of oil, water, and mud - a small price to pay for the shred of cover it provided.

Lying there, heart pounding, I took a moment to catch my breath, the cold, wet ground an uncomfortable contrast to the adrenaline coursing through my veins. The proximity to my goal and the imminent risk of discovery melded into a potent mix of fear and determination. The stakes were clear, the mission critical - not just for me, but for all those counting on me back at Bixbus. In the shadow of the truck, amidst the storm, I steeled myself for what was to come, driven by the knowledge that failure was not an option.

My filthy hands, now canvases of dirt and grass debris, smeared across my face in a futile attempt to wipe the worst of the rain away. Clumps of dirt stubbornly clung to the back of my head, an unexpected but silent gratitude for keeping my hair short whispered through my mind. It was one less thing to worry about in moments like these.

"Who's there?" an authoritative voice shattered the relative silence, slicing through the rain and my thoughts like a cold blade.

Shit! Somebody must have seen me. My heart slammed against my chest with the force of a drum, sending waves of panic coursing through my veins. Panicked eyes frantically searched the underbelly of the truck for any nook, any cranny that might serve as a suitable spot for a quick portal getaway. But there was nothing! The stark realisation hit me like a physical blow, bracing myself for the inevitable discovery of my hiding place.

"Fuck's sake," a deep voice growled, frustration lacing the air with tension.

Water splashed as two sets of footsteps diverged, heading in different directions. "Beatrix!" I whispered under my breath, a sliver of hope igniting at the realisation that the first voice hadn't been calling out to me. My eyes tracked the slow, deliberate movement of the officer's feet as they approached the verandah, each step a measured beat in the cacophony of the storm.

Turning my head to look behind, I caught sight of the driver, continuing to cuss as he chased after a small piece of paper whisked away by the wind. The sight, oddly mundane in the midst of my plight, offered a brief distraction from the direness of my situation.

Sliding myself toward the back of the truck, icy, dirty water seeped through the layers of my clothing, sending shivers down my spine as it finally made its way to my bare skin. The cold was biting, a reminder of the lengths to which I had gone, the desperate measures I was willing to take.

Ignoring the uncomfortable clinging of my sodden clothes to my body, I pulled myself from beneath the truck with a determined grunt. The act felt like emerging from one world into another, a transition from the hidden to the exposed, from the observer to the participant. My movements were quick, calculated, driven by a need to act before any further chance of discovery.

Still distracted! I told myself, stealing another glance at the driver's comedic battle with the wind and paper. I couldn't help but use the moment to my advantage. My fingers fumbled for the Portal Key, the cold metal feeling alien against my skin, numbed from the relentless rain. Stealing a quick glance to ensure I remained unnoticed, I readied myself to fire it against the back of the truck and leave this current debacle behind. The sight of the back of the truck, only half closed, was like a beacon of hope in the gloom. With a fresh burst of adrenaline surging through my veins, I hoisted myself inside, the action more desperate than graceful.

Navigating my way deeper into the dark confines of the truck was like moving through another world, one of shadows and unseen obstacles. My knee connected with a metal pole in the darkness, sending a sharp pain shooting through my leg. I bit down hard on my lower lip, the taste of iron flooding my mouth as I stifled the cursing that fought for release. The silence was my ally, and I could not afford to break it now.

Wrapping my cold, nearly frozen hand around another pole for support, the chain-link fence clinked loudly against its counterpart as I attempted to squeeze past. The sound was unnervingly loud in the enclosed space.

Then, the back door rattled and closed with a definitive thundering that echoed throughout the truck, leaving an unpleasant ringing in my ears. The sudden plunge into even thicker darkness was disorienting, a momentary void that seemed to swallow every sense. I stood still, stunned, with the unexpected realisation that my movements inside the truck had gone undetected. The silence that followed was a tense, pregnant pause before the truck's engine rumbled to life, a low growl that spoke of imminent departure.

As the darkness gave way to the rainbow colours of the Portal, their dancing lights reflecting buzzing excitement around the crowded space, a sense of surreal accomplishment washed over me. Dripping water across the truck with every step, I couldn't suppress the broad grin that spread across my face. The thought of the driver returning, only to find the truck empty, was deliciously satisfying. He would be left grappling with the impossible task of explaining where the goods had vanished to, a puzzle with no logical solution.

The truck, unknowingly, would be used again, becoming another unanticipated resource for a Guardian to plunder at some future time. This interception, executed against all odds, was a silent victory in the shadows. I smiled to myself, the satisfaction of the moment a warmth against the cold, a light in the darkness, a silent testament to the ingenuity and resilience of those who operate in the unseen. This was more than just a mission accomplished; it was a statement, a declaration of our continued resistance and adaptability—*The perfect interception!*

SAFE

4338.211.3

Amid the flickering flames of the campfire, soft voices melded into a comforting but haunting backdrop to my wearied face. The fire's warm glow cast dancing shadows across us, highlighting the deep lines of strain etched across my forehead. These were not just marks of physical exhaustion but silent acknowledgments of the weight of responsibility that now rested on my shoulders. In the dim light, Beatrix's scars seemed to stand out more prominently, each one a testament to the challenges and sacrifices inherent in our roles as Guardians. Observing her, I couldn't help but wonder if my own journey would soon bear similar marks, a thought that both daunted and steeled me.

Bixbus, with its ever-growing settler population and improving living conditions, stood as a beacon of progress in the wilderness. Our recent efforts to fortify the camp with a simple chain-link fence were a testament to our determination to protect what we were building. Yet, despite these advancements, the vast unknown beyond the camp's perimeter served as a constant reminder of danger. The shadow panthers, with their lurking threat, ensured my thoughts seldom wandered far from the immediate concerns of safety and survival.

"That's everyone," Nial's voice broke through my reverie as he secured the metallic gate, signalling the completion of the day's work. Paul's entrance into the small enclosed settlement marked the moment with a gravity that seemed to weigh down the very air around us.

"It feels a bit like a zoo here now," I remarked, attempting to inject a bit of levity into the heavy atmosphere as my brother approached. The comparison, though made in jest, was a reflection of the surreal sense of our situation, enclosed and watched, yet not by spectators but by the unseen dangers that prowled beyond our makeshift barriers.

Paul sighed, a sound that seemed to carry the weight of countless burdens. The heaviness in his demeanour was palpable, a clear sign he was in no mood for humour. "Except this time, I think we are the animals locked in the cage," he replied, his words cutting through the night with a sharpness that left a lingering silence in their wake.

"I'm not so sure that the goat and chickens you've locked in the car and left out there would agree with you," Beatrix's voice cut through the evening air, her tone light yet pointed, drawing a collective gaze toward the direction of the Drop Zone.

"It won't always be this way," I reassured, my hand rubbing at my brow. I turned to Beatrix, determination in my eyes. "Beatrix and I will bring you more supplies tomorrow."

She nodded in agreement, "Yeah. I'll get you as many motorhomes as I can over the next few days."

"And you've got some skilled people here now; you'll have a little village built and buzzing with enthusiasm in no time," I added, my voice tinged with optimism. The vision of a thriving community, one that transcended the boundaries of a makeshift camp, seemed within reach, a tangible goal that spurred me forward.

"I wouldn't go that—" Beatrix began, her pragmatism always a grounding force, only to be cut off by Paul's interjection.

"Speaking of motorhomes and supplies, Luke can give you my house keys." His look towards me sought confirmation, a silent query that I was quick to affirm. "Yeah," I said, "I've got them all in a safe space." The keys, symbolic of Paul's trust in us, felt like a significant gesture, an extension of our community's shared resources and mutual reliance.

"If Claire and the kids really have gone to Queensland, I doubt they'll return anytime soon," Paul continued, his words drawing a curious glance from me.

Either oblivious to or choosing to ignore my unvoiced curiosity, Paul turned his attention back to Beatrix. "You may as well bring anything from the house that looks useful." His directive, practical as it was, spoke volumes of the sacrifices and adaptations we were all forced to make.

"Include furniture with that," Kain added, hobbling over with his new crutches. "I could really do with a good couch to rest my leg."

"Has it still not healed fully yet?" I asked, my concern for Kain genuine.

"No," Kain replied, the simplicity of his answer belied by the complexity of emotions it evoked. "I don't seem to be as privileged as Joel." His words, laced with a tinge of bitterness, hinted at deeper stories of struggle and resilience.

"Any news on that front?" I inquired further, hoping for some positive update on Joel and the others who had become mere whispers and worries in the wind.

"No," answered Kain, the fading daylight doing little to mask the concern etched deeply on his face. "We've not seen anything of Joel, Jamie, or Glenda," Paul added, his voice carrying a hint of resignation.

"Give them a couple more days," I suggested, trying to inject a note of optimism into the conversation. The alternative—giving in to despair—was not an option.

"And then what?" Beatrix asked, her question hanging in the air, a palpable reminder of the uncertainty that cloaked our every decision.

I shrugged, my response a silent admission of the limitations of my foresight. Paul, however, seemed to embody the collective anxiety with another heavy sigh.

"You've really got no idea what you are doing, do you, Luke?" Kain's interjection, though perhaps meant as a jest, shifted the mood perceptibly.

"It's not that easy," Beatrix snapped back, her defence immediate and fierce.

"You don't have to tell me that," Kain retorted, motioning to his recovering leg.

My mouth opened for a rebuttal, the words teetering on the edge of my tongue, ready to defend, to argue, to make my stance known. But it was Paul's timely intervention that cut through the rising tension like a knife through water, his voice calm, redirecting the flow of our conversation towards more practical matters. "My car is still parked at the Adelaide airport carpark. Can you collect it for me and bring it here?" he requested from Beatrix.

"Sure," she muttered.

"Oh," I said, my face lighting up as an idea sparked to life within my mind. The potential for solving multiple problems with a single solution seemed almost too good to pass up. "I am flying from Hobart to Adelaide first thing in the morning. I won't have time to collect Paul's car, but I can register a Portal location to make it easier for you, Beatrix."

"Thanks, but there's no need to fly; I've already registered several locations in Adelaide," she replied, her words effectively rendering my planned effort redundant.

"Oh," I responded, my initial enthusiasm deflating into thoughtful concentration.

Her narrowed eyes studying me, Beatrix's puzzlement at my reaction was evident. She was trying to piece together the puzzle of my intentions, the undercurrents of plans within plans that even I was still navigating. Finally, lifting my head,

I clarified, "I've already got my flight booked. I may as well use it. Besides, I might find something useful at the airport. In any event, it'll give you a much closer point of entry for collecting Paul's car." The words, once spoken, solidified my resolve, painting a picture of a path forward that leveraged every available resource for our collective benefit.

"Alright," she agreed, her acquiescence a relief. It was a delicate balance, managing the myriad tasks and challenges that our situation presented, and her willingness to adapt provided a much-needed sense of solidarity.

My list of tasks in my mental notebook was already burgeoning, each entry a commitment, a responsibility that I bore willingly, yet not without a measure of apprehension for the growing complexity of our lives.

"What are you actually going to Adelaide for, Luke?" Paul's question, tinged with suspicion, cut through my thoughts, a reminder that my actions, however well-intentioned, did not exist in a vacuum.

I hesitated momentarily, the weight of the decision pressing down on me. "I'm thinking I might bring our parents and siblings to Clivilius," I said, feeling a surge of confidence buoy my words. It was a bold move, one fraught with risk and uncertainty, yet driven by a deep-seated belief in the sanctuary we were trying to create, in the potential for a better life that lay within the bounds of Clivilius.

Beatrix gasped loudly. "Is that a good idea?"

Surprisingly, Paul stepped in before I could muster a response, his words cutting through the heavy air with a decisiveness that momentarily lifted the weight from my shoulders. "It'll be a lot more mouths to feed, but I think you are right. I think they could really help us here." His support, unexpected yet unwavering, bolstered my resolve, a reminder of the strength found in our collective determination.

"How many?" Beatrix's question, straightforward and filled with pragmatic concern, prompted me to delve into the specifics, to quantify the challenge we were contemplating.

"Only Adelaide?" Paul inquired.

"I think so, for now," I replied, my mind wrestling with the multitude of considerations the decision entailed.

Paul, turning back to Beatrix with a semblance of clarity, stated, "Parents and three brothers."

"Two brothers," I quickly corrected, a slight mix-up in the family count that needed addressing. The sudden interjection painted a confused expression on both Beatrix's and Paul's faces, prompting me to clarify the situation further. "Eli is still visiting Lisa in the United States." The mention of Eli brought a momentary pause, a brief detour in our discussion as we navigated the complexities of our family dynamics.

"Girlfriend?" Beatrix ventured a guess, her curiosity piqued.

"Sister," came our characteristic unified brotherly response, a chorus of clarification that momentarily lightened the mood.

"Oh, you've got a big family," Beatrix remarked, her fingers moving as if trying to tally the members in her mind.

"Yep," Paul and I chimed in together, another unified reply that underscored the bond between us

"Are you going to bring them to Bixbus tomorrow?" Paul's question brought us back to the immediacy of the challenge, the logistics of integrating our family into this new life we were carving out in Clivilius.

I shrugged casually. "I'm not sure yet. I still haven't worked out the best way to approach them." The admission was a moment of vulnerability, an acknowledgment of the uncertainty that lay ahead. After a brief pause, seeking wisdom in shared counsel, I asked, "Any ideas?"

Paul's initial shrug was a mirror of my own uncertainty, but it didn't last long before a thought seemed to cross his mind, a spark of insight in the growing dusk. "I suspect that all you need to do is find a way to convince dad, and the rest will easily follow."

"Hmm," I mused, the simplicity of his suggestion resonating with a deep-seated truth. Rubbing my chin, I considered his words, a plan beginning to take shape amidst the myriad of uncertainties. "I think you're onto something there."

"Come on, Beatrix," I said, pulling her back from the edge of her wandering thoughts. "Let's get you these keys."

❖

The white painted wardrobe door, now aged and slightly chipped at the edges, rumbled along its worn track, a sound reminiscent of distant thunder rolling over a quiet town. As it begrudgingly gave way, it revealed an assortment of empty coat hangers, swaying slightly as if dancing to a breeze that had snuck into the room. The hangers, devoid of their usual garments, clinked together softly, an eerie chime in the otherwise silent room.

"Where's your clothes?" Beatrix inquired, her voice laced with a mix of curiosity and skepticism. I could almost see the gears turning in her mind, questioning the practicality of my decision to leave my wardrobe barren when the convenience of returning to change was just a mere thought away. Her eyes, sharp and inquisitive, scanned the empty space before her as if trying to unravel a mystery hidden within the void.

On tiptoes, I stretched towards the heavens, or at least towards the top shelf of the wardrobe, my fingers grazing the rough texture of the wood. "They're on the other side of the wardrobe," I responded, injecting a hint of mock frustration into my voice, as though the answer to her question should have been obvious. My tone was light, playful even, but beneath it lay a layer of anticipation, a prelude to the revelation I was about to unveil.

Cringing, I felt the coarse surface of the shelf beneath my fingertips, a sensation akin to dragging one's skin across the rough bark of an ancient tree. "Got it," I declared triumphantly, the sound of a solid clink against wood marking the end of my brief, yet arduous, quest. My prize in hand, I descended back to the solid ground, the plush carpet embracing my heels with a softness that contrasted sharply with the harshness of the shelf above.

Beatrix reached out for the keys now jingling in my grasp, her movements swift and purposeful. Yet, in a moment of silent defiance, I dropped to my knees, the metallic chorus of the keys ceasing as they landed in my open palm. The thrill of the secret I was about to share enveloped me, a cloak of excitement that rendered me almost entirely oblivious to her presence. Only the faint awareness of her curious gaze, tracking my every move, tethered me to the reality of her company.

Pulling several pairs of shoes from the depths of the wardrobe floor, I felt a nervous excitement ripple through me, a current of anticipation that electrified the air around us. It was a moment of revelation, of crossing a threshold into the unknown. The shoes, mundane in appearance, were mere vessels for a secret of greater magnitude, a secret that was about to bind Beatrix and me in a way few could understand. It was time to induct another Guardian into my little secret.

My fingers danced nervously at the edge of the carpet in the back corner of the wardrobe, each thread whispering secrets as they unravelled under my touch. Beatrix's eyes, wide with a blend of curiosity and disbelief, mirrored the flickering lights above as I peeled back a considerable section of the carpet. It was like revealing a hidden world beneath our feet, a shiny, metallic surface winking at us from its discreet haven.

"You have a safe buried in your wardrobe floor?" Beatrix's voice was a mix of incredulity and awe, her tone climbing an octave as she carefully lowered herself beside me.

The key, cold and metallic against the warmth of my palm, slid into the keyhole with a satisfying ease, a testament to the many times I had performed this ritual in solitude. Pausing, I savoured the moment of anticipation, the seconds stretching into eternity before the impending reveal. "Of course," I replied, my voice laced with a mischievous glee, a wide grin splitting my face as I imagined the myriad of possibilities racing through her mind.

With a soft click, the lock yielded under my fingers, and I lifted the lid with a reverence usually reserved for the unveiling of sacred relics. Beatrix inhaled sharply, a gasp escaping her lips as the contents of the safe came into view. It was a treasure trove of the mundane, elevated to the extraordinary by their concealment. The safe was meticulously organised, lined with bulging zip-lock bags that seemed to pulse with the secrets they contained.

"Here's Paul's," I said, my voice a mixture of pride and solemnity as I extracted one of the bags, placing it gently in her hands. The clear exterior crinkled under her touch, a tactile connection to the lives encapsulated within. Her fingers hesitated over the items—a phone, a wallet, scraps of paper—each object a puzzle piece in our interconnected existence.

"Is there a bag for everyone?" The question slipped from her lips, a natural curiosity blooming amidst the garden of her thoughts.

"Yeah. I figured keeping things grouped by owner would be the best way to manage," I answered, my voice steady, betraying none of the inner turmoil that accompanied the guardianship of such secrets.

"Probably—" she began, her voice trailing off as agreement and further questions percolated in her mind.

"Oh, apart from this one," I interjected, presenting another large bag with a flourish. The shift in her gaze was palpable, the light of inquiry narrowing into focused scrutiny as she beheld the small images of faces trapped behind the plastic veil. "Why keep all the driver's licenses separate?" she probed, her voice a blend of curiosity and concern.

In that moment, I felt the weight of her gaze, heavy with questions and the dawning realisation of the depth of my secret. Ignoring her question was not an act of evasion but one of protection, a shield against the barrage of inquiries that would surely follow. Swiftly, I reclaimed the bag, returning it to its sanctuary within the safe. The act was not just a physical retrieval but a metaphorical drawing of boundaries, a line I was not yet ready to cross.

Deciding not to venture further into the enigmatic labyrinth of my thoughts, Beatrix's curiosity turned tangible as she opened the zip-lock bag housing Paul's belongings. "What's all this?" she inquired, her voice a blend of intrigue and confusion. The scrap paper, crinkling under her touch, whispered secrets as she carefully unfolded it, her eyes darting across the jumble of numbers and letters inscribed with hurried strokes.

"It's the notes I've been making for Paul. It includes all the important stuff like the codes to unlock his phone and access his bank accounts," I explained, my voice carrying a hint of pride mixed with a sobering sense of responsibility. These were not just arbitrary numbers but gateways into the private corners of my brother's life.

I jingled Paul's keys close to her, a playful distraction from the gravity of the paper in her hands. The metallic clatter seemed out of place in the quiet of the room, a reminder of the mundane world outside our secret sanctuary. "Even the keys are labelled," I commented, observing her silent gaze lingering on the small tag bearing Paul's name. It was a small detail, but in our world of carefully guarded secrets, every label served as a beacon of identity.

"Feel free to access the safe whenever you need to. Leave the key at the back of the top shelf," I offered, laying down the rules of engagement with a casual authority. It was an invitation into my inner circle, a gesture of trust that bound us closer together.

"Of course," she responded, her voice steady, betraying neither excitement nor apprehension.

"And only turn the mobile phones on when you need to use them," I continued, the weight of each instruction hanging in the air between us. "Why's that?" she questioned, a furrow forming between her brows, the physical manifestation of her puzzlement.

"I don't know whether police really can track our exact locations from a phone when it is turned on, but I'd rather not take any chances to find out." My words were laced with a cautious paranoia, a reflection of the tightrope we walked in our efforts to stay beneath the radar.

Beatrix shrugged, a silent concession to the limits of her knowledge on the matter.

My instructions continued, "And don't reply to any messages or answer any calls unless they are from me." The directive was clear, a non-negotiable term in our pact of secrecy.

She nodded quickly, her expression a mixture of determination and a touch of overwhelm. The information was a lot to digest, a testament to the intricate web we wove in our clandestine endeavours. Yet, beneath the complexity of our operations, there was an underlying simplicity to our goals: protect, preserve, and proceed with caution. In this shadowy dance of secrets and safety, each step was measured, each decision weighed with the utmost care.

"Oh," I interjected, an afterthought catching the tail of our conversation like a leaf caught in a swift stream. "Use the cash sparingly and be sure to make a note of any bank transactions on the relevant paper." The words felt heavy, laden with the burden of our precarious financial situation. She nodded, her understanding silent yet profound, as if the gravity of our fiscal constraints wrapped its chains around us both.

My concerns spilled over like a torrent breaking through a dam. "Finances don't go too far. I'm really not sure how we're going to keep up paying for supplies and materials to help them build the new settlement," I confessed, the stream of my worries unchecked. It was a rare admission of uncertainty, a crack in the façade of composure I tried so hard to maintain.

Beatrix's lips pursed, a silent mirror to the complexity of the puzzle we found ourselves entangled in. Her mind, I knew, was racing through the maze of our financial conundrum, seeking a way out.

"I think we're going to need to get creative," I suggested, a tentative bridge across the chasm of our dilemma. It was an invitation to think beyond the conventional, to dare to dream up solutions that skirted the edges of the impossible.

Suddenly, the tension in her face eased, replaced by a spark of inspiration that lit her eyes with a gleam of possibilities. "What is it?" I asked, curiosity piqued, my own train of thoughts halting to give room to her revelation.

"I know how we can get more cash," she declared, a smirk playing at the corner of her mouth, a harbinger of schemes yet unveiled. "Lots of cash."

"How?" My question hung in the air, a mixture of hope and apprehension. Her response, or rather the lack thereof, sent a chill down my spine. Shaking her head, Beatrix pocketed Paul's keys with a decisive motion and stood. "Never mind about the detail. I think the less you know the better. Leave it to me and Jarod."

"Jarod?" The name sparked a flare of panic, igniting a firestorm of questions. As I rose to join her, the name echoed ominously in my mind.

"Just trust me on this one, Luke," she assured, her grin unwavering, a beacon of her confidence—or recklessness. Without waiting for my consent, she strode toward the living room, her determination palpable.

"Beatrix," I called out, trailing behind her like a shadow tethered to her light. My heart raced, each beat a drum of war against the silence of her impending actions.

Before the Portal, a masterpiece that painted the room in buzzing colours of otherworldly vistas, she halted and faced me. Her silhouette, framed by the kaleidoscope of energies, was both formidable and fragile.

My brow furrowed, a landscape of my worries and pleas. "Please be careful."

"Well, I can't promise that one," she scoffed, her laughter a light note floating atop the heavy air between us. It was a playful dismissal, yet beneath it lay the unspoken truths of our reality—the risks, the dangers, and the unyielding drive that propelled each of us forward.

As Beatrix's form vanished into the swirling vortex of the portal, the room was abruptly reclaimed by an eerie silence, a stark contrast to the fervent energy that had just pulsated within its confines. I found myself alone, the lingering buzz from the portal's activation fading into a quiet that seemed to press in from all sides.

❖

Returning to the bedroom, my gaze drifted back to the safe, its metallic surface catching the dim light and throwing it back in soft glimmers, as if it too held its breath in anticipation of what was to come.

My mind, a tempest of thoughts and emotions, struggled to find purchase amidst the tumult. The outline of Bixbus, with its settlers and the intricate network of connections that bound them, was intricately mapped on paper. It was a tangible manifestation of the delicate web we were tasked with nurturing. Lines that represented lives, resources, and responsibilities intertwined across the sketches, each connection a thread in the fabric of our burgeoning community.

My fingers moved of their own accord, tracing the lines with a reverence that belied their simplicity. Each stroke felt laden with the weight of the lives these lines represented, and within this network of ink and paper, I glimpsed the potential for something greater. It was in this moment of reflection that a plan, nebulous at first, began to crystallise in my mind—a strategy not just for the physical fortification of the settlement, but for the fortification of our bonds, our unity.

"This needs to be more than just a sketch," I found myself saying aloud, the words breaking the silence like a promise to the future. I flipped through the pages of a small notebook, its presence in the safe a testament to its importance. Hidden away from prying eyes, it was a repository of our hopes and fears, a record of the intricate dance of survival we were all engaged in.

"A record of who we are, what we bring, and who we've left behind." The words hung in the air, heavy with implication. It was a declaration of intent, a vow to weave the individual threads of our stories into a tapestry that would tell the tale of Bixbus. This settlement, this dream that we were all daring to believe in, deserved more than to be a mere footnote in the annals of history. It deserved to be remembered, to be chronicled with the depth and reverence its inception warranted.

The idea solidified within me, as clear and brilliant as a diamond forged under unfathomable pressures. It wasn't just a fleeting thought anymore but a vision pulsating with life—a book, a compendium that would encapsulate the essence of Bixbus, serving as a beacon of resilience and a testament to the indomitable spirit of community. As I gathered the scattered papers before me, my fingers inadvertently caressed the cool, leathery cover of the notebook that lay beneath them. *The Book of Kin*, the name echoed through my mind, resonating with a profound significance. It was a title that perfectly captured the essence of the interconnected lives and destinies that would fill its pages, binding them together in a narrative of shared fate and collective endeavour.

Methodically, I shuffled through the papers, each one a fragment of the larger mosaic I was piecing together. "This settlement is more than just structures and resources," I found myself murmuring, almost absent-mindedly. My voice, a soft timbre in the otherwise silent room, carried with it the weight of realisation. It was a recognition of the fact that the true essence of Bixbus lay not in its physical manifestation but in the people who called it home, their stories, and the rich tapestry they wove together through their daily lives and shared experiences.

Envisioning *The Book of Kin* as a living document, I saw it evolving and growing with each new chapter we added to our collective journey. It would not merely be a record but a vibrant chronicle of life in Bixbus—the joy and the struggle, the triumphs and trials, and most importantly, the intricate web of relationships that formed the backbone of our community. Leafing through the blank pages of the notebook, I imagined the stories that would one day inhabit them—narratives of bravery and cooperation, tales infused with hope and underscored by the unyielding determination to thrive against the odds.

"This will be my legacy," I whispered into the stillness, the words a solemn vow to myself and to the fledgling settlement teetering on the brink of the unknown. It was a promise not just to record our history but to honour it, to ensure that the trials and triumphs of Bixbus and its inhabitants would never be forgotten. In the quietude of that moment, with the promise of *The Book of Kin* taking root in my heart, I felt a profound connection to the settlement and its people—a sense of responsibility and purpose that transcended the immediate concerns of survival and construction.

4338.212

(31 July 2018)

UNLOCKING ADELAIDE

4338.212.1

The dawn chorus had barely begun its symphony when the first rays of the sun began their ascent over the Tasmanian horizon, painting the sky in strokes of pink and orange that seemed to bleed into one another, creating a canvas of natural beauty that heralded the start of a new day. The air was crisp, a sharp reminder of the morning's freshness, and with each breath, I felt a mixture of anticipation and apprehension for the journey ahead.

Navigating through the terminal of Hobart Airport, I found myself enveloped in the bustling hum of early travellers. The place, though small by comparison to the sprawling airports of larger cities, pulsed with the same undercurrent of excitement and tension that airports universally possess. The rhythmic hum of distant plane engines provided a constant backdrop, a soothing yet invigorating soundtrack to the myriad personal stories unfolding within the building.

Approaching the security checkpoint, I clutched my boarding pass—a flimsy testament to the impending voyage. The security officer, adorned in the unmistakable uniform that spoke of authority and scrutiny, met my approach with a gaze that seemed to pierce through the façade of casual travellers, seeking out the anomalies in the routine procession of passengers.

"No baggage today?" His voice was neutral, yet the raised eyebrow spoke volumes of his curiosity. The absence of luggage was a deviation from the norm, a blip on the radar of his trained observation.

I offered a chuckle, a sound that felt somewhat hollow even to my own ears, as I scrambled internally for an excuse that might diffuse the spotlight of his attention. "Travelling light, you know? Just a quick business trip," I replied, injecting a note of nonchalance into my voice. It was a plausible explanation, yet the words felt foreign on my tongue, a clumsy fabrication spun on the spur of the moment.

The officer's gaze didn't waver, and I could sense the skepticism that lingered beneath his professional demeanour. It was a silent challenge, a prompt for further elaboration that I hadn't anticipated.

I continued, the narrative flowing more smoothly now, albeit still tinged with the underlying tension of deceit. "I find it liberating, really. Less to carry, less to worry about." The words were a shield, an attempt to project a confidence I was far from feeling.

"Not even a laptop?" The question came, slicing through my pretence with analytical precision.

A broad smile was my immediate response, a façade meant to mask the rising tide of nervousness that threatened to betray me. "There's plenty of laptops in the office," I countered swiftly, my mind racing to lend credibility to the lie. It was a gamble, hinging on the hope that the officer wouldn't dwell on the practicalities—or the improbabilities—of my statement.

Standing there, under the scrutinising gaze of security, I felt an acute awareness of the delicate balance I was attempting to maintain. Each word, each smile, was a calculated move in an intricate dance of deception. The airport, with its cacophony of sounds and flurry of activity, suddenly seemed like a stage on which I played a role that was not my own, a role that required a performance convincing enough to navigate through the layers of security and scrutiny that stood between me and my objective.

The security officer's nod was slow, a tangible manifestation of his lingering doubts. Yet, with a professional detachment, he gestured towards the security scanner. "Fair enough. This way please, sir," his voice was devoid of suspicion, but the undercurrent of scrutiny was palpable. As I complied, stepping through the scanner, a mix of relief and bemusement churned within me. The absurdity of the situation wasn't lost on me—a Guardian of Clivilius navigating the mundanities of Earth's security protocols. The bile that had risen in my throat was a visceral reaction to the tension, but it also served as a reminder of the precarious tightrope I walked between my two worlds.

Crossing the threshold of the scanner felt like stepping through an invisible barrier, one that separated the commonplace from the realm of secrets and guardianship I was a part of. The twinge of amusement at our exchange didn't fully mask the underlying truth: in Clivilius, the essentials of a Guardian were far removed from the earthly belongings scrutinised by the airport's security.

The terminal beyond was a hive of activity, its atmosphere alive with the electronic melodies of departure boards. The litany of destinations and times created a backdrop of anticipation, a reminder of the many journeys that converged in this space. It was against this backdrop that the call of a nearby cafe barista pierced the cacophony, a siren song promising the comfort of familiarity in the form of coffee—a welcome companion for the journey ahead.

Approaching the counter, the aroma of freshly ground coffee beans was like a balm, easing the lingering tension from the security checkpoint. The barista's grin was a beacon of warmth in the sterile airport environment. "Morning! What can I get for you today?" he asked, his cheerfulness a stark contrast to the clinical efficiency of the officer I'd just encountered.

"Flat white, please," I responded, the simplicity of the order a small anchor to normalcy. As I waited, my gaze drifted, taking in the display of pastries and snacks. Each item was a testament to the myriad tastes and preferences that passed through this terminal, a microcosm of the world's diversity encapsulated within the glass display.

The return of the barista with my order was a prompt to refocus. The exchange of cash for caffeine, a ritual so mundane yet so essential, marked the end of this brief interlude. Clutching the steaming cup, the warmth seeping into my palms, I felt a momentary peace. Gratitude, in that moment, was not just for the barista but for the brief respite the coffee promised from the whirlwind of thoughts and responsibilities that awaited me.

As I took that first, savoured sip, the richness of the flat white served as a reminder of the world's simple pleasures. It was a contrast to the complexities of my existence, a life divided between the ordinary and the extraordinary, where each action, each decision, carried weight beyond the immediate. The coffee, aromatic and comforting, was a brief sanctuary, a momentary pause in the dance between the worlds I inhabited, offering a taste of refreshment before the next step of my journey.

The departure lounge served as a microcosm of the world at large, buzzing with the energy of imminent departures. People from all walks of life gathered, each embarking on a journey of their own, yet momentarily united in this shared space of anticipation. I found solace in the robust brew I cradled, its bitterness grounding me amidst the cacophony of conversations and the sweet anticipation that filled the air.

As I savoured the final sip of my coffee, the announcement for boarding cut through the lounge's hum, a clarion call to all those it concerned. I discarded my empty cup and joined the stream of passengers moving towards the gate. The process was efficient, a well-orchestrated dance of travel logistics that swiftly guided us through the jet bridge and into the aircraft.

Stepping onto the plane, I was immediately enveloped by the unique atmosphere of air travel—a mix of excitement, apprehension, and the faint but omnipresent scent of recycled air. The narrow aisle forced a single-file march, and I navigated through the maze of seats with a practiced ease. Finding my seat by the window, I took a moment to appreciate the view that awaited—the plane, a marvel of human ingenuity, sat poised on the tarmac, its engines a silent promise of the skies we were about to conquer.

As I settled into my seat, fastening my seatbelt with a click that echoed the finality of our departure, I couldn't help but feel a sense of departure within myself as well. The engines began their low, comforting hum, a prelude to the adventure that lay ahead. I watched through the window as the ground crew gave their final signals, a choreographed farewell to those of us leaving the safety of the ground behind.

The plane taxied to the runway, and with each moment, the anticipation built. As we lifted off, the transition was palpable—not just in the physical ascent, but in the mental shift from the known to the unknown. The familiar landscapes of Tasmania receded into the distance, the patchwork of hills and fields, once so detailed and vibrant, became abstract art, a blend of greens and browns blurring into the distance below.

As the plane cruised at high altitude, leaving the terrestrial world behind, I found myself captivated by the view outside my window. The sun-kissed horizon stretched infinitely, a canvas of light and shadow that seemed to encapsulate the vastness of the journey ahead. Below, the clouds formed a soft, unbroken sea, hiding the world below and symbolising the myriad uncertainties that awaited in Adelaide. The Portal

Key, a small but significant weight in my pocket, served as a tangible link to the realms beyond, a constant reminder of my responsibilities and the hidden truths of my existence.

My thoughts drifted to Bixbus, the Book of Kin, and the myriad secrets that lay concealed beneath the mundanity of my wardrobe. The journey to Adelaide was not just a geographical transition but a quest for answers, a step closer to the ambitious goal of integrating my family into the complex tapestry of Clivilius. The path to achieving such a feat was shrouded in mystery, the details of the endeavour still undefined. Yet, in what was becoming a hallmark of my role as a Guardian, I resolved to set aside these concerns for another time. There was a certain liberation in acknowledging that not all answers needed to be sought in the immediacy of the moment.

The flight itself seemed to pass in the blink of an eye, the vastness below giving way to the sprawling urban expanse of Adelaide. The city, familiar in its contours and yet alien in the years that had passed since my last visit, evoked a complex tapestry of emotions. I was returning not just to the city of my childhood but to a landscape that had evolved in my absence. The airport, as we approached, symbolised not just a point of arrival but a threshold between the known and the unknown, a nexus of mundane travels and the clandestine operations that now spurred me into action.

Disembarking into the controlled chaos of the airport, I moved with a sense of purpose that belied my internal tumult. The Portal Key, my secret burden, lay hidden, a testament to the dual life I led. Amidst the throngs of travellers, I found an odd solace in my anonymity, a temporary shield against the complexities of my double existence.

Settling into the hard, unforgiving contours of a plastic airport seat, I allowed my mind to wander through the immediate future. The task of registering a new Portal location in Adelaide Airport loomed large, a challenge that required a delicate balance of discretion and decisiveness. The bustling airport, with its incessant flow of people and noise, seemed an unlikely backdrop for such a significant act. Yet, it was within this cacophony that I sought a moment of stillness, a brief pause to collect my thoughts and prepare for the steps ahead.

❖

The Adelaide Airport, a nexus of departures and arrivals, thrummed with the constant motion of people. Each traveller, encapsulated in their own narrative, added to the vibrant tapestry of stories that crisscrossed through the terminal. My own narrative, however, diverged significantly from the rest, a secret mission that propelled me through the bustling crowds with a singular focus. The Portal Key, a beacon of my dual existence, lay securely against the fabric of my pocket, its presence both comforting and daunting.

Navigating through the airport was akin to moving through a living organism. The polished floors echoed the footsteps of countless others, amplifying my own as I sought out the perfect spot for transition. The airport's vibrant atmosphere, while invigorating, posed a unique challenge: finding a location that melded seamlessly into the background, unnoticed yet pivotal for my clandestine activities.

The janitor's closet, an unassuming nook amidst the bustling feet, caught my attention. It was an unlikely sanctuary, yet it perfectly fit the criteria. The slightly ajar door was an invitation, one that I accepted without hesitation. Stepping inside, the shift in ambiance was immediate. The space, cramped and redolent with the sharp tang of cleaning chemicals, offered a stark contrast to the airport's open, crowded spaces. Here, in this confined solitude, I found a moment's respite from the whirlwind of activity just beyond its walls.

The act of activating the Portal Key was now familiar, yet it never ceased to stir a sense of awe within me. The device, unremarkable to the untrained eye, was a masterpiece of otherworldly technology. As it hummed to life, the sound was a soft whisper against the backdrop of the closet's silence. The air shimmered, the particles dancing as if in anticipation, before coalescing into the vibrant swirl of colours that marked the portal's emergence.

This closet, a place of mundane utility, transformed into a gateway between worlds. The portal, with its compact swirl of colours, clung to the back of the door like a secret window to another realm. For a moment, I marvelled at the juxtaposition—a doorway within a doorway, leading not to brooms and mops, but to the mysteries of Clivilius.

As I prepared to cross the threshold into Clivilius, I heeded the unspoken rule that had become a cornerstone of my travels between worlds: one does not simply enter Clivilius empty-handed. With a sense of purpose, I gathered an armful of cleaning supplies from the closet, an odd assortment of detergents and cloths, and, for good measure, wedged a mop between my legs. It was a comical sight, perhaps, but the significance was not lost on me. These items, mundane in this world, could serve unforeseen purposes in Clivilius. My senses sharpened, attuned to the imminent shift in reality as I stepped into the portal's embrace.

The transition was a familiar rush, a blend of exhilaration and momentary disorientation that never failed to quicken my pulse. Then, just as suddenly as it had begun, the sensation subsided, and I found myself standing in the vast, untamed landscapes of Clivilius. The stark contrast between the cramped janitor's closet and the open expanse of this alien realm was breathtaking. The air here held a different weight, charged with the raw essence of a world unbound by the limitations of Earth.

A surge of adrenaline coursed through me as the realisation set in: I had successfully registered a new Portal location within the very heart of Adelaide Airport. The strategic implications of this act unfurled in my mind like a map, revealing new pathways and opportunities for our endeavours. This discreet entry point, nestled amidst the mundane comings and goings of the airport, was now a gateway to possibilities yet to be explored.

Closing the portal behind me, I was enveloped in a sense of dual accomplishment and secrecy. The airport, with its constant hum of activity, remained blissfully unaware of the extraordinary passage that had briefly opened within its walls. My actions, though small in the grand scheme, felt like silent rebellions against the ordinary, each step a dance in the delicate ballet of shadows and light.

Safely tucking the Portal Key back into my pocket, I re-emerged into the world of the airport, the janitor's closet door closing behind me with a soft click that felt like the sealing of a secret. To any passerby, I was just another traveller, another face in the crowd, but hidden in my pocket was the key to worlds untold.

The closet, now just another door in the endless corridor, held its secret close. To the uninitiated, it was merely a storage space for mops and buckets. But to me, it was a testament to the thin veil that separates the mundane from the magical, a reminder of the hidden depths that lie just beneath the surface of our perceived reality.

A RAID IDEA

4338.212.2

Paul's voice cut through the ambient sounds of the Drop Zone, calling me over with an urgency that piqued my curiosity. Making my way to where he stood, the eager glint in his eyes sent a nervous shudder running across my shoulders. That look in his eyes, a blend of determination and barely contained excitement, was a clear signal. *He wants something*, I instinctively knew it, and whatever it was, it promised to be significant.

"Luke," Paul said, pulling me into a hushed conversation near some stacked boxes overlaid with heaping piles of clothes, a makeshift privacy in the midst of our communal space. "Beatrix and I have come up with a plan, something that could really help us." His tone, low and conspiratorial, immediately drew me in, the promise of a plan sparking a mixture of intrigue and apprehension within me.

Intrigued by the gravity of his introduction, I nodded, my interest clearly piqued, urging him to share the details.

"Tonight, we're hitting a Big W store in Elizabeth," Paul revealed, his voice charged with a conspiratorial excitement that was both infectious and nerve-wracking. "Beatrix registered a Portal location in one of the change room stalls." The very notion, bold and fraught with risk, sent a thrill of adrenaline coursing through me.

"So, Beatrix made it to Adelaide safely, then?" I couldn't help but interrupt, the concern for her safety momentarily overshadowing the audacity of their plan.

"Yeah, she's fine," Paul said, his nonchalance brushing aside my concern with a casual wave of his hand, as if the danger she faced was just another day's work for us.

My eyes narrowed as the reality of Paul's revelation sank in. The plan was audacious, bordering on reckless. Paul would rally the settlers at the Portal, and Beatrix and I were to navigate the Clivilius gateway, embarking on a covert operation to pilfer supplies from the store. The depth of the situation, the sheer boldness of our endeavour, was enough to make my heart race.

"How do we know we won't get caught?" The question sprang from my lips almost involuntarily, the logistics of the operation suddenly pressing heavily on my mind.

"I didn't realise that was a matter you thought much about these days," Paul replied, his smirk cutting through the tension.

My eyes rolled at his jest. "That was such a typical older brother thing to say."

Paul chuckled loudly, his amusement filling the space between us. "That's why you love me so much," he jested, the playfulness in his voice a stark contrast to the seriousness of his plan.

A mix of excitement and apprehension settled over me. "When's the rendezvous?" I found myself asking, my reluctance warring with a readiness to embrace the challenge ahead.

"As soon as night falls," Paul's reply was swift, decisive. "Beatrix will coordinate the Portal activation. We'll be here, waiting." His confidence was reassuring, a beacon in the murky waters of the plan.

"Nightfall?" I couldn't help but challenge. "Isn't this shop open until really late?" The practicalities of our operation, the timing, and the risk involved, suddenly seemed all too real.

Paul paused, the practicalities momentarily catching him off guard. My hands gestured, urging him to think through the details more thoroughly, to consider every angle.

The pressure had its desired effect. "I think they close at ten. We'll gather at the Portal at nightfall, and then when the coast is clear, you and Beatrix strike at midnight," he explained, his strategy now more defined, his confidence restored.

"Midnight!?" The exclamation burst from me, a mix of disbelief and dawning realisation of the scale of our undertaking.

"Yeah," Paul replied, his optimism dimming slightly under the weight of practical concerns. "We can't be too careful, you know."

"Fine," I replied reluctantly, my agreement accompanied by another involuntary eye roll. The simplicity of the word belied the complexity of my emotions — excitement, fear, anticipation.

"Great!" Exclaimed Paul, his enthusiasm undiminished as he slapped my shoulder a little too enthusiastically.

Rubbing my shoulder as I retreated from the Drop Zone, the reality of his plan weighing heavily on me, I couldn't help but mutter under my breath, "This is going to be a very long night."

A BLOSSOMING VISION

4338.212.3

The late morning sun spilled its golden radiance across the bedroom, painting what remained in the room with a warm glow. I found myself seated on the edge of my bed. My laptop perched on my knees, the screen flickering with digital landscapes and information. The metallic taste of anticipation lingered in the air as I pondered the upcoming raid on the colossal Big W store.

In front of me, the safe yawned open, revealing an assortment of personal items—belongings of the Bixbus settlers. In this enclave of my thoughts, I grappled with conflicting emotions about the impending raid. The promise of untold treasures within the store beckoned, but the weight of responsibility tugged at the corners of my consciousness.

The laptop hummed softly, a gateway to both the mundane and the extraordinary. My fingers danced across the keys, navigating the digital realm as I embraced the oddity of my surroundings. The clash between the normalcy of admin work and the extraordinary prospect of plundering a retail giant set the stage for the peculiar drama unfolding.

Lost in the labyrinth of my thoughts, the elusive concept of "The Book of Kin" became a persistent enigma. Its ethereal nature teased my imagination, revealing itself in fragmented glimpses that danced at the periphery of my consciousness. In my quiet moments, the mystery surrounding its form and purpose unfurled like the delicate petals of a flower, inviting me into a realm of perpetual contemplation.

The wardrobe, sentinel-like, guarded its secrets, while the open safe in the floor harboured the tangible artefacts of unconventional pursuits. The laptop whirred softly, a modern-day oracle offering both distraction and revelation.

As my fingers hovered over the keys, I delved into the digital landscape, a place where the answers to my curiosities might reside. The concept of "The Book of Kin" remained elusive, its purpose weaving through the tapestry of my thoughts like a subtle undercurrent. Each glimpse left me yearning for more, a thirst for understanding that seemed both insatiable and tantalising.

In this contemplative space, the dichotomy of my existence unfolded — a Guardian navigating the mundane intricacies of admin work while grappling with the profound mysteries that Clivilius whispered to my soul. The room, a unique canvas of my peculiarities, bore witness to the silent dialogue between duty and destiny, the ordinary and the extraordinary.

Submerged in the digital sea of information, I navigated through the vast expanse of the internet, seeking the elusive knowledge required to establish a new settlement. Each click and keystroke propelled me further into the intricacies and complexities. The hum of the laptop, a constant companion in my solitary pursuits, resonated with the echoes of untold possibilities.

As I traversed the various websites, a serendipitous encounter occurred—an unexpected intersection of my quest for knowledge and the peculiarities of Clivilius. A plant website materialised on the screen, its pages adorned with vibrant images that transcended pixels and reached into the recesses of my memory.

The images triggered a recall of a conversation with Karen, the details etched in my mind like delicate brushstrokes on a canvas. Her recounting of coriander seeds germinating and sprouting within minutes of touching the Clivilius soil beneath the hardened crust layer echoed in my thoughts. The miraculous responsiveness of the flora to the unique properties of the new world sparked a fresh idea, an unexplored avenue to enhance the settlement.

In that moment of revelation, the seeds of a new task took root in my mind, a task that required the assistance of Gladys, my ever-reliable confidante in the realm of administrative feats.

11:37 AM Luke: Check out the following website. Use Paul's credit card details that I gave you before. I need you to order as much as you can. Spend several thousand dollars. Critical.

Realising the gravity of my request, I understood that I was entrusting Gladys with a substantial expenditure. However, the potential benefits for the settlement outweighed the financial concerns that lingered in the back of my mind.

11:39 AM Luke: Deliver it to my parents' address in Adelaide. And forward me the order confirmation and expected delivery date.

The delicate dance between practicality and ambition unfolded in the digital ether, and I awaited Gladys's response, confident in her ability to turn the abstract into the tangible.

11:46AM Gladys: What exactly am I getting?

Gazing at the screen, I mulled over the expansive selection before me. The images of plants, each a vibrant testament to life's diversity, beckoned for attention. I weighed the potential benefits for the settlement, my mind teetering on the precipice of practicality and the allure of botanical wonders.

As the cursor hovered over the virtual inventory, I sensed the weight of responsibility in the task at hand. It wasn't just about acquiring plants; it was about orchestrating a symphony of life within Clivilius. A surge of excitement coursed through me, akin to a conductor poised to guide an orchestra through uncharted melodies.

12:11PM Luke: Anything... everything. Surprise me!

In surrendering to the unknown, I opted for spontaneity. The simplicity of the directive concealed a deeper truth—I craved the unpredictability that mirrored the essence of Clivilius. The settlement, an evolving canvas, awaited the brushstrokes of nature's vibrant hues.

With Gladys as my emissary in this green venture, I relinquished the need for meticulous planning. Instead, I embraced the wonder of a botanical surprise, trusting in the resilience of life to forge its own path within our burgeoning settlement.

12:43PM Luke: I'll send you Adrian's credit card details. He has two of them, so max one out. We may as well use it before the accounts get frozen!

DREAMS AND SHADOWS

4338.212.4

Approaching the Drop Zone, the heart of our makeshift operations, I could already sense the shift in atmosphere. The place, usually buzzing with a certain level of organised chaos, seemed to be under a cloud of tension today. My eyes quickly found Paul, his stance betraying a man wrestling with more than just the logistical nightmares of accumulating inventory.

As he turned to greet me, the weariness painted across his features was unmistakable. "Luke," he greeted, his voice laden with the kind of fatigue that sleep couldn't cure. It was more than physical exhaustion; it was the mental toll of leadership.

Joining him amidst the disarray of supplies, I couldn't help but comment on the visible signs of strain. "This looks like it's taking a toll on you," I observed, my concern genuine. Paul wasn't just my brother; he was a pillar of our little community, and seeing him so beleaguered was disconcerting.

"You have no idea," he confessed, the gesture of running a hand through his hair a telltale sign of his stress. "We've hit a snag. Adrian and Nial... they got into some trouble."

Surprised, I raised an eyebrow. "Trouble? What happened?"

Paul sighed, a heavy burden evident in his eyes. "I caught them smoking weed, right here at the Drop Zone. It turned into a mess. Words were exchanged, and now I'm worried about the cohesion of the group. The last thing we need is internal conflict."

Suppressing the giggle that threatened to surface, I recognised the seriousness of the issue from Paul's perspective. "Weed? Seriously? This is the last thing we need right now," I echoed, offering a veneer of solidarity. Inside, I was churning with a mix of incredulity and frustration. Of all the challenges we faced, a rift over something so mundane seemed both ironic and maddening.

Paul's agreement was tinged with a despondency that was rare for him. "I agree. I never expected that we'd have this problem here. It's like they've thrown a wrench into the gears just when we needed everything to run smoothly."

Paul's unfamiliarity with the more hedonistic aspects of Earth culture was evident in his reaction, a blend of consternation and disbelief that such trivialities could disrupt the delicate equilibrium he was working so hard to establish. My hand found its way to his shoulder, a gesture meant to ground and reassure him. "Look, we can't let this derail us. We've come too far to let internal issues jeopardise the raid. Let me talk to them, see if I can smooth things over."

His response, a silent communication of mixed feelings, underscored the burden of leadership he felt. "Luke, I appreciate that. We need everyone focused, especially with the raid approaching. But if this keeps up, I'm seriously considering calling the whole thing off. The risks might outweigh the benefits."

The mention of calling off the raid struck a chord within me, igniting a flicker of defiance against the notion of retreat. My own past, peppered with experiences with substances that Paul might deem reckless, had taught me the value of diversity, of learning from every corner of life's vast tapestry. Yet, I respected his perspective, understanding the rationale behind his caution.

Paul's sudden exclamation, "That's it! Don't bring any more people here, Luke. Enough is enough!" caught me off guard, a bold declaration that underscored his growing apprehension. It was a line drawn in the sand, a limit to the expansion he was willing to tolerate under the shadow of recent events.

"I'm telling you, Paul, this is the chance we've been waiting for," I countered, my voice a cocktail of eagerness and frustration. The idea of closing our doors, of stifling the potential growth and enrichment that new minds could bring to our community, was anathema to me. "We can't thrive in isolation. Our numbers are so small, and our knowledge only stretches so far. By bringing in others, we can pool our talents, our ideas, and our strength. This is how Clivilius intended it, I know it." My argument was a plea for openness, a reminder of the vision that had guided us thus far.

The tension between us was palpable, a clash of ideologies born from the same desire to protect and nurture our fledgling society. As I stood there, advocating for expansion and diversity, I was acutely aware of the delicate balance we tread, the fine line between growth and disorder. Paul's concerns, while rooted in the immediate challenges posed by Adrian and Nial's indiscretion, touched on broader themes of security, cohesion, and the vision for our future.

"Luke, I'm not denying the potential of new perspectives and fresh hope. But we must also consider the realities of our situation. We're still struggling to establish the basics for our camp, let alone expand our housing and food production. Every new member adds to the strain on our already limited resources. We have to be practical, not just optimistic." His words, steeped in the pragmatism born of hard-won experiences, struck a chord within me. For a fleeting moment, doubt clouded my resolve, the limitations of our predicament tempering my zeal.

Yet, within me, the flame of belief in Clivilius' potential refused to be extinguished. "Paul, I understand your worries,"

I responded, striving to infuse my voice with both empathy and conviction. "But we can't let fear of the unknown hold us back. Clivilius has a way of providing, even in the most challenging circumstances. I've seen it, felt it." My mind cast back to the visions that had visited me in dreams, vivid tapestries woven from the fabric of our collective destiny. "The dream I had, it's a sign that there's a greater purpose guiding us. It's a story of how our community can grow, how we can all thrive." I offered these words not as mere comfort, but as a testament to the faith that had guided me thus far.

Paul's gaze, unwavering and probing, seemed to search my very soul for the conviction behind my words. It was a moment of truth, a crossroads where the path of our future hinged on the power of belief and the strength of our shared vision.

"You've had another dream?" His inquiry, laced with curiosity, broke through the tension, signalling an openness, however tentative, to the possibilities I proposed.

I nodded, a gesture that carried the weight of my hopes and fears. The admission was not made lightly; to share one's dreams is to lay bare one's innermost hopes. "Tell me about it," Paul's command, though simple, felt like an invitation to traverse the boundary between what was and what could be.

Gathering my thoughts, I prepared to recount the dream that had so profoundly affected me, a vision that promised not just survival but flourishing. In sharing this dream, I sought not just to convince Paul of the practicality of expanding our ranks but to rekindle the spark of hope within him.

"In my dream, I found myself standing in the vast, barren expanse of the Clivilius desert. The monochromatic sands stretched endlessly in all directions, and a feeling of desolation enveloped me. It was as if time itself had forgotten this place, a realm of emptiness.

As I stood in the desolate desert, the first tendrils of a magnificent garden began to emerge from the lifeless dust. A single green shoot, fragile and tentative, pushed its way through the arid soil. It was a beacon of hope in this harsh landscape. I watched in awe as it grew taller, its leaves unfurling with vibrant, shimmering colours.

The garden around me seemed to materialise out of nothingness, as if the very essence of creation was at work. Flowers of unimaginable beauty blossomed in an array of shades I couldn't name. Their petals swayed in a melody of their own, whispering secrets to the breeze. It was a revelation of life from the ashes, of awareness dawning amidst the desolation.

As I wandered deeper into this lush garden, I became acutely aware of my surroundings. Every sensation was heightened. The colours were more vivid, and the fragrances more intoxicating. I could feel the coolness of the earth beneath my feet, and the warmth of the sun kissing my skin.

The garden was not a solitary sanctuary. Others stood among the blossoms and foliage, each one lost in their own moments of enchantment. It was a tapestry of connections, where we were all threads, interwoven in a grand design. I felt an overwhelming sense of connection, of shared existence, and the realisation that we depended on one another for our mutual prosperity."

I paused, my eyes searching Paul's face for acceptance.

"Go on," Paul nodded.

"The dream moved on, and I found myself atop a towering peak, the wind playing through my hair. I looked out at the horizon, which stretched infinitely in all directions. It was a panorama of boundless possibilities, a canvas for self-discovery. The world was my oyster, and I was imbued with the profound sense of freedom, understanding that my choices and actions had the power to shape my destiny.

Next, I was transported to a bustling marketplace. Laughter and joy filled the air as people celebrated the bountiful harvest of life. The stalls overflowed with an abundance of goods and services, all designed to satisfy not just physical needs but the deeper cravings of the heart. It was a festival of gratification in all its forms, a testament to the intricate web of human desires and the sheer pleasure of fulfilment."

I suddenly found my pace quickening as the excitement at recounting my dream grew.

"The dream shifted again, and I found myself in a grand library. It was a place where knowledge knew no bounds, where the wisdom of the ages mingled with contemporary insights. I felt like an explorer in this vast ocean of information, my mind a willing vessel to absorb the riches of understanding. I was on a quest for self-actualisation and the pursuit of my full potential."

"Finally-" I paused, a sharp pang pierced my chest, eliciting a painful gasp.

"Luke, are you okay?" Paul asked, reaching to grab me as I stumbled forward.

"Yeah," I replied, forcing myself to regain my composure, and tentatively I continued recounting the dream.

"Finally, the dream led me to a sanctuary that embodied the principle of survival. But this was survival with a higher purpose. It was about the preservation and flourishing of an entire society. I witnessed a community that worked together seamlessly, ensuring the well-being and longevity of their world. Basic needs were met, but more importantly, they had constructed a foundation for a thriving, sustainable society.

As the dream ended, I awoke with a profound sense of enlightenment and purpose. The interplay of these principles, both at the individual and societal level, was the key to creating a harmonious and thriving society. The dream had been a revelation, a glimpse into a world where these principles were not just aspirations but lived realities. It left me with a deep sense of awe and inspiration."

"That's really quite some dream," Paul said, his continued concern for my well-being clear in his tone.

A sudden image, like a bolt of lightning in the dead of night, seared through the canvas of my consciousness—*Detective Karl Jenkins*. The grip of fear tightened its vice around my heart, its tendrils reaching into the very core of my being. Karl's countenance bore the weight of an inscrutable burden. His face, etched with a stoic resolve, became an ominous portrait, triggering a sense of unease that crawled beneath my skin.

The unease deepened into a visceral fear, a primal instinct warning of an unseen menace lurking within the shadows of familiarity. I strained to shake off the feeling, but it clung to me tenaciously, wrapping me in a heavy shroud of darkness that eclipsed the very essence of hope. It was a suffocating void, where the line between reality and nightmare blurred, and the sense that one of our own was lost loomed over my mind like a haunting spectre.

In that chilling moment, the air crackled with an unspoken tragedy, and the weight of a deep sorrow pressed down on me, threatening to pull me into the abyss of uncertainty. Each heartbeat echoed a mournful refrain, painting the canvas of my mind with strokes of fear, darkness, and an irreparable sense of loss.

Paul's eyes, a mirror reflecting the concern etched across his furrowed brow, locked onto mine as if searching for an elusive truth. "Luke, you really don't look so well," the weight of his scrutiny pressed down on me, and for a moment, the line between dream and reality blurred.

"I'm fine," I repeated, my voice a feeble attempt to anchor myself in the present. My gaze, however, wandered into the unfathomable depths of the Clivilius landscape, as if seeking solace in the alien terrain that mirrored the tumult within. A haunting silence lingered, the unspoken acknowledgment that the nightmares now invaded the waking realm, a reality that sent shivers down the spine of my consciousness. "Normally the nightmares only come when I'm asleep," I mumbled.

Paul's sharp inquiry pierced through the stillness, cutting to the core of my unsettled state. "What was that?" he demanded, a note of urgency threading through his words. The shadows of Karl's stoic face continued to dance in the recesses of my mind, and a heavy sigh escaped me as I waved off Paul's concern with a nonchalant gesture.

"Never mind," I muttered, the words carrying the weight of the unspoken and the fear that dared not take form. My hand, trembling imperceptibly, moved in a dismissive wave, attempting to ward off the tendrils of darkness that clung to my consciousness. "I think I just need to sit down for a while," I added, the weight of the unseen burden urging me to retreat from the harsh gaze of reality into the solace of contemplation.

HARVEST OF PLENTY

4338.212.5

The pale glow of bonfires, scattered like beacons in the void, flickered across the Drop Zone. Their light cast eerie shadows, turning the ground beneath my feet into a patchwork of darkness and soft, orange hues. Clivilius, wrapped in the inky cloak of night, felt more isolated than ever, the darkness almost tangible, pressing in from all sides. In my hand, the fire stick felt like a lifeline, its flame a small rebellion against the overwhelming dark.

Paul and I moved through this obsidian expanse, our footsteps shuffling through the dust, oddly loud in the encompassing silence. It was as if the world held its breath, waiting for something momentous to happen. The Portal, our destination and the gateway to what lay beyond, emerged ahead. It stood, an otherworldly silhouette against the void, its presence both awe-inspiring and slightly nerve-wracking. The firelight from our sticks barely made a dent in the surrounding darkness, creating an aura of mystery around it.

Breaking the silence, Paul's voice, tinged with excitement and a hint of the unknown, cut through the night. "Luke, this is going to be epic! Supermarket raid at night, just like old times!"

"Old times?" I repeated, my voice laced with amusement. "What supermarket raids have you participated in before?"

"Well, none," he admitted sheepishly, a grin audible in his voice. "But we've done plenty of other exciting stuff growing up."

I couldn't help but scoff at his undying optimism, yet it was impossible not to be drawn into it, to smile at the animated way he clung to our teenage antics as if they were battle honours. "Remember the time that we poured maple syrup and flour all over the missionaries' car in the middle of the night? From what I heard, not even the car wash could get it off. They were scrubbing it all weekend!" he reminisced, laughter bubbling under the surface of his words.

My smile widened into a grin, the memory a bright spark in the darkness. Yet, beneath the humour and nostalgia, a weight settled in my stomach, a reminder of the gravity of our current endeavour. "Yeah, but remember, Paul, this isn't a game. We need to be quick and careful," I cautioned, my tone sobering. The flickering light of my fire stick painted my face with dancing shadows, reflecting the mix of emotions within.

Undeterred, Paul clapped me on the back, his own fire stick casting wild patterns of light and shadow. "Trust me, it'll be both. Late-night shenanigans, brother! Embrace it!" His confidence was unwavering, a beacon as bright as the bonfires around us.

As we approached the Portal, the air seemed to thrum with energy, anticipation coiling in my gut. The sight of Nial and Adrian waiting for us only heightened the sense of an impending adventure. Their silhouettes, illuminated by their fire sticks, were like guardians of the threshold we were about to cross. My heart raced, not just with the thrill of the raid, but with the understanding of what lay beyond. This was more than a mere escapade; it was a step into the unknown, a challenge we had to face together.

Unexpectedly, Adrian's intense gaze cut through the flickering shadows, fixing me with a stare that felt like a physical force. His eyes, lit by the erratic dance of firelight, bore into me with clarity and urgency. "Luke, take us back home. Now," he demanded, his voice carrying a weight that seemed to push against the very air between us.

Paul seemed to glide over the tension, his cheer undimmed by Adrian's grave tone. "Hey there, fellas! Ready for the midnight adventure?" he chimed, his voice a stark contrast to the seriousness of the moment.

Adrian, unswayed by Paul's attempt at lightening the mood, kept his focus locked on me. "This is not an adventure. Take us back, now!" His words were a command, not a request, and they hung heavy in the night air.

I sighed, a mixture of frustration and resignation settling in. "I've told you, Adrian, you can't go back. It's not possible."

Adrian's frustration boiled over then, his hand gripping my arm with a desperation that was almost frightening. "Activate the damn Portal, Luke!" His voice was edged with a panic that I hadn't heard from him before.

Paul tried to diffuse the escalating tension. "Come on, guys, it's late. Let's all calm down and have a bit of fun. The night is young!" His words, though well-intentioned, felt strangely out of place against the backdrop of our growing dilemma.

Knowing that resistance would only fuel the fire, I reluctantly acquiesced. "Fine." As I initiated the Portal, my voice was a mere mutter, "Go on, step through."

Nial approached the Portal cautiously, his movements hesitant, while Adrian, releasing his grip on me, joined him. What happened next was a predictable reminder of the reality they faced: both were violently thrust back by the Portal's unseen force, a clear rejection of their attempts to defy Clivilius' will.

They stumbled back, wide-eyed and visibly shaken, cowering in the dim light of our fire sticks. As I had anticipated, yet dreaded, Clivilius had made its stance clear. Nial turned to me, his eyes filled with a desperation that was palpable. "I need my family here," he pleaded, his voice cracking with emotion.

A wry smile played on my lips. Clivilius had worked its persuasive magic. "The settlement isn't ready yet," I explained. It was a diplomatic response that I hoped would ignite their commitment to supporting and developing Bixbus. When the time was right, I knew that I wouldn't hesitate to bring Nial and Adrian's families to Clivilius.

Adrian, recovering from his initial shock, found his voice, his next words offering an unexpected proposal. "We'll help you build it." His tone was different now, determined, perhaps a sign of acceptance of our situation.

As the tension lingered in the air, palpable and thick, Paul's infectious enthusiasm seemed to falter for the first time. I met his gaze, and in that moment, we shared an unspoken understanding that this mission, our presence here, was far more than just a late-night escapade. It was a commitment, a challenge we were all bound to, whether we liked it or not.

❖

The night air, thick with anticipation and the distinct scent of adventure, enveloped us as we stood at the brink of something that felt both exhilarating and slightly reckless. Kain's crutches, a constant reminder of the resilience and determination that permeated our small community, tapped out a rhythmic cadence against the barren ground, a sound that seemed to echo in the quiet of the night as he approached. Beside him, Grant and Sarah, the newest faces in our midst, wore their eagerness like a cloak, albeit one lined with the nervous energy of stepping into the unknown. Their arrival felt like a fresh surge of energy, adding to the palpable excitement that buzzed through the air.

"Luke," Kain greeted, his voice steady, a nod accompanying his words. The siblings, standing close to Kain as if drawing strength from his unwavering spirit, had their eyes lit with the spark of unspoken excitement, the kind that comes from being part of something clandestine, something bigger than oneself. Their gaze held mine for a moment, reflecting a myriad of emotions—anticipation, curiosity, perhaps a hint of apprehension at the adventure that lay ahead.

"Grant, Sarah," I responded, offering them a nod in return. My acknowledgement was met with bright, eager eyes, their expressions a mirror to the whirlwind of emotions I sensed swirling within them. It was a look I recognised, one that spoke of the thrill of the unknown, of stepping into a story that was still writing itself.

As our small assembly took shape in the shadowy light, Paul, with his natural inclination for leadership, stepped forward, his presence cutting through the pre-raid tension like a beacon. "Where's Karen and Chris?" His voice carried across to us, his gaze sweeping over the familiar faces gathered, searching for the couple known for their determined spirit, yet noticeably absent tonight.

Kain chuckled, the sound rich and warm in the cool night air, his crutches supporting him as he leaned into the conversation. "Decided to turn in early. Figured the supermarket raid was a job for the younger night owls." His words, light and tinged with humour, brought a ripple of laughter through the group, a shared moment of levity that momentarily lifted the weight of anticipation.

Paul shook his head, a mock expression of disappointment playing across his features. "Well, more spoils for the rest of us." His words, spoken in jest, carried an underlying truth—we were a unit, a makeshift family bound together by circumstance and the shared thrill of the night's endeavour.

As we stood together, the camaraderie among us was palpable, each of us illuminated by the soft, flickering firelight that sent shadows dancing playfully across our faces. This moment of banter, filled with light-hearted jests and laughter, served as a brief respite from the gravity of what lay ahead. Paul's leadership, always with a hint of the unspoken promise of adventure; Kain's easygoing presence, a steadying force amidst our ragtag group; and the newcomers, Grant and Sarah, whose enthusiasm seemed to ripple through the air, all combined to momentarily lift the weight of the impending night from my shoulders. Even Nial and Adrian, caught in the throes of grappling with the surreal reality of the Portal, seemed to find a moment of solace in our shared mirth, exchanging glances that spoke volumes of their silent contemplation of the unknown possibilities that awaited us.

Kain, his crutches a testament to his resilience, surveyed the group with a discerning eye. His next words, laced with humour yet underscored by an unspoken understanding of the risks involved, broke through the transient lightness of our mood. "Alright, I'll keep watch out here. Although I reckon if we're going to face off against shadow panthers, a supermarket's just a walk in the park, isn't it?" His attempt at humour was not lost on us, drawing a collective chuckle from the group. It was a comparison so absurd, yet so fitting for the peculiar situation we found ourselves in, bridging the gap between the extraordinary and the mundane aspects of our mission.

Paul's laughter, tinged with a hint of nervousness, echoed Kain's sentiment. "Just hope they don't have security guards as fierce as those panthers," he jested, his smirk reflecting the underlying tension of our undertaking. The nods of assurance that followed from the rest of us were more than mere agreements; they were silent pledges of solidarity, acknowledgments of the shared risks and the unspoken promise to watch out for one another.

❖

As Beatrix emerged from the Portal, the dim light of the bonfires cast her features in relief, shadows playing across her face, revealing the toll of her unseen efforts. My heart tightened at the sight, concern weaving its way through my words almost involuntarily. "Beatrix, where have you been? We've been waiting for hours." My voice carried the weight of worry, an echo of the collective tension that had built in her absence.

She met my gaze squarely, the light from the fires reflecting in her eyes, revealing a depth of exhaustion that went beyond the physical. "Luke, we don't have time for this now. We need to focus on the raid." Her words, though firm, carried an undercurrent of urgency that belied the calm she projected.

The tension between us tightened, an invisible thread pulling taut. My concern for her well-being, for the unity of our group, pressed against the barrier of her privacy. "We're a team. We should know where each other is."

Beatrix's eyes flashed, a spark of irritation cutting through the fatigue that had dulled them moments before. "Look, I was taking care of something important. Drop it, okay?" Her sharpness, a rare glimpse of vulnerability veiled in defiance, hinted at the weight of whatever task she had undertaken alone.

The air was thick with unspoken questions, the tension palpable, a storm brewing on the horizon of our unity. It was Paul who intervened, his voice a calm in the brewing storm. "Hey, Beatrix, why don't you go check on the Big W store? Make sure everything's clear for our grand raid." His suggestion, tactfully placed, offered a momentary bridge over the chasm that was opening between us.

Her eyes, locking with mine once more, conveyed a silent promise, an acknowledgment of the need to revisit this conversation, to bridge the gap that worry and secrecy had carved between us. "Sure thing. I'll be back shortly." With those words, she turned, disappearing through the Portal once again, leaving behind a trail of questions yet unanswered.

In her wake, a hushed anticipation settled over the group, the vibrant colours of the swirling vortex casting dynamic shadows across our faces, painting us in the hues of uncertainty and excitement. The shadows mirrored the tumult of emotions within us, a dance of anxiety and anticipation for the raid that lay ahead.

The atmosphere was thick with anticipation, every second stretching into what felt like minutes, each minute an hour. The hushed whispers of our small gathering and the occasional crackle of bonfires punctured the heavy silence.

Kain, leaning on his crutches, broke the silence. "Sure is taking her a while. You think everything's okay over there?"

Nial, Adrian, Grant, and Sarah exchanged nervous glances, their excitement tempered by the growing uncertainty. I forced a reassuring smile. "Beatrix knows what she's doing. Let's give her a few more minutes."

Yet, as the minutes ticked by, an invisible weight bore down on us. The flickering light of the bonfires played tricks on our senses, casting elongated shadows that seemed to dance with the nervous energy in the air.

Paul attempted to break the tension. "Maybe she's found a secret stash of chocolate, and she's debating whether to share it with us."

A hesitant chuckle escaped the group, a fleeting moment of relief in the midst of our collective unease. But as the laughter faded, the silence returned, heavy with unspoken questions and the anticipation of what Beatrix would report upon her return.

As Beatrix stepped back into our realm from the swirling hues of the Portal, her silhouette momentarily framed by its vibrant dance of colours, an expectant hush descended upon us. The Portal's luminous display gradually dimmed, resigning us to the subdued, flickering glow of our bonfires. The air around us seemed to hold its breath, thick with anticipation and the faint, smoky scent of burning wood.

The settlers' gazes, including my own, were locked on Beatrix, every pair of eyes reflecting a blend of hope and anxiety sharpened by the extended wait. A wave of relief washed over me, mingling with a keen sense of curiosity as she stepped closer. "Well?" I prompted, my voice betraying my eagerness for her report, for any hint of delay or warning of peril.

Beatrix's eyes met mine across the flickering firelight, and a sly smile, the harbinger of good news, teased the corners of her mouth. "It's clear," she announced, her voice a beacon in the night, slicing through the tension with the promise of success.

The response was instantaneous—a burst of spontaneous cheers from our small band of settlers, a sound so full of joy and relief that it seemed to momentarily fill the barren landscape with life. Each cheer, each shout of jubilation, felt like a personal victory against the challenges we'd faced, a collective defiance against the scarcity that shadowed our existence.

As our group erupted into celebration, my gaze found Beatrix's once more. There was a silent exchange between us, a mutual recognition of the significance of this moment. The raid's success wasn't just about the supplies we'd gain; it was a testament to our resilience, to our ability to carve out a semblance of normalcy in this unforgiving world. The Portal, now subdued yet still pulsating with the potential of untold riches, stood as a testament to the bridge we'd built between our desperate need and the world of consumer plenty lying just on the other side.

Paul's voice cut through the celebration, rallying the settlers. "Well, folks, it looks like we've hit the jackpot. Let's get those trolleys loaded up. Time to bring home the harvest!" His words, infused with excitement, reignited the sense of purpose in everyone, transforming jubilation into action.

The settlers mobilised with a newfound energy, each person assuming their role in what was about to become a meticulously orchestrated raid. It was an unfamiliar dance, yet charged with the thrill of the venture.

The Portal beckoned, its pulsating colours an invitation to a clandestine treasure trove. United Beatrix and I stood, two Guardians against the vastness of the night, ready to venture into the unknown aisles of the Big W store. In the shadows of Clivilius, the promise of abundance swirled, an intoxicating cocktail of triumph and anticipation.

And with that, we stepped through the Portal in turn, leaving the barren landscape behind, plunging into the mysterious world of consumerism.

❖

The sterile lights of Big W flickered as Beatrix and I stepped through the Portal. We were bathed in the soft artificial glow of the department store, surrounded by towering shelves stocked with goods. The distant hum of electronic devices underscored the potential riches at our fingertips.

"This place is massive," Beatrix whispered, eyes wide with awe.

I nodded, caught between a child in a toy store and a thief in the night. An unexpected surge of conflicting emotions bubbled within me. The thrill of acquisition mingled with a tinge of guilt, a reminder of the world we left behind. The sterile surroundings of Big W transformed into a surreal canvas of possibilities.

Beatrix, sensing the ambivalence, placed a hand on my shoulder. "Luke, we're Guardians. This is about ensuring our people have what they need to thrive in Clivilius. It's not theft; it's adaptation."

Her words, though rational, did little to completely assuage the unease. I took a deep breath, pushing aside the lingering doubt. In the grand scheme, our mission was a necessity, an unconventional means to a vital end.

The expansive space seemed both daunting and inviting, and we began to weave through aisles laden with forgotten treasures. Our senses heightened, attuned to the soft rustle of packaging and the occasional creak of settling shelves.

As we moved through the labyrinthine aisles, our arms filled with items, Beatrix's voice cut through the hushed ambiance. "Trolleys. We need trolleys."

Her idea ignited a spark of brilliance. Trolleys would be our silent steeds, carrying the weight of abundance. We sought out the metal chariots, the rhythmic clatter of their wheels accompanying our growing excitement.

With each aisle, the trolleys multiplied, a caravan of liberation. We loaded them with provisions, the metallic echo of packaged goods and boxes resonating like a symphony of plenty. The realisation that we were pioneers in a consumerist frontier brought a grin to my face.

The trolleys, once lifeless sentinels of commerce, now served a clandestine purpose. Their handles, cold and indifferent, became conduits of hope. We filled them to the brim, the contents a testament to our journey—staples, luxuries, and the occasional guilty pleasure.

The procession of trolleys rolled toward the Portal, a silent convoy of plenty. The load required precision, an artful arrangement to maximise both quantity and variety. Beatrix's meticulous planning ensured each cart bore a mosaic of provisions.

As we approached the Portal, the rhythmic clinking of trolley wheels created a mesmerising cadence, a clandestine symphony heralding our return to Clivilius. The night seemed to hold its breath, a conspiratorial silence embracing our audacious venture.

The first trolley breached the Portal's threshold, vanishing into the void with a whisper. The hum of energy intensified, a celestial symphony greeting our plundered spoils. One by one, the trolleys followed, disappearing into the cosmic gateway.

Back in Clivilius, the settlers awaited the fruits of our labour. Beatrix and I emerged from the Portal, faces flushed with triumph. The trolleys materialised, their contents a beacon of abundance amidst the arid landscape.

A collective gasp swept through the settlers as they beheld the spoils. Trolleys laden with sustenance stood as monuments to our audacity, our rebellion against the shadowy claws of scarcity.

Under the soft radiance of Clivilius, Paul assumed a role of leadership, his voice cutting through the night like a beacon.

"Move those trolleys fast, people! We need to sort and relocate them to the Drop Zone. Nial, get your hands on the health supplies first. We've got priorities!"

The settlers, energised by the arrival of abundance, hastened to obey Paul's directives. The Portal-lit tableau became a hive of activity, and amidst the bustling settlers, Paul approached Beatrix and me with an approving nod.

"Fantastic work, Paul. You're turning this place into a thriving settlement, step by step," I told my brother, giving him an encouraging thump on his shoulder.

Beatrix beamed, satisfaction etched across her face. "We've got more than just clothes and essentials. There are household goods, blankets, even some toys for the kids."

For a brief moment, Paul's eyes narrowed, and I cast Beatrix a nervous glance. I knew my brother well enough to know the thought that had sprung to the forefront of his mind - *but we don't have any kids here!*

Thankfully, Paul remained silent, and his eyes sparkled with gratitude. "Every bit counts. You've given us a glimpse of what Clivilius can become."

As the settlers continued their fervent activity and went to collect more spoils, I grabbed Paul's arm and leaned in, my voice a conspiratorial whisper. "Paul, this is just the beginning. We're laying the foundation of a new life here. People are really looking to you as their leader."

Paul nodded in agreement. "I'm doing my best, Luke. For Clivilius."

I clapped Paul on the shoulder. "That's the spirit. Keep this momentum going."

As Paul strode off, his commands echoing through the night, I surveyed the busyness. The glow of accomplishment warmed my heart, a testament to the shared resilience against the encircling shadows. *Bixbus, born from adversity, will thrive under Paul's watchful gaze,* and in that moment, I knew our journey was far from over.

As the night unfolded, the once barren landscape of Clivilius transformed into a realm of plenty. The settlers, faces illuminated by the soft radiance of Portal's colourful vibrance and the constant crackling of strategically-built bonfires, revelled in the spoils of our audacious raid. And in the shadows, we found solace, knowing that for a fleeting moment, we had outwitted the darkness that sought to encroach upon our haven.

4338.213

(1 August 2018)

THE PATRIARCH

4338.213.1

The taxi's abrupt manoeuvre around the sharp corner violently jerked me back to reality, brutally interrupting the fragile peace of my light slumber. With the remnants of sleep barely clinging to me, my mind waded through a fog of exhaustion, a direct aftermath of the night's escapade at Big W. The events had unfurled into the wee hours, leaving me ensnared in a state of mental fog and physical lethargy.

Due to the early hour of the morning, the logistical impossibility of using the Portal location at the Big W store for my entry point to Adelaide had forced me to adapt. The store remained closed, a barrier to the seamless transition I had hoped for, and hence, I wouldn't have been able to leave the store upon arrival. So, I had settled on emerging from the cleaner's cupboard at the Adelaide Airport, a less than ideal but necessary choice. From there, I had decided to catch a taxi, a mundane continuation of a journey that had started in anything but ordinary circumstances.

"Thank you, have a good day," I mumbled, my voice barely more than a whisper as I clumsily disentangled myself from the confines of the back seat. My hand lingered on the door for a moment longer than necessary, the act of closing it behind me felt like sealing off the outside world. As the taxi faded into the distance, its engine's grumble dissolving into the early morning, the air around me felt heavier, laden with a misty drizzle. It caressed my face with cold, wet fingers, a stark contrast to the warmth I longed for but knew I wouldn't find here.

There it stood, the house I once called home. Its familiar silhouette loomed through the veil of drizzle, yet it felt alien, as if the years had erected an invisible barrier that time alone couldn't dismantle. The memories, bitter and jagged, clawed their way to the forefront of my mind, each one a reminder of the turmoil that had driven me away. The taste of those recollections was acrid, coating my tongue with regret and unresolved sentiments.

Shaking my head, I attempted to scatter the gathering storm of emotions, much like one would try to dispel the morning fog with a mere gesture. Drawing a deep, steadying breath, I sought to anchor myself in the present. "Let's do this," I whispered, my own voice a lifeline in the tempest of my thoughts.

"The plan is simple," I muttered, the words a mantra against the rising tide of apprehension as I trudged up the driveway. The concrete beneath my feet felt unyielding, a reflection of the resolve I was desperately trying to muster. "Keep the visit short and simple. Play to the absurdities of their religion, although don't tell them that." The irony of my own intentions wasn't lost on me, a bitter chuckle escaping my lips at the thought.

Standing at the threshold, I paused, allowing myself a moment to compile a mental checklist. It was more than a mere strategy; it was a survival guide for navigating the emotional minefield that lay beyond the door. The plan was to start with Dad, to reveal the Portal's secrets in a way that would bridge not just the physical gap between our worlds, but perhaps, on a more optimistic note, the emotional chasm that had widened over the years.

Yet, as my hand hovered over the doorbell, a silent admonition whispered through my mind. *Don't tell them it's a one-way trip.* The weight of this secret, heavy and ominous, settled on my shoulders. It was a burden I had chosen to bear alone, a testament to the lengths I would go to ensure they journeyed to Clivilius, even as I stood on the precipice of revealing a truth that would forever alter the fabric of our family.

Knocking loudly, the sound echoed like a thunderclap in the still morning air, slicing through the veil of silence that shrouded the house. My heart hammered against my ribcage, a frenetic rhythm that mirrored my escalating nerves. The suspense stretched into an eternity as I stood there, my breath suspended in a tight hold within my chest, the anticipation coiling tighter with each passing second.

Then, the door creaked open, a sliver of the familiar interior peeking through the widening gap. The sight of it, so unchanged, momentarily transported me back in time, blurring the lines between past and present.

"Luke!" The utter shock in my father's voice was palpable, his features contorted in a mix of astonishment and disbelief, as if he'd seen a ghost rather than his estranged son. His jaw slackened, hovering precariously close to the threshold, a physical testament to his stunned state.

"Hi—" I stumbled over my greeting, trying to cloak the whirlwind of emotions under a guise of nonchalance. It felt like walking a tightrope, balancing between the desire to reconnect and the raw edges of past grievances.

"What are you doing here?" Dad's voice broke through my reverie, his question laced with a confusion that mirrored the scattering of my thoughts. His eyes, wide with awe, searched mine for an answer, as if I were a puzzle he couldn't quite solve.

Stay calm, Luke. The internal command was a lifeline, pulling me back from the brink of emotional turmoil. "I know it's been a few years, but that's hardly the warm welcome I was expecting," I replied, my laugh tinged with nervousness. It was a brittle sound, one that barely masked the undercurrent of bitterness that time had failed to erode completely.

"I'm sorry," Dad stammered, a sheepish acknowledgment of his unintended brusqueness. "I just wasn't expecting it to be you at the door."

"Is it Charles?" The sound of my mother's voice, distant yet unmistakable, a distant echo from the hallway, sought clarification.

Dad's response was to swing the door wider, an unspoken gesture of welcome that felt as significant as any formal invitation. "No, it's Luke," he projected back towards the unseen depths of the house.

"Thank you," I murmured as I crossed the threshold, a tangible wave of relief washing over me. Stepping into the house felt like crossing into another world, one where the rules were dictated by religious values and familial bonds—their most sacred space. *Well, apart from the Temple*, that is, I mused, a silent nod to the complex tapestry of belief and tradition that had always loomed large in my family's life. This house, with its familiar corners and shadows, held a sacredness of its own, a sanctity that was both comforting and confining in equal measure.

"Luke!" The sound of Mum's voice, charged with a blend of surprise and joy, cut through the quiet tension like a beacon, illuminating the once familiar passageway. She surged towards me, her arms wrapping around me in an embrace that was both unexpected and overwhelmingly tight. It was a physical manifestation of the myriad emotions we both harboured, a tumultuous mix of relief, love, and the unspoken grievances of years past.

"Where's your brother?" she asked almost immediately, her focus shifting with the rapidity that I had come to expect from her. It was a hallmark of her demeanour, this ability to pivot her attention on a dime, leaving one feeling simultaneously acknowledged and overlooked.

And there it is, I thought to myself, the echo of resignation soft in my mind. The transitory nature of her focus was a familiar dance, one that I had learned to navigate with a blend of patience and detached acceptance.

"Ah," I replied, easing myself out of her embrace with a gentle firmness. The need for space was as much about reclaiming my physical autonomy as it was a metaphor for the emotional distance I sought to maintain. Turning to Dad, I found my voice imbued with a newfound resolve. "I need to talk to you in private," I stated, the weight of my request hanging between us, a silent plea for understanding and discretion.

Mum's response was immediate and loud, her scoff a tangible wave of disapproval that seemed to fill the space. "Anything you need to say to your father, you can say to me too. You know we have no secrets in this family," she declared, her words sharp, a reminder of the unyielding framework within which our family dynamics operated. It was an authoritarian stance, rooted in the belief of transparency, yet often felt more like a mechanism of control.

My eyes rolled involuntarily, a silent testament to the frustration that bubbled beneath the surface. The familiar dance of matriarchal dominance was unfolding once again, a reminder of the dynamics that had, in part, driven me to seek solace away from what was once home.

"Come into the study with me," Dad's voice, unexpectedly firm, cut through the tension. It was a moment of uncharacteristic defiance on his part, a deviation from the norm that caught me by surprise and offered a glimmer of hope that this conversation might unfold differently.

Mum huffed loudly, her displeasure manifesting in the sound of her departure, the soft thud of her ugg boots against the tiles a rhythmic backdrop to her retreat. "So much for a happy return," she muttered, her words laced with a mixture of disappointment and resignation. Her departure, marked by the diminishing sound of her steps, left a lingering echo of discontent in her wake, a discordant soundtrack to the unfolding scene.

The journey from the bustling life of the hallway to the secluded quiet of the study felt like crossing into another world, where the air was thick with anticipation and the history of countless discussions that had preceded this one. As the door clicked shut behind us, sealing off the outside world, the sound seemed to echo a finality, a demarcation of before and after. The familiar space, with its walls lined with bookshelves and the scent of aged paper, suddenly felt like a stage set appropriately for a pivotal scene about to unfold.

"What's going on, Luke?" Dad's voice, tinged with a mixture of concern and confusion, cut through the silence. His dressing gown, a worn and comforting garment, clung to him awkwardly, as if trying to offer protection against the unknown.

Caught in a maelstrom of emotion, I found myself at a crossroads. The echoes of Mum's discontent seemed to bounce off the walls, a ghostly presence that added weight to the already heavy air. The secret I was about to divulge felt like a physical entity, its presence in the room almost suffocating. Yet, beneath the tumult of apprehension, a steady current of resolve urged me forward. It was time to lift the veil on the secret I'd harboured.

"I've had a vision," I confessed, the words slipping out into the tension-filled room. It felt like releasing a breath I didn't know I was holding. The term 'vision' felt archaic yet apt, encapsulating the profound and otherworldly nature of my experiences. It was a bridge between the mystical and the tangible, embodying the dual heritage of our family's legacy and the forward thrust of my own journey.

Dad's reaction was a mix of bewilderment and concern, his brow creasing as if trying to decipher a code from my words. The concept of visions wasn't foreign to us; it was a part of our family lore, a mystical inheritance that had always been more fairy tale than reality. Yet here I was, bringing it into the realm of the tangible, challenging the boundaries between the known and the unknown.

"What was the vision about?" he inquired, his voice steadier now, curiosity piercing through the initial shock.

"The building of a new civilisation," I announced, the words resonating in the space between us. It was more than a statement; it was a declaration of a newfound purpose, a vision that stretched beyond the confines of our reality into the realm of possibility. The excitement that vibrated through me was palpable, a stark contrast to the apprehension that had clouded my thoughts just moments before. I was poised on the edge of revelation, ready to share the blueprint of a future that was already unfolding in Clivilius, a future where the dreams of today were becoming the foundations of tomorrow.

Dad's gasp sliced through the charged atmosphere of the study, a sound that seemed to reverberate off the walls, amplifying the gravity of the moment. "The New Jerusalem," he whispered, the words imbued with a reverence that filled the room, echoing against the backdrop of our family's deeply rooted religious convictions. His eyes, wide with the dawning of realisation, searched mine, seeking confirmation, validation, perhaps even salvation.

"You could call it that," I replied, carefully choosing my words to bridge the vast expanse of our beliefs and hopes. It was a delicate dance, indeed, threading the needle between the tangible and the spiritual, between the visions of a new civilisation I harboured and the prophetic imagery that resonated with him. This interplay of truth and interpretation, a subtle manoeuvring to align our perspectives, felt like navigating a labyrinthine path toward mutual understanding.

The spark of hope that ignited in Dad's eyes was unmistakable, a glimmer of belief rekindled in the face of my revelations. It emboldened me, urging me to press on, to leverage this newfound connection. "I know you believe in miracles," I said, our gazes locking in a moment of profound connection. The history of faith that wove through the fabric of our relationship provided a backdrop to my words, a reminder of the common ground we shared despite the years and differences that lay between us.

Just as Dad seemed poised to share something pivotal, a piece of news from the Temple that hung in the air like a promise, the tide of the conversation took an unexpected turn. My sense of urgency, a pressing need to keep the focus on the revelation I was about to unveil, spurred me to cut in. "I have a miracle to show you," I declared, redirecting the flow of our exchange with a determination that felt foreign yet necessary.

His response, laden with emotion, "You being here is a miracle enough for me," was a balm to the years of distance and silence. It was an acknowledgment of the momentousness of our reunion, yet beneath the surface, it hinted at the layers of complexity, the unsaid words, and the shared history that shaped our relationship.

The swift motions to clear the study for what I was about to reveal seemed to beat in time with my racing heart, each action heavy with the urgency of the moment. As I gripped the edge of the computer desk, a sturdy fixture that had witnessed countless hours of work and contemplation, I felt a surge of resolve. "Help me clear some space," I commanded, my voice more assertive than I intended, as I wrenched the desk from its longstanding position against the wall. It felt symbolic, like I was physically tearing down the walls of secrecy that had long stood between us.

The desk moved with a reluctant scrape, its bulk resisting before giving way to our combined effort. Loose papers, remnants of past projects and forgotten tasks, fluttered to the floor in a chaotic whirlwind, their flight a visual echo of the upheaval I was about to introduce into their lives. It was a mess, yes, but a necessary one, reflecting the internal turmoil that had been brewing long before this moment.

Dad joined in, his movements syncopated with mine as we pushed and pulled at the furniture. The physical strain of the task was mirrored in the strained contours of our relationship, yet as we worked together, a small, almost imperceptible smile found its way to my lips. It was a complex smile, woven from threads of determination, nostalgia, and a faint hope for reconciliation. For a brief spell, as we shared the labour, there was a semblance of unity, a fragile bridge being built over the chasm that had widened between us over the years.

With the space cleared, the wall that had once been obscured by the trappings of everyday life now stood empty, a blank slate awaiting the ultimate revelation. My heart hammered with anticipation as I retrieved the Portal Key from my pocket. This small device, seemingly mundane to the unknowing eye, was the key to unlocking the visions that had haunted and inspired me. Holding it in my hand, I felt the weight of the moment, the precipice on which I stood between the known and the unknown.

Activating the Portal Key, the wall before us transformed, the once mundane surface now alive with an otherworldly display of swirling colours and pulsating energy. The portal, a mesmerising spectacle of light and motion, beckoned to realms beyond, a visible breach between worlds.

As Dad's arms encircled me in an embrace that was both unexpected and overwhelmingly tight, I found myself momentarily breathless, caught off guard by the intensity of his reaction. His grip was fierce, as if by holding me closer, he could somehow anchor the fleeting, magical reality that had unfolded before his eyes. "I always knew you would be the one to lead our family to the New Jerusalem," he whispered, his voice thick with emotion. The fervour in his words was palpable, echoing with a blend of prophecy and pride that I found both bewildering and hopeful.

The concept of the New Jerusalem had always been a fixture in our family's narrative, a symbol of ultimate salvation and redemption. Yet, hearing it invoked in this moment, against the backdrop of the portal's swirling energies, lent it a new weight, a new urgency that I couldn't fully grasp. I hugged him back, my own arms wrapping around him in a gesture that was as much about seeking comfort as it was about offering it. Within me, a whirlpool of emotions churned, love, confusion, and a dawning realisation of the vast chasm that lay between our understandings of destiny.

As we separated, I found myself confronting the widening gap between us, driven by an urgent need to take advantage of the rare opportunity it presented. "Does this mean you'll follow me?" I asked, my voice laced with a hopeful tremor. The anxiety that gnawed at my insides was almost overpowering, a visceral response to the fear of rejection, of misunderstanding.

Dad's answer, when it came, was like a blow, his eyes alight with a fire that spoke of convictions and paths diverging from my own. He spoke of righteousness, of a pilgrimage to Salt Lake City, his words painting a picture of a journey rooted in the physical, starkly contrasting the metaphysical odyssey I had envisioned. This deviation, this vastly different interpretation of our future, left me reeling, trying to reconcile our shared blood with our disparate dreams.

A lump formed in my throat, hard and unyielding, as the full magnitude of our dissonance dawned on me. The anxiety morphed into a tidal wave of realisation, the profound disconnect between father and son laying bare the emotional and ideological rifts that had, perhaps, always been there, simmering beneath the surface. My stomach churned painfully, mirroring the turmoil within, as I stood on the precipice of this new, uncertain divide, grappling with the implications of my bungled attempt to entice him to Clivilius.

As the study door swung open with a jarring squeak, the fragile equilibrium within the room shattered, replaced by the abrupt intrusion of Mum's presence. Her hands were planted firmly on her hips, her posture radiating impatience and a demand for inclusion that could not be ignored. "Are you two done with your secret man's business yet?" she asked, her tone slicing through the tense silence that had settled between Dad and me.

The urgency of the moment, the pressing need to weave a narrative that could encapsulate the profound revelations and the visions of new beginnings, spurred a desperate response from me. "The New Jerusalem is just beyond the Portal of colour," I blurted out, grasping at the threads of their shared faith and the imagery it conjured, hoping it would be enough to bridge the gap between our worlds.

I watched Dad closely as he reached for Mum's hand, a silent plea for unity in the face of the unknown. "Do you love me?" he asked her, his voice carrying the weight of years, of shared dreams and challenges faced together.

Mum's attention, momentarily captivated by the mesmerising display on the wall, shifted back to Dad as she responded with a softness that belied the strength of their connection. "You know I do," she said, her words a testament to the enduring love that had weathered much before this moment.

Dad's next words, "Then we will follow Luke, and he will lead us to the New Jerusalem," felt like a beacon of hope in the tumult of emotions and fears that swirled within me. It was a proclamation of faith, of a willingness to venture into the unknown, guided by the visions that had haunted and inspired me.

The confusion that clouded Mum's face was palpable as she grappled with the implications of this sudden shift in her reality. "But what about Salt Lake City?" she questioned, her voice tinged with uncertainty, seeking clarity amidst the whirlwind of revelations and decisions.

In that moment, I found myself silently pleading with her to see beyond the physicality of the journey, to understand the metaphysical leap they were about to take. *Just touch the colour*, I urged in the silent recesses of my mind, desperate for her to embrace the simplicity and the profound transformation that awaited with just a single touch.

But then, Dad's words about a dream, about being God's elect, buoyed the fragile hope I had harboured. As they, hand in hand, stepped toward the portal, I was struck by the surreal realisation of what was unfolding. Inwardly, I praised the unpredictability of faith and fate, my heart racing as I watched Mum and Dad, united in their decision, walk through the Portal, leaving me grappling with the magnitude of what I had set into motion.

As Jerome's voice, laced with panic and confusion, broke the silence of the aftermath, I felt a resurgence of the urgency that had propelled my actions up to this point. "Mum? Dad?"

he called out, standing in the doorway, his figure a sharp silhouette against the backdrop of the ordinary world that lay beyond the study. The sight of him, so suddenly thrust into the midst of this unfathomable journey, reignited my sense of responsibility.

"Quick, you'd better go after them," I urged, my voice a mix of command and desperation. I reached out to him, physically steering him towards the portal's mesmerising display. The swirling colours seemed to pulse with anticipation, a visual echo of the heartbeat of my parent's leap of faith. Jerome's look of bewilderment, his eyes wide with the shock of what he had witnessed, met mine. It was a silent exchange, a momentary connection filled with unanswered questions and unspoken fears. Then, with an almost imperceptible nod, he stepped forward and vanished into the vibrant maelstrom, leaving me in the sudden, profound silence of his absence.

Alone I stood there, the weight of the moment settling around me. The portal's colours danced with wild, untamed energy, sparking and colliding in a display that was at once beautiful and chaotic. It was a visual metaphor for the tumultuous journey my family had now embarked upon, a journey into Clivilius driven by faith, hope, and a quest for a New Jerusalem of our own making.

A scoff, unbidden but not entirely unwelcome, broke free from my lips. "Mormons, impulsive and non-questioning buggers when they think they're following the promptings of the Spirit," I remarked, a wry smile tugging at the corners of my mouth.

NOSTALGIA

4338.213.2

As I approached the trio of the latest Smith family members to step through the portal, the mix of emotions swirling within me was difficult to untangle. The sight of Paul among them sparked a twinge of relief that he was here, safe and sound—a beacon of familiarity. The thought, *Oh good, Paul is here,* flitted through my mind almost whimsically, a brief respite from the weight of what had just occurred.

Interrupting their animated conversation, my voice carried a sharper edge than intended, "Where's Charles?" The urgency behind my question sliced through the air. Their synchronised response, "Seminary!" rang out in perfect harmony, a testament to the ingrained routines and shared experiences that bound them. Despite the seriousness of the moment, their collective turn and the sing-song delivery of their answer coaxed a brief, involuntary smile from me— *some things never do change.*

However, any semblance of amusement was quickly overshadowed by Mum's reaction. Her scowl was a dark cloud on the horizon, and her voice, sharp as a whip, "Luke! What have you done!?" The accusatory note in her screech, laden with fear and confusion, was a jarring reminder of the finality of my actions.

My response, a nonchalant shrug paired with a light-hearted, "I did what was necessary," was an attempt to diffuse the situation, to offer some semblance of control or justification for the upheaval I had caused. But even as the words left my lips, I knew they did little to address the underlying tumult of emotions and questions.

Paul's incredulous reaction to our parents' attire—a mix of disbelief and concern—brought a moment of comic relief to the surreal situation. "You didn't think it was necessary to let them change from their pyjamas first?" he asked, his eyes wide with disbelief.

Observing Mum and Dad, standing there in the unfamiliar landscape of the Clivilian dust, dressed in nothing but their nightwear, was an absurd sight. Dad, clutching his dressing gown as if it were a lifeline, and Mum, her pink flannelette pyjamas adorned with happy Jesus faces, seemed out of place and time.

"It didn't really cross my mind, to be honest," I admitted, my grin widening despite the seriousness of Paul's question. The humour in the situation was undeniable, a bizarre juxtaposition against the backdrop of their extraordinary journey.

Dad's question, tinged with a mix of hope and uncertainty, "And where's the New Jerusalem?" echoed the longing and faith that had propelled him here. His unwavering belief in the promise of a new beginning, even in the face of such disorientation, was both heartening and daunting.

As Paul shot me a disapproving look, a silent reprimand for my cavalier attitude, I couldn't help but respond with a nonchalance that belied the complexity of the situation. Gesturing towards the horizon with a casual wave, I offered, "It's just over the hill." The simplicity of my response, the promise of discovery just beyond their reach, was a leap of faith in itself—a belief in the possibility of finding their New Jerusalem, whatever and wherever that might be.

Paul's reaction was a perfect storm of incredulity and exasperation, his body language screaming disbelief as his hands flew up in a gesture that could only be described as bewildered surrender. The expression on his face, a rich tapestry of confusion and annoyance, spoke volumes more than words ever could. Each furrow on his forehead, each tightening of his jaw muscles, was a silent testament to the chaos I had seemingly thrust upon him.

"Paul will take you there," I announced, directing my words towards the trio who stood a mix of bewildered and expectant, casting Paul in a role he was clearly unprepared to accept. The simplicity of the statement belied the complexity of the situation, a fact made immediately evident by Paul's vehement reaction.

"What!?" The word burst from Paul like a dam breaking, his disbelief splashing across the conversation and soaking us all in its intensity. His posture, previously one of reluctant acceptance, now radiated a defiance that caught me slightly off guard.

As frustration with Paul bubbled to the surface, my patience began to wear thin, my expression mirroring his as my brow furrowed in irritation. "I don't know why you're getting in such a huff. I told you I would bring them here," I retorted, aiming to cut off any further protests. The words, though true, felt hollow, an inadequate explanation for the whirlwind of events that had unfolded.

Paul's attempt to articulate his thoughts, the laptop clutched in his hands as if it were a lifeline, was abruptly interrupted. "Yeah, but I thought-" he started, the confusion palpable in his voice, his stance one of a man desperately seeking solid ground amidst shifting sands.

"Oh, plans changed," I interjected smoothly, a calm façade masking the underlying tension. "Dad wanted to go to the New Jerusalem instead," I added, my tone laced with a mocking sarcasm that I couldn't quite suppress. The sardonic edge to my words was a defence mechanism, a way to navigate the surreal reality of our situation while also acknowledging the absurdity of it all.

"What is she doing?" Jerome asked, drawing our gazes to the distant figure of a woman navigating the Clivilian dust with a shopping trolley. It was a surreal sight, one that momentarily distracted us from the underlying tensions that simmered beneath the surface of our makeshift gathering.

"Hey, Karen!" My voice broke the silence, carrying across the barren landscape with a mixture of hope and eagerness. The opportunity to shift the focus from our familial discord to something, or rather someone, external was a welcome one.

Karen paused, her posture betraying a moment of hesitation before she turned to face us. The distance did little to mask the evident fatigue that seemed to weigh her down, her shoulders drooping ever so slightly—a testament to the burdens she carried. "I'm busy, Luke!" Her response, though laced with a thread of irritation, couldn't dampen my resolve.

Undeterred, I pressed on, my determination piercing the dusty silence between us. "It'll only take a few minutes!" I insisted, hoping to convince her of the urgency and brief nature of our interruption.

With a sigh that seemed to carry her resignation across the expanse, Karen capitulated, abandoning her trolley to approach us. Her stride, though reluctant, bridged the gap with a sense of inevitability. "Karen, meet my parents, Noah and Greta. And this is my younger brother, Jerome," I introduced them, eager to forge a connection, however brief, between my family and this woman who had unwittingly become part of their narrative.

Mum's response was immediate and effusive, her arms enveloping Karen in an embrace that was as surprising to our guest as it was characteristic of Mum's unguarded warmth. "Lovely to meet you, Karen," she declared, the enthusiasm in her voice wrapping around Karen like the hug she bestowed upon her.

Karen's reaction was one of polite restraint, her hands remaining at her sides as she navigated the unexpected display of affection. Her eyes, sharp and calculating, found mine, silently conveying a mix of amusement and plea for rescue. The silent exchange, laden with unspoken understanding, brought a chuckle to my lips.

Observing Dad adjust his dressing gown in the background provided a moment of comic relief, a reminder of the absurdity of our current predicament. It was these small, human moments that grounded me, a counterbalance to the weight of the unknown that lay ahead.

"I suppose I'd better get you some clothes to change into," I mused aloud, finally acknowledging the practical needs that had been overlooked in the rush of our departure.

Jerome's question, voiced with a mix of longing and confusion as he edged closer to the portal's mesmerising display, struck a chord within me. His innocence, juxtaposed with the gravity of our situation, underscored the surreal nature of our predicament. "Can't we just go home?"

"Well," said Karen, seizing the moment as her exit cue, and gently extricating herself from Mum's enthusiastic embrace. "I guess that's my cue to keep moving. These garden supplies won't move themselves," she said, gesturing towards the trolleys near the Drop Zone.

As Karen made her departure, Paul redirected the focus to Jerome's question, a gentle reminder of the immediate challenges ahead. "It's not quite that simple," he offered, his arm around Jerome in a gesture of support and guidance. "How about I explain it on our way to camp?" he suggested.

"Great idea, Paul," I agreed, encouragingly motioning for Mum and Dad to follow them.

"And Luke," Paul said, pausing mid-step to address me. "Bring their clothes to camp, would you? Don't leave them at the Drop Zone this time."

I nodded in agreement, "Of course." Although not particularly thrilled about lugging extra items to camp, I acknowledged that it was the least I could do for bringing them into this barren world with only their pyjamas.

"Although we are born with less," I muttered to myself with a bemused grin. I brought the Portal's colours to life and returned to the home of my childhood, the familiar surroundings carrying the weight of memories and new responsibilities.

❖

The task of finding two suitable suitcases in the house morphed into an impromptu odyssey through the labyrinth of my past. Each corner turned, every closet opened, seemed to pulse with the residue of bygone days, as if the very walls were imbued with the essence of my family's history. This was more than a mere search; it was a pilgrimage through the sacred halls of my childhood, each room a shrine to different chapters of our collective story.

As I sifted through the rooms, stumbling upon old board games and faded photographs, memories cascaded through my mind with the vividness of a waking dream. I could almost hear the laughter and playful arguments that accompanied our family pizza and game nights, the air rich with the scent of tomato sauce and melted cheese. These were the moments when happiness felt as tangible as the dough we kneaded with our own hands, a blissful simplicity that now seemed as distant as the stars.

A chuckle escaped me as I unearthed an old pair of bright yellow socks, a relic from the days of our indoor sliding escapades. Paul's antics, his laughter echoing down the hallway as he glided with reckless abandon, came flooding back. The memory was bittersweet, tainted by the aftermath of Lisa's accident. The imposed ban on our slippery pursuits, while a necessary measure, had felt like the end of an era, a stark reminder of the delicate balance between joy and the potential for sorrow that underpinned our lives.

However, not all recollections were swathed in the soft glow of nostalgia. The darker undercurrents of my youth, the nightmares that once seemed as real as the daylight, also made their presence felt. The shadowy figure that haunted my dreams stood as a metaphor for the fears I faced, both real and imagined. More tangible, though, was the memory of the turmoil that had engulfed my final year at home. The struggle to reconcile my personal beliefs with the doctrines of our faith had driven a wedge between me and my family, a chasm deepened by Mum's silence in those last, tense weeks.

That silence had been a heavy cloak, smothering and impenetrable, marking my departure with a solemnity that had remained unchallenged until now. The weight of those days, the unsaid words, and the unresolved tensions, lingered in the air, a silent testament to the journey I had embarked upon since. As I continued my search for the suitcases, the task at hand felt imbued with a greater purpose, each step a tentative bridge over the gulf of years and silence, a chance to reconcile the past with the hope of a new beginning.

Extracting two suitcases from the shadowy recesses of the food storage room cupboard felt like unearthing relics from a bygone era. Dust motes danced in the sliver of light that invaded their long-standing sanctuary, swirling around me as I disturbed their rest. Coughing, I waved away the cloud of particles that had settled on these objects of transit. Dragging the suitcases behind me, their wheels stuttering against the threshold, I felt a poignant mix of nostalgia and reluctance with each step.

Placing them upon the expanse of my parents' king-sized bed, I approached the task of unzipping each case with a reverence usually reserved for rituals of significant personal meaning. The sound of the zippers parting the fabric was almost ceremonial, echoing softly in the room filled with shadows and memories.

The discovery of daddy-long-legs spiders scuttling away from the light, seeking refuge in the corners of the suitcases, grounded the moment in an everyday reality. Yet, even this small, mundane occurrence seemed laced with symbolism, a reminder of the normalcy that life outside this task continued to hold.

Filling the suitcases, each garment and personal item selected became a piece of the mosaic that comprised my family's history. The act of packing socks, mundane in its nature, became laden with meaning as my gaze inadvertently drifted to the dresser drawer I had been consciously avoiding. The hesitation that gripped me was palpable, a tangible expression of the internal debate that raged within. The unspoken question lingered—*should I pack them?*

Voicing my thoughts aloud, I wrestled with the decision. "They don't really need them in Clivilius," I mused, attempting to rationalise my reluctance. The counterargument, that these items might offer a semblance of familiarity, at least initially, felt equally valid. It was a moment of indecision, where logic and emotion collided.

Opening the drawer and adding the sacred underclothes to the suitcase felt like capitulating to a part of myself I had long since battled and subdued. The act was swift, almost automatic, but the flood of memories it unleashed was neither. Memories of rejection, of the pain that came from stepping away from the church and the life I had known, washed over me with a bitterness that was hard to swallow.

The sharpness of my own declaration cut through the haze of reminiscence. "No," I stated, a surge of clarity and resolve propelling my actions. The garments were returned to their drawer, a symbolic rejection of the past and its hold over me and, by extension, my family. As I closed the drawer, the finality of the gesture was not just a physical act but an emotional closure.

"Clivilius is a new world, a world without their god. They'll need to grow up and adapt, just as I had to," I affirmed, my voice carrying a mix of defiance and determination. It was a declaration of independence, not just from the tangible symbols of a faith left behind but from the weight of expectations and the legacy of conformity. In that moment, packing the suitcases became more than a mere preparation for a journey; it was a rite of passage into a future unencumbered by the shadows of the past.

The act of dragging each heavy suitcase from the room felt like a physical manifestation of the emotional baggage I was attempting to leave behind. Yet, as I stood in the bedroom doorway, I was met with a new, unexpected confrontation. The scent of freshly washed clothes wafted towards me, carrying with it a flood of memories so potent, so intimately tied to a past I had struggled to distance myself from. It was a distinct aroma, one that time had been powerless to dilute or erase, etched deeply within the recesses of my memory.

Reflecting on those earlier years, I couldn't help but acknowledge the innocence that once permeated my existence. At ten, innocence wasn't just a trait; it was my reality, a shield against the complexities and contradictions that would later seep into my life. The peculiar practices of my youth, once sporadic moments of curiosity and exploration, had gradually morphed into sources of deep internal conflict as I grew. What had felt natural and right became entangled with the stringent teachings that had been rigorously ingrained in me, creating a chasm between my inner experiences and the outer doctrines I was expected to adhere to.

With each step towards the dresser, I endeavoured to push those burgeoning memories to the back of my mind. "Now isn't the time for such indulgence," I chastised myself, attempting to erect a mental barrier against the onslaught of reminiscence. Yet, my efforts proved futile, as the concept of the "one true way" haunted my thoughts, a reminder of the only method I had known to navigate the complex web of emotions and beliefs that had ensnared me.

The question of whether he still possessed any of those forbidden items tugged at me with an irresistible allure, pulling me towards the dresser with a force that felt beyond my control. Resistance, it seemed, had crumbled beneath the weight of curiosity and unresolved feelings.

Kneeling before the drawer, the physical reaction of my body was undeniable. My heart raced, a testament to the anticipation and trepidation that coursed through me, sending warmth spreading through my limbs. My fingertips grazed the wooden knob, the anticipation of uncovering what lay within sending a shiver of excitement mixed with apprehension down my spine.

"This is ridiculous," I found myself muttering, a laughable attempt to dismiss the intensity of the moment. Standing up, I was acutely aware of my body's response to the mere thought of crossing a boundary I had long since erected between my past and present. The realisation of my reaction, the physical embodiment of a myriad of forbidden thoughts and desires, left me standing in a moment of profound reflection, questioning the very nature of the barriers we construct and the secrets we keep hidden, even from ourselves.

The impulse that drove me back to my knees was as unexpected as it was compelling. With a swift motion, I yanked the drawer open once more, my actions fuelled by a mix of desperation and hope. The white garments I had previously dismissed lay forgotten as my hands delved deeper, searching through the fabric sea for something—something quite specific—that might offer the solace or connection I was so desperately seeking. Yet, as my fingers grazed the familiar textures, none of the items within provided the refuge I yearned for, leaving a faint shadow of disappointment to cloud my resolve.

"It's probably just as well," I found myself whispering into the quiet of the room, a self-soothing mantra meant to temper the rising tide of unmet expectations. With a sigh, I closed the drawer, the finality of the gesture marking the end of my search.

With no small amount of sexual energy now pulsing through my veins, I rubbed my hand across my bulging jeans. "It's such a shame," I softly told my dick, closing my eyes as I released a soft moan of anticipated pleasure that I feared would never again be actualised.

Standing up, I was momentarily caught in the web of contemplation regarding my next steps. The pressing matter of Charles's return from school loomed large in my thoughts. The idea of him coming home to an empty house, the absence of our parents a silent, gaping chasm, sent an involuntary shiver coursing through me. The potential for misunderstanding, for fear, or even the bureaucratic nightmare of another missing persons report, was a scenario I was keen to avoid at all costs. "Not now," I admonished myself, attempting to quell the rising anxiety with a dose of pragmatism. Yet, a part of me couldn't help but wonder, with a hint of dark humour, if Charles might find some solace in the unexpected solitude, a brief respite from the drama of family life.

It was then that a sudden spark of memory illuminated a previously overlooked possibility. "The second set of drawers!" The words burst from me with the force of revelation, echoing off the walls of the now silent house. I remembered the drawers in the built-in robes, a place where Dad stored his oldest clothes. These were ones that had long since ceased to fit, yet he clung to them with a sentimentality that had always baffled me. Perhaps, within those drawers, lay the piece of the past I was unconsciously seeking—a tangible link to the emotions and memories that had propelled me to leave home.

As I approached the wardrobe, a palpable sense of anticipation coursed through me, a sharp contrast to the tumult of emotions I had experienced moments before. The act of sliding open the mirrored door felt like an invitation to a hidden world, one that held the potential for revelation or disappointment.

My heart raced, beating a frenetic rhythm against my chest as I reached for the drawer, a silent prayer whispered to the void for something, anything, that might connect me to a simpler time. The drawer creaked open, revealing its contents like a time capsule of my father's fashion missteps. Familiar grey trackpants and garishly striped polo shirts lay in wait, relics of a bygone era. "I can't believe he still has these," I muttered, my voice tinged with disbelief and a hint of disdain, as I held up a particularly egregious t-shirt, its ugliness transcending time.

Yet, even as I voiced my distaste, a part of me dared to hope for more, to believe that this search could yield something truly meaningful. My actions became more frantic, a frenzied discard of each unwanted piece, as if the very act of searching could summon the item I so desperately sought. And then, my fingers encountered something different—an anomaly amidst the mundane—a touch of silk that sent a jolt of recognition through me.

"The onesie," I whispered to myself, a mixture of awe and incredulity in my voice as I unfolded the garment. It was more than just fabric; it was a vestige of innocence, a remnant of a past self untouched by the complexities and disappointments of adult life. The sensation of saliva pooling in my mouth was reflexive, a physical response to the anticipation and longing that the onesie evoked.

Compelled by a ritualistic reverence, I quickly shed my current attire, each movement deliberate, an unspoken homage to the transformation I was about to undergo. Slipping into the onesie felt like stepping into a new yet familiar skin, a seamless fusion of past and present. My hands traced the contours of my body, the silk clinging to my flesh, amplifying every sensation. The act of lying down on the bed, the fabric tightening around me, was not just a physical experience but an emotional journey—a reconnection with a part of myself that I thought lost to time.

Closing my eyes, I surrendered to the moment, my breath finding a deep, rhythmic cadence that seemed to resonate with the silence of the room. My hands moved with a gentleness born of reverence, tracing the lines and contours of my form encased in the silk garment. Each touch, each caress, was a deliberate act, a silent homage to moments of pure, unadulterated joy that had become all too rare in the complexities of adulthood.

The exposed head of my penis rubbed against the silken material, the sensation sending my brain intense pulses of satisfaction, which merely encouraged a stronger physical response. It was an endless cycle that aptly reflected the situation I found myself - a sensitive adult now returning full-circle to the sensual innocence of childhood.

Unlike earlier times where, to maintain my sacred secrets, I had to take care where and how I culminated, this time, thanks to the miracle of my parents in Clivilius, such restrictions did not exist. Nor did I care. Now, I was free to explore, to experience without the weight of judgment or expectation. My breathing deepened, a natural response to the increasing intensity of my experience, my hands moving with a purpose that was both personal and profound.

As I neared a state of complete immersion in the sensation, the silk garment became more than just a piece of clothing; it was a cocoon, a protective barrier that held me safe within its embrace. The fine material, now damp with sweat and the first emergences of my life-force, seemed to fuse with me, an extension of myself that offered both comfort and exhilaration.

In that moment of absolute surrender, for the first time in my life, I ejaculated my seed beneath the pure whiteness that enveloped me like a shield. The world beyond the confines of the garment, the room, even Clivilius itself, ceased to exist. There was only the here and now, the purity of experience that carried me to the edge of consciousness.

The garment clung to me as though we were one entity, the resulting combination of sweat and semen. And then, with a final, deep breath, I allowed the waves of intoxicating pleasure to wash over me, leading me into a state of restful slumber, a blissful escape from the complexities of the world.

❖

Waking with a startle, it took me a few moments to remember where I was - laying practically naked on my parents bed, and growing rapidly cold.

Unable to control the lingering urge, my cool hand moved across my dick, and massaged it firmly into the soaked, silky garment. As arousal began to manifest itself again, my breathing deepened momentarily before being interrupted by a heavy sigh.

"Duty awaits," I murmured, rolling myself from the bed. The sensual feel of the silky white sent shudders down my spine as I removed the initiated garment, and without much thought, left it in a scrunched heap on the bed. *They're all in Clivilius anyway, I reasoned with myself as I began to dress into my own clothing. It's not like I run the risk of anybody finding them. Even if months from now, somebody happened to stumble across them, they'd have no clue nor reason to believe that it was covered in my spunk.*

Once more fully clothed and standing in the doorway of my parents bedroom, I cast a glance back at the object of my childhood's fantastical infatuation. *Besides,* I told myself with a wide grin and a teasing pleasurable moan, *I may need to return for a reprisal.*

❖

With the suitcases now meticulously prepared and stationed in the study, a testament to the imminent journey ahead, I turned my attention to the solitary bag that had been momentarily cast aside during my earlier indulgence in nostalgia and personal reflection. The task at hand was clear, a straightforward collection of items for Jerome, yet it held a weight of responsibility that I couldn't ignore.

As I emptied Jerome's schoolbag onto his bed, the contents sprawling in a disorganised array, I couldn't help but overlook the mound of what appeared to be dirty laundry accumulating on the floor. My actions were swift, lacking the meticulous care one might expect, as I selected the basic necessities and shoved them into the backpack. The precision of the packing seemed inconsequential in the grand scheme of things; after all, the entirety of the household would eventually make the transition to Clivilius. The exception, of course, was Dad's drawer of old clothes, a thought that brought a fleeting, cheeky smirk to my lips, a private joke shared with no one but myself.

With Jerome's backpack now secured and resting heavily upon my shoulders, a testament to the physical and metaphorical load I carried, I returned to the study. There, before the grandeur of the Portal, I stood—a lone figure caught between two worlds, a suitcase clutched in each hand. As I stepped forward, a sense of déjà vu enveloped me, a reminder of the previous occasions I had undertaken this very task for Paul and Jamie. The familiarity of the action, juxtaposed with the strangeness of its context, sent an involuntary shiver coursing through me, a physical manifestation of the internal conflict I faced.

The contemplation of how many more times this ritual would be repeated lingered in my mind, a haunting question that seemed to echo in the silence that surrounded me. *How many more lives would I disrupt, only to reestablish them within the unfamiliar confines of Clivilius?* The magnitude of the undertaking was not lost on me, yet it was a path I had chosen, a path I believed in.

With a shrug that belied the depth of my thoughts, I reconciled myself to the uncertainty of the future. "Who knows, but it'll all be worth it in the end," I concluded, a whisper of resolve amidst the cacophony of doubts.

❖

The journey through the Clivilius dust felt like an odyssey, each step laden with the physical weight of my family's belongings and the metaphysical weight of our collective hopes and apprehensions about this new chapter.

Paul's impatient inquiry, sharp and piercing in the stillness of our new world, jarred me from my contemplative reverie. "What's taken you so long!?" His words, laced with urgency, served as a reminder of the practical realities we faced. "We've been waiting ages for you!"

"Sorry," I offered quietly, my gaze anchored to the dust beneath my feet, half-searching for an excuse, half-pondering the enormity of the step I had taken. Despite the tension, a mischievous smirk found its way to my lips, a private revolt against the seriousness of the moment.

My attention was abruptly drawn to Mum, her appearance sparking curiosity and concern. "Who's clothes-" The question hung in the air, unfinished, as Karen's voice interjected with a practicality that was both welcome and surprising.

"I've lent her some of mine, since you were taking so long," Karen's voice, emanating from somewhere behind me, carried a mix of reproach and helpfulness. Her intervention, stepping in where I had faltered, was a testament to her character.

"Thanks, Karen. That's very kind of you," I responded, striving for a tone of gratitude amidst the whirlwind of emotions. My voice, however, betrayed the effort it took to maintain composure under the circumstances.

Karen's stern retort hinted at an underlying tension I hadn't anticipated. "I'm not sure that your mother agrees that it was a suitable compromise," she observed, her seriousness a stark counterpoint to my internal amusement.

The thought of Karen and Mum, two distinctly strong personalities, navigating this unexpected situation was both amusing and slightly alarming. Suppressing the urge to laugh, I couldn't help but consider the dynamics at play. Karen's blunt candour seemed destined to clash with Mum's sensibilities. The idea of them forming an alliance, however temporary, was fascinating. Karen's straightforwardness, a trait I admired, was likely to ruffle Mum's feathers.

Paul's words sliced through the air, redirecting our collective focus towards the practical matters at hand. The suitcases, momentarily forgotten in the wake of our interactions, were swiftly reclaimed and redistributed under his watchful eye. "We're expecting the first of the sheds to be completed today, so why don't you bring us some of the food storage at home?" His directive, while simple, stirred a mixture of emotions within me. The thought of contributing something tangible to our new community in Clivilius brought a fleeting sense of purpose, a momentary reprieve from the complexities of our familial dynamics.

"Food storage?" Karen's inquiry into one of our family's many religious practices caught me off guard, her curiosity piercing the bubble of familiarity that surrounded our family's preparations.

Mum, basking in pride, responded, "Our church leaders have always taught the diligent Saints to have twelve months of food storage." The way her gaze softened as she looked at Dad, her voice a mixture of pride and reverence, spoke volumes about the shared values that had guided their decisions. "It's always been Noah's pride and joy. We've been ever so obedient."

Karen's skepticism lingered, contrasting with Jerome's matter-of-fact confirmation. "She's not lying. There's literally an entire room dedicated just to food storage."

Dad, ever the patriarch, took evident pride in detailing the contents of their storeroom. "Tins of vegetables, pasta varieties of almost every kind, containers of flour and sugar, and-" His listing of their supplies, a testament to years of careful planning and provision, was interrupted by Karen's interjection.

"Well, it looks as though that obedience of yours is about to actually pay off," she said, her skepticism giving way to a grudging acknowledgment of the value of their preparations. Her glance towards me, accompanied by a sideways smirk, sparked an involuntary chuckle. The interaction, though brief, highlighted the unique dynamic at play – Karen's candidness, juxtaposed with my family's steadfast adherence to their beliefs, promised to add an intriguing layer to our shared experience in Clivilius.

Paul's initiative to pivot our attention to the more immediate, tangible tasks at hand was a welcome shift. "Karen's been busy emptying a lot of shopping trolleys from last night's shopping raid. Could you take them back to Earth and fill them with the food stuff?"

"Yeah," I found myself responding, a spark of enthusiasm igniting within me at the thought of such a straightforward, actionable plan. "That should work."

"Jerome and I will collect the empty trolleys and bring them to the Portal for you," Karen offered.

Jerome's loud sigh echoed his reluctance.

"Go and make yourself useful," Mum commanded, her directive leaving no room for argument. The efficiency of her dismissal, while not unexpected, was a reminder of the roles she expected each of us to play within the family dynamic—a dynamic that I was grateful to have distanced myself from.

The temptation to challenge Mum's concept of "usefulness," to push back against the expectations placed upon us, lingered on the periphery of my thoughts. Yet, recognising the futility of such contemplations in the moment, I chose to let it go. With a nascent plan beginning to take shape, I signalled to Karen and Jerome to follow me, a silent leader shepherding my flock towards the Portal.

CONSPIRATORIAL CURRENCY

4338.213.3

The day unfolded in a rhythmic dance of productivity. Time lost its distinct edges as I methodically filled trolleys with an array of long-lasting provisions—canned goods, essential packages—all stacking up in a meticulous choreography. Baked beans, an unrelenting cascade, provided an amusing, albeit cringe-worthy, familial undertone that clung persistently.

As each tin of baked beans fell into the trolley, I couldn't help but wince. The sheer volume reminded me of an undeniable truth: the baked bean influence was ingrained, an inescapable legacy of my family. It wasn't just about sustenance; it was a marker of the eccentricities that had bound us together. Regardless of how much I had tried to distance myself from them, and the church's influence, I had to admit that it would always be a part of me.

"Although I guess not all of that is bad," a chuckle escaped my lips, a playful gesture over my crotch accompanied by a self-warning, invoking a cascade of playful memories. The storage room bore witness to more than the mere stacking of supplies. The echoes of past indulgences lingered, a mischievous smile lingering on my lips.

Hunger, a persistent force, gnawed at my stomach. A stroke of luck led me to leftover lasagne in the fridge, a serendipitous feast shared with Karen and Jerome.

Seated in the dust near the Portal, the aroma of leftover lasagne wafted through the air, creating a brief oasis of comfort amid the challenges of the day.

"Mum may be protective of her leftovers," I teased, a mischievous grin playing on my lips as I observed the communal act of indulgence. "But at least there's always leftovers to be protective over."

Jerome, always ready to take advantage of a good opportunity, added with a conspiratorial glint in his eye, "Quick, let's finish it before Mum develops some sort of leftover radar. Doesn't matter where we are; she'll find a way to protect her food."

Playful banter ensued as we exchanged boasts of our stealthy manoeuvres, relishing the lasagne without falling victim to Mum's scolding. Laughter mingled with the warm aroma, creating a momentary escape from the demands of the day. Karen, the perceptive outsider to our familial dynamics, observed the interaction with a mix of amusement and bemusement.

As we revelled in the small victory of successfully savouring the lasagne, Karen's gaze shifted. Her eyes caught sight of mum near the Drop Zone. The realisation sparked a sense of urgency in our banter—

"Better eat quickly," I suggested with a wink, acknowledging Karen's observation. "Mum's on the move. We wouldn't want her to discover the missing lasagne before we've had our fill."

"She'd surely take it from us, no doubt convinced in grand delusion that the small portion of food could miraculously feed everyone in the camp," Jerome added, shoving the food into his mouth like it was going to be his final meal.

The banter took on an added edge of haste, transforming our impromptu feast into a race against time, all under the watchful eyes of our ever-vigilant mother.

With the hunger abated, the act of adding more tins of tuna to the burgeoning collection brought about a profound sense of satisfaction. Each can placed in the trolley seemed to embody a small victory, contributing to the growing cache that would sustain the settlers for months. However, an unspoken caveat lingered in the background, a subtle murmur contemplating the pace at which the settlement could continue to expand. The utopian vision of forging a new civilisation revealed itself to be a more complex reality than my initial optimism had envisioned.

Amidst this contemplation, the day's seamless productivity was abruptly disrupted.

"Beatrix, close your damn Portal," I cursed, my fist shaking at the vacant wall that stubbornly resisted its usual vibrant illumination. The unexpected halt, a stark contrast to the rhythmic progress of the day, jolted me from the steady flow of activities. A sudden obstacle disrupted the comforting routine, introducing an air of boredom into the previously well-orchestrated sequence of events.

❖

Emerging into the dazzling Clivilius sunshine, I felt the warmth bathe my face, a stark contrast to the irritation boiling inside me. The light, almost too bright after the dim confines of my parent's storage room I'd just left, cast sharp shadows on the ground, exaggerating every detail of the scene before me. Beatrix, oblivious to my presence at first, was entirely engrossed with an exorbitant pile of cash that seemed to glow under the sun's scrutiny. The vibrant sunlight, unforgiving and relentless, seemed to mock the absurdity of the situation, highlighting the ludicrousness of the moment.

"Finally! What the fuck have you been doing, Beatrix?" The words erupted from me before I could temper them, laced with a cocktail of frustration and confusion.

"Sorry, Luke," she replied, her actions betraying a sense of urgency as she continued adding more money to the growing stack. "But this was super important."

My eyes narrowed, taking in the scene – the mound of money, a colourful aberration against the pristine clarity of the Clivilius sky. It was almost too much, too vivid, too surreal. Without thinking, my confusion vocalised itself, "What could possibly be that important that you had to keep your Portal active for almost an hour!"

"It wasn't my Portal that was active," Beatrix explained, nodding towards a familiar face I couldn't quite place. *It was Jarod's Portal!*

"We have another Guardian?" The words tumbled out, my voice a mix of incredulity and surprise. My mind raced, trying to piece together the implications of her words, the significance of Jarod's involvement.

"We are going to be the envy of all other Guardians!" Jarod's enthusiasm was palpable, his actions bordering on the theatrical as he joyfully showered himself with a handful of notes. It was a display of triumph, of victory, albeit in a manner most peculiar and flamboyant.

"What the heck?" The thought echoed in my head, a silent plea for some semblance of logic amidst the chaos. The situation unfurled like a scene from a dream, the elements too disparate to weave into a coherent narrative. My brain struggled to connect the dots, the absurdity of cash showers and an unexpected Guardian in the bright Clivilius sunshine painting a picture that defied logic, yet here we were, standing at the precipice of something extraordinary, something utterly bewildering.

As Jarod made his way toward the Portal, his steps confident and unhesitant, the air vibrated with a tension that was palpable. "Jarod, wait!" Beatrix's voice pierced the heavy atmosphere, a touch of practicality lacing her tone, grounding us momentarily in the midst of our fantastical dilemma. She held herself with a poise that suggested careful consideration, a contrast to the whirlwind of chaos that seemed to follow us. "I think we're better off storing the money here in Clivilius, rather than your safe." There was a pause, heavy with contemplation, before she added with a tinge of hesitancy, "That isn't so safe," her words tinged with a hint of doubt that seemed to hang in the air between us.

My fingertips rubbed at my brow, an automatic gesture born of deep-seated confusion and weariness. The sunlight, relentless in its intensity, seemed to mock my attempt to find clarity, its brilliance almost too much to bear.

"We should only take the money when we actually need it," Beatrix reasoned with Jarod, her voice a beacon of sanity in the madness that enveloped us. Her attempt to instil a semblance of order was admirable, yet seemed almost quaint in the face of our surreal circumstances.

"I'm sure I need this much already," Jarod retorted, his cheeky grin cutting through the tension. His nonchalance, so characteristic yet infuriating, added layers to the absurdity of our situation. With that, he departed, leaving a trail of bewilderment in his wake.

"Beatrix!" My exclamation was a desperate attempt to anchor myself to some semblance of reality, my voice a cocktail of frustration and disbelief. The situation was slipping through my fingers like sand, the more I tried to grasp it, the less I seemed to understand. "What the fuck was that all about?"

"Come on, Luke," Beatrix's response was tinged with resignation, a weary acceptance of the mayhem that seemed to be our constant companion. "You know Jarod. He works to his own agenda. You can't be too surprised."

"I'm not surprised with Jarod's behaviour in the slightest," I found myself retorting, the frustration bubbling inside me like a tempest. "But I am gobsmacked that you've chosen to make him part of our Guardian crew!"

Beatrix sighed, a sound heavy with unspoken words and shared burdens. "Look," she said, a hint of defiance in her gesture as she tossed handfuls of cash into the air. The bills scattered like confetti, dancing in the vibrant sunlight, a moment of surreal beauty. "It's not all that bad."

My eyes rolled involuntarily, a silent testament to my exasperation. "It could be worse, I suppose," I muttered, though the very nature of our situation, surreal and beyond comprehension, made it hard to imagine how. The scattering cash, shimmering in the sunlight, seemed to underscore the absurdity of our lives, a vivid reminder of the fine line we tread between order and insanity.

The ground beneath our feet betrayed us without warning, a sudden shudder that rippled through the serene chaos of Clivilius. Beatrix's screech, "Earthquake!" sliced through the air, a sharp contrast to the previously muted sounds of our surroundings. Her reaction, swift and instinctive, saw her dropping to the ground in what could only be described as an armadillo-like posture. Despite the severity of the situation, I couldn't suppress a chuckle at the sight, her form curled protectively, a beacon of humour in the unexpected tumult.

The quake itself was mercifully brief, a fleeting yet forceful reminder of the unpredictability of our world. As the tremors subsided, a disorienting silence enveloped us, the kind that follows a storm, filled with the echo of what just transpired. It was in this silence that a new spectacle unfolded before us —a giant Portal screen, materialising out of thin air. Its emergence, grand and imposing, seemed to dwarf everything in its vicinity. An irrational thought flickered through my mind, a trivial concern in the grand scheme of things: *Her Portal is bigger than mine!*

"Well, that was unexpected," Beatrix's voice cut through the silence, her tone laced with a nonchalance that belied the extraordinary nature of the event. Her ability to remain unfazed, or at least appear so, in the face of such anomalies was something I both admired and envied.

"You don't say," I retorted, my words dripping with a sarcasm born out of confusion and intrigue. The lack of forewarning, the sheer suddenness of the quake and the Portal's appearance, left a myriad of questions swirling in my head. "Do you think this is normal?" The question escaped me almost without thought, a genuine curiosity pushing past the initial shock.

Beatrix's shrug, a simple gesture, mirrored the uncertainty that clouded my own thoughts. "No idea." Her response, succinct, somehow encapsulated the unpredictability of our existence in Clivilius.

The gears in my mind whirred to life, a lightbulb moment that seemed almost too perfect. "Prepare your Portal Key, Beatrix. There's testing to be done!" My voice carried a mixture of excitement and determination, the prospect of experimentation a welcome distraction from the oddity of our situation. The surreal had become our playground, and it was time to explore its boundaries.

❖

In Jarod's conspicuous absence, the pieces of the puzzle began to align with a clarity that was previously elusive. Beatrix and I deduced the ownership of the Portals – the first being exclusively mine, a solitary gateway that I had grown accustomed to, and the newly emerged giant, a shared conduit between Beatrix and Jarod. Annoyance pricked at me, a thorn of realisation that, despite the grandeur of our discoveries, we were still rationing resources among the Guardians. My Portal, though uniquely mine, paled in comparison to the colossal newcomer. This realisation was a double-edged sword; while the sting of having the smaller Portal was undeniable, the solace in not having to share provided a balm to my bruised ego.

"Unless you are sharing with Jarod," Beatrix's voice snapped me back to reality, her words laced with humour yet cutting through my contemplations like a knife. Her teasing, though playful, unearthed a scenario I hadn't fully considered, one that didn't sit well with me.

"For your sake, Beatrix, you'd better be hoping that I'm not sharing a Portal with Jarod," I retorted, my words carrying a weight of warning, my gaze locking onto hers with an intensity that was meant to convey the seriousness of my statement. The air between us crackled with the unspoken implications of what sharing a Portal with Jarod could entail, a prospect I certainly didn't find particularly appealing.

Then, as if struck by lightning, a realisation dawned on me – Charles! The thought hit me with the force of a freight train, a crucial piece of our intricate familial puzzle that had momentarily slipped my mind in the whirlwind of recent discoveries.

"Jarod's your responsibility now, Beatrix," I declared with finality, a hint of desperation perhaps colouring my tone as I turned my attention to my Portal. I left her standing amidst her piles of cash, a visual reminder of the madness that had become our norm.

Stepping through the Portal and arriving in the familiar confines of the Smith house, a sense of stupidity washed over me. *How could I have overlooked Charles?* The comfort of the study, with its walls lined with books and the faint smell of aged paper, did little to ease the gnawing feeling in my gut. Beatrix, with her new shared Portal and her piles of cash, suddenly seemed miles away. A silent plea hung in the air, unspoken yet fervent – *Beatrix had better save me some of that cash!*

CHARLES

4338.213.4

The moment I stepped into the living room, the air was thick with tension, a sharp rebuke slicing through the silence and setting my nerves on edge. "Ah! You freakin' imbecile!" The words, harsh and unyielding, hung heavy, a discordant note that made me pause, an instinctive reaction thinking perhaps I had walked into a personal storm. However, a swift survey of the room dispelled that notion; the vitriol wasn't aimed at me.

It struck me as amusing, the casual disregard for the absence of family, as if the solitude granted him a kingdom where his frustrations were the only subjects. I couldn't help but let a cheeky grin play across my lips, the situation unfolding into an unexpected moment of levity.

With a confidence born from years of camaraderie, I made my way towards the source of the outburst. Charles, oblivious to my approach, was ensconced in his digital world, fingers dancing a furious ballet across the keyboard, completely immersed in whatever virtual battle was unfolding before him. The faint, tinny echoes of his game filtered through his headset, a soundtrack to his intense concentration.

"Charles!" My voice boomed, a deliberate contrast to the focused silence, as I clasped his shoulders with exaggerated drama. The effect was instantaneous and exactly as intended. His reaction was a symphony of surprise, a near orchestral leap from his seat, headphones flung aside in a moment of pure, unadulterated shock. My laughter, genuine and unrestrained, filled the room, a shared moment of humour that momentarily lifted the weight from my shoulders.

"Luke!" His scolding morphed into a declaration of surprise, the initial annoyance quickly giving way to joy upon recognising me. Watching him clutch at his chest, the rapid rise and fall indicative of his startled state, I couldn't help but feel a twinge of affection for the scene. His wide grin, so reminiscent of the carefree moments of his youth, was infectious, drawing me further into the familiarity of our brotherhood. "I didn't know you were coming to visit."

My casual shrug was a thin veil over the complexity of emotions swirling within. "It was a last-minute plan," I said, words floating in the air like leaves carried by the wind, aimless and unanchored. Charles, ever the master of multi-tasking, split his attention between our conversation and the digital world laid out before him, fingers deftly closing tabs and silencing the virtual chaos that had consumed him moments before.

"Did Mum and Dad pick you up from the airport?" His question, innocent and routine, hinted at the normalcy of a life I felt I was slowly drifting away from. Opting for evasion, a tactic becoming all too familiar, I redirected the conversation towards safer waters. "I'm guessing you're not supposed to be on there," I remarked, a nod towards the backpack slung carelessly beside the chair, an unspoken symbol of the everyday battles fought over screen time.

"Not unless it's for school work," Charles admitted, a trace of resignation in his voice as he closed the last of his game screens, the final act of a well-rehearsed routine. His compliance, though reluctant, was a reminder of the simple rules that governed my life before the complexity of Guardians and Portals had taken hold.

Following Charles into the kitchen felt like stepping back in time, a return to the mundane yet comforting rituals of home life. He reached atop the fridge with a familiarity bred from countless similar acts of culinary defiance, retrieving biscuits from an old tin—a tin that held more than just treats, it held memories. "Want one?" he offered, his generosity as automatic as his earlier evasion of household rules. My acceptance was met with a grumble of approval from my stomach, a reminder of the simple pleasures that had become overshadowed by the weight of my responsibilities.

Leaning against the doorway, Charles's question about our parents' whereabouts echoed through the silent hall, a reminder of the conversation I had been dreading. "Yeah, about that," I stuttered, the words catching like thorns. *This should be easy*, I chided myself, Charles's nature as the family clown, his intelligence wrapped in a perpetual refusal to take life's dramas too seriously, should make this easier.

"I need to show you something, Charles," I declared, a seriousness creeping into my voice that felt foreign in the comfort of our kitchen. The crumbs from the biscuits, now scattered down my top, seemed a metaphor for the messy situation I was about to reveal.

"Oh, goodie. You've brought us presents!" Charles exclaimed, gleeful.

"You could call it that," I responded, a smile tugging at the corners of my mouth despite the gravity of what lay ahead. Leading him into the study, the cleared wall awaiting us felt less like a preparation for a demonstration and more like a stage set for the unveiling of a new reality. This was more than a simple reveal; it was an invitation into the unknown, a step towards sharing the burdens and wonders that had become my new normal.

The weight of the moment settled on my shoulders as I stood there, pondering the best way to bridge the gap between his everyday reality and the unfathomable truths I was about to unveil. Opting against a preamble, I decided that the sheer spectacle of the Portal would speak volumes more than any introduction could. With a deep breath, I activated the Portal Key, and the once blank study wall burst into life, awash with the mesmerising dance of colours that heralded the opening of the Portal. It was a sight that never failed to stir a sense of wonder in me, yet now, it bore the weight of revelation.

"Whoa! What the heck is that?" Charles's reaction was immediate, his voice tinged with a mix of astonishment and disbelief. His eyes, wide with a childlike wonder I hadn't seen in him for years, were fixated on the vibrant spectacle before us.

"That is a Portal," I stated, the simplicity of the term belying the complexity of what it represented. It felt almost mundane to call it by its name, yet there was no other way to describe the gateway to worlds unknown that shimmered on the wall.

"That's amazing," Charles breathed out, his attention wholly captivated by the display. The soft sounds of awe that accompanied his observation of the energy swirls and the sparks they sent flying into the air were a testament to the Portal's inherent allure, its beauty undeniable even in the face of its daunting implications.

"That's where Mum and Dad are," I found myself saying, the words tumbling out in a rush. The reality of their location, so casually disclosed, hung between us, a palpable tension in the air.

"Huh?" The confusion that snapped Charles's gaze back to me was as clear as daylight, his wide eyes searching mine for clarity, for some semblance of sense in the midst of the extraordinary.

"And Jerome and Paul," I added, feeling the need to include them in the revelation, to paint a fuller picture of the situation.

"Huh?" His repeated query was more than a question; it was a plea for understanding, for a foothold in the rapidly shifting ground of his world.

"I know it doesn't really make much sense, but this device," I said, holding up the Portal Key, an object so small and yet so pivotal, "opens a portal to a new world." The significance of the Portal Key, its role as the bridge between our world and another, felt heavier in my hand than ever before.

"And that's where Mum and Dad are?" Charles's skepticism was palpable, each word heavy with doubt. His skepticism served as a mirror to my own initial disbelief when I was first confronted with the reality of the Portal. Standing there, faced with his incredulity, I realised the enormity of what I was asking him to accept, to believe. It was a leap of faith that went beyond the physical realm we understood, into the very heart of what we considered possible.

"Here, let's do an experiment," I told him, playing to his love for the scientific method.

"Okay," he responded, a newfound enthusiasm lacing his voice, a testament to his innate love for understanding the world through evidence and experimentation.

"You get the laptop working, and I need to go through that Portal quickly and grab something," I instructed, laying out the plan with a simplicity that belied the complexity of what I was about to do. Charles's gaze lingered on me for a moment longer than necessary, a silent plea for caution that I understood all too well.

Leaving Charles to his tasks, I stepped into Clivilius, the familiar yet always changing landscape unfolding before me. The thought of Charles potentially following me didn't worry me; in fact, the idea seemed almost appealing. The simplicity of companionship in this bizarre new world was a comforting thought, yet the caution of pacing our revelations won the day. Sometimes, introducing someone to a new reality required a gentle hand.

"Are you ready to speak with Charles?" I asked Jerome, finding him in a moment of quiet solitude amidst the dust of Clivilius. His reaction, a swift rise to his feet, was marked by a readiness to act, a testament to his own sense of responsibility in our shared plight.

Jerome handed me the network cable, his movements deliberate, as we walked and talked. His question, "Are you really sure that we should do this? This place is dangerous, isn't it?" was laced with genuine concern.

I paused, considering his words. "And Earth is a safe place?" I countered rhetorically, challenging the notion of safety in a world as unpredictable as our own. My response, though not entirely satisfying to Jerome, was meant to put things into perspective. The real clincher came with a more personal appeal, "Do you really want to be left here alone with Mum and Dad?" The suggestion of isolation, of being left to navigate this world without the camaraderie of siblings, struck the right chord.

Jerome's face, a canvas of emotions, briefly displayed panic before settling into resolved agreement. "You're right," he conceded, the urgency of his conviction pushing us to bridge the physical and emotional distances that separated us from Charles. "Let's bring Charles here too."

I couldn't help but smile at his conclusion, a knowing smile that spoke volumes of the unspoken bond between siblings. Our parents were indeed great, a constant in their lives filled with love and support. But the unique connection shared between siblings, with its blend of rivalry, camaraderie, and unbreakable bonds, held a different kind of magic. In this moment, in this strange new world, it was this bond that felt like the most powerful force of all.

The moment I stepped back into the study, the shift in atmosphere was palpable. My return was marked by a sense of urgency, a directness that didn't allow for any dilly-dallying. "Have you got it working yet?" I asked Charles, my tone laden with anticipation.

"Yep. It's all good to go," Charles replied, his eagerness a mirror to my own. The simplicity of his response, the readiness with which he embraced this new venture, brought a momentary sense of calm to the whirlwind of emotions swirling within me.

Connecting the network cable, I instructed Charles to log in to whatever app he and Jerome used the most to talk to each other.

Charles looked at me, a bemused expression on his face. "Why would we use an app to talk to each other when we live in the same house?"

My rhetorical comeback, "I thought that's how all kids operated these days?" was met with Charles's quick wit. "Don't worry, I'm just messing with ya," he joked, his wide grin serving as a brief respite from the whirlwind of events.

Within moments, the sound of Jerome's voice echoed around the room. After initial greetings were done, I excused myself, allowing Charles time to talk with Jerome alone. It wasn't just that I thought Jerome had a better relationship with Charles and could sweet-talk him into anything much better than I could, but the taste of the remaining biscuits in the tin beckoned me to devour them.

And I wasn't disappointed. Each new biscuit that crumbled inside my mouth tasted even better than the last. Before long, I realised that once again, another day was passing by where I hadn't eaten properly.

"Hey, Luke!" Charles's voice, vibrant and tinged with excitement, summoned me from the cozy confines of the study. With the biscuit tin cradled in my arms, I hastened towards the source of the call, eager and slightly amused. As I entered the room, a half-chewed biscuit escaped its confines, dribbling clumsily from the corners of my mouth. The taste of chocolate chips still melting on my tongue, I managed a muffled, "Yeah?"

Charles, his eyes alight with a mix of determination and an almost childlike wonder, rose to his feet. "I'm ready to enter Clivilius," he announced with a firmness that belied his usually playful demeanour. At his words, a broad smile erupted across my face, spreading warmth and pride through my chest. *Well done, Jerome,* I thought, silently applauding his effectiveness.

"So, what do I do?" Charles's question, laced with a slight shrug, betrayed his uncertainty. He gestured towards the Portal, its colourful swirls dancing like a living abstract painting, captivating yet mysterious. "Do I just walk into that?"

Distractedly, I reached into the biscuit tin, my fingers brushing against the remaining treats as I selected another. "Yep," I answered, voice muffled by the fresh crunch of biscuit between my teeth.

Taking a deep breath, Charles braced himself, his shoulders squared yet his eyes betraying a hint of apprehension. "Okay," he exhaled, taking a tentative step forward, his gaze fixed on the swirling vortex that promised a journey to Clivilius.

"Charles, wait!" My voice, louder than intended, echoed sharply in the room, halting him mid-step and eliciting a startled jump. The sudden interruption drew a confused, "What is it?" from Jerome, his voice emanating from the laptop with a mix of concern and curiosity.

I glanced down at the half-eaten biscuit in my hand, its sweetness a stark contrast to the gravity of the moment. Then, looking back at Charles, a curious idea sparked in my mind, lighting up a path to a new plan. "I need Charles to help me first," I announced, more to myself than to the awaiting audience.

"Help with what?" Jerome's voice, now tinged with frustration, demanded clarity.

Squatting in front of the laptop, I leaned in close. "Hey, Jerome, can you go and get some empty shopping trolleys for me? I'll bring them in here, and Charles can help me finish bringing all that food storage into Clivilius." The words spilled out, framing a task that seemed mundane yet essential.

Charles turned to me, his expression a mix of surprise and mild annoyance. "You're going to make me do work already?" he gawked, disbelief colouring his tone.

"Better get used to it, little brother," I said, the affection clear in my voice. I slapped him across the shoulder playfully, a gesture meant to reassure as much as to motivate. "You wait here; I'll grab a few trolleys for us."

❖

"You and I make a great team, Charles," I remarked, the words floating between us like a shared secret as we unloaded another batch of toilet paper into the waiting trolley. The activity, mundane in any other context, felt charged with an underlying excitement given our current venture. A sense of camaraderie, thick and palpable, enveloped us, binding our fates together in this bizarre, yet thrilling, undertaking.

"I can't believe any of this feels normal already," Charles mused, his voice a blend of wonder and disbelief. He paused, a pack of toilet paper in hand, his gaze lost somewhere between the reality of our actions and the surrealism of our situation. "I kinda feel like I'm having some sort of vivid dream, and any minute now I'm going to wake up and find Mum standing over me, glaring as she demands I get up for seminary again."

The image he painted was so vivid, so ordinary in its domesticity, that it momentarily grounded me back to our less adventurous, pre-Clivilius life. "She can do that tomorrow," I quipped, the humour light and teasing. Our laughter mingled, an easy, lighthearted chuckle that briefly dispelled the finality of our task.

"Don't jinx me, Luke," Charles laughed in response, his eyes sparkling with mirth and a hint of mischief.

In the midst of grabbing another pack of loo paper from the top of the cupboard, my fingers brushing against the rough packaging, a sudden idea gripped me. It was as if a light had flicked on in a previously dark room, illuminating a path I hadn't seen before. "Charles, I think I have a much better use for you," I declared, my voice infused with a newfound purpose.

"Oh no," Charles muttered playfully, the words dripping with a feigned dread that couldn't quite mask his underlying curiosity. His expression, a mixture of amusement and faux apprehension, was priceless. "Can't I just go to Clivilius already?"

"Nope," I asserted, my grin broadening at his mock despair. The prospect of this new diversion, whatever it might be, sparked an unspoken challenge between us, a silent acknowledgment of the adventures and trials that lay ahead. "Follow me." My voice was the beacon, leading us away from the routine task at hand towards something unknown, something new.

Charles, with a mixture of curiosity and resignation, trailed behind me. The air between us crackled with anticipation, the mundane world of toilet paper and seminary mornings fading into the background as we ventured towards the next chapter.

INTER-DIMENSIONAL RUN

4338.213.5

Grunting and panting, the physical exertion felt almost primal as Charles and I wrestled with the fifth large white barrel, its daunting weight a test of our determination. This wasn't just any task; it was a trial, a tangible measure of our resolve. The barrel, its surface smooth and unyielding under our sweat-slicked palms, seemed almost a beast to be tamed as we strained to tilt and rotate it along its round bottom edge. Each movement was a calculated effort, a dance of strength and balance, as we slowly inched our way toward the Portal.

The Portal itself had been strategically relocated to the glass sliding door separating the living room from the outdoor patio, a threshold between worlds both literal and metaphorical. Emerging from the large garage, the cool air of the afternoon kissed our flushed faces, offering a brief respite from the stifling confines we'd just left. Our tremendously heavy loot—this particular container filled with rice, each grain a potential lifeline in the world of Clivilius—seemed to mock us with its inert weight.

Amidst our concerted struggle, Charles abruptly halted, his sudden stop nearly causing me to lose my grip on the barrel's thick plastic edge. The abrupt cessation of movement threw me off balance, both physically and mentally, as the ambient sounds of our efforts were abruptly replaced by an eerie silence. It was as if the world itself had paused, holding its breath in anticipation. The only sound that remained was the muffled thumping of our own hearts, a result of the exertion and the sudden spike of adrenaline coursing through our veins.

"What's—" I began, the confusion clear in my voice, my mind racing to understand the sudden change. But Charles swiftly shushed me with a gesture, his index finger pressed against his lips, his eyes wide with a mix of caution and curiosity. It was a look that immediately set my nerves on edge, a clear signal that something was amiss.

"Did you hear that?" he whispered, his voice barely audible over the now apparent silence that enveloped us. The question sent a shiver down my spine, a premonition of something unseen and perhaps unfriendly lurking in the shadows.

I shook my head, my senses straining in the silence, trying to pierce the quiet with sheer will. "Hear what?" I whispered back, the words barely escaping my lips. My eyes darted around the dimly lit garage, seeking out any anomaly, any sign of the source of Charles's alarm. The air felt charged, thick with the tension of unseen dangers, a stark contrast to the mundane task we had been so focused on moments before.

A sudden, loud bang echoed against the garage door, its force reverberating through the air and sending a jolt of fear straight through me. The announcement that followed, "Police. Anyone in there?" carried with it the unmistakable weight of authority, its words slicing through the silence and casting an ominous shadow over our clandestine activities. The reality of our situation crashed down on me, the thrill of our adventure now tinged with a sharp edge of danger.

An unsettling chill raced down my spine, momentarily paralysing me as the implications of being discovered threatened to overwhelm my thoughts. Beside me, Charles, his youthful face etched with a mixture of fear and determination, delivered a hushed directive. "We must go, now," he hissed, his voice barely a whisper yet imbued with an urgency that propelled me into action. Without a second thought, we abandoned our heavy cargo, the barrel of rice suddenly insignificant compared to the threat looming just beyond the garage door.

My heart hammered in my chest as Charles led the way. We moved with caution, navigating the narrow path between stacked boxes and forgotten items, remnants of a life less complicated. The thumping of police on the garage door grew louder, an unsettling percussion that seemed to echo with each beat of my heart, urging us to hasten our escape.

Reaching the end of the garage, Charles abruptly stopped and turned back to me. His eyes, wide and questioning, bore into mine. "Aren't you coming too?" he hissed, the urgency in his gaze mingling with a hint of fear. The sounds of the police, their authoritative knocks growing ever more insistent, seemed to punctuate his question, lending an acute sense of immediacy to our predicament.

Shaking my head, I silently mouthed, "No," my decision made in the span of a heartbeat. My eyes briefly darted toward the source of the rhythmic echoes of authority that seemed to be closing in with each passing second. I returned my gaze to Charles, ensuring our exchange remained as discreet as possible under the circumstances.

"I'm going to hang around a bit longer," I whispered back to him, my voice a mere breath against the backdrop of the intensifying drumming of police fists on metal. The resolve in my voice belied the turmoil churning within me. "I need to know what the police know and why they are even here." The words felt heavy, laden with a mix of courage and recklessness. In that moment, I was acutely aware of the gravity of my decision, the potential consequences it could have not just for me, but for Charles, Jerome, and our entire undertaking.

Charles eyed me with a look that was hard to decipher, his expression caught somewhere between concern and the uncertainty of our predicament. The dim light of the garage cast shadows across his face, making his youthful features appear more solemn than usual.

"It could have huge implications," I found myself whispering, the words barely escaping my lips as I glanced nervously towards the closed garage door. I wasn't entirely sure of the exact implications myself, but the urgency of staying informed and ahead of any potential threat pressed heavily upon me.

"I don't think you should," Charles insisted, his voice carrying a weight of fear and protective concern that was uncharacteristic of his usually adventurous spirit. His eyes, wide and searching, seemed to probe for reassurance in mine, looking for a sign that might dissuade me from what he perceived as a risky course of action.

"It's okay," I reassured him, trying to muster as much confidence into my voice as I could. My hands moved almost of their own accord to close the Portal, severing the visible connection between our hidden Clivilius and the outside world.

Charles looked perplexed, torn between his trust in me and the fear of the unknown that loomed just outside our sanctuary. "They can't enter without a warrant," I assured him, trying to sound more convinced than I felt. The rhythmic pounding of authority outside served as a stark, unnerving reminder of our vulnerability, the thin veil of security that hung precariously between us and them.

Biting his lower lip, a nervous habit he'd had since childhood, Charles's fingertips absently scratched at the eczema in the crook of his elbow—a telltale sign of his growing anxiety. "Are you sure they don't already have one?" he whispered, his voice barely audible over the growing cacophony outside. The question, simple yet loaded with fear, caught me off guard, sending a jolt of panic through my veins.

"Why would they?" I retorted almost defensively, my brain racing through potential scenarios, searching for a rational explanation that could quell the rising tide of fear. The truth was, I had no way of knowing for sure, no solid ground upon which to base my reassurance.

Charles shrugged, a gesture that felt heavy with implication. His eyes, reflecting the dim light, mirrored the unsettling reality we found ourselves in. "Why would they even be here in the first place?" he asked, his voice barely more than a breath.

The tight knot in the pit of my stomach twisted tighter, a physical manifestation of the dread that crept along the edges of my mind. My youngest brother had a very valid point—one that I couldn't ignore. *What are they even doing here?* The uncertainty of it all felt overwhelming, a nebulous threat that loomed larger with each passing second.

The roller door rumbled to life, its mechanical growl a sudden and jarring herald of the urgency now coursing through my veins. "Shit!" I hissed under my breath, the expletive slipping out almost reflexively as my fingers tightened around Charles's arm. With a firm grip, I pulled him along, our escape from the garage propelling us onto the expansive patio. The cool air of the afternoon brushed against my skin, and the heated rush of adrenaline flooded my system.

Charles, breathless from the sudden exertion, whispered sharply in my ear, "Crap, they're inside the house!" His words, laced with panic, sent another shock of fear through me. Without taking a moment to confirm his claim, I pressed on, guiding us around the corner of the shed. Here, we were concealed from the garage and the clear glass of the backdoor, our movements as stealthy as shadows in the dim light of the mottled sky.

Time seemed to stretch into an agonising eternity, each moment elongated as we strained to avoid detection. The adrenaline coursing through me heightened my senses, making every sound, every shadow, feel like a potential threat. What felt like hours transpired in mere minutes, the distorted passage of time a testament to the intensity of our predicament.

Then, the sliding door of the house glided open, its movement accompanied by a low hum that signalled the approach of a formidable presence. My breathing deepened, unconsciously matching the erratic thump of my heart as the sound of heavy police boots clomped around the patio. The deliberate pace of those boots, the authority they commanded with each step, felt like a noose tightening around us.

"Can't we go to Clivilius now?" Charles pleaded, the fear evident in his shaky voice cutting through the tension. His eyes, wide and searching, looked to me for a solution, a way out of this increasingly dire situation.

My head shook in response, my eyes scanning our immediate surroundings for any possible advantage. "There's nowhere to activate the Portal here. I need a flat surface," I told him, running my hand along the shed's undulating exterior to emphasise the point. The rough texture of the shed's surface under my fingertips felt grounding. "A surface big enough for a person to fit through," I added, the weight of our limited options pressing heavily upon me.

"Crap!" Charles hissed, his eyes widening in a realisation that mirrored my own. The blunt reality of our situation was clear—we were trapped, with no immediate means of escape to Clivilius. The realisation hung between us, heavy and foreboding, as the sounds of the police presence drew nearer.

In that moment, the shed wasn't just a barrier between us and them; it was a reminder of the thin line we walked between freedom and capture.

Another set of footsteps joined the symphony of sounds on the patio, the crisp clarity of their approach cutting through the tense silence. "Have you found anything?" the firm voice asked, its authoritative tone slicing through the air like a knife. The presence of another, confirming the search was intensifying, sent a fresh wave of anxiety coursing through me.

"There appears to have been recent activity here, but there doesn't appear to be anyone here now," the female officer replied. Her voice, professional and detached, offered a stark contrast to the racing thoughts in my head. An exhale I hadn't realised I was holding escaped me as a temporary reprieve settled over us, the tension in my shoulders easing ever so slightly at her words.

"Would it really be so bad if we, or at least I, reveal myself to them?" Charles whispered, his voice barely audible, laden with a mix of desperation and naivety. The question, innocent in its asking, belied the complexity of the further complications such an action might cause.

My eyes narrowed, and I frowned at him. "The rest of the family is in Clivilius. Do you think the police will let you join them so easily? Imagine all the questions they'll force you to answer." My words were sharp, not out of irritation with Charles, but from a place of protective urgency. The thought of entangling him further into this web of complexity and danger was unbearable.

Charles sighed. I could see the internal conflict playing out on his face, a tumultuous sea of realisation and resignation. "You're right," he admitted, his voice a murmur of acquiescence to the harsh truths of our situation.

The male officer spoke again, his voice cutting through our whispered exchange. "Let's go. There's nobody inside either. There's an almost empty room at the back of the house, and a shopping trolley full of toilet paper. No idea what that means." The casual dismissal of our carefully laid plans, represented by that trolley full of toilet paper, felt like a mockery of our efforts.

"Judging by all the Jesus pictures on the walls," a third voice spoke condescendingly, "I'd say they're preppers." The scorn in the statement, the reduction of our lives and fears to a stereotype, stung with an unexpected intensity. It was a reminder of how easily misunderstood our actions could be, how quickly our attempts to protect and prepare could be trivialised by those looking in from the outside.

The footsteps on the patio, once a distant threat, began to move again, each step a palpable echo of our escalating fear. "Wait!" the female officer's voice pierced the tense silence, a command that froze me in place. The urgency in her tone suggested she had discovered something significant.

"What is it?" The inquiry from her colleague was laced with curiosity and concern, reflecting the gravity of her interruption.

"Somebody was here very recently," the woman officer replied, her tone indicating a discovery that piqued her interest and heightened the stakes of our precarious situation.

A pause hung in the air, thick with anticipation, before the second pair of feet stepped onto the patio once more. The moment stretched on, each second a sharp note of suspense. Then the female officer continued, "It looks like there is blood on the edge of the shed. It's fresh too." Her observation, clinical and detached, sent a jolt of fear through me.

"Shit!" I hissed under my breath, the word slipping out as a reflex. My gaze locked with Charles's, his eyes wide with panic. Quickly, we checked ourselves over and I found a small cut near my left elbow, the skin there tender and slightly parted—a minor injury that now felt monumental. "I think it's my blood," I told Charles, the words heavy with dread. My blood pressure skyrocketed at the realisation that this inadvertent clue could lead the police directly to me, that they would have my DNA.

"I'll call for backup," an officer stated, his voice carrying the weight of authority and the promise of an escalating situation.

"Detective Santos is already on his way. He's not far. I'll call in forensics too," the female officer called out, her voice echoing slightly as she communicated the need for further investigation.

The mention of Detective Santos and the decision to call in forensics solidified the seriousness of our situation. My mind raced, trying to piece together a plan, any plan, that could help us evade detection and the mounting legal complications. The implications of leaving behind such a personal trace as my own blood were staggering, transforming our attempt at escape into a nightmare scenario of potential capture and interrogation.

Tugging on my arm, Charles's actions spoke louder than words as he gestured toward the fence, a silent proposal that we make our escape by vaulting over it. His eyes, wide with the immediacy of our situation, conveyed a sense of urgency that was hard to ignore. However, the reality of the blood they had discovered—an undeniable trace of our presence—anchored me to the spot. Whispering sharply, a hint of frustration laced with fear colouring my tone, I reminded him, "I need to destroy the evidence."

In response, Charles pulled out his smartphone, a tool that had become an extension of our modern lives, now repurposed as a means of survival. Using the camera to carefully survey the corner of the shed, he assessed our situation with a critical eye. "I don't think they're going anywhere," he remarked, his voice low but clear.

I sighed, a mix of resignation and acknowledgment of Charles's assessment. He was right; the officers seemed to have settled in for a thorough investigation. "Wait," I whispered hastily before he could dismiss the utility of his phone in this moment.

Charles looked at me, confusion momentarily clouding his expression. His silent 'what'? hung in the air between us, a question mark that demanded an answer without the luxury of spoken words.

Responding in kind, I gestured for him to take some photos, my hands mimicking the action of snapping pictures. The necessity for visual documentation dawned on me as a crucial tactic—not just for our immediate needs, but for validating the assumption that they were simply police officers. In a world where appearances could be deceiving, and every detail mattered, these photos could prove to be invaluable.

Charles's face broke into a brief smile, a flicker of understanding crossing his features as he grasped the unspoken necessity of the action. The smartphone, a device so often used for mundane captures of daily life, was now our tool for gathering evidence, a silent witness to the unfolding drama. In that moment, the roles we had assumed—of fugitives, of survivors—were crystallised, underscored by the simple act of documenting our actions.

"Okay," I whispered to Charles, the word barely leaving my lips as I prepared us for what came next. The urgency of our situation had condensed into this single moment, a pivotal leap that could mean the difference between capture and escape.

Almost instantly, Charles lunged forward, his body tensed for action. But my quick reflexes caught hold of him and dragged him back. He turned to me, his face etched with questions, the silent 'why' clear in his eyes.

Not wanting to risk any unnecessary noise that could betray our position, I held out the Portal Key. The small device, unassuming to any unknowing observer, was our lifeline. Employing our years of childhood charade gaming, I mimed the action of activating the Portal swiftly after crossing the fence. The gestures, exaggerated and precise, were a language all their own, one that Charles and I had mastered over countless hours of play and practice.

Charles responded with a nod of acknowledgment, his features hardening with determination. He understood the plan without needing words to cloud the air between us. Then, with a leader's clarity, he signalled for me to follow his lead. He held up three fingers, a silent sentinel marking the beginning of our final countdown.

Two fingers now. My heart hammered against my ribcage, adrenaline surging through my veins like wildfire. The world seemed to narrow down to this very instant, every sense heightened, every thought focused on what needed to be done.

As the final finger closed into a closed fist, a signal as potent as any starting gun, Charles and I launched ourselves off the side of the shed. We were like lightning, our bodies propelled by a mixture of fear, hope, and sheer will. Bolting toward the back fence, every muscle fibre in my body screamed with the effort. Our footsteps clanged loudly against the metal, a cacophony that seemed impossibly loud in the quiet of the afternoon.

I landed with a heavy thud on the other side, the impact jarring yet exhilarating. Quickly, I scrambled to my feet, my first thought to check that Charles was still with me. The relief that flooded through me when I saw him land, albeit with a graceless thud of his own, was palpable. We were together, we were on the other side, and for a moment, that was all that mattered.

Yelling echoed not far behind us, a vocal reminder that our escape was far from secure. The sound, sharp and urgent, spurred us forward even as we glimpsed the first officer's head peering over the high fence. The sight sent a shock of fear through me, the realisation that we were barely a step ahead of capture.

"Keep going," Charles instructed, his voice a mix of determination and urgency as we sprinted through a small gum tree-filled reserve. The trees, with their twisted trunks and sprawling branches, offered scant cover but did little to dampen the sounds of our pursuers. The reserve, usually a place of tranquility and natural beauty, had transformed into the backdrop of our frantic flight for freedom.

Barely waiting for a gap in the traffic, we darted across the busy main road, our actions driven by desperation. The roar of engines and blare of horns filled the air as we made our daring dash, the danger from the vehicles almost as palpable as that of the chasing officers. Our destination—the shopping centre—loomed directly in our line of sight, a beacon of relative safety in the mad dash of our escape.

Glancing over my shoulder, the sight of at least one officer in pursuit added weight to the fear gnawing at my insides.

"This way," Charles said, his voice cutting through my spiralling thoughts as he pointed away from the bustling shopping centre. His quick thinking directed us around the back of the complex, away from the prying eyes of the public and, hopefully, our pursuers. The less attention we drew to ourselves, the better our chances of slipping away unnoticed.

Soon, we found a secluded alley, a narrow passageway hidden from the main thoroughfares of the shopping centre.

The alley, with its shadows and silence, felt like a temporary sanctuary. With a hefty sigh of relief, we silently slipped into Clivilius, the familiar sensation of the Portal enveloping us in its embrace. The transition from the tangible, frenetic energy of our escape to the serene realm of Clivilius was initially disorienting, yet welcome.

WORLDS APART, TIES INTACT

4338.213.6

The relentless sun bore down upon us with an intensity that seemed to highlight the surreal transition from our world to Clivilius. As Charles and I emerged from the portal's kaleidoscope, the lingering hues of our passage—reds, blues, and greens—dissipated into the Clivilius air, like watercolour paints blending into the fabric of this new reality. The vibrant tableau that was Bixbus unfolded before us, its colours and sounds a stark contrast to the grey monotony of the chase we had just escaped.

A hive of activity enveloped the settlement, a bustling hub of life and motion that captured the essence of Clivilius's spirit. Karen orchestrated the rhythmic dance of trolleys shuttling between the Drop Zone and the newly erected shed, her movements precise and commanding. The metallic resonance of barrels being hoisted onto a waiting ute reverberated through the air, a symphony of industry and cooperation that underscored the community's unity and purpose.

In the heart of this orchestrated chaos, Paul, Jerome, and Dad saw to the loading operation with the focused intensity of a well-rehearsed team. Their figures, illuminated by the harsh sunlight, moved with a purpose that was both urgent and methodical. Adrian and Nial, who had momentarily abandoned their work on the second shed, lent their strength to the effort, their laughter and banter adding a layer of camaraderie.

The scene unfolded against the peculiar backdrop of grazing livestock—a goat and a handful of hens, blissfully oblivious to the extraterrestrial choreography around them. Their presence, so mundane and yet so incongruous, lent an air of surreal normalcy to the landscape of Bixbus. It was a vivid reminder of the duality of our existence here in Clivilius, a blend of the extraordinary and the everyday.

Standing there, at the threshold of this new world, the weight of our recent escape began to fade, replaced by a burgeoning sense of belonging and purpose. The challenges we faced, the dangers we escaped, seemed to shrink in the face of the vibrant life that was beginning to pulse through Bixbus. Yet, beneath the surface, a current of apprehension remained—a silent acknowledgment of the unknowns that lay ahead.

We navigated the lively scene before us at a deliberate pace, each step measured, allowing ourselves to savour the moments of tranquility that punctuated the buzzing energy around us. The air was alive with the sounds of productivity and the gentle hum of conversation, a stark contrast to the adrenaline-fuelled silence of our recent escape.

Jerome, whose movements weaved with a dance of practiced efficiency, greeted us with a nod—a silent testament to the camaraderie and understanding that had long defined our relationship. "Good to see you, lil' bro," he said, his voice carrying over the din. His greeting was punctuated with a playful thump on Charles's shoulder, a gesture that spoke volumes of their bond.

Charles, who had been a silent observer until now, absorbed the spectacle with wide eyes, a mix of fascination and trepidation colouring his gaze. His eyes, constantly moving, betrayed the unspoken question that lingered on his mind – what sort of world had we entered? The sights and sounds of Clivilius, so vastly different from anything we had known, seemed to both allure and unsettle him.

Dad, momentarily detaching from the loading duties, approached us with open arms, enveloping Charles in a robust embrace that seemed to momentarily lift the weight of uncertainty from his shoulders. His words, laden with a touch of resigned humour, resonated deeply. "Stuck together as a family forever in this bizarre place." The sentiment, while humorous, carried an undercurrent of solemnity—a recognition of the strangeness of our new reality and the unbreakable bond that tied us together.

A pang of guilt flitted through me at Dad's words, the assumption that Paul had filled him in on the unsettling truth gnawing at the edges of my conscience. *Clivilius isn't the New Jerusalem*, a thought that had haunted my quieter moments, casting a shadow over the wonder of our new beginning. The reality of Clivilius, with its newness of life and daunting unknowns, was a far cry from the utopian dreams that had filled my father's imagination.

Paul, ever attuned to the subtleties of our family dynamics, met my gaze across the bustling expanse. In that silent exchange, volumes were spoken—a mutual understanding that a private conversation was pending, one that promised to delve into the complexities of our current predicament. But for now, amidst the whirlwind of survival that had enveloped us since our arrival in Clivilius, we remained mere players in the intricate dance of establishing a foothold in this new world.

"Let's take a short break," Paul announced, halting the operation with a commanding presence that seemed to momentarily still the air itself. His words, simple yet authoritative, prompted collective sighs of relief from the group, as the work paused.

"You've cut yourself," Paul observed, his eyes briefly flickering towards the inconspicuous wound on my elbow. The casualness of his observation belied the concern lurking beneath the surface.

"Yeah," I admitted cautiously, feeling the tension escalate as unspoken words hovered in the air between us.

Dad seized the opportune moment, suggesting a retreat to the camp with an air of light-heartedness that only a parent can muster in times of stress. "Come on, let's get you to the camp. Mum will be wanting to interrogate you," he said to Charles, his tone imbued with a touch of resigned humour that hinted at the familiar rituals of family life. Paul readily endorsed the idea, his nod a silent agreement to the temporary division of the group.

As they departed, the space between Paul and me seemed to grow more pronounced, the weight of unresolved conversations hanging heavily between us. With the others moving towards the camp, a bubble of privacy formed around us, a rare commodity in the communal life taking shape in Clivilius.

"We need to talk, in private," I asserted, the urgency in my voice cutting through the ambient clamour of the Drop Zone. The words, spoken aloud, seemed to carve out a space for the forthcoming dialogue, a recognition of the need to address the swirling undercurrents of our situation.

❖

Amidst the rhythmic clatter of barrels being loaded onto the ute, a backdrop of industrious sound that had become the heartbeat of Bixbus, I guided Paul away from the bustling activity. The air around us seemed thick with unspoken questions, a tangible tension that was mirrored in the mix of concern and curiosity in Paul's eyes. His gaze was sharp, dissecting, always seeking the deeper meaning behind words left unsaid.

Jerome trailed behind us. Just as I considered requesting some privacy, Paul intervened, his voice carrying an undertone of authority that demanded attention. "It's okay," he assured, his approval of Jerome's presence reinforcing the gravity of our situation. "Everyone here in Clivilius will need to pull more than their own weight if we stand any chance of surviving out here." His gaze then shifted to Jerome, firm and unyielding. "That makes you a man now, bro." The weight of his words seemed to settle on Jerome's shoulders, his face oscillating between awe and trepidation, caught in the liminal space between young adulthood and the mantle of responsibility now placed upon him.

"Paul," I began, my voice a hushed murmur designed to carry weight yet not travel far, "we had to leave the house in a hurry. It's not safe there anymore." The admission felt heavy, laden with implications of unknown dangers.

Paul's reaction was immediate, his brow furrowing in a silent inquiry, his face a canvas of concern and confusion. Taking a deep breath, I continued, my words measured and deliberate, each one chosen to convey the seriousness of our predicament. "The police showed up, seemingly out of nowhere. And there's a Detective Santos involved."

The mention of a detective, a figure of authority far removed from the routine patrols we might have anticipated, seemed to strike a chord with Paul. Surprise and alarm flitted across his features, his eyes widening in response. "Detective? That's no beat cop. What were they doing there?"

"I've got no idea," I confessed, the admission a heavy weight in the silence that followed. Meeting his gaze, I conveyed the depth of my uncertainty, the unease that gnawed at the edges of my resolve. "I can't risk going back right now. Something feels off about the whole situation."

The words hung between us, a stark acknowledgment of the peril that had driven Charles and me from the family home.

Paul nodded, his expression mirroring the weight of our shared concerns. Then, suddenly, as if a switch had been flipped, his demeanour changed, an idea igniting in his eyes. "Claire!" he blurted out, the name slicing through the tension like a knife.

I gasped, the implications of his outburst dawning on me with unsettling clarity. "You think Claire would have gone to the police?" The question tumbled out, heavy with disbelief and a burgeoning sense of betrayal.

Paul's response was a pout, condescending in its delivery, as if the answer should have been obvious to me from the start. "Well, I have been missing for almost ten days now," he stated, matter-of-factly.

My brow furrowed, the revelation sinking in. *Had it truly been that long?*

"Has it been that long already?" Jerome echoed my unspoken thoughts, his voice tinged with surprise and a hint of alarm.

"Apparently so," Paul answered, a touch of weariness in his voice. "To be honest, I'm struggling to keep track of time here."

"But a Detective?" I pressed, grappling with the notion. "Would anybody take Claire's claims seriously enough to warrant spending Detective resources on her?" The skepticism in my voice was palpable, a reflection of my struggle to reconcile the image of Claire with the expense of law enforcement's involvement.

"Oh, come on, Luke. You've met Claire. She's the most skilled manipulator I've ever met," Paul retorted, his words carrying a mixture of respect and wariness for the woman he had chosen as a partner.

"Lucky you married her, then," I joked, an attempt to lighten the mood, to find some semblance of levity in our predicament. However, the humour fell flat, the gravity of the situation cementing itself further with Paul's unamused reaction.

"So, what's the plan?" Paul shifted the conversation towards action, his face etched with seriousness, the moment for jest long passed.

"For now, I need to steer clear of the house," I advised, the decision a difficult but necessary concession to the dangers that now lurked within the once-safe haven.

Paul, ever the strategist, pressed further. "Can you try and dig deeper into it? See just how messy things are getting?"

"Oh, things are definitely messy," I said, half serious, half light-hearted, as I thought about my blood on the shed and the semen-soaked garment I had left on my parent's bed.

"To lighten the mood," Jerome chimed in, his suggestion cutting through the heavy air with a hopeful note. "Let's have a celebration tonight at the bonfire. Welcome the Smith Clan properly. What do you think?" His eyes sparkled with the prospect of unity and joy, an antidote to the tension that had momentarily ensnared us.

A faint smile touched Paul's lips, softening the hardened lines of concern that had settled there. "That's a damn good idea. A celebration might be just what we all need." His voice, infused with a newfound warmth, acknowledged the weight of Jerome's proposal—not just as a diversion, but as a vital reaffirmation of our communal spirit and resilience.

With the three of us in agreement, a wave of relief washed over me, and I clapped my hand on Paul's shoulder in a gesture of brotherly camaraderie. "I'll leave the two of you to organise it. We should have plenty of supplies between the raid last night and the food storage I've managed to bring through." The mention of our preparedness, the tangible results of our efforts to secure our survival, bolstered my confidence in the plan.

"Yeah, there's heaps here now," Paul responded, his smile broadening, the shadow of earlier conversations momentarily forgotten in the light of our collective resolve.

"I'll let Beatrix know too," I added, the logistics of the celebration beginning to take shape in my mind.

"And Jarod?" Paul couldn't resist adding, the gleam in his eye betraying his awareness of the complexities that lay within our interpersonal dynamics. My distaste for Beatrix choosing Jarod as a Guardian was no secret, a sore point that Paul, ever the observer, had not missed.

"Sure," I muttered, conceding to the necessity of inclusivity, even if it meant involving those I harboured reservations about. "I guess we should involve him too."

"This is going to be awesome!" Jerome's enthusiasm burst forth, untainted by the undercurrents that flowed beneath the surface of our planning. His cheer, genuine and infectious, elicited contagious smiles and chuckles from both Paul and me, a much-needed reminder of the joy and strength found in our collective spirit.

❖

As our paths finally crossed by the Portals, Beatrix's energetic strides matched her lively greeting. "Hey, Luke!" she called out, the excitement evident in her voice. "This Guardian stuff is so much fun. I can jump between all these locations on Earth where we've registered Portal locations. It's awesome!"

"It is," I agreed, a subtle smile finding its way onto my face in response to Beatrix's infectious enthusiasm. Her ability to find joy in her responsibilities, to marvel at the capabilities bestowed upon her as a Guardian, offered a momentary reprieve from the weight of my own concerns. Her vibrant energy served as a beacon of light in the long and challenging day that had been consumed by the efforts of bringing my family to this new world.

Curiosity piqued by her interactions with my family, I ventured, "Have you met my family yet?" The question was tinged with a mix of hope and apprehension. The integration of my family into the fabric of Clivilius was paramount to me, and Beatrix's impressions would serve as a valuable gauge of their settling in.

"I've met your father. He seems to hang around the Drop Zone a lot with Paul," she shared, her chuckle resonating warmly in the air between us. "Oh, and Jerome. He's a cute one."

"Beatrix!" I snapped, the hint of protective older brother surfacing with a force that surprised even me. "He's only twenty-one. He's too young for you." The words spilled out, a reflexive defence, a barrier erected to shield Jerome from complications he didn't need.

Beatrix pouted playfully, undeterred by my warning. "That doesn't mean I can't enjoy his company," she retorted, her teasing smirk a challenge to my protective stance. Her ability to parry my concerns with humour was both frustrating and endearing, a testament to the complexity of our interactions.

"Don't even think about it," I warned, my tone firm and brooking no argument. "He's my younger brother." The declaration was more than a statement of fact; it was a line drawn in the sand, an assertion of my role in Jerome's life, even here in the uncertain terrain of Clivilius.

She scoffed in response, her expression a blend of defiance and playfulness that seemed to dance in her eyes. "He wouldn't go there, anyway," I continued, trying to lay the issue to rest with a fact I thought would deter any further teasing. "He's Mormon."

"Oh?" Beatrix probed, her eyebrow arching with curiosity, as if this piece of information added a new layer of intrigue rather than serving as a deterrent.

I chuckled, unable to resist the amusement that bubbled up at her persistence. Her curiosity, always as boundless as the worlds we could now traverse, had a way of making even the most steadfast facts seem like the beginning of a debate rather than the end. "He only dates other Mormons," I elaborated, hoping to paint a clearer picture of Jerome's world view, one steeped in faith and tradition.

"Give him time," Beatrix suggested, her voice laced with a confidence that suggested she saw this not as a barrier but as a temporary state of affairs. "Besides, I don't intend to bring any more Mormons to Clivilius. Do you?"

Her logic, flawed yet delivered with such unabashed assurance, drew a laugh from me, a sound that felt lighter than the air around us, but her question had planted a seed of thought. "Well, no, but..." I trailed off, the conversation veering into territory that was both familiar and foreign. The mention of Mormons in Clivilius, of integrating our Earthly identities and beliefs into this new world, evoked memories of Sunday School lessons and stories of the early pioneers. My mind wandered, drawn to tales of resilience, faith, and communal strength that had been ingrained in me since childhood.

As I stood there, lost in thought amidst the backdrop of Clivilius's bustling activity, the notion of a Mormon community in this extraterrestrial settlement took root in my mind with an unexpected clarity. Images of covered wagons and handcart treks flickered through my consciousness, vivid and compelling. The pioneers, those forebears who faced untold hardships and forged paths through uncharted territories, had clung to their faith and community for survival. Their narrative, one of perseverance, faith, and collective strength in the face of adversity, resonated deeply with me. It was a testament to the enduring importance of unity and shared beliefs, especially when confronted by the unknown.

The stories of those who had crossed the plains, seeking refuge and religious freedom, echoed in my thoughts, their echoes blending seamlessly with the sounds of Clivilius. Could Clivilius, this alien world that we were slowly making our own, become a new gathering place? A haven for those seeking not just refuge from Earth's challenges but also a different kind of sanctuary—a sanctuary of purpose, of shared vision?

The parallels between the pioneers' journey across daunting landscapes and our current quest for survival in this new environment were striking. Both were tales of leaving behind the familiar in search of something greater, of facing the vast unknown with little more than faith and each other.

Actually, I mused, my contemplation deepening in the silence that surrounded me, *it might not be such a bad idea.* The early pioneers, despite—or perhaps because of—their challenges, forged a community that was tightly knit, resilient, and imbued with a sense of higher purpose. They relied on each other, their shared values providing a compass through their trials. Maybe that's precisely what we need here in Clivilius—a sense of community that transcends mere survival, a shared purpose that binds us together not just as individuals fighting to adapt, but as a collective, united in our quest to thrive in this new world.

"Hello, Earth to Luke," Beatrix quipped, her voice slicing through my reverie like a beacon. Her fingers snapped in front of my face, an effective, albeit startling, method to reel me back from the depths of my contemplation.

Shaking off the remnants of my thoughts, I found myself momentarily disoriented by the abrupt return to the present.

"We're not on Earth," I retorted, a half-smile playing on my lips as I anchored myself in the reality of Clivilius, not just geographically but metaphorically as well.

"Aren't we?" Beatrix fired back sharply, her quick wit a constant reminder of the complexity of our situation. Her question, though posed in jest, resonated with a deeper, more existential inquiry.

"I'm really not sure," I admitted with a gentle shrug, conceding to the ambiguity of our existence in Clivilius. It was a place that defied simple definitions, a world that was neither fully alien nor entirely reminiscent of Earth.

Beatrix chuckled, a sound that seemed to celebrate her banter victory, a playful acknowledgment of our ongoing verbal sparring. "Anyway," I redirected the conversation, eager to share the news of the impending celebration, "they're organising a big celebration at the bonfire tonight to welcome all the new people that have arrived in the last few days."

"That sounds like a great idea," Beatrix agreed cheerfully, her enthusiasm genuine.

"You'll be coming along then?" I asked, my question laced with an undercurrent of curiosity about her willingness to partake in community gatherings, especially given the Guardians' notorious tendency to avoid such events after dark.

"Yeah. Sounds like fun," Beatrix replied, her voice carrying a hint of something akin to relief. "Could do with a bit of fun."

"Oh, come on," I interjected, grinning, seizing the opportunity to tease her. "You loved plundering that Big W store last night." The memory of the raid, a blend of adrenaline and necessity, was a vivid one, marked by Beatrix's particular flair for the dramatic.

"It's my specialty," Beatrix acknowledged with a mischievous grin, her pride in her unique skills apparent. "Leave it to me, Luke. I'll make sure it's a night they won't forget." Her confidence was infectious, a beacon of optimism in the uncertain terrain of our new world.

"Let's make it memorable, Beatrix," I said, my voice imbued with a newfound determination. "A celebration to anchor them here, in the heart of Bixbus."

"Agreed," she said. "Anyway, there's Guardian work to be done," she added, her tone shifting to one of resolve as she activated her Portal and disappeared, leaving me alone with my thoughts once more.

"Shit," I muttered to myself, a twinge of frustration laced with concern bubbling up as I realised I had forgotten to ask her about Jarod. Beatrix's sudden departure through the Portal left me with a lingering unease. Jarod's silence since his arrival was troubling, a silent alarm bell that rang faintly in the back of my mind. My knowledge of Jarod was limited, but the bits and pieces I did know painted a picture of complexity and potential turmoil, especially in his interactions with Beatrix. Together, they formed a duo that was as dynamic as it was unpredictable, and the uncertainty of their influence on each other—and on Clivilius—was a puzzle I was yet to solve.

LIGHT THE FIRE. SHARE THE LIGHT

4338.213.7

As the golden orb of the evening sun began its descent, it bathed Clivilius in a warm, enchanting glow, a prelude to the grand celebration unfolding beneath its benevolent gaze. The bonfire, a focal point of communal spirit, crackled with unabashed enthusiasm, its dancing flames sending shadows on a lively canvas of faces. Settlers, momentarily liberated from the demands of daily chores, converged around the flickering beacon, their eyes reflecting the communal joy that pulsed through the gathering.

The air resonated with the melodies of lively tunes, the rhythmic beats stirring an infectious energy that coursed through the assembly.

A symphony of laughter and chatter interwove with the music, creating a tapestry of sound that mirrored the diverse tapestry of the community itself. Faces aglow with anticipation and delight turned towards the source of the culinary symphony, where the irresistible aroma of delectable dishes wafted through the air. The tantalising scent, a siren's call, beckoned settlers to indulge in the abundance of food that adorned communal tables, each dish a testament to the collective effort that had gone into preparing this feast.

Under the benevolent gaze of the evening sun, Clivilius transformed into a haven of celebration. The warmth, both literal and metaphorical, embraced every soul present, fostering a sense of unity that transcended the mundane.

Navigating through the lively gathering, my eyes caught a glimpse of a cluster of unfamiliar faces just beyond the secure embrace of the fence. A surge of initial panic pulsed through my chest, the kind that tightens your grip on reality for a fleeting moment. However, the recent addition of Guardians and Portals around Bixbus had taught us all to temper our fears, to hold back the tide of hasty assumptions about potential intruders that once might have sent us into a frenzy.

Intrigued by the enigma beyond the fence, I manoeuvred through the crowd toward Beatrix, engrossed in conversation with Paul. The warm radiance from the bonfire cast an ethereal ambiance over the settlers, dancing on their faces like whispers of light, transforming the mundane into something otherworldly. The scene felt suspended in time, a living painting illuminated by the flickering flames.

"Beatrix," I interjected, catching her attention along with Paul's. The words felt heavy, loaded with the weight of our communal safety, "did you or Jarod bring those people here?" My voice carried a hint of urgency, not quite accusing but teetering on the edge of suspicion.

"No," Beatrix replied, her expression mirroring my unease. It was a look that spoke volumes, a shared concern momentarily dimming the light in her eyes. The flickering shadows seemed to play on her worried features, casting a spell of doubt that momentarily enveloped us.

Paul chuckled softly, the sound blending with the music in a way that seemed almost incongruous with the tension of the moment. "It's okay. I know them," he assured us, his voice a lighthouse in the fog of our apprehension.

"You do?" Beatrix and I chorused in disbelief, our gazes locked in a dance of shared skepticism. It was as if our simultaneous response bridged the gap between worry and the possibility of relief, a single question mark hanging in the air between us.

"Yeah. They're members of Charity's Chewbathian Hunter team. They were hunting the Shadow Panther pack that attacked us recently," Paul explained, his words painting a picture of allies in the shadows, of warriors united against a common enemy. It was a narrative twist, turning the unfamiliar into the familiar, the feared into the friend.

He ushered us toward the fence gate, his stride confident, a man on a mission to bridge worlds. He waved over a tall, rugged man, eager to introduce us. The man approached with the ease of a seasoned warrior, his presence commanding yet not imposing, the kind of person who carried stories in every scar and gesture.

As the figure approached, the bonfire's glow heightened the contours of his face, emphasising a stern yet composed countenance that seemed to carve him out of the night itself. "What are they still doing here?" I whispered sharply to Paul before the man arrived within earshot, my voice laced with a blend of curiosity and concern that seemed to vibrate in the cool night air.

"Luke, Beatrix, meet Alistair. He's the commander of the Chewbathian Hunter Group," Paul announced the man as he stepped into the circle of light, his presence almost commanding the shadows to retreat.

Alistair extended a firm handshake, his grip strong and assured. His gaze was unwavering, piercing through the flickering dance of flames reflected in his eyes, creating an intensity that seemed to echo the seriousness of his mission. The bonfire's flames played in his eyes, lending a fiery depth to them that was only accentuated by his thick Scottish accent. "Paul has briefed me on the situation here. We've decided to offer our protection for the next ten days. Consider it a token of goodwill between settlements," he said, his voice carrying a weight that seemed to ground his words in a reality far removed from the festivities around us.

Surprise and curiosity flickered in my eyes, a testament to the unexpected turn of events. "Your settlement is nearby?" I inquired, my mind racing with questions about these strangers and their sudden appearance.

"No, we've travelled a considerable distance. You've got a few small settlements in the area, but with this vast desert and the dangers lurking in the darkness, they're all struggling," Alistair elucidated, painting a picture of the world beyond our gates that was both vast and fraught with unseen challenges. "Your group is doing well to be growing so rapidly," he added, acknowledging our efforts with a nod that seemed to bridge the gap between our disparate lives.

"Thank you," Paul responded, pride lighting up his face. The bonfire's glow seemed to amplify the warmth in his expression, and I couldn't help but chuckle internally at his eagerness for praise in this moment of unexpected camaraderie. It was a side of Paul that felt both endearing and slightly amusing.

"So, what happens after ten days?" Beatrix asked, her voice cutting through the night with a clarity that mirrored my own curiosity. Her question hung in the air, a poignant reminder of the transient nature of this newfound alliance.

Alistair's expression remained grave, and the shadows from the bonfire lent a gravity to his words that felt almost prophetic. "You build bigger fences," he stated simply, his advice resonating with an ominous undertone that seemed to echo the harsh realities of our existence on this frontier.

I swallowed, the warmth of the bonfire's glow a stark contrast to the weight of Alistair's words. A chill that had nothing to do with the night air crept up my spine. *Are things truly that dire and dangerous here?* The question echoed in my mind, a persistent whisper amid the crackle of flames and the distant hum of celebration. It was a reminder of the fragile veneer of safety that cloaked our existence, a thin layer that could be shattered by the realities of our world.

"I'd better get back to my post. Paul can keep you abreast of developments," Alistair announced, breaking the moment. His voice, firm and resolute, seemed to pull me back from the edge of my ruminations. He stood, a sentinel against the uncertainties that lay beyond our light.

"Thank you, Alistair," I expressed gratitude, the words heavy with recognition of the significance of solidarity in these uncertain times. "We're grateful for your assistance and protection. Hopefully, this is the start of something positive - a chance for our settlements to connect and support each other." My voice carried a hopeful note, a desire for a future where alliances forged in the shadow of adversity could blossom into enduring bonds.

"Light the fire," said Alistair, placing three fingers of his right hand against his right temple.

"Share the light," replied Paul, reciprocating with the three fingers of his left hand pressed into his left temple.

Alistair nodded, uttering a grunt before heading back to the outer perimeter of the settlement. His departure was marked by the shifting shadows that played on his figure, casting him in a light that seemed both heroic and enigmatic. As he moved away, the mystery and solemnity of his presence lingered, leaving an air of mystery in his wake.

"He seems a bit odd," Beatrix remarked, her gaze lingering on Alistair's retreating figure, a silhouette gradually merging with the night's embrace.

"What was that all about?" I found myself asking Paul, my curiosity piqued by the ceremonial exchange I had just witnessed.

Paul stared at me blankly for a moment, as if the significance of my question was lost in translation between our worlds. His expression, usually so open and readable, was momentarily a blank slate, a rare occurrence that only served to heighten my curiosity.

"The whole, light the fire, share the light thing," I clarified, hoping to pierce the veil of his momentary detachment.

"Oh, that's what everyone says," Paul answered, his voice casual, as if explaining a commonplace tradition. Yet, the simplicity of his response belied the depth of the ritual's significance.

"And the three fingers?" Beatrix prodded further, seeking to decode the symbolism behind the gesture.

Paul shrugged, a nonchalant gesture that seemed at odds with the solemnity of the tradition he was explaining. "It's a gesture, a symbol. Light the fire represents unity and strength. It's about igniting the flame within ourselves, our community, and nature. Share the light signifies spreading that strength, sharing it with others, connecting settlements and hearts. I believe it's been around for centuries."

Understanding dawned on Beatrix's face, and she nodded appreciatively, her initial skepticism giving way to a recognition of the profound meaning embedded within the simplicity of the gesture. It was a moment of revelation, a glimpse into the depths of tradition and solidarity that bound these communities together.

Intrigued by the revelation of a phrase and gesture with such profound symbolism having been around for a very long time, but seemingly with no more answers left to learn, I decided to steer the conversation towards a more practical inquiry. "Have you spoken much with him?" I asked Paul, the flickering glow of the bonfire reflecting the curiosity that danced in my eyes.

"They keep their distance. They're very military-focused. It's what they've trained their whole life for," Paul explained, his voice carrying a note of respect mixed with a hint of distance.

Beatrix gasped. "They've lived their entire lives here in Clivilius?" she questioned, her voice tinged with a mix of astonishment and curiosity. The revelation seemed to hang in the air between us, as tangible as the smoke that curled upwards into the night sky.

Paul nodded. "Yes. Chewbathia is the military hub of New Edinburgh. It was founded by the Stewart sisters several centuries ago."

"That explains the Scottish accent, then," I added with a smile, the warmth of the bonfire reflecting in my amused expression.

"I still don't really know much about them, but Alistair has promised that before they leave, they'll take some time to give us some real intel - tell us who is nearby. Who we can trust. Who to stay away from. That kind of thing," Paul shared, the bonfire's glow outlining the seriousness of his revelation.

"That actually sounds pretty exciting," I said, feeling a surge of anticipation at the prospect of newfound knowledge and connections. The darkness beyond the bonfire's reach suddenly seemed less foreboding, more like a canvas awaiting the strokes of new alliances and understandings. My heart quickened with the thought of expanding our horizons, of forging paths through the unknown with the help of our Chewbathian allies.

"It is," Paul agreed. "And also terrifying. Everything is just so unknown."

"You'll keep us updated?" I asked Paul.

"Of course," he assured.

"Come on then," I rallied Paul and Beatrix with a light-hearted tone, the bonfire's glow flickering in the background, "Let's grab ourselves some of this food before it's all gone!"

❖

The night unfolded with the bonfire celebration reaching a crescendo, the flames casting a warm glow on faces wrapped in laughter and camaraderie. As settlers gathered around, the air was filled with the sharing of funny anecdotes that wove a tapestry of stories, each thread tightening the bonds of our growing community. It was in these moments, amidst the laughter and the shared memories, that the essence of Clivilius truly came alive.

Charles, a master storyteller whose voice could command the attention of any crowd, took centre stage. His dramatic retelling of the Smiths' arrival at Bixbus painted a vivid picture that danced in the flames of the bonfire. Chaos, surprise, and an unexpected surplus of toilet rolls became the subjects of a tale that had us all chuckling, the absurdity and warmth of the story encapsulating the spirit of our community. I found myself laughing along, the familiarity of the tale a comforting reminder of our shared experiences.

Chuckling at the embellished tale, I sensed the impending mention of another infamous toilet paper incident, and Jerome didn't disappoint. "Speaking of toilet rolls," Jerome interjected playfully, his voice laced with a mischief that immediately piqued everyone's interest. I muttered an anticipatory, "Uh oh," knowing full well the direction in which the evening was veering.

"Is this that time in Broken Hill with the Clarke's?" Paul asked, a grin playing on his lips, his anticipation palpable in the flickering light. The mention of Broken Hill sparked a wave of curiosity and amusement that rippled through the gathered settlers.

A broad smile adorned Jerome's face as he confirmed, "Yep. That one," his excitement barely contained. It was a story that, while familiar to some of us, never failed to amuse with its recounting.

Mum, sensing the mischief that was about to unfold, narrowed her eyes at Jerome. "Is this really something I want to know?" she inquired, her tone a mix of warning and curiosity. Her maternal instinct, always on alert for tales that might tread into the realm of the infamous or the scandalous, added an extra layer of anticipation to the story.

"Oh, come on!" Kain exclaimed, his enthusiasm echoing around the bonfire. "You have to tell us now." His insistence, a testament to the allure of a good story, especially one shrouded in the promise of humour and past misadventures.

Jerome, struggling to maintain his composure amidst the rising tide of laughter and expectant faces, began his tale. "It was when we were living in Broken Hill. I was still quite young, but Paul and Luke let me come along."

"If you promised not to get us caught!" Paul interjected, his words prompting gasps and laughter around the campfire.

"I bet they got caught," Karen teased, her voice laced with amusement.

Jerome chuckled, his voice rich with the thrill of reliving the past, sharing excessive details until Paul halted him. "Forget the irrelevant stuff. We t-pee'd the Clarke's house, and then—" His words, a blend of impatience and nostalgia, cut through the laughter, directing us back to the heart of the story.

"Hang on!" Nial interrupted, his confusion breaking into the flow of the tale. "What's t-'peeing?" His question, innocent yet filled with curiosity, echoed around the campfire, drawing a mixture of chuckles and raised eyebrows.

Mum, ever the voice of reason and slightly unimpressed by our juvenile antics, clarified, "It means they threw toilet paper all over their house in the middle of the night." Her explanation, succinct and tinged with a hint of disapproval, laid bare the mischief of our youth.

"Oh," Nial chuckled, his earlier confusion replaced by a spark of amusement. "That actually sounds like a bit of fun."

"But that's not the best part," Jerome teased, his voice dancing with anticipation. He had us, every one of us, captured in the palm of his hand, waiting for the climax of the tale.

"We... we..." Jerome struggled, the words catching in his throat as if the memory itself was too big to escape.

Grinning widely, unable to contain my own part in the story, I chimed in, "Paul and I sent Jerome to knock on their front door while we went into hiding just over the small garden fence." My admission, gleeful and conspiratorial, drew gasps and laughter from around the fire.

The attention shifted back to Jerome, all eyes on him, eager for the next piece of the puzzle. "I knock on the door, and..." Jerome tried to continue, the anticipation building with each word.

Paul, barely able to suppress his amusement, took over. "And then you just stood there!" His interjection, filled with incredulous laughter, painted a picture of Jerome, frozen in the moment, a statue of confusion and panic.

"Paul and I thought we were done for," I added, the memory vivid in my mind. The tension of that night, the fear of getting caught, mingled with the exhilaration of the prank, was a feeling I'd never forget. It was one of those moments that seemed to define the reckless freedom of our youth.

"And what happened? Did Jerome get caught?" Sarah asked eagerly, her voice a catalyst, propelling the story forward.

"No," Paul answered, the amusement evident in his voice, breaking through the suspense of the moment. "I had to sprint to the front door to grab him and drag him behind the fence. He nearly tripped me up on the way." His recounting brought chuckles from the group, the image of Paul, usually so composed, in a desperate dash to rescue Jerome, painted a picture so comical it was irresistible.

"And then the front door opens," I continued, leaning into the collective anticipation that had built around the fire.

"And the family comes out and finds that their house has been t'peed," Paul chimed in, his tone shifting to mimic the bewildered reaction of the Clarke family. "They were so confused. They had no idea who had done it or why."

"They came so close to finding us behind the fence," I added, the memory of that near discovery sending a shiver down my spine even now.

Maintaining his composure with effort, Jerome continued, "But then one of their kids was like, I know who it was." He paused, a giggle escaping him, a prelude to the punchline we all knew was coming. The suspense, the build-up, it was all part of the storytelling dance we were engaged in, each playing our part.

Glancing at Paul, we silently agreed to let Jerome finish the story, a mutual acknowledgment that this was his moment, his finale to deliver. Encouragement echoed around the campfire, a chorus of eager anticipation for the climax of the story.

"And he was like, 'it must be the Smith's. They use home brand'." The punchline landed amidst us, the absurdity of the accusation, the innocence of the conclusion drawn by the Clarke's child, it was too much. Laughter filled the camp, rolling in waves of joy and disbelief. Even Mum couldn't resist a chuckle, her stern façade finally breaking under the weight of the humour. Her laughter, rare and precious, was a testament to the power of the story, to the joy found in shared memories and communal folly.

Amidst the mirth and banter that swirled around the bonfire, a moment of transformation unfolded as Paul initiated the symbolic gesture that Beatrix and I had just learned from Alistair. Placing three fingers against his right temple, he declared with a voice that cut through the laughter, "Light the fire." It was a call to action, a reminder of our shared purpose and commitment.

As attention shifted uncertainly, with the jovial atmosphere momentarily suspended, Beatrix and I exchanged a glance of understanding. It was a silent agreement, an acknowledgment of the importance of this tradition. Mirroring Paul's gesture with three fingers on our left temples, we responded in unison, "Share the light." Our voices, intertwined, carried a weight that seemed to anchor the moment in something deeper, something profound.

A hush fell over the group, a tangible sense of significance lingering in the air, as if the very night itself paused to recognise the importance of our words. The playful banter that had filled the air moments before gave way to a solemn reverence, a collective acknowledgment of the bond we shared as a community.

To reinforce the expression and perhaps to ensure that the message was felt by every heart present, Paul repeated the gesture with even more conviction. "Light the fire!" he exclaimed, his voice echoing into the night, a beacon calling us back to our core values. It was more than a statement; it was a declaration, a reaffirmation of our commitment to each other and to the ideals that bound us.

Beatrix and I, feeling the surge of unity and purpose that coursed through the group, encouraged everyone to join in. And then, in a spine-tingling unison that seemed to rise from the very earth beneath us, "Share the light!" erupted triumphantly into the dark Clivilius sky. The words, spoken by every voice present, melded into a chorus that transcended individuality, solidifying our unity, a beacon of hope in the night.

❖

As the night wrapped its arms around the lively celebration, transforming joy into a canvas of shadows and light, a subtle tension crept through the air like a hushed murmur. The shift was almost imperceptible at first, but as Mum, the stalwart enforcer of our family's values, approached Dad, Paul, and me, the change in the atmosphere became undeniable. Her furrowed brow was like a beacon of concern, casting a small shadow over the warmth of the bonfire's glow.

"Noah," she murmured, her voice a delicate whisper amidst the vibrant chatter that filled the air. "I'm getting a bit worried about the drinking. It's too much, and I don't like it." Her words, though softly spoken, carried a weight of concern that was hard to ignore. Observing the scenes of jubilation and laughter, so beautifully illuminated by the warm dance of the bonfire, I couldn't help but feel a twinge of apprehension. I hoped that I wasn't about to regret bringing her to Clivilius, to this place of newfound freedom and community.

"I don't really like it either," Dad confessed, his voice low, glancing at Paul and me. It was a rare admission, a shared concern that momentarily bridged the gap between our worlds. "But I don't think there's a lot we can do about it." His words were a resignation, an acknowledgment of the complex fabric of community life that was not easily altered.

Mum insisted, with a determination that was both admirable and slightly daunting, "I think we should leave now. Will you get the kids," directing Dad with a firmness that brooked no argument. It was a command, not a request, fuelled by her protective instincts.

"Are you sure that's really necessary?" Dad attempted to reason, sensing an imminent 'mum outburst.' His attempt to mitigate the situation was a delicate dance, a balancing act between respect for Mum's concerns and the desire to stay.

I tactfully stepped back, leaving the matter in Paul's capable hands. *He's good at managing Mum*, I reassured myself. In moments like these, Paul's calm demeanour and diplomatic touch were invaluable. He had a way of navigating the stormy waters of family dynamics with a grace that I often found elusive.

As Mum's concerns echoed in my mind, I retreated from the heart of the celebration, seeking solace in the shadows. Reflecting on my own rebellious journey against family and church, a new idea blossomed within me. Amidst flickering shadows, I sought the company of our two other Guardians – Beatrix and Jarod – in a quieter corner of the gathering.

In the relative seclusion of our quiet corner, away from the bonfire's boisterous glow and the settlers' lively discussions, a glance between us conveyed more than words could. It was a silent acknowledgment of our unity. I unfolded a fresh plan, a mission shrouded in the secrecy of night, to retrieve the Smiths' belongings from their family home before the police could seize them entirely.

"We need to bring everything from the Smith house to Clivilius," I explained, my voice a hushed whisper to ensure our conversation remained just between us. "I don't want the police to have any of it."

Beatrix's eyes gleamed with a determination that mirrored my own, her spirit undaunted by the prospect of what I was proposing. And Jarod, ever enigmatic in his expressions, gave a subtle nod that signalled his agreement. It was clear; *we were doing this!*

"It'll be a covert entry into the Smith house from the inside, ensuring we can operate undetected," I continued, laying out the plan with precision. "And I don't want a word of this to anyone else. Not yet." The importance of discretion, of keeping our plans under wraps, couldn't be overstated.

"When are we doing this?" Beatrix's inquiry cut through the night, her readiness evident.

Glancing back at the campfire, where settlers were engrossed in their own worlds, their attention diverted from our clandestine gathering, I made the call. "Now," I replied, the word heavy with resolve.

"Now?" Jarod repeated, his surprise momentarily breaking through his usually composed demeanour, as he glanced down at his almost full beer.

"You can bring that with you," Beatrix answered for me, her smile playful, a spark of adventure lighting up her eyes.

"You love this, don't you, Beatrix?" Jarod teased, his tone light, finding amusement in Beatrix's enthusiasm for the new mission.

Beatrix chuckled, her laughter a soft sound in the darkness. "Stealing stuff in the middle of the night. Of course, I love this shit." Her candid admission, though made in jest, spoke volumes of her spirit.

"It belongs to my family, so technically we're not really stealing anything," I pointed out, needing to clarify that our actions, though covert, were rooted in a sense of justice, of reclaiming what was rightfully ours.

"Whatever. Same difference," Beatrix retorted with a playful pout. "We're still doing secret stuff while trying not to get caught." Her words, light and teasing, belied the seriousness of our undertaking.

Jarod and I chuckled at Beatrix's response, her ability to find levity in the moment a welcome relief from the tension that had begun to build.

"Come on, then," I encouraged the pair, feeling the weight of responsibility settle over me. "Let's go before we get dragged into another conversation." It was time to act, to step into the shadows of the night and undertake our new mission.

Avoiding direct eye contact from anyone else, the three of us, Beatrix, Jarod, and I, approached the gate in the fence that encircled our small encampment. The metal hinges let out a soft squeak, a sound so at odds with the jubilee of the night, it seemed almost like a protest against our departure into the unknown. As we stepped beyond the threshold, the familiar warmth of the bonfire's glow was replaced by a realm of darkness, a world painted in shades of mystery and intrigue that stretched out before us like an uncharted territory.

Pausing as I gently closed the gate behind us, ensuring it made as little noise as possible, I turned to my fellow Guardians. The significance of the moment felt as heavy as the darkness that enveloped us. Pressing the three fingers into my right temple, I reaffirmed our bond with the words, "Light the fire." It was more than a command; it was a reminder of why we were here, of the light we sought to preserve and protect.

Beatrix and Jarod, ever my partners in this night's endeavour, mirrored the movement with their own hands. "Share the light," they whispered back, their voices barely audible yet laden with determination. In the silence of the night, our whispered vow felt like a powerful echo of our commitment to unity and shared purpose, a beacon of hope in the enveloping darkness.

Our only sources of light were the torches we carried with us, their flames flickering like distant stars borrowed from Earth's night sky. These torches guided us through the obsidian expanse, casting elongated shadows that stretched out on the sandy ground beneath our feet. The shadows danced with every flicker of the flame, intertwining with the uncertainty that the night held. Yet, there was a certain beauty in the way the light and shadow played together, a visual metaphor for the duality of our mission — the interplay of risk and resolve, of darkness and the light we sought to reclaim.

Each step taken was resonant with purpose, a testament to the urgency that drove us. We were not just moving through the darkness; we were moving against it. In this mission, we were more than just individuals; we were shadows ourselves, moving silently, ensuring that the only secrets the night would hold were our own.

UNDER THEIR NOSES

4338.213.8

The tension in the air was more than just palpable; it was a tangible, electric current that enveloped us, an invisible force that hummed with anticipation and danger. As Guardians, Beatrix, Jarod, and I were slowly getting accustomed to the weight of responsibility that cloaked our shoulders, a mantle we bore with silent resolve. Tonight, our mission was clear, and we utilised our Portals with practiced ease, materialising directly within the shadowed confines of the Smith family home. The study, a room that bore witness to countless moments of my childhood, now lay shrouded in darkness, its familiar contours bathed in the soft, eerie glow of moonlight that seeped through the half-closed blinds.

Navigating the Smith house, a place that once resonated with the vibrant energy of family gatherings, now felt like traversing a mausoleum. Each step we took was accompanied by the faint echoes of the past—ghostly laughter and the distant sound of conversations that once filled these rooms. The study, with its walls lined with shelves heavy with aged books, had always been a sanctuary of knowledge and warmth. But tonight, it harboured a different atmosphere—one laced with an undercurrent of apprehension and the stale scent of abandonment.

Before we could commence our intended raid, we conducted a thorough sweep of every room, moving with a precision that spoke of our need to assess the situation. Our senses, already sharpened by the nature of our task, were heightened further by the knowledge of the risk that cloaked our every move. Beatrix, with her keen eye and ever watchful stance, approached the living room curtains with a caution that was almost palpable. The sudden, sharp intake of breath and the gasp that slipped from her lips shattered the silence, a clear indication of an unexpected discovery. "We've got eyes on us," she murmured, her voice barely above a whisper, yet it cut through the stifling air with the sharpness of a knife.

A wave of frustration washed over me, tightening its grip around my jaw as the reality of our situation sank in. The invasion of our privacy, the sanctity of my family's home being violated, was a betrayal that stung with a bitterness I couldn't shake off. My childhood home, a place that once stood as a bastion of safety and family, had been transformed into a cage. The very idea that the authorities had infiltrated this space, turning it into a battleground for their cloak-and-dagger activities, was a violation of everything I held dear. The realisation that this haven, once sacred and inviolable, was now under the scrutinising gaze of those who sought to control and dominate, left me with a sense of loss that was profound. The shadows that danced across the walls seemed to mock us, a stark reminder of the battle lines that had been drawn within the very heart of what was once a place of refuge.

"Close the curtains," I directed, my voice a low growl, tinged with the urgency of our situation. The words left my lips in a whisper, but they carried the weight of command. "We stay in the shadows. No unnecessary risks." My eyes, adjusted to the darkness, watched as Beatrix moved with a grace that belied the tension of the moment. Her hands, steady and sure, swiftly drew every curtain, wrapping the house in an impenetrable veil of darkness that mirrored the uncertainty and danger of our mission. The action was swift, a testament to our shared understanding that in the shadows, we found our strength.

"The food storage room," I declared, leading the way through the darkened rooms. "We'll do it there. Less chance of prying eyes catching a glimpse." The familiar scent of preserved goods greeted us as we entered the room, now almost bare thanks to the earlier efforts of myself and Charles.

Stadning in the food storage room, a heavy silence enveloped us, the weight of defiance and determination hanging thick in the air. A sombre realisation settled over me, pressing down with the gravity of our future actions. The room, with its sparse shelves and the remnants of our preparedness, was a physical manifestation of the risks we were taking. It was here, in this room that the tangible danger of our covert operation became all too real.

I took a moment to gather Beatrix and Jarod, pulling them close for a hushed conversation. Our heads bowed together, our whispers barely audible over the pounding of our hearts. The seriousness of our undertaking was reflected in their faces, illuminated by the portal's colourful light that oversaw our secluded space. "This is it," I whispered, the weight of leadership heavy on my shoulders. "We do this smart, we do this quietly. We're in and out before they even know we're here."

In the swirling light, I could see the resolve in Beatrix and Jarod's eyes, a mirrored reflection of my own determination. The food storage room, once a place of preservation and hope, now served as our staging ground for defiance.

"We need to be cautious," I whispered, my voice barely a breath against the stillness that enveloped us. The words hung in the air, a tangible reminder of the peril that shadowed our every move. The police—at least I hoped that it was only the police— had their gaze fixed upon us, a scrutiny we could ill afford. "The shed, where I cut myself, is compromised. They found my blood, and that's a vulnerability we can't ignore." The words felt heavy on my tongue, each syllable a stark echo of our increasingly precarious situation.

Jarod's expression tightened, his features etched with the gravity of our circumstances. His eyes, a mirror to the turmoil churning within, sought mine. "What are the chances they'll connect any of this to Beatrix and me?" His voice, though steady, carried an undercurrent of concern that mirrored my own apprehensions.

I sighed, the weight of leadership and the burden of our collective safety pressing down on me. "If they're as thorough as I fear, they might link it back to Clivilius. We can't underestimate them." The possibility loomed over us like a dark cloud, threatening to unleash a storm that could sweep us away. I paused, my gaze drifting, haunted by the thought of unseen eyes and ears prying into our lives. "They've even taken the shopping trolley full of loo paper we had to abandon." The absurdity of the detail, juxtaposed with our dire situation, lent a surreal edge to the danger we faced.

And then, with a hesitation that felt like a betrayal of my own resolve, I added, "And," my voice faltered, the next words catching in my throat as my head dropped, the weight of shame and fear mingling in the silence that followed. The decision to leave my thoughts unvoiced, about the soiled garment from my parents' bed now in their hands, was a testament to the depth of our vulnerability.

Beatrix shot me a concerned look, her eyes conveying a depth of understanding that words could scarcely encompass. A silent communication passed between us, a shared recognition of the tightening noose the authorities had looped around our efforts. The knowledge that they had confiscated not just physical items but pieces of my families personal lives, felt like an invasion far more insidious than a simple breach of privacy.

Beatrix's moment of hesitation was like the calm before a storm, a brief pause in which the sanctity of our situation hung suspended in the air. She turned to Jarod and me, her resolve reflected in the set of her shoulders. "Okay, let's make this quick and quiet. We don't want any unexpected guests." Her voice, a whisper in the vast silence of the night, was a command that set us into motion.

As Beatrix busied herself with gathering the smaller items, Jarod and I turned our attention to the heavier pieces of furniture. The silence of the house amplified every sound, from the soft shuffle of our feet across the floor to the occasional clatter of a falling object—a jarring note in the otherwise hushed symphony of our movements. Amid this quietude, Jarod's voice cut through the silence, bringing with it a question that hung heavily in the air.

"Why are we doing this, Luke?" he asked, a mix of curiosity and challenge in his gaze. "We don't have proper storage in Clivilius. Most of this stuff will just gather dust anyway."

I met his gaze, feeling the weight of my conviction anchor me. "It's not about where we keep it. It's about not letting them have it," I responded, the determination in my voice as solid as the ground beneath our feet. "After what happened today, I'd rather see my family's treasured belongings in the dust of Clivilius than in the hands of those meddling in our affairs." The words were a testament to my resolve, a declaration of our right to protect what was ours from those who would take it from us.

Jarod held up an old tin of powdered mashed potato, its expiration date several decades past. With a grin tinged with mischief, he read the date aloud, his chuckle breaking the seriousness of our endeavour. "This is a treasured belonging?" he teased, his levity a brief respite from the seriousness of our mood.

Despite the frustration that bubbled up at his jest, I couldn't help but defend our actions, albeit with a huff. "We're taking all of it," I insisted, the stubborn set of my jaw a silent challenge to any who would question my motives.

"Keep your voices down!" Beatrix's scold cut through our exchange, a reminder of the need for stealth. As she passed by, laden with belongings, she added, "Regardless, imagine the confusion on their faces when they realise an entire houseful of stuff vanished right under their noses! It's a little payback for the intrusion." Her words painted a picture of our small victory, a blow against the forces that sought to undermine us.

A nervous laugh escaped me at the thought, the absurdity of our situation momentarily lightening the heavy atmosphere. "Assuming they're just normal police doing their normal police jobs and don't know a thing about Clivilius. But let's make sure they stay clueless." The shared understanding between us solidified our resolve, binding us together in our covert operation. "Besides," I added, pausing briefly as the weight of my thought settled in my gut. "We may only get one shot at this. Once they, whoever 'they' are, realise that it was infiltrated during their watch, who knows what they'll do to this place. So let's make it count."

With that, we continued our work, each movement and decision transforming the Smith house from a mere structure of walls and memories into a stage for our rebellion. It was more than just an act of defiance; it was a statement, a silent challenge to those who dared to control our fate. The weight of our determination filled the air, a testament to our unwillingness to bend, to break, under the scrutiny of those who sought to claim dominion over us.

❖

In the dim, undercover darkness of the Smith house, as it neared its transformation into an echo of emptiness, a hint of dark humour danced around us, ethereal and fleeting, like a spectre amused by our defiance. Amidst the heavy air of solemnity, Beatrix, with a sly grin painting her features, began to unhinge the curtains from their rods, her movements deliberate, a mischievous glint sparkling in her eyes. Confused by her actions, both Jarod and I turned our heads towards her, our expressions a mirror of bewildered curiosity. Almost in perfect harmony, our voices melded into one as we questioned, "Why are you taking the curtains?"

Her response, delivered with a deadpan seriousness that belied the humour in her eyes, was succinct. "Luke, you said to take everything. So, I am." Her words, simple yet profound in their literal adherence, hung in the air, a testament to her unwavering commitment to our cause.

Soft chuckles broke free from us, the tension that had knotted our shoulders unwinding as we surrendered to the unexpected twist in our operation. The gravity of our situation, for a fleeting moment, seemed to lift, replaced by the lightness of shared amusement over Beatrix's literal interpretation of my earlier directive.

But then, as if inspired by Beatrix's commitment to our cause, Jarod, moved by a sudden revelation, made his way to the corner of the now-bare living room. With a determination that caught me off guard, he dropped to his knees and began to pull at the edges of the carpet. My eyes widened in surprise, the action so unexpected that it rendered me momentarily speechless. "What?" I managed, my voice a mix of astonishment and curiosity, as I watched him fervently work to free the carpet from its moorings.

Without pausing in his efforts, Jarod's actions spoke louder than words, his determination a silent echo of Beatrix's earlier sentiment. Beatrix, now openly smirking at our collective realisation, added, "You did say everything, remember?" Her words, a playful challenge, reignited a spark of enthusiasm within me.

Caught up in the infectious spirit of our newfound resolve, I joined Jarod on the floor, Beatrix following suit. Together, we worked to strip the house of its carpeting, our actions a physical manifestation of our rebellion. The absurdity of what we were doing - dismantling the very fabric of the home - resonated deeply within the hollow rooms, each tug and pull a symbol of our refusal to leave behind any part of the past for them to claim.

In those moments, as the shadows played across our faces and soft giggles punctuated the silence, the Smith house transformed. No longer just a structure of wood and brick, it became a testament to the unconventional rebellion of Bixbus' Guardians. Our laughter and the sound of the carpet ripping from the floorboards were the final notes in a symphony of defiance, a melody that sang of resilience, of the strength found in unity, and of a commitment to protect what belonged to Bixbus, no matter how unconventional the method.

❖

In the cloak of night, we melded with the shadows, moving with a precision and silence that made us indistinguishable from the darkness itself. The backyard of the Smith house, familiar to me, yet transformed under the cover of darkness, became the final stage for our silent rebellion. The tension in the air was palpable, a thick presence that wrapped around us as we approached the patio, a trio of Guardians united in a clandestine mission to erase every trace of Smith Clan existence from this place that once echoed with the vibrancy of life.

The patio, which had once been a riot of colour and life with its vibrant plants, now served as a backdrop for our stealthy operation. Beatrix, with the grace and precision of a seasoned thief, moved among the potted greens, her hands gently but efficiently gathering them. The soft rustle of leaves, a whisper in the night, was nearly inaudible, as if the plants themselves were complicit in our mission. Jarod and I joined in, each of us silently contributing to the collection, our actions synchronised in the quiet ballet of our endeavour.

Our next target was the hen house, a structure that seemed to stand sentinel in the quiet of the night. Undeterred by the potential for noise, while Beatrix and I gathered the sleeping hens, Jarod deftly gathered the straw bedding, his movements quick and assured. The night air around us felt charged, holding its breath as we worked in unison, the silence our accomplice.

The shed, however, posed a new challenge. Standing before its locked door, we hesitated, the realisation that we lacked the means to unlock it hanging between us like a tangible obstacle. The thought of abandoning our quest to clear it out was a bitter pill, a pause in the rhythm of our mission. But then, in the silence, Beatrix's ingenuity shone like a beacon.

Her eyes, alight with the spark of an idea, found a small gap in the join of the shed. "I have an idea," she whispered, her voice a soft murmur of promise in the darkness. With the precision of an artist, she wedged her Portal key into the gap, her movements deliberate. The moment she activated the device, registering a location within the shed itself, was a testament to her brilliance. "You're a pure genius," I whispered, admiration and gratitude mingling in my voice, awed by her quick thinking and resourcefulness.

"Nah, she's just an expert thief," Jarod interjected with a sly grin.

As Beatrix assumed the role of the keymaster to our impromptu heist, she vanished into the shed's depths, her presence marked only by the sounds that floated out to where Jarod and I stood in the cool night air. The soft shuffling of items being moved, the occasional thud as something was inevitably displaced, and even a muffled curse when she unexpectedly encountered a nest of black spiders—all painted a vivid picture of her endeavours in the pitch-black interior. Jarod and I, stationed outside, continued our task with a focus that matched the intensity of our mission, our actions seamless against the backdrop of the night, as if we were nothing more than shadows ourselves.

When we finally regrouped, our stolen bounty in tow, there was a palpable sense of accomplishment that seemed to radiate from us as we made our retreat through the Portals to Clivilius. The weight of our nocturnal escapade bore down on us, a mix of exhilaration and fatigue, as if we had just pulled off the most significant heist in history. The beds we had liberated, now lying near the Portals, stood as silent witnesses to our daring mission, encircled by the various spoils of our rebellion.

Collapsing onto the beds, the fatigue from our endeavours washed over me in waves. It was a moment of quiet reflection, the adrenaline of the heist slowly ebbing away, leaving behind a sense of surreal accomplishment.

Jarod's observation cut through the silence, his voice tinged with a mixture of awe and exhaustion. "It looks like a war zone out here," he remarked, his gaze sweeping over the chaotic arrangement of our spoils. His words resonated with me, echoing my own sentiments. As I lay there, surrounded by the tangible evidence of our audacious mission, I couldn't help but agree. The scene did resemble a battlefield, albeit one where the combatants fought not with weapons but with wits and resolve against the encroachment of forces that sought to strip us of our autonomy.

"Paul can deal with it in the morning," I chuckled, the laughter bubbling up from a place of deep-seated satisfaction mixed with the undeniable weariness that draped over my shoulders. The night's escapades had drawn much from me, and now, as I lay amidst the scattered Smith house, the reality of my exhaustion began to firmly take hold.

"I'd love to see their reactions on their little police faces when they discover that the house is totally empty," Beatrix added, her voice infused with a mischievous glee that perfectly captured the spirit of our adventure. Her amusement was infectious, a light in the darkness that surrounded us.

"Me too," Jarod and I said together, our voices a harmonious echo of shared sentiment.

Beatrix, still riding the high of our great adventure, continued to weave her thoughts into the night air, her voice a soft murmur against the backdrop of our makeshift camp. Her words were like sparks in the darkness, illuminating the shadows with the tale of our defiance. But as her voice began to fade, succumbing to the pull of exhaustion, Jarod's snores took over, a rhythmic sound that spoke volumes of the night's toll on us all. It wasn't long before the soft cadence of Beatrix's voice joined the chorus of sleep, her final words trailing off into the silence.

Lying there, my gaze fixed on the vast, empty sky above Clivilius, a profound sense of awe washed over me. The audacity of what we had accomplished — the sheer scale of our actions — was something I couldn't quite grasp in my tired state. Yet, there it was, undeniable and indelible. In the quiet of the night, I found myself hoping, almost praying, that the temporary fencing we had erected around the Portals would hold, would keep us safe through the vulnerable hours that stretched before dawn.

4338.214

(2 August 2018)

FROM HEISTS TO AGREEMENTS

4338.214.1

As the veil of sleep began to lift, the remnants of our audacious escapade lay scattered around me, a tangible echo of the night's rebellion. The beds we had appropriated from the Smith household served as makeshift resting places for us, guardians of our own fate, amidst the spoils of our midnight heist. Beatrix and Jarod, still ensnared in the remnants of their dreams, began to stir, their movements slow, as if the weight of our actions tethered them to the realm of sleep. Our glances met, bleary and heavy with the realisation of what we had dared to do under the cover of darkness.

"Did we really do all this?" The words slipped from my lips, a murmur that broke the quiet of the morning. The reality of our actions, bold and irrevocable, began to seep into my waking consciousness, a tide of awareness that filled me with a mix of pride and disbelief.

It was then that a figure approached, his presence casting a long shadow over the chaotic landscape of reclaimed belongings. "You three look like you've had a busy night," Dad's voice, laced with amusement and an undercurrent of concern, broke the silence.

"Yeah," I replied, my voice thick with sleep, as I struggled to bring the world into focus. "Is Paul here?" The question, born of a half-remembered concern, hung in the air between us.

"No," Dad responded, his calmness a stark contrast to the tumult of our recent actions. "We had a good talk this morning. We've decided that I'll take charge of the Drop Zone management from now on." His announcement, unexpected and significant, hinted at changes that stretched beyond the physical boundaries of our night's work.

"Oh," was all I could manage, my surprise at the sudden shift in roles evident in my voice. Dad, however, seemed almost amused by the situation, a sly smile playing at the corners of his mouth. "He took one look at all of this and decided he couldn't handle you anymore." His chuckle, soft and tinged with dry humour, filled the space between us.

I frowned, the humour of the situation eluding me. As I glanced around at the dusty expanse of Bixbus, the reality of our actions and their consequences began to truly settle in. The desolate sanctuary that had once offered solace now bore witness to our defiance, a silent testament to a night that had changed the very fabric of our existence. The laughter and light-hearted comments did little to dispel the sense of solemnity that had begun to weave itself into my thoughts. Our actions, though born of necessity and a fierce desire for autonomy, had also ushered in a period of uncertainty, the future of which lay as yet uncharted before us.

As Dad's demeanour shifted towards a more serious tone, his gaze piercing through the early morning light, I felt the realness of our actions settle around us like a dense fog. His words, though calm, carried an undeniable weight, underscoring the consequences of our midnight escapade. "You three may have pulled off a spectacular vanishing act, but we can't afford such recklessness. Going forward, there will be more stringent controls."

Our collective groan, a natural response to the prospect of tighter restrictions, seemed to hang in the air, a tangible representation of our shared discontent. The dim light of dawn did little to soften the stern lines etched into Dad's face, a clear indication of his serious take on the matter.

"It won't happen again," I found myself saying, the words a mix of determination and a nagging guilt that clung to the edges of my resolve. My attempt at assurance, however, felt hollow, even to my own ears.

Jarod's laughter, light yet edged with an underlying truth, broke the heavy silence. "I'm not so sure you can promise that," he said, his glance towards Beatrix sparking a silent exchange filled with an unspoken acknowledgment of our inherent nature to push boundaries.

"He's right," I conceded, feeling the weight of reality press down upon me. Turning to face Dad, I admitted, "I really can't promise that this won't happen again." The admission was difficult, not only for its truth but for the disappointment it would surely bring.

Dad's expression shifted, the look of disappointment in his eyes striking a chord deep within me. It was a look that always seemed to cut deeper, more profoundly than any show of anger could.

"But I can make sure that you are better prepared and equipped to deal with it when it does," I added quickly, a desperate attempt to offer some semblance of consolation, to show that despite our recklessness, there was a willingness to learn, to adapt.

The intensity of Dad's gaze did not waver, his eyes narrowing as if to scrutinise the sincerity and resolve behind my words. It was a silent exchange, one that acknowledged the inevitable challenges ahead but also the undercurrent of understanding that bound us. The resolve in my gaze, reflecting back at him, was a testament to my commitment to face those challenges head-on, to learn from our actions and to adapt in ways that would safeguard us all. In that moment, despite the looming spectre of stricter controls, there was an unspoken agreement that growth often comes from facing the consequences of our actions, from navigating the fine line between freedom and responsibility.

❖

Standing amidst the tangible reminders of our night's activities, the sudden intrusion of Kain's voice into the contemplative silence was almost jarring. His approach, marked by an agility that seemed to defy his recent reliance on crutches, signalled a change, not just in his physical condition but perhaps in the dynamics of our interaction as well. As he called my name, there was a clarity and purpose in his tone that immediately piqued my interest.

Shifting the weight on my feet, I felt the stiffness of my muscles protest, a physical testament to the exertions of the night. Stretching, I braced myself for the conversation ahead, sensing the significance of what Kain was about to share.

"Luke, we need to talk," Kain's words, simple yet laden with an unspoken gravity, effectively captured my full attention. His deliberate positioning, placing himself between my father and me, not only underscored the personal nature of the discussion but also seemed to draw an invisible boundary, momentarily isolating us from the curious gazes of those nearby.

"In private," he added, his voice low, imbuing our imminent conversation with an added layer of seriousness.

"Sure," I responded, my curiosity now fully engaged. As we moved away from the group, the air between us felt charged, heavy with the anticipation of a conversation that promised to be both significant and potentially transformative.

Kain's proposal, as it unfolded, was unexpected. The festivities with the Smith Clan had evidently left a profound impact on him, igniting a desire to cultivate a similar sense of family and community within Clivilius. As I listened, I found myself wrestling with how to articulate the complex dynamics of my own family life. The harmony we presented to the outside world was genuine, yet it was not without its underlying tensions and challenges.

"Luke, I get it," Kain interjected, his understanding cutting through my hesitations. The resolute glint in his eyes spoke volumes, reflecting a depth of conviction and a clear vision of what he hoped to achieve. "Every family has its struggles. But what I saw last night—your family, the Smiths, all of it—it's more than just a façade. It's genuine, and I want that for Brianne and our child."

His words, sincere and forthright, struck a chord within me. The notion that the warmth and unity we had shared could serve as inspiration for Kain's aspirations was both humbling and profoundly moving. The realisation that our actions and the way we interacted as a family could have such a meaningful impact on others was a powerful reminder of the importance of community, of the bonds that tie us together, and of the potential for those bonds to inspire and foster a sense of belonging and togetherness in others.

Yet, it was vital to make sure that Kain understood the repercussions of what he was asking. I studied his expression, recognising the sincerity in his words. "It's not always easy, Kain. We've been through a lot, and sometimes it feels like we're barely holding it together," I found myself saying, the words heavy with the reality of our experiences. The struggles and triumphs that had shaped us were not just stories; they were testaments to our resilience.

He nodded, a gesture that conveyed understanding and acceptance of the complexities involved. "But that's what makes it real. I don't want a perfect paradise; I want a place where we can face challenges together and come out stronger on the other side. Clivilius seems like that kind of place." His words resonated with me, echoing the very essence of what we had built and hoped to continue building in Clivilius—a community forged in the fire of adversity, strengthened by its trials.

As the conversation turned towards the logistical aspects of bringing Brianne to Clivilius, I outlined the necessities—coordination of transportation, securing a suitable living space, and ensuring she received the care needed throughout her pregnancy. The complexity of the situation was not lost on either of us, especially considering the void left by Glenda's departure. "Are you up for the challenge?" I asked, my concern for their well-being etching lines of worry across my face. The absence of a qualified medical professional to assist with the birth was a significant hurdle, one that underscored the critical nature of their decision to join us.

Kain's response was a testament to his resolve. "I'm ready, Luke. I've seen what we're building here, and I believe it's the right place for us. We'll figure it out together." The determination in his gaze was unwavering, a clear indication of his commitment to not only stay in our community but to actively contribute to its growth and resilience.

When I broached the subject of timing, his immediate response took me by surprise. "Today!" The urgency of his reply underscored the depth of his conviction, and yet, the rapid timeline added an additional layer of complexity to the already daunting task ahead.

"No pressure, then," I joked, the levity of my remark a brief respite from the weight of our discussion. The prospect of welcoming Kain's fiancée into our midst was a significant step for Clivilius, one that brought with it a mixture of excitement and apprehension. It marked the dawn of a new chapter, not just for Kain and his family, but for our entire community—a chapter filled with the promise of growth, the challenge of adaptation, and the continued quest for a life built on the principles of unity, resilience, and shared purpose.

As Kain and I navigated the complexities of his fiancée's impending transition to Clivilius, his next words introduced an unexpected twist to our already intricate plans. "And there's one more thing, Luke. I want Hudson and my motorbike. They're family too." The earnestness in his declaration caught me off guard, prompting a moment of silent contemplation.

I raised an eyebrow, a mix of amusement and surprise colouring my reaction. "A dog and a motorbike? Seriously?" The question slipped out, tinged with incredulity, not out of judgment but from the sheer unexpectedness of his request.

Kain's response was immediate and unwavering. "Absolutely. Hudson's been with me through thick and thin, and the bike, well, it's my freedom. Can't imagine starting this new chapter without them," he said, his tone imbued with a deep sense of loyalty and attachment to both his faithful companion and his cherished motorbike.

I couldn't help but chuckle, the sound a mixture of admiration and the burgeoning realisation of the unique challenge Kain's request presented. It was a reminder of the personal attachments and the seemingly small, yet profoundly significant, elements that compose the tapestry of our lives. Kain's definition of family, inclusive of his loyal dog and the symbol of his independence, resonated with me, highlighting the varied connections that anchor us.

"Alright, Hudson and the motorbike it is. I'll find a way to make it happen," I promised, the words a testament to my commitment to Kain. The resolve in my voice was not just about facilitating the physical relocation of a dog and a motorbike; it was an acknowledgment of the importance of preserving those elements that define our sense of self and home.

BRIANNE, DISRUPTED

4338.214.2

The atmosphere was charged with a palpable sense of anticipation, a silent pressure that seemed to amplify the significance of what I was about to do. I found myself repeating a silent mantra—*it's the best way*—to quell the rising tide of doubt and anxiety that threatened to overwhelm my resolve. In a moment of quiet determination, I took a deep breath, the air heavy with the scent of old secrets and the dust of forgotten spaces. The musty aroma seemed almost comforting, a reminder of the hidden depths and layers within our lives.

As I lifted the heavy metal lid, hidden beneath the wardrobe floor, it groaned in protest, a sound that echoed the hesitance in my heart. Yet, my movements were deliberate, guided by a sense of purpose that outweighed my trepidation. My fingers, accustomed to the touch of technology yet laden with the significance of the moment, found their way to Kain's phone with an ease that belied the complexity of the emotions swirling within me.

Holding the device in my hands felt like holding a Pandora's box, teeming with messages and missed calls that pulsed with the urgency of unspoken words and unmet needs. As I navigated through its interface, a sense of urgency propelled my actions, each tap and swipe on the screen a careful step in a dance of discretion and speed.

Crafting the message to Brianne, I felt the weight of every word, aware that the simplicity of the text belied the depth of trust and hope it was meant to convey:

Kain: *I am safe. Luke is on his way. You must trust him!*

Sending the message was akin to releasing a bird into the unknown, hoping it would find its way and deliver the promise of safety and connection. The confirmation of its receipt was a small beacon of success in the murky waters of my plan, a momentary relief in the storm of uncertainties that lay ahead.

Powering off the phone, I slipped it into the pocket of my worn jeans, its presence a constant reminder of the role I now played in bridging the distances and fears that separated Brianne and Kain. The device, though inanimate, felt almost alive with the weight of its mission, a tangible manifestation of the trust Kain had placed in me and the delicate thread of hope that he was desperately clinging to.

As I moved forward, the weight of the phone against my thigh was a constant companion, a physical reminder of the stakes involved and the importance of every step I took toward reuniting a family. It was a burden I accepted willingly, driven by a determination to see this through, to navigate the complexities and challenges with a resolve that was as much about honouring Kain's trust as it was about weaving the fabric of our Bixbus community even tighter.

❖

Fifteen minutes after setting off, the scene transformed dramatically as a cloud of dust announced my arrival, the tires of the borrowed vehicle murmuring secrets to the gravel beneath. I stepped out, immediately faced with the formidable ascent before me—a path littered with gravel, winding its way up to the imposing figure of Jeffries Manor, which sat like a sentinel atop the steep hill. A twinge of regret nagged at the edge of my thoughts, the realisation that a previously recorded portal positioned closer to my destination would have significantly eased my current burden. The irony of the situation didn't escape me, prompting a muttered commentary to the empty air, "Timing and fast action are critical," a reflection of the urgency and precision required, yet here I was, contemplating the physical challenge that lay ahead.

With the Portal Key in hand, a symbol of the technological marvels at my disposal, yet also a reminder of the limitations I faced, I began the ascent. Each step was measured, the effort more pronounced with the steep incline, and my breath became a rhythmic huff, a testament to the physicality of the journey. The shadows cast by the bush-lined driveway offered a semblance of concealment, a strategic advantage I was tempted to utilise to its fullest.

As I navigated the path, a mantra took shape in my mind, a rehearsed narrative to cloak my true intentions: "Brianne and Louise are unaware of my ulterior motives. I am simply Jamie's partner coming to speak with Brianne. They have no reason to suspect anything else." This internal repetition served as a mental shield, fortifying my resolve and focusing my thoughts on the task at hand. It was crucial that my appearance and demeanour mirrored the innocuous cover story I had crafted. Every gesture and expression would need to align with the narrative of a simple visit, concealing the deeper, more urgent purpose driving my actions.

As I stood before the grandeur of the manor's front door, my pulse raced with anticipation, each heartbeat a drumroll to the momentous encounter that awaited. The act of pressing the buzzer felt like a declaration of intent, the sound slicing through the silence and resonating deep within me, mirroring the tension that gripped my heart.

The door creaked open slowly, revealing Louise. Her presence was like a tangible barrier, her stance guarded, embodying an unspoken challenge that filled the space between us. "What do you want?" she demanded, her voice laced with skepticism that seemed to thicken the air around us.

Before I could weave my prepared narrative into the conversation, Louise cut in, her suspicion casting shadows across her features. "And where's Jamie?" The question, sharp and probing, threatened to unravel the delicate web of deceit I had spun.

Choosing to navigate around her inquiry, I steered the conversation towards my intended purpose. "Is Brianne home?" I asked, injecting a note of casual interest into my voice. The urgency of my mission for Kain momentarily cast aside the fact that, in Louise's eyes, her brother's whereabouts remained an enigma.

"And Jamie?" she persisted, her focus unwavering. The necessity of maintaining my cover compelled me to respond with a fabricated truth. "He's still in Melbourne," I stated, the falsehood slipping from my tongue with practiced ease, a testament to the role I had assumed.

"But he's still not answering my..." Louise's voice faltered, her concern for her brother momentarily surfacing before being swallowed by the unfolding drama.

Seizing the moment, I produced a white envelope from my back pocket, holding Louise's gaze with a resolve born from the gravity of my task. "I received this strange letter in the mail. It's addressed to Brianne, but for some reason, it was posted to my address," I explained, introducing a new element of intrigue into our exchange.

"Can I see?" Louise's interest piqued, her hand reaching out towards the envelope with an instinctive curiosity. Anticipating her reaction, I pulled it back, just out of her reach. "I think I'd better give it to Brianne myself," I insisted, my stance firm, understanding the importance of delivering the message directly.

Louise's reaction was a mixture of indifference and frustration, her huff a clear sign of her waning patience with the peculiarities of the situation. Despite the oddity of my request, the urgency of my mission rendered any concerns about appearing eccentric secondary.

"Fine," she grumbled, resigning herself to my request. "I'll go and find her." Her acquiescence, though grudging, marked a small victory in the intricate dance of deception and necessity.

"Thank you," I responded, my gratitude barely audible against the backdrop of the tense silence that had settled around us.

Left in the echoing stillness of the entryway, the sound of the door closing behind Louise felt like a solemn punctuation to the moment, a heavy silence settling around me. The weight of what I was attempting to do pressed down with an almost physical force, the seconds ticking by marking the intensity of the situation, each one a reminder of why I was here and the delicate balance I was trying to maintain.

Time seemed to warp, stretching out into an agonising wait that tested the limits of my patience and resolve. Questions churned through my mind, a turbulent sea of doubts and what-ifs. *Is Brianne coming?* The question pulsed in the forefront of my thoughts, mingling with concerns over the message I'd sent from Kain's phone. *Had it been convincing enough?* The uncertainty of whether Brianne could discern its true origin gnawed at me, a silent spectre of potential failure looming over the mission.

As the minutes dragged on, my patience frayed at the edges, giving way to a creeping unease. It occurred to me that perhaps a further nudge from Kain, albeit through my own fabrication, was necessary to coax Brianne into action. Retrieving Kain's phone once more, I powered it on, the screen's glow casting my features in sharp relief against the dimness of the entryway. Brianne's response was immediate, a beacon of her concern: *Kain, where are you???*

Choosing to remain silent to her query was a decision made with the ease of someone who had become all too familiar with the art of evasion. An internal acknowledgment of this habit brushed my consciousness—*I'm getting good at this*, I noted wryly, a reflection on the evasive manoeuvres that had become an integral part of navigating these complex situations.

The necessity for further prompting from Kain was clear. I crafted another message, hoping to bridge the gap of trust between Brianne and myself through the guise of Kain's reassurance.

Kain: *Is Luke there yet?*

Her swift reply indicated her awareness of my presence: *Yes, he's at the front door.*

Pushing further, I sought to confirm the dialogue between us, to ensure that our planned interaction would proceed.

Kain: *Have you spoken to him yet?*

Brianne's response was tinged with caution, a testament to the uncertainty and mistrust that clouded the situation: *No. I barely know him. Are you sure I can trust him?*

With a deep breath, feeling the weight of the responsibility to both Kain and Brianne, I responded with a simple affirmation that carried the weight of my promise to them both.

Kain: *Yes!*

In the silence that stretched between each digital message, time seemed to slow, each minute amplifying the tension and uncertainty that hovered around me like an unwelcome shadow. It became increasingly clear that a more empathetic approach was needed to bridge the chasm of silence and worry that had undoubtedly enveloped Brianne. Her partner's sudden disappearance into a void of no communication would naturally leave her fraught with anxiety and fear.

Guided by this realisation, I let Kain's persona reach out through the digital ether once more, injecting a note of contrition and vulnerability into the conversation: *I'm really sorry that I haven't been in contact sooner. To be honest, I've gotten myself into a bit of trouble.* The words, though not my own, were laced with a sincerity I hoped would resonate with Brianne, offering her a sliver of understanding amidst the swirling vortex of her concerns.

Her response came quickly, a wave of worry breaking through the virtual barrier: *What sort of trouble?* The simplicity of her question belied the depth of her concern, a concern that now teetered on the edge of panic.

The brief pause that followed felt like an eternity, a moment suspended in time as I deliberated over the path our conversation should take. Finally, I chose to navigate towards a resolution that would bring this delicate dance to a close: *Probably best we speak in person.* The suggestion, veiled in Kain's voice, was both an olive branch and a lifeline, a means to transition from the impersonal realm of texts to the tangible reality awaiting us.

Her response was immediate and fraught with urgency: *Where are you?!?* The desperation in her words echoed the tumult of emotions I imagined swirling within her.

It was then that I decided to anchor the conversation in the reality of my mission, to firmly link my presence to Kain's and to the promise of reunion that I bore: *Go with Luke. He knows where I am. He'll bring you to me.* The message, cryptic yet imbued with a directive, was intended to pave the way for the trust and action needed to move forward.

As the digital exchange faded into a momentary lull, my attention remained riveted to the screen, a silent sentinel awaiting a sign, a confirmation, a decision. *Did Brianne...*

The sudden noise of the front door creaking open jolted me from my reverie, a stark reminder of the reality that lay beyond the virtual world I had been navigating. Instinctively, Kain's phone was tucked away into the sanctuary of my back pocket, its secrets momentarily concealed as I braced myself for the next phase of this unfolding drama.

The anticipation, the strategy, the careful weaving of words—all of it converged in that moment of interruption, leaving me momentarily adrift in the sudden shift from anticipation to action. The opening door was not just a physical entryway being crossed; it was a threshold between plans laid and actions to be taken, between the uncertain and the tangible, between doubt and the possibility of hope being realised.

Brianne's presence in the doorway was like a physical manifestation of the tension that had been building within me. Her voice, sharp and laden with urgency, sliced through the stillness, demanding an answer I knew would be difficult to provide convincingly. "Where's Kain?" she asked, her eyes searching mine for a truth I was tasked to obscure.

"He sent me to collect you," I replied, my voice steady, though inside, I was anything but. I held up Kain's keys, a gesture meant to symbolise my legitimacy and urgency, yet feeling acutely aware of its potential inadequacy in truly convincing Brianne of Kain's safety.

Brianne's persistence cut through my thoughts, her repeated question, "Where is he?" pulling me back to the reality of my immediate challenge. As she stormed through the doorway, effectively sealing us off from the house, a silent acknowledgment passed between us—a shared, albeit reluctant, agreement to proceed.

"I'll take you," I reiterated, my pace quickening to match hers as we navigated the open space before us. The urgency lent speed to our steps, a mutual recognition of the stakes at play propelling us forward.

However, our hurried movement was abruptly interrupted by Brianne's sudden stop. "Where's Kain's ute?" she demanded, her body language shifting into one of heightened alertness as her gaze swept our surroundings. The question hung heavily in the air, a startling reminder of the discrepancies in the narrative I had woven.

"We need to take your car," I declared, a note of decisiveness cutting through my initial hesitation. The realisation that Kain's keys—and by extension, the plan I had carefully laid out—were irrelevant for accessing the ute already secured in Clivilius, sent a rush of adrenaline through me. It was a moment of truth, a pivot point where the absence of Kain's ute became not just a logistical hurdle but a test of trust and willingness to embark on an uncertain journey.

As Brianne marched determinedly towards the large shed where her red Mazda was parked, her actions spoke volumes of her resolve. Without hesitation, she directed me to unlock the car, her urgency palpable as she tugged at the passenger door. My initial confusion must have been evident, a silent question hanging between us: *Where was her key?*

Her impatience cut through my momentary stupor. "If you've got Kain's keys, he has a spare for my car too. It's the chunky square one that says Mazda on it," she explained with a hint of exasperation. Her words snapped me back to reality, the realisation that I was indeed holding the means to move us forward in this tense situation.

"Of course," I managed to say, my voice steadier than I felt. My fingers quickly sifted through Kain's keys, seeking the one she described. The urgency in Brianne's actions served as a catalyst, sharpening my focus despite the whirlwind of stress and determination that threatened to overwhelm me. With the correct key finally identified, I pressed the unlock button, and the sound of the doors opening in unison offered a brief respite from the tension.

Settling into the car, the discomfort of the phone in my back pocket became too much to ignore. I retrieved it, placing it in the console beside me. The Mazda roared to life under my hands, the sound a stark contrast to the growing suspicion in Brianne's narrowed hazel eyes.

"Why do you have Kain's phone?" she demanded, her voice carrying a weight of accusation that made the car's interior feel even more confined. Her gaze, fixed on the phone as if it were a tangible manifestation of her growing doubts, added a layer of complexity to the already charged atmosphere.

"From Kain," I responded, the words tumbling out in a rush of sound that barely masked my growing anxiety. The revving of the car's engine under my palms did little to hide the clamminess of my hands, a physical testament to the tension that weaved its way through every word and gesture.

Brianne's reaction, a visceral blend of fear and accusation, sliced through the already tense atmosphere within the car. Her eyes, wide and shadowed by a growing terror, fixed me with a stare that felt like it could bore right through my soul. "You sent me those messages from Kain, didn't you?" The accusation, sharp and filled with a trembling unease, left me scrambling for a response, my heart hammering against my ribcage.

"I can explain," I stammered, the words barely forming above the rush of adrenaline and the unpleasant sensation of sweat breaking out across my forehead. The situation was spiralling, the delicate thread of trust I'd hoped to maintain unravelling with each passing second.

"Let me out!" The plea, desperate and filled with a raw fear, echoed within the confines of the Mazda. Brianne's panic manifested physically as she pounded against the locked door, her actions a reminder of how quickly fear could turn to frenzy.

"I can't," was all I could muster in response, my voice a mix of determination and regret as I shifted the car into reverse. The car's movement, rather than soothing the tension, seemed to act as a catalyst, escalating Brianne's distress.

"Let me out!" Brianne's urgency escalated, her fist connecting with a forceful thump against my shoulder.

"Fuck! Just trust me!" I found myself shouting, the strain of the moment pushing me to the brink. The plea, born out of desperation, was met with a gaze that reflected my own turmoil, desperation mirrored in both our eyes.

"Let me out, you fucking psychopath!" Brianne's shrieks filled the car, her fear transforming into outright panic as she struggled against the locked door. The intensity of her fear, her attempts to escape, it all coalesced into a palpable sense of dread that seemed to suffocate the air around us.

As the car's back wheels churned against the gravel, the reality of our situation struck me with chilling clarity. Pausing only to switch the car to drive, the small Mazda lurched forward, each moment stretching into infinity as the realisation dawned on me: this journey, driven by a mix of fear, misunderstanding, and desperation, was teetering on the edge of catastrophe.

The urgency spiked as my eyes caught Louise's figure emerging through the manor's front door in the rearview mirror. "Shit!" escaped my lips, a reflexive curse as the situation escalated beyond my initial calculations. My hands, guided by a mix of panic and determination, manoeuvred the car in a sharp turn towards the large shed, the tires screeching a protest against the gravel. Another rapid turn concealed us behind the shed, the driver's side window lowering as part of a desperate gambit for escape.

Brianne's frantic efforts to thwart my actions filled the car with chaos. Her attempts to grab the wheel or halt our desperate flight were palpable signs of her panic and distrust. Amidst this turmoil, my right hand fought for control, breaking free from the struggle. The moment was fleeting, and before the shadow of regret could darken my resolve, the Mazda burst through the Portal, enveloped in a grateful wall of rainbow colour that signified our passage to another reality.

As we emerged on the other side, I was met with the immediate necessity to halt our unintended flight. I slammed on the brakes, the sudden deceleration sending plumes of fine dust swirling around us and causing Brianne to recoil back against her seat. "Sorry, can't stay," I apologised, the words feeling hollow given the whirlwind of actions and reactions we were caught in. Swinging the car door open, I didn't bother to close it behind me as I sprinted towards the still-open Portal, driven by the need to complete the mission that had brought me to this moment of chaos and confrontation.

Brianne's screech, "You bastard!" pierced the air, a haunting echo of the turmoil and betrayal she must have felt. Her voice, laden with anger and confusion, followed me as I vanished into the swirling colours of the Portal.

The rush of adrenaline rendered every thought fleeting, every decision a blur on the edge of rationality. I had achieved the immediate goal of bringing Brianne to Clivilius, yet the pursuit by Louise added layers of complexity and urgency I hadn't fully anticipated. The internal debate was brief—*should I stop now?* The question echoed in my mind, a whisper of caution drowned out by the necessity of the moment.

With a strategist's mind and a fugitive's urgency, I opted for the path less predictable, moving in the opposite direction of where I anticipated Louise would expect me to go. The strategy was simple: avoid direct confrontation, maintain the element of surprise. As I neared the corner of the shed, caution reasserted itself, urging me to slow down and assess before proceeding. *Better to peek first*, the voice of caution advised, a rare moment of prudence in a sea of haste.

Louise's distant screech, calling out for Brianne, propelled me toward the manor, my actions driven by a mix of desperation and determination. Her screams, though fading into the background, underscored the urgency of my actions.

Rounding the far side of the manor, each step felt like a gamble, a dance with fate itself. And then, the unexpected sound of familiarity in this maelstrom of mayhem—Hudson's barks of recognition and joy. The sight of him, so full of life and oblivious to the situations desperation, brought a momentary lightness to the heaviness that weighed on my shoulders. Yet, the realisation that silencing his excited barks was a battle I couldn't win added another layer of complexity to my mission.

The sudden sound of a door slamming shut snapped my focus back to the immediate challenge. Pressing myself against the brick wall, I took a moment to survey the scene through the sliding glass door into the sunroom, a space that held its own secrets and memories. With no one in sight, I seized the opportunity, moving swiftly towards Hudson's enclosure.

Unlatching the gate, I was met with an onslaught of affection from Hudson, his enthusiasm untempered by the situation at hand. With a firm grip on his collar, I made a split-second decision, driven by the need to ensure his safety above all else. Activating the Portal Key as I ran, I propelled Hudson through the shimmering doorway of the sunroom, sending him to a place of safety, away from the immediacy of pursuit and danger.

Having sent Hudson through to safety and closing the Portal behind him, the rush of adrenaline still coursed through my veins, a relentless surge that refused to subside. With the immediate threat of Louise's pursuit momentarily at bay, my next objective loomed dauntingly ahead—retrieving Kain's motorbike from the large shed. The urgency of the situation led my steps, quick and determined as I navigated towards the cluttered sanctuary where the bike was stored.

The shed, a maelstrom of shadows and shapes in the dim light, offered little in the way of orientation. In my haste, I left the door slightly ajar, a small concession to the darkness as I frantically searched for the motorbike. Amidst the contents, the bike was a beacon, its identifiable form standing out against the backdrop of disorder. Positioning myself awkwardly on the seat, a sinking feeling took hold as my gaze fell upon the empty ignition. The expletive slipped out, a vocal acknowledgment of my oversight. The realisation that the key, now left in Brianne's Mazda, was literally a world away from where I desperately needed it, sparked a wave of self-reproach. "Idiot!" I chastised myself, my frustration manifesting in a physical outburst against the handlebars.

Louise's voice, cutting through the tension of my predicament, carried with it a new wave of urgency. "The police are on their way." The words, laden with fear, echoed ominously within the confines of the shed. "Shit!" The curse was a reflex, a verbal marker of the escalating stakes.

Surveying my surroundings, the logic of escape battled with the limitations of my situation. The possibility of activating the Portal loomed as a tantalising escape but came laden with risks. Louise's inevitable witness to such an event posed a significant threat to the veil of secrecy surrounding our existence in Clivilius. And the thought of involuntarily dragging Louise into the fold of our hidden world weighed heavily on me, a burden I was loath to consider. *I really don't want to bring Louise with me*, I mused, the silent sigh a testament to the complexity of my dilemma.

As I disengaged from the motorbike, turning to confront the reality waiting at the entrance, the sight that greeted me sent a jolt of shock coursing through my body. Louise, her figure framed by the dim light of the doorway, held a large kitchen knife in her hand, a silent declaration of her desperation and fear. *What the fuck!* The exclamation was a silent scream in my mind, a mix of disbelief and rising panic. The knife, a stark symbol of the precarious turn the situation had taken, posed an unspoken question of intent and desperation. *Would Louise really use it?*

BYE, KARL - PART 2

4338.214.3

The distant wail of the approaching police siren cut through the tension like a knife, its ominous sound a chilling reminder of the rapidly closing window for action. The cold air around me seemed to thicken with anticipation, each breath a heavy sigh as I frantically scanned the shed for any avenue of escape. My gaze darted across the cramped space, the corrugated iron walls, adorned with tools and shelving, offered no solace, only an unsettling reminder of the confines within which I was trapped. The clutter and dust that filled the shed provided a meagre barrier between me and Louise, whose presence at the entrance, knife in hand and movements unpredictable, added layers of complexity to an already dire situation.

As I contemplated my next move, the silence was abruptly broken by Louise's voice, her betrayal ringing clear as she alerted the outside world to my presence. "He's in here!" The desperation in her voice, whether feigned or genuine, shattered the last vestiges of silence, propelling me into action.

"Shit!" The curse was a whispered echo of my frustration as I realised the futility of a straightforward escape. The arrival of Detective Karl Jenkins, his voice authoritative and commanding, brought a new player onto the field, complicating the dynamics of my predicament. Louise's compliance with the detective's demand to surrender the knife was a small relief, but her next words sent a shockwave through me. "I've got the bastard trapped inside," she declared, her voice breaking with emotion. "I can't find Brianne!"

The mention of Brianne, Kain's fiancée, and the insinuation of my involvement in her disappearance left me reeling. Louise's portrayal of the situation painted me in a light far removed from the truth, casting shadows of doubt and accusation that I had never anticipated facing.

I know Louise doesn't like me, but the thought that she might truly believe I was capable of harm was a bitter pill to swallow. The accusation, hanging heavy in the air, forced me to reassess not only my immediate situation but also the relationships and perceptions that had led me to this point.

As Detective Jenkins issued his orders, directing Louise to retreat back into the safety of the house, I found myself at a crossroads. The authority in his voice offered a brief respite, a momentary pause in the unfolding drama that allowed me to gather my thoughts.

Darting back into the shadows of the shed, the weight of Louise's accusations and the imminent arrival of law enforcement forced me to weigh my limited options.

From my concealed position, I observed Detective Jenkins as he stepped into the shed, his form outlined by the backlight from outside. The idea of using the Portal to escape, a tactic I had relied on before, seemed suddenly fraught with uncertainty against an adversary like Jenkins. "I'm unarmed," I declared, aiming to set a tone of non-aggression. Despite the delicacy of the situation, I clung to the hope that a peaceful resolution was possible, bolstered by the fact that, in technicality, I hadn't committed any crime.

Jenkins moved forward with a cautious grace, his hands visibly empty and raised slightly—a gesture that seemed to bridge the gap between authority and understanding. "I just want us to talk," he stated, his approach measured, almost inviting dialogue rather than confrontation. *Could the resolution to this be so straightforward?* The thought flickered through my mind, a glimmer of cautious optimism amidst the storm.

"I'm Detective Jenkins. You must be Luke Smith?" His introduction was formal yet lacked any edge of accusation. "Yes, I am," I answered, finding a small measure of relief in his direct yet seemingly open demeanour.

"Where is Brianne?" The question came swiftly, a direct pivot to the heart of the matter. "With Kain," I responded, the truth of my words mingled with the complexity of their implications. Jenkins' follow-up was expected. "And where might that be?" Jenkins probed deeper into the specifics of their whereabouts.

"I am not exactly sure," I confessed, threading a line between honesty and the necessity of vagueness. "Kain sent her a message about an hour ago with an address of where to meet him. That's why she took off in his car earlier when I arrived."

"So why is Louise so concerned about her safety?" Detective Jenkins probed further. "I don't know. I guess she is just confused and scared. I suppose I would be too if people around me were going missing and being secretive," I reasoned, painting a picture of misunderstanding and fear that, while not entirely untrue, was designed to deflect from the deeper truths at play.

"Are you being secretive?" Jenkins' question cut deeper, challenging the façade I had carefully constructed. "No. I really don't know what's going on," I lied, a sudden departure from the nuanced dance of half-truths I had been performing. The assertion was bold, perhaps too bold, but it was a line I had crossed with the utterance, stepping firmly into the realm of deceit in a desperate bid to protect the larger secrets that lay just beneath the surface.

Jenkins' unwavering gaze felt like it could unravel the fabric of my carefully constructed narrative, each question pulling at threads I desperately wished to keep intact. "And what about Jamie?"

"Jamie is safe," I found myself saying, the words a blend of truth and necessity, the sigh that followed a release of tension I hadn't realised I'd been holding.

The shed, dimly lit and filled with the remnants of our confrontation, suddenly felt smaller, more oppressive, as Jenkins prepared his next question. The pause that preceded it was heavy with implication, a silent herald to the scrutiny that was about to intensify. "I do have one question for you." His voice, steady and expectant, filled the space between us with a palpable sense of foreboding.

"What's that?" My response, an attempt at nonchalance, betrayed a flicker of uncertainty.

"We tracked your movements to Adelaide just yesterday. How did you manage to sneak past all of our surveillance and back into Hobart?" Jenkins inquired, the question striking a chord of alarm within me. The implications of his inquiry were clear—he was dangerously close to peeling back layers I had fought hard to keep covered.

I opted for silence, a nonchalant shrug my only reply to a question that dug too deep, threatening to expose more than just my own secrets. The realisation that my actions were under such close scrutiny sent a wave of dread crashing over me. *How much did they really know, and how close were they to discovering the existence of Clivilius?*

Karl's observation, "You are a cunning little bastard, aren't you?" carried with it a change in tone, an edge that sliced through the false calm of our conversation. His words, though perhaps intended to provoke a reaction or an admission, only served to highlight the precarious nature of our interaction. The stakes had indeed escalated, his acknowledgment of my evasion a clear sign that our cat-and-mouse game was nearing a critical juncture.

The impulse to flee, to evade the looming threat of detention and the unravelling of Clivilius' secrets, surged within me with an intensity that bordered on desperation. My hand, almost of its own accord, edged towards the sanctuary of my back pocket, seeking the Portal Key that had become my lifeline in situations far less dire than this.

"Don't move!" The sharpness in Karl's voice, amplified by the acoustics of the shed, halted my movements instantly. The sight of his hand moving towards his holster was a stark reminder of the reality of our confrontation, a reality I had hoped to avoid. My involuntary startle, a reflex born out of surprise and fear, sent an unfortunate chain reaction through the shed, culminating in the crash of a nearby motorbike. The sound, loud and jarring, shattered the already fragile silence, marking the end of any pretence of a peaceful resolution.

Karl's response was swift and decisive, a testament to his training and instincts. The force of his tackle was unexpected, the impact with my chest sudden and breathtaking, quite literally. As we tumbled to the floor, the breath was forced from my lungs in a whoosh that left me gasping for air, my mind racing even as my body struggled to cope with the immediate physical demands of the situation.

The application of a wrist lock to my right arm was both precise and painful, a clear demonstration of Karl's control over the situation. The pain was sharp, a white-hot line of fire that seared through my nerves. Instinctively, I reacted, a jerk of motion driven by pain and the primal urge to escape. Our struggle on the floor was desperate and disorienting, a physical contest of strength and will that left us both slick with sweat and grappling for dominance.

Ultimately, it was Karl's strength and technique that prevailed. I found myself immobilised, sprawled on the cold concrete floor, my arms secured above my head in a position that left me vulnerable and exposed. The weight of his body pinned me down effectively, a physical reminder of the precariousness of my situation and the seriousness of the consequences now looming over me.

Lying there, the cold seeping into my bones, I was acutely aware of the sudden shift in our dynamic. Karl's physical dominance was not just a matter of strength; it was a clear message, a demonstration of the lengths to which he was willing to go to secure his objectives. The realisation that my options were rapidly diminishing, that my usual means of escape and evasion were no longer viable, filled me with a sense of dread and helplessness I had not anticipated.

Exhausted and uncertain of my fate, our eyes met, a silent clash in the dim light of the shed. "Well, this is awkward," I managed to say, the words slipping out in a feeble attempt at humour. In that moment, I was grasping for any semblance of leverage, a way to diffuse the tension or perhaps create an opening for escape.

"You're enjoying this, aren't you?" The disgust in his voice was palpable, a clear reflection of his feelings towards the situation and, by extension, towards me. His disdain acted as a sharp reminder of the seriousness of my predicament, a contrast to the levity I had attempted to inject.

Despite the intensity of the moment, a wild grin found its way across my face, an involuntary reaction to the absurdity of our standoff. It was then that Beatrix's face momentarily appeared in the doorway, a fleeting glimpse that sparked a flicker of hope. *Perfect timing!* The thought raced through my mind, her presence a potential game-changer in the deadlock between Karl and me.

"And what about you?" I shot back, seizing the opportunity to probe Karl's resolve, to keep him mentally off-balance even as he maintained physical control. His retort, a declaration of restrained violence, sent a chill down my spine. "If my hands weren't pinning you down right now, I'd punch you in the face."

A shudder rippled through me at his words, a visceral reaction to the threat they represented. "Well, ain't that a shame," I replied, the remark accompanied by an inadvertent wink as dust irritated my eye, adding an unintended layer of insolence to my response.

Karl's whispered accusation, "You're a fucking psychopath," delivered so close, carried with it a weight of panic and realisation. The immediacy of the danger, the potential consequences of my actions, and the fine balance between escape and capture became overwhelmingly clear. The surge of panic was palpable, a tangible force that threatened to overwhelm my senses. Yet, despite the fear, the necessity of maintaining my composure, of finding a way out of this predicament without being arrested or worse, became the singular focus of my thoughts.

"What makes you think I'm a psychopath?" I shot back, my voice laced with a mix of defiance and curiosity. Beatrix's fleeting appearance at the door had injected a sliver of hope into the dire situation, yet her intentions remained a mystery, leaving me to navigate this precarious dialogue with Karl on my own.

Karl's next words came as a hammer blow, his voice heavy with accusation. "Do you have no remorse for what you have done? You've murdered at least four people!" The claim sent a jolt through me, a visceral reaction to the seriousness of the charges he laid at my feet.

"I haven't murdered anyone," I retorted, my denial immediate and forceful, yet internally, I was besieged by a tumultuous flood of images. Visions of Cody, of Karl dressed in ominous black, the haunting memory of a swinging chair and a harrowing tumble down stairs—the echoes of snapping bones and the visceral sight of dark blood pooling ominously. These fragments of memory, disjointed and disturbing, assaulted my mind, blurring the lines between reality and perception.

A sudden, gripping fear took hold. "Have you?" The question slipped out, a reflection of the turmoil within, turning Karl's accusation back upon him in a moment of desperate confusion.

The intensity of our confrontation seemed to shift then, with Karl's grip on my arms loosening slightly, a small concession in the physical struggle that mirrored the complex dance of our conversation. "So how do you want to do this?" he asked, the question marking a pivotal moment in our encounter. It was an opening, a potential path to de-escalation that I hadn't anticipated, yet one that carried with it the weight of decision.

Before I could formulate a response to Karl's probing question, an abrupt interruption shattered the tense atmosphere. The crackle of the radio attached to Karl's belt pierced the silence, a harbinger of external intrusion, while the shed's lone light flickered ominously, casting our shadows in stark relief against the cluttered walls. Panic surged through me like a live wire, sparking a frantic thought: *I can't go through Beatrix's Portal.* The reality of my limited escape options settled heavily upon me, a suffocating cloak of dread.

Then, as if summoned by my desperation, Beatrix's voice cut through the chaos, a beacon of unexpected hope. "Luke!" The sound of her voice was the precursor to the door closing with a definitive thud, revealing behind it not the expected darkness of the shed's exterior but a wall of brilliant, swirling colours—the Portal, activated and inviting.

The moment of distraction was all I needed. Acting on instinct, I delivered a swift knee strike to Karl's groin, a desperate bid for freedom. Our bodies became entangled in the struggle, a messy tangle of limbs and determination. My hand scrambled for the Portal Key in my pocket, its familiar shape a promise of escape. With a sense of urgency bordering on panic, I aimed it towards the floor and pressed the button, a silent plea for it to transport us away from this confrontation.

What followed was a chaotic descent into the unknown. Objects crashed around us, their sounds muffled by the thick, Clivilian dust that enveloped us in a disorienting cloud. The wrestle between Karl and me continued unabated, our struggle undiminished by the transition through the Portal. Finding myself once again on my back, with my hands pinned by Karl's superior strength, a whisper escaped my lips, "Bye, Karl." It was a whisper filled with the taste of a fleeting victory, a momentary triumph savoured in the face of overwhelming odds.

But victory was short-lived. Swift and precise, Karl's counterstrike was the last sensation I felt before my world plunged into darkness.

TO BE CONTINUED...